SUNFIRE

DAN KENNER

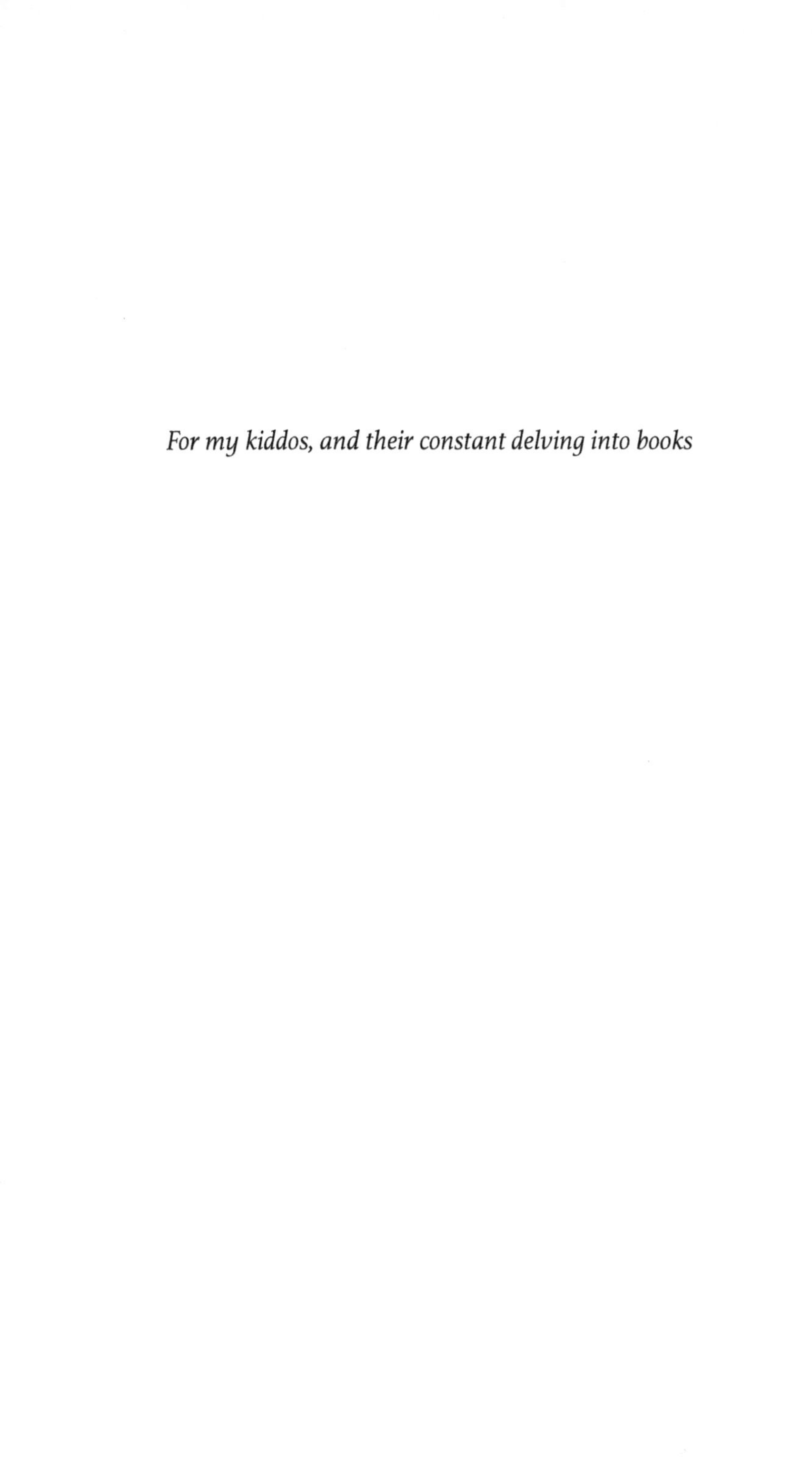

For my kiddos, and their constant delving into books

1

The alarm rings in my ear, shocking my whole system awake as it does every morning at 6:00 a.m.

I groan and roll over just enough to smack the table where an alarm clock *should* be. Instead, my hand smacks the metal side table jutting out of the wall there. I wince at the slight sting that comes from hitting the cold metal. The lack of an alarm clock makes me think about how I got here in the first place. Guilt reminds me that I'm the one who put my family into this situation.

Squinting my eyes open, I can see that the artificial light overhead is slowly coming on, white and dull. Unfortunately, the light will be full and bright in only a few minutes.

Stupid mornings—I think—*why do they have to wake us up so early?*

Rather than jump out of bed and rush to get dressed, I yank the wool blanket back over my head. It is a neutral color, grey and thin, but warm enough to keep me comfortable at night. The alarm continues to ring overhead from the speakers in the ceiling, loud and imposing. It reminds me of when my brother Sean pesters me throughout the day, persistent and annoying.

The sound of the alarm stops and a pleasant voice comes out of the speaker instead.

"Citizens of Safety. It's time to wake up. Get dressed and prepare for the day. If you have not yet risen from your bed, motivation can be provided to assist you in doing so."

I mouth the words to myself as I hide under the warm and comfortable blanket. It's the same every morning for everyone in this unholy place. Well, maybe not *everyone*. They have programmed the rooms here to deliver the same message each morning, but only to those who haven't gotten up yet.

Breathing out a sigh of annoyance, I count to three in my head before throwing the blanket off of my body, sucking in a sharp breath and practically jumping out of bed. If I don't do it this way, I would probably fall back to sleep and have to suffer the 'motivation' that they spoke of in the announcement.

The 'motivation' just happens to be an electric shock that comes through your bed and zaps you awake if you aren't up and out of it by 6:05 a.m. No one wants to be subject to that type of motivation, except maybe my crackpot best friend, Charlie. He says you get used to the feeling. Waking up has never been one of his strengths. He told me the electric shock actually helps him get up for the day, almost like his own kind of routine that gets him going in the morning. I think he's foolish, but to each their own.

I shudder as I recall the first time I experienced the shock. I hadn't slept well that night and thought I could get a few more minutes of shut-eye before breakfast. I remember the fizzing feeling started low, then filled my whole body, locking my joints and muscles and causing me to cry out. It was short, but it felt so long and terrible because of the pain—that horrible pain.

I almost expected the shock to come this morning, even though it's only 6:03. The beds are weight sensitive, so they know the moment you get up. The information is put in your log as well, so if you don't wake up on time, you get a demerit. If you get too many of those, then it gets pretty bad—for you, and your family. Charlie racks demerits up so fast, but he's without a family here in Safety. Perhaps that's why he's so casual about accumulating them.

Ever since Safety was built for people like us, the Creators have put us in 'family' units with parents and two kids. Apparently this takes a lot of time, so about the time Charlie and I were born, they decided to try something new. Charlie was part of this experimental unit where he wasn't assigned parents to watch him. Instead, they threw him and a bunch of other kids together in a nursery to be mass raised by scientists. The Creators hoped to have success with it so they didn't have to waste so much time with the family unit organization. It wasn't as successful as they'd hoped. Rather than assign the kids in the group to parents, they just let them live together. So, Charlie doesn't have a family. For him, demerits just mean some of his personal luxuries get taken away. Recently he lost access to extra provisions between meals, but he still acts as happy as ever.

I cringe at the thought. When you get demerits, and the punishments from gathering too many of them, they don't just affect you. The Creators take it out on your whole family as well.

My mind wanders back to our prior housing assignment. My room there had an alarm clock I could turn off at will. It was still programmed to ring at 6:00 a.m. and I couldn't change it. I was still expected out of bed by 6:05, but having an alarm clock to switch off had a sweetness to it that made waking up easier. The soft carpet in the room also provided a comfort I couldn't explain. Now I am acutely aware as my bare feet touch the cold metal ground of my current room.

I shudder at the coolness but force myself to get moving,

regardless. I cross my room to the wall where drawers hold my clothes. As I touch the top drawer, a hissing noise pushes into my still-awakening senses and it slides open on its own. I see a selection of light grey clothes, all made from the same dull cotton. The fabric is soft to touch, but boring to look at.

I put my finger to my lips and make a show of trying to decide what to wear. The Creators are watching and I know it will bother them. Tapping my foot, I run my finger over the options. Grey pants with a grey short-sleeve? Grey skirt with a grey long-sleeve? Grey shorts? After a few moments, the voice rings from the overhead speaker again.

"Citizens of Safety. Breakfast will soon begin in the mess hall. Please proceed to dress yourselves and make your way to the hall. Eating will begin promptly at 6:30 a.m."

I roll my eyes and snatch a pair of pants and a long-sleeved shirt from my drawer. I don't dress quickly because I know that I have plenty of time. I opt to not shower this morning because I'm not in the mood. Admittedly, the clothes that the Creators give us are comfortable, so I can't complain too much. It would be nice to see more color here though. All the clothes are the same boring grey and everything we see here is made of the same silver metal. It gets old, to be honest.

A hissing sound behind me announces my door opening. As usual, every person's bedroom door opens at 6:20 a.m. regardless of how prepared you are for it. I suppose they figure it's more motivation for us to be dressed and ready so we aren't caught naked when the doors open on their own.

I walk out of the room to see my father coming out of his room. My mother is already awake in the kitchen nook of our housing assignment. She always gets up early, though I can't fathom why. Even though we are required to get up by 6:05, there are no rules for getting up early if you want to. I find her humming a familiar lullaby to herself and washing a mug, which likely held her morning tea.

"Good morning dear," she says to me, without turning away from the sink, "did you have a good night's sleep?"

I snort at her. "I slept as much as I usually do, let's just say that."

"Don't give us any of that attitude, Korinne, it's got us in plenty of trouble already," my mother snaps at me. I glare at her and stick my tongue out like the mature fifteen-year-old that I am.

My father chuckles while shaking his head, but makes no move to correct me.

"You should say something, Blaine. She shouldn't be picking up on those gestures. What if she started directing them toward the Peaceholders?"

He rolls his eyes at my mother, then gives me a thumbs-up. "I'll give her a friendly pat on the back for it." He grins at me.

I grin back. My father is like me, always pushing against the grain; fighting back against the Creators in the smallest ways. Of course, my father knows his boundaries better than I do, which makes it so he can get away with his rebellion. Me, on the other hand . . . well, let's just say I am not as good. I did get us kicked out of our more comfortable living quarters and put into this iron place.

"We'd best be getting to breakfast. It started just a minute ago," my mother suggests.

The Creators don't expect us to get to all meals exactly on time, which is unlike anything else in our schedule. Meals are exactly forty-five minutes long. Despite the start time being flexible, if you miss it, you are out of luck. Of course, they provide victuals in our home assignments, though not many. These provisions are only restocked once a week which elimi-nates the problem of people skipping meals altogether.

My brother comes out of his room half dressed, eyes bleary. His top half is the dressed half, but his bottom half sports only his grey underwear. I wrinkle my nose at him and make a disgusted sound. He chuckles and shakes his hips at me.

"What, don't like what you see?"

I gag in response.

"Put your pants on Sean, we don't have time for this," my mother, Elaine, says to him.

He rolls his eyes but does as he's told. As a family, we make our way to the mess hall. It only takes five or so minutes. The hallways are all full of standard white lights which reflect off of the metal walls and ceiling. The floor is metal grate, as if they are preparing for the halls to flood and have installed drains below just in case. This isn't a comforting thought to me.

The mess hall is busy, as expected. The large room is full of lunch tables and benches, set in rows down the length of the room. It is long and deep, so far that I can't quite make out the other side of the room as I come in the side entrance, which is the closest to our housing assignment. I grumble at the crowd as we push our way to the closest line. There are about ten different lines in the room, all serving the same thing. It still takes forever to get through just one of them.

I grab a tray and wait my turn. After what seems like ages, we finally make it to the front of the line. At this point, my stomach is grumbling and my annoyance is growing. I marvel at how they haven't built another mess hall to make our lives easier. Then again, I don't think that is their first priority here. The irony of the name for this place, *Safety,* is not lost on me. Sure, we're safe from the sun, but punishments come easily for breaking *any* simple rules. That, plus the constant watch from the cameras and the presence of the Peaceholders makes me feel anything but truly safe.

As usual, I pick up the first thing that is served: my vitamins. The small cup contains a multivitamin, some other pills I can't recall, and vitamin D, which we get none of from the biggest natural source, the sun.

I have never seen the sun, never felt it. You see, we're allergic to it. A couple hundred years ago, there were so-called sun events that wiped out a huge part of Earth's population. Some of us who survived had our genes mutated in a way that made us vulnerable to the sun. In short, it makes us explode in flames and die, instantly. At first, they didn't know what was happening, but then they figured out that those with the mutation who stayed out of the sun's rays didn't burst into flames. They found out how to recognize the gene at birth, so they test every new baby for it. From what we're told, the hospitals had to be sun-proofed extensively to give doctors a safe space to test the babies. If they find the gene, the baby gets put here. They've told us it's an allergy, but they refuse to explain what that even means scientifically. All I know is that we're stuck here in Safety.

Safety, you see, is what this place is called. It's a place closed off from the sun. As in, not even the slightest bit of sun can peak through any crack. Where we are, I have no idea. I assume somewhere deep underground, which freaks me out, to be honest. In any case, the people who put us here and provide everything we experience—even the horrid schedule we have —are called Creators. Some are the original inventors who made this place, others are the scientists maintaining it and building on it.

I hate them. Maybe it's the fact that I haven't experienced the reaction which comes with the allergy, but I hate this place, so of course I also hate the ones who put us here. My mother says that's not fair; they put a lot of time and money into this place and we ought to be grateful. I'm definitely not grateful.

For one thing, I resent that my family isn't a generational one like normal people on the outside. Essentially, my mother and father were both put here at birth, and so were my brother and I. The Creators pulled each of us from our actual families outside of Safety when the doctors found the sun allergy gene in us. The Creators formed family units from these people taken from the outside world. There aren't any blood families here. When we come of age, they give us pills that prevent us from having kids. The effects of the pills aren't permanent, so we have to take them every day until they tell us we can stop. Women do get to stop taking these pills at some point, but the men have to keep going. It's kind of a point of contention for many people here who want to have families. The Creators say that they don't want us to pass on the allergy to any offspring, if that's even possible. Also, they don't want to overpopulate the compound protecting us. I think it's just rude.

My brother bumps me with his elbow to get me to move forward. I nudge him back, but move forward with the line.

Ooh, French toast and eggs, I think.

This is one of the better breakfasts and I smile in glee. They do portion control our food, so I can't take as much as I want. Each person gets a different amount based on their age and weight. Apparently the Creators are concerned about us overeating. The server scans my access bracelet, then reviews the screen next to her before weighing my food on the plate.

After we pick up our food, we locate our table. It takes a bit of walking, but we soon find our assigned table. At this point, I'm so hungry that I've been sneaking bites on the way to our table.

"So who's excited for another fabulous day today?" my father teases.

Sean pipes up first, but only because my mouth is so full of food.

"Oh, I'm *thrilled*. Nothing like a good day's learning and work."

My mother sighs. "It isn't all bad, is it?"

I snort, which causes me to choke on my food. I cough loudly and spit the food out on my plate. Our neighbors, ones I don't know well, stare at me. My noises are loud enough that I even get the attention of a Peaceholder standing at the side of the room. His metal body armor glints in the lights and his eyes stare at me hard.

I wink at him.

His glare darkens, and he turns to look away from me.

"How many times have I told you to chew your food, Korinne?" Elaine scolds.

"As I was *trying* to say before my food so rudely interrupted me," I say, matter-of-fact, "an entire *day* of learning one subject? It's just *such* a joy."

"At least they take the time to invest in your learning," my mother attempts.

I roll my eyes at the comment and open my mouth to respond, but am interrupted by an announcement on the overhead speakers.

"Breakfast ends in ten minutes. Please complete your meal and proceed to your assigned classes or job assignments promptly at 7:30 a.m. The regular schedule for the children's jobs is posted on the bulletins at the sides of the cafeteria, as well as in each classroom."

Unfortunately, I already know what today is for my age group—cleaning the facilities.

I groan, making sure as many people hear me as possible. The Peaceholder's jaw tightens and I see him try not to glare at me from behind his helmet.

At least they know how unhappy I am about this whole situation, I think.

As soon as I'm done with the food, I pat my belly to show my approval, then stand up and walk toward the ramp that takes our trays away. Those assigned to clean up meals for the day will have already been sent back to take care of the mess. I envy them. I would much prefer cleaning up meals than cleaning up the facilities, but char, it's only once every couple of weeks that we do it, so I'll suck it up. The only good thing about my jobs is that Charlie is on the same rotation as me, so at least I can gripe to him.

The ramp is past the Peaceholder who just glared at me, which pleases me. I stand up straight and walk as closely as possible to him just to annoy him. I put on my best haughty face and puff out my chest to show that he doesn't bother me. Right as I walk past him, my foot catches on something and I pitch forward in shock. I soon realize I've tripped on the Peaceholder's boot.

Oh blazing flesh, I'm an idiot, I think, gritting my teeth as I try to right myself.

The moment my foot strikes his, the Peaceholder's hands fly outward and snatch me by the arms. A scream escapes my lips as his hard hands grip my shoulders.

"Let me go! It was just an accident, for heaven's sake!" I shout at him.

The entire room turns to look at me and the guard.

"Insubordination is not to be tolerated. We have been recently instructed to eliminate all signs of rebellion. You step out of line one more time, *girl,* and we'll throw you *and* your family out in the sun to burn and die," the guard scolds me.

I knit my brows in shock. I don't know what he means by 'eliminate all signs', but I don't have time to think about it much because of how flustered I feel now. This Peaceholder has always had it out for me. I don't know what his deal is, but he never ceases to take any bit of anger out on me. Most of the other Peaceholders make me uncomfortable, but they are at least cordial. Part of me fears him, another part of me wants to spit in his face. Still, his reaction is way more heated than normal, which gives me pause. All I can wonder is what changed to make him act this way.

"Yes, sir. I will be more careful where I walk from now on."

My words are kind, but my eyes are not, and he knows it. He lets me go and I toss my platter angrily on the ramp, food splattering on the floor. I'll avoid getting close to him and the other Peaceholders today because I know I won't be able to hold my temper any longer.

Let's get this over with, I think as I head for one of the facilities.

2

By the time I make it to the first set of facilities, Charlie is already there. I don't know how he beats me to our work assignments every day, but he always does.

"Decided to get up early today, then?" I tease him.

He laughs. "I'm assuming you're joking. I waited until seconds before the 6:05 shock today, but it didn't get me. So sure, I guess I woke up early." He sticks his tongue out at me, then laughs again.

"Wow, I'm impressed. You didn't take the shock today. You deserve a prize."

He grins at me. "It doesn't take me that long to eat. You know I can snarf it down fast," he says.

I roll my eyes at him, then turn to our group leader as they explain how we should work this morning. Each work station has several leaders. These are other members of Safety who have been good boys and girls for long enough to get the role. I've been too unmotivated to even try for it. This one is a woman, and I remember her. We cycle through the jobs every couple of weeks, so we see her often. She seems happy again this morning, her blonde hair pulled tight in a high bun, not a hair out of place. Her smile is perfect, her eyes a dark brown.

I very much dislike her.

My hair is stringy and strawberry blonde. My eyes are blue, just like the sky. Well, that's what I'm told by the outsiders hired to help in Safety. I've never seen the sky, of course. We've seen videos in our classes, sure, but that's the closest thing that I can compare it to. Scorch me, I wouldn't even be able to know if the videos are fake or not.

"Alright, please pick a partner to work with. The facilities will be closed as we work on them, so don't be afraid to pick a partner different from your own gender."

The woman keeps speaking, her voice bouncy and cheerful. I turn and fake a gag at Charlie, who grins at me. We've heard this all before, yet this woman continues to talk to us as if we don't know how it works. I stop listening to her and start looking around. Our group has twenty kids and we are all the same age. They group us together by age because they assign jobs according to our developmental stage. Cleaning the facilities started when we turned eight, and in my opinion, that is too early for kids.

I notice someone is missing. These people aren't all close friends, sure, but I can tell we aren't all here.

"Wait, where is Therese?" I whisper to Charlie.

He glances around and shrugs. "Maybe she's sick today. Or maybe she got pulled into another group for some reason," Charlie says back, a little too loudly.

We are awarded with a scolding look from the leader, so we both mumble apologies.

"Be quiet, don't you know how to whisper?" I hiss at him. He shrugs again.

It wouldn't be the first time someone from a lower age group got pulled up into another group, but it wasn't common.

Therese was nice, but she wasn't the smartest person in the group either.

"Maybe she's sick," I whisper, largely to myself, but I make sure Charlie can hear me.

He nods in affirmation then looks back to the leader, pretending to be interested in what she is saying.

People do get sick here in Safety, but not normally sick enough to have to miss work. They pump us full of medicine and vitamins every day, so sickness rarely makes it very far. Still, I can't think of any other reason Therese is missing. People just don't go missing.

My fingers fumble in front of me, my anxiety tugging at my chest. I can't describe why, but this change is freaking me out.

The leader stops talking and I move forward with the group to get our supplies for cleaning. It's first-come first-served, and I wasn't very early to arrive. Charlie is kind enough to have waited for me, so even though he was early, he stayed back to partner with me. That means we get the toilets, as usual. I groan, bringing snickers from the kids around me. They know me. They know I won't be quiet with my disapproval.

"If you got here earlier, you could get a better pick," the snooty woman says to me.

I look up at her and narrow my eyes. "Don't be so high and mighty. You're a group leader over the toilet cleaners. I don't think that's such a prestigious job."

She blushes at my words but continues staring at me, hard. "At least it's a station higher than your own. Remember, I can award demerits. You can't afford to get your family more demerits at this point, can you?" she asks hotly.

I continue glaring, but say nothing back. She is right, after all. I don't want to push buttons too hard. It just has to be enough that those who run this place know I'm annoyed.

Charlie nudges me with his arm and I turn to see him holding the buckets, rags, and cleaners for the toilet. His hair is black and messy. His eyes are green—so beautifully green. He's taller than me, but only by a few inches.

"Shall we?" he says.

My heart skips a beat as I stare at him. This annoying thing called puberty has been a recent development for me, and it's really getting in my way. Charlie's been my friend for years, but now I can't look at him anymore without wanting to kiss him.

It's even more frustrating to know that we don't pick our matches. The Creators do it for us. Even if I wanted to be with Charlie someday, it probably won't happen.

My face gets hot and I shift my eyes away. At the same time, I reach out and grab one of the buckets, cloths, and cleaners.

"Thanks. Let's get this over with."

We both rush to catch up with the rest of the kids in our group. They are whispering excitedly, and I want to hear what they are saying. With all of our shoes pounding on the metal floors, there are too many echoing footfalls for me to hear from this far away. There are no windows in this place, but the fluorescent lights above and at the edges of the path make it easy to see where we are going.

"Did you hear about Therese?" a girl in front of me whispers.

"No! What happened?!" the small girl next to her says.

My ears perk up, and I try to focus on their voices over the echoing sounds of our feet.

"I heard her father did something rebellious. Now they are confined to prison."

I shake my head. I have no idea how she could have heard something like that, but then I remember this girl's mother is employed in the Peaceholder quarters. Maybe she heard something from the guards. There's been no actual proof of a prison existing, but there have been rumors. No one has ever been sent to prison before that I know of, so this is an odd development.

"That's terrible. What did he do?" the other girl asks.

"I don't know, but something horrible, probably. Why else would Therese and her entire family be absent today? I didn't see any of them in the mess hall this morning!" the first girl replies.

I frown, realizing I didn't notice that myself.

"Do you think the Creators threw them in the sun? I mean, that's what the Peaceholder threatened Korinne with this morning. They seem more serious about punishment nowadays." The girl looks thoughtful as she speaks the words.

I blush at her words. I don't know why I do. It wouldn't be the first time I've made a scene, after all, but being connected to the strange absence of Therese and her family makes my stomach twist. What she says is true, though. Sure, that particular Peaceholder has always had it out for me, but his reaction this morning was extreme.

"We are right here you know," Charlie blurts, making me stare at him in awe.

The two girls turn around, embarrassed. "Sorry, Korinne, we didn't mean to be rude."

I nod at them. "S'okay, I know what you mean. That Peaceholder was not having any of my lip this morning."

Sure, I am continually pushing against the grain and rebelling in small ways, but I mostly just get angry looks and grunts, not death threats.

We pass a couple of Peaceholders stationed in the hallway and we fall silent, not wanting to provoke them with our conversation. I squint as we pass, trying to see through the tinted glass of the face shields that come just over their noses. When their visors are down, you can't tell anything about them other than what you can see from their chins. One of them is a man, I can tell by the brown beard he is sporting on his chin. The other is a woman. Her tight uniform on her chest gives that away.

They glare at me and I wonder if the Creators told them about the incident in the mess hall this morning.

When I think about that, I force myself to look forward, averting my eyes.

At length, we make it to the first set of facilities and Charlie and I start working on the toilets. With all the high-tech gadgets in this place, I wonder why they couldn't just get self-cleaning toilets. That has to be a thing nowadays, right?

"What do you think happened?" I ask Charlie, trying to make conversation. My mind won't let this whole Therese thing go.

"Hm? Uh, I cleaned that one already if that's what you mean," he says to me.

I look at the toilet and shake my head. I am hardly paying attention to my work.

"No, not the toilet. I'm talking about Therese," I say, trying not to let him see my irritation.

He furrows his thick black eyebrows and shrugs again. That is his favorite gesture. Holding back a sigh, I continue working on the next toilet which is set into the wall a few paces from the one Charlie works on.

"I don't know. I mean, they keep us pretty well taken care of here in Safety, so I don't think anything awful happened. They'll be back tomorrow. I bet they're just sick today."

I purse my lips but don't disagree. My gut still tells me something is off, but I know that is unreasonable. People don't go missing in Safety.

We clean for a few hours, Charlie and I enjoying each other's company. It's the same thing every morning, just lots of work and chores until a chime rings on the speakers overhead.

"Thank you for your diligence this morning. Lunch will be provided in the mess hall at 12:05. Please proceed there now. School will begin promptly at 1:00 p.m. as usual."

The voice sounds so pleasant that I want to scream.

She must not have been cleaning toilets for the past few hours, I think grumpily.

Before long, we make our way to the mess hall and I see my family grouped up near the back of one line. The Peaceholders don't know each of the family units well enough, but they have a list on their digital devices with the assigned tables. If they catch you not sitting with them, you can get a demerit. They require that we sit with our families for every meal.

"How was your cleaning today?" my mother asks.

I shake my head. "As good as cleaning toilets can be. How do you think it went?" I practically spit out.

My father chuckles. "Well, at least it's something easy. I was having a hard time wrapping my brain around certain problems today," he says to me.

"Oh please, your job sounds so easy," I say, rolling my eyes.

My dad works with technology here. Thousands of machines and other bits of tech stuff run this place. He has a knack for that sort of thing so they assigned him to support and build new technology to help Safety run more smoothly. It would be cool, except that means he and his team are also in charge of maintaining things like the electrical shockers that force us out of bed every morning and the automatic doors that make sure we don't have privacy.

Still, I can't hate my dad for it, he's just doing his job like the rest of us.

"Sweet! It's chicken fried steak today! Love me some foooood," my brother exclaims, elongating the word. It's clear he's very excited.

I wrinkle my nose. We stay on a three-week food cycle and all I can think is why they can't make that cycle longer. I swear we just had this meal yesterday. Unfortunately, there aren't a ton of other options. They provide salads and a type of soup at every meal, but the different types are only on a one-week cycle, so you get sick of those quick.

I decide to grab the main course, but I make sure to drop a word with the servers about increasing the rotation of food options for variety. As usual, they shake their heads at me and say they'll 'let the higher-ups' know. Before long, I'm picking through the better parts of the food, which ironically, are the vegetables. They are always fresh from a garden somewhere. It makes me wonder where we actually are in the world, since they haven't told us where Safety is. We know it's somewhere in the United States, but other than that, we have no idea. I can only guess that gardens grow somewhere nearby.

"Are you going to eat that?" my brother asks eagerly, pointing at my picked-over fried steak.

"No, by all means." I push my tray over to him.

The speakers above us crackle, making the room fall silent. There aren't generally announcements during lunch, and it's too early to say that the mealtime is almost done. I look at my parents curiously.

"Citizens of Safety, we are sorry to interrupt your meal, but we must inform you of the passing on of some citizens within our facility. The Larsson family has taken ill and have been removed from the facility by peaceful means to prevent the spreading of the illness. Know that they died with little pain. We will miss them greatly."

My skin suddenly feels chilled.

That's Therese's family, I realize, my stomach turning. I saw her only yesterday. How could they have gotten that sick so quickly? Murmurs spread around the lunch room as people hear the news.

I look at my dad, who has paled. He keeps his face hard and continues eating, trying to hide his emotions. I narrow my eyes at him and he shakes his head ever so slightly.

I get the message: *Later, now is not the time.*

"That is so sad," my mother says next to me. "I didn't know them well, but wasn't the daughter in your age group, Korinne?"

I nod and open my mouth to say something, but stop when I see that one table across the room is in a fuss. My eyes shift to my dad and back to the table. He hardens his jaw and resists the urge to turn toward them.

The family there, the Grilivans, I think their last name is, are arguing with each other, though I can't hear about what. A Peaceholder has moved closer to the table, his hand on his gun. A few other Peaceholders are moving in now and I can't help but stare. Most of the other families are doing their best to not watch the scene, but I don't care. One guard—I realize it's the one I tripped on at breakfast—sees me watching. He flips up his visor and glares at me.

I turn my eyes away.

"Yeah, I wasn't close to Therese, but she's been in my group since the beginning. It's weird that she's gone now."

The words are hollow as I say them. People don't just die in Safety. They keep us healthy and strong. Sickness seldom breaks out, and with our seclusion from the outside world, diseases from there don't usually make their way in here. Every external employee is tested and checked thoroughly before entering the facility.

My mother sighs but keeps eating. "At least they died peacefully, that's a comfort."

My father stiffens at the words, but nods again.

I know he's hiding something but doesn't want to say it here. The problem is that there isn't anywhere that's free of cameras or microphones. Our eyes lock again, and I see longing in them. He knows something but can't share it with me.

I fall into the rhythm of eating my food until the announcement sounds to get to class. Today is math day. I hate math.

3

JUST AFTER LUNCH, I FIND CHARLIE AS QUICKLY AS I CAN. I KNOW he is probably uneasy about the announcement as well. He is closer to everyone in our group than I am, so someone dying would have affected him more. I don't bother trying to get closer to people because I know my poor attitude about this whole place just annoys them. When I find him, his eyes are red. I feel a pang of sadness. It isn't because I see he's been crying, though that's part of it. I didn't realize he cared enough about Therese to cry about her being gone. I am jealous of him. I start to think about losing one of the few people that are close to me and shy away from it.

People don't get lost here, I think, *I don't need to worry about that*.

Despite my attempt at alleviating my own concern, that very thing just happened.

"Are you going to be okay, Charlie? I know you are closer to everyone in our group," I say, shifting on my feet.

He looks at me and smiles, appreciative of my attempts to console him.

"It's just that we were talking and laughing together in class yesterday, and now she's gone. I don't understand how she could get sick so fast."

I bite my tongue. I want to tell him I think something is off and that I want to dig into it more, but I know it will not help him right now. Instead, I put my arm around his shoulder and lean my head against his cheek.

"I'm sorry, what can I do for you?" I say.

He shakes his head, then puts his arm around my waist. "This is helpful."

My heart thunders in my chest and I think I might throw up. His firm hand against my hip is making my skin tingle. I can barely breathe.

"You will tell me if I can help, right?" I ask.

He nods this time and lets me go. Part of me is grateful that he pulls his hand away. The other part mourns that the time was so short.

Ugh, these dumb hormones, I think, trying to push the lingering feelings away. It doesn't work.

"Let's just get to class. It's math day, I know that's your favorite," he says, punching my shoulder in jest. His eyes are still teary, but it's clear that he doesn't want to talk about it anymore.

I roll my eyes.

"Yay, I can't contain my excitement."

When we get to class, however, the teacher looks grim. Charlie and I exchange curious looks before we move to our seats. Luckily, our teachers allow us to choose our seats at this age. When we were kids, they arranged us alphabetically first, then shifted us around if we were disruptive. As C and K aren't close, we pretty much never got to sit together until last year.

"Hello class. As you know, today is typically math day, but given the circumstances—it might be best if we change the subject—just for today." Murmurs spread through the class at her words.

The circumstances? Is that all she can say about it? I think.

Reaching toward my desk, I put my thumb on the keypad and it scans my print. A little light flashes green before a hissing sound announces the top of my desk opening. I pull open the lid and take out my school holopad and stylus. They give each of us a new pad at the start of every year. It's preloaded with each year's curriculum. They deliver all of our school work here, and we send our completed tests and assignments through them as well. I guess that's why they want us to lock them in security desks. The Creators are very serious about cheating. They make it almost impossible to do it.

I detach an earbud from the holopad and stick it in my right ear. All around me the students do the same thing. A small square at the bottom of the black pad scans my thumb again before it chirps in my ear through my earbud and says, "*Welcome to school today, Korinne.*"

The screen flashes on and I see that once again, the battery is fully charged. The desks wirelessly charge the holopads every time they sit inside. Still, I've never gotten close to empty before. Sure, I sometimes have to take it out for a night or two to finish my assignments, but the battery seems to last forever.

My eyes shift over to the empty desk in the second row, and a nervous feeling runs through my gut again. Therese used to sit there, but not any longer.

I'm not the only one that steals glances over to her desk. Even so, it's clear everyone is trying not to show the others what they are thinking.

"As you all heard, the Larsson family has unexpectedly left us. Because of the nature of their sickness, it was important that they were taken care of quickly and efficiently. They died to save us all."

The room is quiet.

I stare at the small badge on our teacher's left shoulder. It's an image of two crossing domes, intersecting at the center like the Venn diagrams we've learned about in school. Everyone that runs Safety wears it. My mind shifts to why all the teachers are hired from outside the compound, rather than from within the Citizen ranks. I still don't understand. Some jobs, mostly manufacturing, cooking, and maintenance jobs are taken care of by us—those with the allergy to the sun. Teachers aren't.

I glance over at the female Peaceholder who stands at our door. She has the same badge as our teacher.

"It seems prudent that we take the time to remember the history of our people, and the sacrifices made by the government to keep you and your families safe, despite your ailment."

My mind is spinning. *Sure, we go over this history regularly, but why now? How does this relate to the Larssons?*

My thoughts are soon answered by Mrs. Pimm's next words. "There has been unrest from citizens here in Safety as to the Larsson family's sickness and how the Creators handled it. It is important to understand Safety's dedication to keeping you and your families safe from not only the spreading of sickness in the facility, but also in protecting you from the dangerous rays of the sun. Please direct your attention to your holopads for the video."

A chime in my ear lets me know that the video is starting. Charlie and I exchange glances. I think about what happened after the announcement in the mess hall earlier. *There was that one family putting up a fuss after the news of the Larssons . . . the Grilivans?* This place is normally so quiet and boring. My heart races as I think of the possibility that something bigger is happening. As a fifteen-year-old, I shouldn't be worrying about this kind of stuff; I have schoolwork and job assignments to worry about, but I hate this place. Couldn't they have come up with a better solution for our allergy?

My screen buzzes to life and I know that the other kids' holopads are doing the same thing. An image of the earth appears in front of us and a deep voice talks.

"Earth: a peaceful place for all humans to thrive and live. For years, the sun's cycles continued without trouble, until the solar anomalies began."

The image flashes and different scenes of chaos and fire appear on the screen.

"Many of us didn't know what to do when technology was no longer reliable. The earth's resources were burning up before our eyes. Our only solace was that the solar events didn't last more than a few days."

The video zooms out and we see the earth from a distance. There are black spots everywhere from mass fires, red flickers showing huge flames that still hadn't been extinguished.

"These events particularly afflicted a small percentage of the remaining population worldwide. When exposed to the sun, their new ailment made them spontaneously combust."

A man walks out of a post office and explodes in flames, screaming like crazy. I flinch and look away for a moment. Ever since they started showing us these videos when we were younger, that scene has always made me uncomfortable. I'm terrified, knowing that if the sun touches any of us, we'll die in the same way.

"The United States Government had mercy on you and the others afflicted. They created Safety as a sanctuary for you—a security from the sun. We here at Safety are working tirelessly to produce a cure for your ailment. We hope to someday return you to the outside, where you will be able to enjoy the freedoms of the world once more."

The video ends with beautiful videos of forests and mountains, rivers and deserts. Just before it shuts off, a woman in a smart-looking white uniform smiles at us. Her olive-skinned face has deep-set wrinkles, her hair black and wavy.

"As the Creators, we will work to ensure that you will be cured."

A burning enters my chest. Natalie Yurislav, the head of the

Creators and leader of Safety, smiles back at us. Me? I'm just annoyed. Not once have we seen her in person, only videos of her and her merciful actions.

The sound ends in our earbuds and we look up at our teacher. She's smiling.

"We are so grateful that we could save each of you at birth, secluding you here in this compound for you and your families' sakes."

I grumble sarcastically under my breath.

I used to mourn the fact that I'll never know—never *meet* my actual parents. Still, I was a baby when they brought me to Safety. My mother and dad here are as real as ever, so I try not to dwell on it much anymore.

Our teacher launches into more explanations on how they are working to resolve our ailment. They want to cure us so we can get back to normal life. They claim they are just teaching us how to work hard, to work as a combined human race so that when we are released someday, we can integrate back into humanity with no laziness or trouble.

I just think they want to work us to death.

I've stopped listening to my teacher since my eyes wandered back to Therese's desk. It still sits there, empty, the thumb pad on the bottom of the desktop blinking, waiting for a student's thumb to open it. I jealously think of the way her dark brown hair fell around her shoulders, curly and wild, unlike my stringy strawberry hair. She was never unkempt, but always looked beautiful. Therese wasn't egotistical, either, and everyone liked her. That fact makes me feel even more guilty at her being dead—my petty jealousy over her beauty and popularity seeming so silly now.

She was the nicest person in the class, except Charlie, of course. I can't imagine how her family got some strange sickness that put us at risk.

I chuckle to myself. We are already in danger from the

primary source of energy for our planet, yet they got themselves into more danger.

"—and that is why the changes need to be made to procedure."

I perk up at my teacher's words.

"As you know, the testing that we perform on you doesn't typically begin until age eighteen, but given the circumstances of the Larsson family, it is imperative that we find a cure for your allergies as soon as possible. So, by decree of our leader, Natalie, testing is to begin once a person reaches age fifteen."

My stomach sinks. That means our entire group, plus the other few groups of fifteen-year-olds are going to start the tests. Charlie stares at me in horror. I clench my jaw, trying to not be nervous, but I know I am not doing a great job of hiding it.

The class shuffles and murmurs around me.

"Now, now, calm down, class. The tests aren't anything to be worried about. They are simply a set of medical tests and blood work—various things that will give our researchers more time and opportunities to learn about your ailment. By changing the age, we are providing more data for our extensive research team to use."

The tests—that's all we ever heard about them. When you turn eighteen—or now fifteen, according to the changes—they start taking you away a few times a week to a part of the compound that no younger kids even know about. After your tests, you can't talk about it. All the adults have to swear to not tell anyone any details, which only makes the rest of us more nervous for them.

"The tests will begin for our group this afternoon, thus class will end early so you can begin your service to the research. Questions?"

Everyone is silent for a moment before a tall boy in the back raises his hand.

"Yes, Jimmy?"

"Do we need to prepare for this—test?" His voice is shaking.

Our teacher smiles, her teeth perfect in her mouth.

"No preparation needed, just be you."

I want to ask what the tests actually are, but I know she won't tell us anything about them. One of the other kids doesn't seem to care.

"What are the tests? What are they going to do to us?" a girl next to me asks.

I roll my eyes. Our teacher purses her lips and peers down at the girl.

"You know I cannot disclose that. It will not matter, because soon enough you will get tested. You will also be sworn to the same secrecy that the others in the compound have undergone. Measures will be put in place to ensure your compliance."

Whatever they make the adults agree to must be serious for them to keep their mouths shut. Even my rebellious dad won't tell me. Normally he'd tell me anything, even rumors about what's going on in the compound, but he keeps the tests to himself.

"Your testing schedule is Monday and Thursday. Groups often get three days, but with the increased numbers of subjects, we can reduce that to two days a week."

What a horrible way to start a week, I think to myself.

Sure, weekends are pretty much the same as weekdays. On Saturdays and Sundays, though, school is shorter, and they give us limited free time in the afternoon to play or worship any of the religions we choose. I usually just sleep since they allow us to take naps on those days.

The history lesson ends and we lapse into math. Ordinarily, I'd be hating the day, but I can't stop thinking about the tests. My eyes flick to the clock every few minutes as my teacher tries to teach us algebra. Before long, the bell rings above and in our earbuds.

"Class is over. Please continue to the hallway where you will be escorted to your test locations." My teacher eyes us sternly.

My stomach lurches. I'm scared, so scared that I can feel myself shaking. I don't know why I'm scared, it's not like people get hurt or killed. My father and mother don't have any marks that I can tell from these tests, but it's the unknown that gets me.

I move to Charlie's side and grab his hand. The moment I do, he looks over at me and gives a wry smile. I know he's scared too, because he squeezes my hand. Butterflies spring up in my stomach and a nervous happiness bursts in my chest.

Several Peaceholders are in the hallways waiting for us. Two are female and two are male.

"The girls and boys split up now. We separate testing facilities for privacy reasons."

Charlie and I exchange glances again.

"Why can't my best friend be a girl?" I grumble, teasing him. Even as I say the words, I know they aren't sincere. I wouldn't feel this way about him if he were a girl.

He grins at me. "Because then I wouldn't be as nice as I am," he teases back.

I stick my tongue out at him and we laugh.

"See you on the other side, I guess," I say.

"Yeah, good luck," he responds.

I'm not sure luck is what I need for this test.

4

The group of girls, roughly half of our fifteen-year-old group, is led down the hallway toward the mess hall. For some reason, the fluorescent lighting on the ceiling and the floor is buzzing even more loudly than it regularly does. My nerves are apparently making me crazy.

I know every one of these girls, but I am not close to any of them. I shift my gaze among my classmates until I land on Susan. My gut wrenches when I see she's leering at me. She's someone who has terrorized me from the moment we could talk. I narrow my eyes at her, but look away quickly. We huddle together, our collective fear making us temporarily forget about anything that made us dislike each other. When we get to the mess hall, the leader stops suddenly and speaks out loud.

"Our first round of new subjects is here, ready to go."

A set of Peaceholders, these ones both male, nod and push a few buttons on the wall. As they do, hissing sounds echo against the metal hallway and a set of double doors protrude from slits in the wall. There are doors like this throughout the compound. They'll close off hallways or rooms for construction or maintenance all the time. I find it annoying when I'm late for my job or class and I have to take a detour because they've closed off a path.

When the two sides of the door slip together, one of the female Peaceholders reaches down and holds her key card to the floor. A loud and continuous beeping echoes around us. Just then, a panel in the floor in front of the newly closed-off hallway opens.

I'm not the only one who gasps at the revelation.

There is a door in the ground.

I peer around, wondering how many hidden doors exist in the floors of the hallways.

"I will lead; each of you follow single file," the other guard says. She's tall and bulky, the visor of her helmet flipped up. Charred, I'd have thought it was a man if I couldn't see her face and hear that her voice was a woman's. She turns and steps into the square hole in the floor. There must be hidden stairs because as she walks, she descends little by little.

We stand there, no one volunteering to go first.

"Hop to it! We don't have all day," the other guard shouts at us.

I'm glad I didn't put myself in the front of the group, for the blonde girl there looks like she'll pee herself when the guard shouts at us and she's forced to start the descent. My nerves get worse as I get closer to the opening in the floor. It looks dark inside, which isn't making it better for me. I somehow manage to wedge myself near the back, but I'm not the last. The idea of having my back exposed freaks me out.

Soon I see the top step and I use it, trying not to overthink what's happening for fear that I'll trip and tumble down the steep stairs that are now coming to light.

There are small dome lights, blue and dim, stuck to the walls along the top of the narrow spiraling stairs. Sure, it's enough for me to see the steps, but it's not bright enough for me to feel able to move too easily. I'm surprised by how soon the stairs end. The way they looked made it seem like they'd go on forever, descending into some pit of doom that is always described by the pastors the Creators let in here on occasion.

At the bottom, I'm surprised to see another metal hallway, pretty much exactly like the one that we left above. I'm not sure why I expected anything different. The hallway appears the same as the ones we use every day, except there are far more doors on both sides. The hallway extends forward pretty far, but there is a definite ending, a single door marking it.

"This is where you will be tested every week. You will not have access to enter. You will have to be escorted, just like this, every time it is your turn. Since you will be in class before your tests, that shouldn't be a problem," the lead-guard says to us.

The guard behind us speaks then, and it makes more than just me jump in surprise. She'd been so quiet up to this point, we'd forgotten she was there.

"To the left is the locker room. Enter and locate your locker. It will be unlocked via your fingerprint, similar to your school holopads and home doors. Undress and put on the robes that are inside."

I blush, tucking my hair tightly behind my right ear. I realize I've been doing this continuously. This habit of mine happens when I'm nervous. I reflect on the directive to undress and think about the rest of our class.

Ah, that's why they took the boys away from us.

I am suddenly grateful that Charlie isn't part of this group. I don't think I could handle the idea of him seeing me without clothes.

The blonde girl in front hesitates for a moment before moving to the door. As she gets closer to it, the door slides open automatically with a hissing sound. Our footsteps echo, even more so with the hallway being closed on the other end. The sounds echo back to us, making the situation seem more dire.

Soon I enter a large room with the other girls. Lockers are

spread out along the sides. They are tall, a few inches taller than me. For a moment we all stand there, unsure of how to tell the difference between them. Then red flashing lights appear above a screen on top of the locker. A picture of Lauren, one of the other girls in the group, appears on the locker to my left.

We are silent, no one wanting to offer encouragement or even comment on the place. Everyone's too nervous. I see my face on another locker, freckled and framed by my stringy strawberry hair.

Charred, is that what I look like to them?

The picture is recent, so they must have pulled from the most recent round of citizen pictures. They insist on taking our pictures every six months. Our home unit doesn't have mirrors anymore, so I haven't seen myself in a long time. Mirrors were another one of the luxuries we lost when I got us demoted to a simpler living space. I'm glad the Creators took pictures a couple weeks ago, because the one before looked even worse than this one.

I move to the locker and search for the finger pad. Sure enough, I see a small black square embedded in the blue metal of the locker at my chest level. I look up again at my face to make sure that I'm in the right place. Lockers open up with slight hisses around me and I sigh, knowing that the inevitable is coming.

The moment my finger touches the pad, I hear a ding, then a hiss as the locker opens up at my touch. Inside is a simple blue robe, made of some shiny material on the outside and some comfortable looking fluff on the inside.

Hmm, at least we'll be walking around in style, I think sarcastically.

They are positively hideous. I am sure that if it were dark in the compound, the slightest light would reflect off of these things. My only solace is knowing that everyone will also be wearing this horrible piece of clothing.

I look around, sheepish, as the girls around me undress to put on their robes. I always hated not having privacy for things like this. Exercise is and always has been my least favorite class for this exact reason.

Couldn't they have provided stalls or something? I think.

Sighing, I pull off my clothes as quickly as possible and put on the blue robe. The insides are even more comfortable than I thought. If it weren't for the ridiculous look of it, I might actually be pleased with the clothes.

"Please take the ear buds," a mechanical voice sounds in front of me.

I jump at the sound, not expecting it. The girl laughs nervously next to me. Her name is Charlotte, that much I know, but I've not taken the time to get to know her much.

"I think everything is going to make me jump here. This is so creepy," she says.

"No, Korinne is just a baby about everything," Susan's voice sounds above the others. I shrivel inside, turning red. Normally I'd fight back, but I'm feeling too overwhelmed to say anything.

Snickers sound from some of the others, but Charlotte gives me an apologetic look.

I smile wryly at her, knowing she didn't mean it to go that way.

"Oh, thank heavens someone said it. This place is terrifying," another girl replies.

I'm relieved that someone said what I've been thinking. The fact that we've all been too terrified to talk has made this even worse. I suspect the others feel the same way, for quiet conversations spring up around me. Snagging both of the earbuds, I shove them in my ears. The moment they enter, I hear a small chime.

"Hello, Korinne of family 46B. Please confirm your identity by saying your name."

I open my mouth and say my name, but I can't hear myself

talking, not even in my head. These earbuds have somehow muted everything from the outside. It freaks me out so much that I want to tear out the devices to get my hearing back. Before I can, the woman's voice is speaking in my ears again.

"Voice match confirmed. Please continue to examination room 12 down the hall."

I furrow my brows and look at the other girls. Some of them have put in the ear buds and some are still getting their robes on. No one appears to be making a move toward the hall, so I am the first to do it. Despite my anxiety from the whole plight, I know that waiting will not help me.

When I get to the hall, I find myself even more uneasy. Ordinarily I can at least hear the slight buzzing of the lights above and below in the metal hallway, but not now. The surrounding hall is silent. I can feel my feet hitting the metal floor, but can't hear it.

Is this what it feels like to be deaf? I wonder.

There is a small section of Safety for the deaf or hard of hearing. I see them signing to each other from time to time, but I've never been curious to know how it feels for them. I'm not appreciating the experience as much as I probably should.

As I walk, I note that each room has a screen above it with a number. I pause for a moment, trying to remember which room the voice told me. This is all so distracting, my memory doesn't seem to be working.

"Please go ahead to room 12," the robotic voice in my ear says again.

Perfect timing, I think, knowing that it couldn't have been a coincidence that the moment I stopped to consider my room number, it spoke. The technology in here is so creepy sometimes.

I soon make it to room 12 and stand in front of the door. There isn't a pad for a fingerprint, but I hear another chime in my earbuds and it slides open silently. I imagine hearing the familiar hissing sound of the doors just to calm my nerves. It doesn't work.

I step inside and find that the room is very small. There is just an examination chair, similar to the ones in the dentist's room when we visit him every year. It's white and looks new and clean, as if I was the first and only person to step foot in the room.

That's not true, however, as I see that there is a woman in a scientist's coat and a massive black helmet.

"Hello, Korinne!" a cheery voice says through my ear buds. "I am Lucia, your examiner. We'll be spending a lot of time together, so I hope that we can get to know each other well."

I'm irked by her words. She sounds so chipper, but looks like she is protecting herself from toxic gas, like the kind we've learned about in History when they discuss wars.

"Um, sure." Once again, I can feel myself speaking, but I can't hear it.

"You can hear me, right?" I ask.

The black helmet bobs up and down. "Yes, I can hear you just fine. Your earbuds pass the sound to speakers here in my helmet. You can turn off the sound-blocking on the head-phones if you want. Just tap the left bud four times."

I try it, and the moment I do, it's like my whole world opens up again. I hear the slight buzzing from the surrounding lights, and I can hear the scientist shuffling in her seat. The first thing I notice, other than the fact that she is wearing what looks like a bug head, is that she doesn't have the Safety badge.

For a moment I think I might ask her why, but then I decide I probably shouldn't.

"Have a seat," she says. I hear it both through my earbuds and muffled from outside of them now that the sound-blocking is off.

I move to the chair and with some effort, pull myself up. It is more stiff than I might have guessed from the way it looks. I lean back in the chair and put my feet up on the rest.

"Alright. Korinne, the first thing that you must know is that I do not want to hurt you. There are a few tests, however, that we need to try which might not be the most comfortable. We will take it slow to see how things go, is that alright?"

I nod.

For a moment, I consider turning on the sound-blocking again, just to get rid of the muffled sound of her voice through the helmet, but I decide not to.

"I'm going to get a blood sample from you first. We'll do this every time since we need as many samples as we can get from each of you."

I shrug. I've never had my blood taken before, but it doesn't sound like it will be too awful.

I'm wrong.

She pulls out this long needle that looks like it will poke right through my arm, and sticks it into my skin. My stomach clenches and I stare at the dark red liquid as it oozes into the vial above the needle. I feel like I'm going to throw up. My head gets light and I'm getting dizzy.

"Korinne, you can look away if you need to."

I hear her, but I can't tear my eyes away.

Oh charred, I'm going to throw up, I think.

I shoot up in the chair and retch. Lucia somehow gets a bowl in front of my face as I throw up.

"I'm sorry, I should have told you more about what it would be like. Are you going to be okay?" her voice echoes in and out of my earbuds.

I nod, though my mouth and throat burn as my eyes water.

"Unfortunately, I still need more. If you'd like, you can turn on music using the holopad to your right."

I look over to see that a small holopad is embedded in the chair's arm. I tap it, trying to distract myself as I feel the needle shift in my arm. I force away the nausea again and focus on the music. It's only a bunch of instrumental music, but I turn it on anyway. As it plays, I reach up and tap the earbud four times. The outside sounds disappear and I can only hear the music.

"Alright that is enough blood for today," Lucia's voice echoes over the music. "I am sorry about the helmet. It is just a precaution. We are reasonably sure that your ailment is not contractible, but we do various experiments with your blood and expose ourselves to your bodily fluids. It's best to be safe, after all."

I nod, but I don't really care. I kind of wish she'd stop talking, but I know she won't.

"Alright, see this?" I hear her say.

I open my eyes and see a small vial of something yellow.

"It looks like pee," I say, not caring what she'll think.

I hear her laugh in my earbuds and see her body shake with laughter. I don't know why she left her mic on for the laugh, but I'm guessing it's because she thinks it will make me feel more at ease.

"It is a serum that we derived from the sunlight. We can't truly capture sunlight in a tangible form, but we can imitate it in a way that helps us test a less-potent form on your body."

I gape at her. "You are going to put that on me?!" I say, horrified.

She nods and I can hear a motherly tone to her voice. "I know it sounds dangerous, but it won't affect you too terribly. We are just testing to see how adverse your reaction would be to the sun if you were exposed."

I'm shaking now. *My entire life I've been told the sun will kill me, and she's going to put some on my skin? What is wrong with these people?*

"Ready?" she asks.

I almost say something sarcastic about how nobody could be ready for having something they're allergic to put on their skin, when she pops the small bottle and tips it over my arm. A few yellow droplets land there.

Heat flares up on my skin, and I shout in surprise. It's not painful, but it's like I've got a fever of 104 and I'm feeling myself from the outside. The effect is quite shocking.

I bite my lip nervously, trying to adjust to the feeling of the heat. I look over to see that my skin is now red and swollen there.

"Hmm, your allergy is severe, indeed. We see various responses to the serum, but yours is volatile. I am glad we could keep you here in Safety."

She puts the bottle away and I end up turning off the music. The stimulation from the instruments and the feeling of heat on my skin is too much.

"Alright, we'll now put a bit inside your body. Of course, if we exposed you to the sun, you'd be hit externally, like I tested with the serum, but whatever antibody or antigen we create will help you from the inside. So let's see what resistance you have to it. Before that, however, let's attach this here."

She pulls a metal arm from below the chair that is attached to the backrest. It is made of some shiny material and has a strap on the end. I look at her, feeling more nervous.

"It will not hurt, it's just going to measure your heart rate and vitals as I administer the serum."

I nod, but I'm not sure I believe her. She fastens the thick strap to my arm and I feel a slight buzz from it, as if electricity is coming from inside the fabric. It makes the hairs on my arm stand up.

"Alright, here we go." She pauses and I see her helmet turn toward me. "You may want to look away."

I see what she means. She has another huge needle, though this one is connected to a vial with the yellow stuff in it.

I follow her instructions and close my eyes.

The moment I do, I feel the pin prick and a warm rush of

something into my arm. I gasp as heat runs up and down my arm. It's not painful, nor as overwhelming as when she dropped the serum on my skin, but it's still uncomfortable. I grit my teeth and think of eating my favorite meal, or taking a restful nap and dreaming of seeing the outside.

I hear her humming as she works.

"Hmmm, yes, your reaction is really strong to the serum, even more so than many other citizens of Safety."

Partially because I'm curious, and partially just to distract myself, I ask her something.

"How many people do you experiment on?"

"Just two per week. I get Saturday and Sunday off like the rest of you."

The hot feeling is running in my chest now and I hold my breath instinctively until I have to gasp for air. Lucia inspects the monitor before her, the screen reflecting off the black of her visor. As the heat travels slowly through my limbs, I try not to panic at the odd sensation. I focus on other things while we sit in silence for what seems like forever. When the heat has spread everywhere inside me, I start to shake, not from the serum, but at the strange reaction as my nerves take over once more. A small gasp escapes my lips and Lucia's helmet turns toward me.

"Are you okay? Can you breathe?" I hear Lucia say. She sounds worried.

I nod with uncertainty. *How should I know if I'm okay? She's the scientist.*

"Perhaps we should be done for the day. We usually have an hour together, but this should be enough. I'm going to put a calming agent in to counteract the serum."

I close my eyes again and feel another needle enter. This time, it cools the nagging heat that's running through my body. I sigh in relief.

"Alright. As you know, it's important that you don't speak

about what happened today, or any day in the testing period, to anyone. Not even family. To aid with that, I've just inserted microbots into your bloodstream. In a few moments, they will attach to your brain stem. If you try to speak of this to anyone, it will activate and trigger your pain response immediately."

My eyes snap open.

"What do you mean? What did you put in me?" I ask, terrified.

"It's nothing to worry about—just follow the rules, and you'll be okay. I am hoping to get to know you better, Korinne, and I look forward to our future sessions. You may go now," she says as she pulls the strap off my arm.

Her hand lingers there for a moment and my body chills. I pull my arm away sharply and look the other direction.

I'm so shocked by the entire experience that I say nothing. I move silently to my locker to redress, or at least it feels that way because of the sound-blocking.

Two other girls trickle in early and I notice there's a wide range in their reactions. One appears thoughtful, the other even intrigued. I just feel sick. Most of the others must be stuck for the full hour, because I'm dressed and out before I see them.

I can't wait to hear what they did to the boys, I think as I get ready to find Charlie.

5

WHEN WE COME UP FROM THE HIDDEN BASEMENT, THE THREE OF us don't know what to do next. The other girls stare aimlessly at the wall or wander around for a moment. I am grateful I'm not the only one affected like this. We were told that sometimes the tests end early, and sometimes they might go long. Today, we were let off early. Now the three of us have unexpected free time.

Free time outside of the weekends just doesn't happen, so that's part of why we stand in the hall together. I'm staring at the floor where the trapdoor closed not too long ago. The halls are empty, save for a few adults passing here and there for their jobs.

"Are you alright, Korinne?" someone says beside me.

I start and turn to see my father looking at me. I've known my entire life that he isn't my birth father, but the idea is more potent today, after having gone through the tests. It makes me wonder how I got landed with this dumb sickness and how my parents, wherever they are, could be safe from it. I'm just happy that I love him so much.

"Oh, hey dad. Just—thinking," I respond.

"Whatever you are thinking about looks terrifying."

He smiles, clearly making a joke. I give him a half smile before my eyes unfocus from him and I shift my gaze away.

"Kor, what happened? You look worried."

I start to speak, but then remember how I'm not supposed to talk about the tests. I'm not sure where the line is for that.

"They started the tests on us today."

His eyes jump open wide at the news. "They what?" he says, staring at me.

It's hard not to react to his shock. It's freaking me out enough already that they just pumped me full of sun-imitating serum and hooked me up to machines. Now he's panicking about the whole thing too. He must see it on my face, because his eyes get smaller and he appears concerned again.

"What changed? Did they say why?"

I shake my head. "Not really. Something about needing to speed up finding a cure for our allergy. I don't know."

My dad narrows his eyes and looks away. "Are you okay? Did they hurt you in the tests?" He shakes his head as he asks, putting a hand to his forehead.

I don't immediately respond, so he tries again. "I know you can't say what they did, but you can at least tell me if you're alright."

I smile wryly at him. "I'm okay. No pain, just weirded out by it."

He smiles in relief at me then.

"You'll get used to it, Kor. It is odd, and you might never fully understand what they're doing, but normally the examiners are chill. You'll have the same one for years, if not forever."

I nod, curious why what we've said so far isn't off limits. My dad has had no trouble speaking about the tests so far. My curiosity gets the better of me and I open my mouth to say something more potent.

"Do they also—"

I try to ask if they also poke him with seemingly endless needles when I feel the back of my neck and head tightening painfully. I gasp and put my hand there, tears filling my eyes as I ride out the pain. Soon it's gone, no pain left. I have fallen to my knees in shock and my dad is down at my level.

"Kor, you can't talk about it, remember? It's not worth trying. Those bots in our heads are effective." He says this like he knows from experience.

"I know, I remember, I just had to know what it would be like to go against it."

His dark brown eyes twinkle at my words, and I sense pride in his face. "That's my girl."

He kisses the top of my head, and I wrap my arms around him. I think that under normal circumstances, a person might feel strange that they never knew their actual parents, but the love for my father I feel right now makes me forget the curiosity about my birth parents. In reality, I'll never know them. I don't think the Creators will ever find a cure for our allergy. I'm expecting to stay in Safety until I die. Until we all die.

"Hang in there, Kor. The tests are alright. Try not to dread them. They come, they go, and we move on with life," my father says. "Dinner still isn't for an hour, so take a moment to relax. Maybe take one of those naps that you are so fond of."

I stick my tongue out at him. He and my mother have tried to get me to go to one of the religious services every Sunday, but I can't resist the urge to sleep. I wonder if they'll ever stop giving me char.

He smiles at me again before it melts away. "One thing, Korinne."

My smile disappears as I sense something foreboding on the edge of his lips.

"There is something going on here in the compound. I'm not sure what to make of it, though."

He furrows his brow and looks left and right. His eyes then shift to a camera hanging from the top of the wall a few paces away before they return to me.

"Just—be careful. While I understand your curiosity about the bots in there," he taps my head lightly with his finger, "try not to break any rules, okay? It's safer here for everyone if we just keep living the way we're being asked to."

The words hang heavy in the air between us. I'm filled with confusion and disappointment. Practically my whole life, especially now that I am in my teen years, my father has always been encouraging me to push against the grain, to fight against the odd treatment and oppression that we experience here in Safety. Now he's telling me not to?

He smiles one more time at me, and I look in his eyes. The way he stares at me for so long is different this time. There is something there, something he's hiding.

The cameras, I think—*he's holding back because of them.*

It's hard to say why I know that's the message he's sending, but I just know. His outright words of 'follow the rules' here in the open are very different from the behavior he normally encourages at home. There are cameras there too, so the fact that we are not in our domicile doesn't change that fact.

What I do know is that the testing age change is bothering him. A lot. Before, the tests didn't begin until we turned eighteen, and now it's fifteen. None of this happened until the Larsson family disappeared. Something feels wrong about the whole thing. Families don't just disappear, not from Safety. Sure, this is the first time a life-threatening disease has made its way into the compound. Despite that, something isn't right.

My father nods at me and turns to leave.

"Go hang out with Charlie or something. You look like you need to do something fun to get your mind off of the tests," he says lightly.

I nod, but only for show. My mind is spinning now. I can tell my father has information, something from his technical maintenance job he isn't telling me. My curiosity tugs at me to run back to him and ask outright, but there is a fear inside me now because of how he glanced at the camera. I wonder if he knows what happened to the Larsson family when they got sick. He worked with Mr. Larsson in technical maintenance.

I realize it's odd that I stood here staring for so long, and decide to move on. I need to find Charlie to see if he's okay. All I can wonder is if he's as worried about all this as I am.

Turning toward the mess hall, I make my way around the corner to find him.

6

I'm walking down the hallway when a group of older kids pass me.

"Why do you think they changed it?" one girl asks the few others with her.

"We're only sixteen. What if we don't pass the tests because we are too young?" another girl wonders.

For the first time since they broke the news about the lowered age, I'm amused. They have no idea what the tests are, and they are assuming it's a school test.

"You'll be fine, Clara. You're the smartest in the class," a blond boy replies. It's clear he likes her by the way he stares at her.

I know they are from the class above me because I've seen them in various places at school, and they are in the classroom next to my own. I walk past them with my head down, not because I'm scared, but because I am not in the mood to make eye contact. They notice this, and one boy reaches out to touch my shoulder.

"Hey, you're from the fifteen-year-old class right?" he asks. I look up into his eyes and nerves strike me. I've seen him before like pretty much everyone else here at Safety, but I don't know his name.

"Yeah, just got done with my testing," I say.

His eyes widen and he backs away as if I've been exposed to a disease or something.

"Did you pass—how was it? Oh, you can't talk about it, can you?" he says quickly, the sentences running together.

I know I can't say anything, but I decide to have a little fun. I have zero intention of actually giving away any information, and somehow the microbots in my brain know. I don't feel the pain attack me like when I was talking to my father, but there is an odd buzzing there as if they are waiting.

"It's horrible, they—" I say, then I grab my stomach and bend over as if I'm in pain.

"It hurts! I can't tell you, or they'll kill me!" I say, exaggerating.

I probably shouldn't joke like this, but I can't help it. The boy turns white and I hear the two girls behind him whimper.

"Can't—say—anymore," I pretend gasp.

They are backing away now, fear in their eyes. I compose myself and just walk away, not wanting to continue the charade, but also quite pleased with the results. They don't know who I am, but they'll remember me now. Who said we can't have a bit of fun with the tests?

I continue through the hallway and as I get closer to the mess hall, I see a group of the boys from my class. Charlie walks behind them, appearing grim. His hair is disheveled, even more than usual. He looks kind of cute, I think.

The moment he sees me, his face brightens and he walks quicker. I hear him say goodbye to our classmates, then he's there and I'm throwing my arms around his waist. I don't know why I am doing it, but after the stress of the past hour, it feels good to hug my best friend.

Inside, I know he's more than that to me.

"Well, gee, it's only been a couple hours. Did you miss me that much?" he teases me.

I pull back and slap his arm in jest.

"Are you trying to tell me you felt completely okay and at ease with the entire testing process?" I ask incredulously.

The buzzing flares up again in the back of my mind. It is as if the microbots in my brain can sense my proximity to the subject of the tests.

"No it was pretty freaky—I'm glad we're done for the day, to be honest," he confirms.

I nod and we walk around, unsure where to go before the meal. It's still twenty minutes before the mess hall will start serving food, so we decide to walk to the art hall.

The Creators must feel at least a little bad that we can't enjoy nature at all. So they've set up a hallway with a few pictures of the outside world. I go there occasionally when I need to see something else besides metal, grey fabric, and fluorescent lighting. There are only five pictures, and one of them is pretty terrible, but it's better than nothing.

"Why do you think they changed the age for the tests?" I say, speaking the question that's been on my mind all afternoon.

Charlie looks at me sideways, a thoughtful look on his face.

"I mean, didn't our teacher say something about them wanting to develop a cure for us quicker? Maybe because the Larssons got sick, they are realizing how hard it will be to keep us healthy and safe."

I gape at him before gathering my thoughts for a response. "Somehow, I just don't believe that. Have you seen the medical technology they have here? No one's going to die from a medical issue unless they get their heads chopped off. How long has it been since anyone got sick?" I say.

Charlie stares at me in horror before it shifts and he gives me a look like I'm stupid.

"Yesterday, remember?" he says.

I blush but try to play it off.

"I mean before that, silly."

He smiles and crosses his eyes at me.

"I'm just being a smart alec," he chuckles, "but you have a point, I don't know if or when someone has gotten sick in Safety. But the workers come from the outside. They could bring something in here."

I shake my head. My instincts want me to come up with an argument, but I can't think of any.

Soon we round the corner into the short hall with the pictures. The first one I see is my favorite. It's a picture of a large pool of water, colors spreading in rings outward. It is apparently an image of a landmark or something in a place called Yellowstone. I of course couldn't point out where that is on a map, but it's somewhere out there.

I take a few moments to admire it, letting my thoughts wander as much as possible away from the events earlier and the news about Therese and her family.

"Do you think the world is really so colorful out there?" Charlie asks. I turn to see him touching the picture across from my favorite one. It is an image of a giant mountain, trees of many colors spreading on the steep surface, the sun is half hidden behind one peak and the beams from the sun shine toward the viewpoint, as if they are reaching out for us.

I shrug.

"Probably—I don't think they made these up. Then again, no one here has ever seen anything outside, so it could all be a lie."

Charlie snorts. "I doubt the Creators would bother lying to us about what the outside world looks like. It doesn't seem like it's worth their time."

Even as he says it though, we both contemplate the picture.

It's not a painting, so it's a picture of somewhere, but when or where, we don't know.

We move down the line and see one picture showing a forest covered in white stuff. We're told that it's snow, but I have no concept of what it literally means. Our science teachers taught that it's when rain freezes, but we haven't seen rain either. The fourth picture shows a bunch of beige colored blobs and it's labeled a desert. This is the one picture that has zero beauty to me. *Why would anyone choose to live in such a place? Especially when the other pictures show more beautiful colors.*

When we get to the last picture, I want to throw up. Amidst the other pictures, they've placed one that depicts anything but beauty. It also happens to be the only one with a time and name plate below it. It shows a tall building, made of what looks like stone. Windows line it all the way to the top. People in the streets are staring in horror at a man that is on fire. The sleeves of his shirt and his hat are blazing with yellow flames and he's screaming.

I shudder at the image.

The plate below reads, *The solar flares of 2120 and their destruction of the world.*

"Why the char do they have this one here?" I say, disgusted.

"My guess is to remind us that even though there are beautiful things in the world, it's not a good idea for us to go out to see them," Charlie says grimly.

I scowl at him, but it's because I know he's right.

"When did you become so wise, oh lanky one?" I tease.

He laughs, then shoves me to the side. "We both know that you are the smart one. I may not be booksmart, but at least I know how to play nice," he jokes back.

I wrinkle my nose and punch him in the arm. He grabs it, pretending to be in pain. Then we both start laughing.

The speakers crackle above us and I'm surprised how quickly the brief break went by. I'm not upset though, because the fact that our schedule was different and we had free time today made me uncomfortable.

"Citizens of Safety, please proceed to the mess hall for your dinner. It will begin promptly at 6:05 and last for 45 minutes."

"Well, I guess it's time to get going. Wow, that free time went fast, didn't it?" Charlie says, turning away from the pictures.

As I turn to follow him, my eyes linger on the picture of the man on fire. He looks terrified and in pain. My lips press into a thin line as I consider what that must have been like for him. I don't often consider what would happen if we went out of the compound and the sun hit us. I'm struck by the fact that we haven't been told the exact details of how our allergies to the sun react if we go out. This bothers me so much that I run to talk to Charlie.

"Why do you think they've never told us what our reactions to the sun would be? I mean, if we are allergic to it, don't you think they'd have given us more detail than just 'you'll just die'?"

"That's an interesting point," Charlie says, cocking his head as we make our way to the mess hall, "Maybe because they've shown us that image back there time and time again. They do say that pictures speak louder than words, right?"

I am still distracted by the question as we join a growing group of people in the hallways.

"I gotta get going. It gets tricky finding the other orphans when too many people are packed in the room," he says to me.

I nod in agreement, then say I'll talk to him later.

Weaving through the people, I take advantage of the fact that I am still smaller than most of those around me. It helps me get to the edge of the room where my family and I typically meet. I'm the first one here, which is unusual. I rarely make it first to the meals and have to wait for my family. Today I will be spared the lecture from my mother about being on time to things.

At length, my mother and brother join me as we wait for my dad. As she sees me and gets closer, there is an obvious look of surprise on her face. It's as if she can't believe that I am really here waiting for her.

"Well, I think that's a first in the history of Safety: Korinne making it first to a meal. What changed today?" she asks.

"I had some unexpected free time today. Didn't know what else to do with it, so I wandered around."

My brother stares at me. "Free time? How did you get away with that?!" he asks, jealousy in his eyes.

I don't feel like telling them how the Creators started the testing on kids fifteen and older. I'm still so freaked out by the experiments that I'm afraid by just saying something to them, I'll get the pain in my head. My brother doesn't take this well, and he pokes me and asks over and over.

"What's the secret? Did you get away with it? Are you going to get us demerits?"

My mother watches me warily, as if she thinks that I've for sure done something wrong and am going to get us into deep trouble.

"Dude, stop talking. I'm not going to say anything to you," I say to Sean.

He glares at me, then sticks out his tongue, reminding me just how young and immature he is at the ripe age of nine. A pang of jealousy hits me when I realize that he still, despite them lowering the age, won't have the experience I've just had for six more years.

I hope so, at least.

I see my father's head poking above the crowd as he pushes through them. He is generally earlier than this to meals, and I wonder what may have happened. He looks normal, though, as he approaches us.

"Hello there, family. Did we all have a great day of doing the same thing we do every other day in our monotonous lives in this mindless compound?"

I snort at his comment.

My mother purses her lips. Sean completely misses the jibe on our conditions.

"Yeah! I learned some pretty great things about World War II today and it was soooo interesting."

My father smiles at him and puts his arm around Sean's shoulders, leading him away to a line that is forming for the food. My mother still stares at me.

"Korinne, please don't tell me you tried to get out of school early again. We can't take another demerit for our family, we've had enough as it already is."

I shake my head. "I didn't, Mother, I promise. We got out of class with permission though because—" I pause, still not sure how to say the words. " . . . they started tests on us today."

Her eyebrows shoot up in surprise and her mouth drops open.

"But you're so young—?" she says, her eyes glazing over slightly. "Are you okay? When did this happen?"

I just nod, still afraid to give any more details about the whole thing. With my silence, I think she realizes I don't want to talk about it, so she just nods. My dad returns, curiously eyeing our reactions.

"Did you want to get food sometime today?" my dad suggests.

I roll my eyes, but we get in the line. It's nothing good today. Chili with thawed scones and lots of toppings. I don't like this meal so much that I decide to go get salad from the bar there. Since we're earlier than usual, I actually get the good things to go on top. Croutons are almost always out by the time I make it through, but today the bowl is brimming with them.

Maybe being earlier to meals is worth it after all, I think.

There are a few people with white lab coats and clipboards

walking around to make sure that all the citizens are accounted for. If you are missing, it's a demerit or two for you and your family.

When I sit at the table, my brother and dad are debating over the best way to eat the chili. I wrinkle my nose as my brother puts the thick chili in a cup and drinks a large gulp. He's trying to convince my dad that it's the best way to eat it. It only makes me more glad that I went with the boring salad for dinner today.

My mother is hiding her face as they debate. I chuckle at the idea that she thinks she could hide her association with us. We're stuck with her until the death time. Unless we do get out of here, at which point I have no idea what would happen to our odd-knit-together family.

"Attention, all Citizens of Safety."

My skin crawls at the sound of the speaker. This is the second time in one day that it has come on during a meal when it shouldn't have. My eyes shoot to my father and he gulps down his bite heavily. He seems nervous as well.

"We regret to inform you that the Grilivan family has been relocated to a high security location within our compound. It is of utmost importance that we as Creators keep you citizens safe from the sunlight, but also from the dangers of rebellious peers. Their table will remain empty for the time being. They have received fifty demerits for their actions and are subject to the lowest level of work and conditions. As such, their table will remain empty for the foreseeable future."

I eye the table that this morning was full of worked-up people and then look away quickly. I am not the only one that looks, but I don't want any Peaceholders to associate me with whatever they did. In my peripheral vision I see something shaking. I see my father's head droop down as he's trying to casually get another bite, but I see the source of the movement: his hand quivers uncontrollably.

"Dad, is everything okay?" I whisper, concerned.

He shakes his head. "Oh, I'm fine, just sad that I won't be working with Stan Grilivan anymore. He was a nice guy," he says, still staring at his plate.

I feel frozen cold on the inside. I had forgotten that the Grilivan father also worked in tech maintenance with my dad and Mr. Larsson. Staring at my dad hard for a moment, I proceed to pick at my food.

I'm not even a little bit hungry anymore. Hearing that the Larsson family is dead and now they've punished the Grilivan family to seclusion and terrible living conditions makes me nervous. My father worked with them, and now it feels like our family has a target on our backs, but I can't even explain why.

Nothing is happening. My dad isn't in trouble, I tell myself.

Even as the thoughts spin through my brain, I know that I'm lying to myself. I wonder what my father has gotten himself into, and I know my mother feels the same. She glares at him from next to me and puts a small bite of chili in her mouth, chewing heavily on it.

Still, my father just eats with his eyes angled down. My mind shifts to the conversation I had with him in the hallway after my tests, and it confirms my thoughts. There is something bigger going on in Safety.

7

We finish dinner in silence, and so does most of the mess hall. It seems no one knows how to handle the news that two families have been removed from the populace in one day. The fact that multiple people in our secluded compound have disappeared feels very ominous.

My family and I make our way back to our housing unit then, dinner extending just past 7:00 pm. We aren't required to be back in our domiciles until 8:30, but we decide we don't feel like doing anything else. Since we aren't on meal cleanup duty, we figure we'll take the time to be together in our home and head in early. Each night, the rules require us to spend at least 30 minutes of 'quality time' with our families before we work on homework, or whatever other free activity we choose until lights out at 10:00 p.m.

"Well I tell you what, I've had a day. Working in the processing plant has been exhausting. We've been canning meats for the past week and I don't know if I can look at or even think about beef the same," my mother is saying when we walk through the metal door into our unit.

My father chuckles. "You didn't have a problem with it

while we were eating chili this evening," Blaine says, a twinkle in his eye.

My mother isn't pleased. "Oh sure, you can joke with me all you want. We know your job is to tip tap on computers all day," she jibes.

Elaine, my assigned mother, is bitter because she had to get back to work now that Sean is nine. Mothers are to stay home in the domiciles with their children until they turn nine, at which point they start the longer mandated school and start working like the rest of us.

Sean has adjusted well to the change, but my mother is less than pleased that she had to return to the food processing part of the compound. Food is brought in from farms somewhere and our people prepare and can it. The work sounds kind of methodical, yet soothing in a way, but my mother hates it.

"Hey, my job isn't all perfect and easy. We have to deal with a lot as well," he says back.

I'm not sure why his choice of words strikes me the way it does, but I freeze, causing my brother to bump into me.

"Hey, you dummy, why'd you stop like that?" Sean complains as he pushes past me.

I mumble an apology, which is unlike me, but I'm distracted.

"Didn't you work with Mr. Larsson and Mr. Grilivan?" I blurt out, just getting to the point.

My dad pauses before our kitchen counter and turns sharply to me. He has a smile on his face, but I can tell it's forced.

"Yes—yes, I worked with them. Interesting guys, that's for sure. I liked Stan Grilivan—good man—I guess he should've been more mindful of the information we come across," he says with a shrug.

He moves behind our small counter and opens a cupboard there, pulling out a glass. He then fills it up and pours it into our coffee machine. It's a tradition of his to drink coffee after each meal, and I have never understood it.

"What does that mean?" I say, unsatisfied.

He shrugs. "I don't know much about it. I was working in a different server station than them for the past few days. But the Creators weren't thrilled with whatever they found."

I can tell my father is keeping information from us. I eye the camera above his head swiveling back and forth slowly. The Creators have always been there, sure, but I'm even more aware of them now. It's mostly because of how my father glanced at them in the hallway earlier.

Before I can say anything else, my mother plops down on the couch.

"How about some world trivia?" she suggests.

Sean and I both groan at the idea.

"Please no, we don't care about the dumb facts of earth's history. It doesn't make sense to me anyway," Sean complains.

I nod in agreement. "Mother, we appreciate that you learn about the world outside of Safety, but the rest of us don't have time to memorize weird dates and facts." I wrinkle my nose for emphasis.

"Fine, what do you suppose we do for our family time today?" she asks me with an eyebrow raised.

"Um, can't we just skip it?"

My father eyes me, knowing that she will not take it well. As expected, my mother pouts and she looks at me.

"This time is important for us as a family. We need to get to know each other better. Yes, we've had each of you since birth, but we still have to get along. You know, there are other families who aren't coping with the arranged family situations well. I heard the Coplin family got demerits for their incessant fighting."

She says the last part in a whisper, as if she's telling us a huge secret she's learned from work. I can see a tear dripping from her eyes.

She clearly feels sensitive about family stuff, doesn't she? I think.

As a teenager, I can't say that I don't have my own share of family sensitivities myself. Sure, I wish I knew my parents, and sometimes I wish I knew if I had any siblings, but right now I'm too distracted by the state of Safety and what went on today in the compound. Still, I feel bad for making my mother unhappy, so I move next to her and put my head on her shoulder.

"I'm sorry, Mother, I'm just distracted with all that's been going on in Safety today. I can't get it off my mind."

I turn to see my dad raising his eyebrow at me. He knows I'm laying it on thick for my mother. I know I'm being a bit over the top. I'm not actually a touchy-feely person, but I feel like I need to make it up to her. I stick my tongue out at him, and he covers a smile.

"What do you mean? Seems like a normal day to me," Sean replies, fingering the small bits of string that poke up from the rug in our only living space. The floors in the rest of our domicile are metal, so this is the only spot that's comfortable to hang out in except for chairs and our beds. Right now I'd love to go to bed early, but I know that will make my mother even more upset. Besides, I want to see if I can get more information from my father.

"I just wish I knew what happened with the Grilivan family," I say pointedly.

I shift my gaze to my father to see his reaction, and I can tell he's trying to hold back. His eyes flick to the camera, then he takes a sip of his mug, long and drawn out. I see him slightly shake his head. The movement is almost imperceptible to even me.

He does know something but can't tell me, I think, frustrated.

"I'm just glad it didn't happen to us. I've only just started getting used to these living conditions. I can't fathom getting put somewhere worse," my mother says, wiping the tear from her face and shooting me a pointed look.

My eyes shift down at the comment. It's my fault we are here. I have always hated conforming to the rules, especially when they make no sense. Sure, I will get out of bed on time, but that's only because of the shock. There were a couple times I was intentionally late to a meal because I was just being stubborn, then one time I threw a baked potato at a Peaceholder who was being a jerk. He didn't take that well. That one gave us three demerits.

It's not just me, though. My father rebels in his own ways too, just usually with more subtlety than I do. My demerits, along with his one or two got us dropped to this lower housing unit. We used to have carpet in every room.

I sigh at the thought of waking up and stepping on the hard, cold metal every morning. Plus we don't get as many extra provisions between meals. It's a lot smaller too. I'm just grateful that we still have hot water. Honestly, that is the only thing that's keeping me from racking up the demerits for my family. My shower may be short, but I sure as charred refuse to shower in the cold.

"I'm sure whatever the family did, the punishment was merited. The Creators know when to give demerits and I believe they know what they're doing," my father says, taking a sip of his tea.

A lie. I know my father well enough to know he wouldn't give any credit to the Creators like that. I wonder why my dad is acting so weird and feels uncomfortable with the camera. His behavior makes me think we are on thin ice, about to get in trouble, though I can't say why.

I stare at him and he notices my gaze. "So, big day for you today, huh, Korinne?"

Changed the subject. Clever.

"Sure, I guess so. Just the tests and whatnot, but you knew that," I say, trying to act casual.

"It's very odd that the Creators would lower the age for the experiments. I can't imagine what would cause them to do that," my mother says, pulling out a holographic board game and raising her eyebrows at me.

I shake my head.

"Oh, fine—I'll play something with you, Mom," Sean murmurs, settling next to the small table we have between the furniture.

"It's fine, it wasn't that bad," I lie, still subconsciously feeling the heat under my skin. The fact that they injected me with manufactured sunlight still freaks me out, but I don't want to let it show for Sean.

My mother isn't dumb. She purses her lips at me and raises an eyebrow. I eye my brother meaningfully and she nods as if she understands. It's fine because I know I can't give details about the experiments anyway, so we let the subject drop.

I move to the closet and pick up a holopad assigned to our domicile. Moving my thumb over the pad, the fingerprint scanner grabs my thumb and opens.

"Welcome, Korinne. What do you wish to do?"

A series of options appear on the screen and I select the book icon. I figure I'll just settle down with a book until I can figure out how to pry information out of my dad. I glance up at the camera and wish I could just turn it off. However, that would be punishable by lots of demerits. One family's teenager thought it would be fun to unplug it. That got them enough demerits alone to drop two levels in housing, just below our own.

I shiver at the thought. I move to the couch and sit next to my dad, who stares off into the distance as if he's deep in thought about something. Putting my feet to the side, I lean into him and feel the warmth of his arm under my head. If anything, I'm grateful that they placed me in his care as a baby. I've gotten so close to my father that I can't imagine ever caring much for a relationship with my real dad. Sure, my mother is okay, but I have grown closer to my father.

I read the Tale of Two Cities, apparently a standard work in the outside world. I've begun reading it before, but I can't get past the first thirty pages. The writing style feels weird to me.

The book appears on the holopad and I scan through the text, though my mind isn't in it. I keep thinking about the scientist who poked me a bunch of times and stuck me with weird liquids, all of which I feel like she shouldn't have been putting inside me.

A chime in the speakers above makes me look up. *"A visitor has arrived at the door. Please respond."*

I look at my father curiously and I see his jaw harden, but he forces a smile.

"How strange, who'd visit us at a time like this?" he says before standing up to go to the door.

I'm frozen inside. People don't visit domiciles at night, and if they do, it's pretty much guaranteed to not be a citizen. Every citizen should be home by now. I glance at the clock and see that we are still a little early, but I still dread what we'll see when he opens the door.

My father pauses before opening the door and turns around to look at us. He very pointedly looks at me and puts a finger to his lips, telling me to not get us in trouble. I scowl at him, but I'm still terrified. My stomach clenches and I feel like I might fall over if I was standing.

He casually opens the door and I see two Peaceholders with their helmet visors retracted. One of them looks like he's had a bad enough day to kill someone. The other one smiles.

"Sorry to disturb you at this hour," the friendly-looking one says. I've seen him before, but then again, I've seen most of the Peaceholders; I don't think they get new ones very often.

"No problem, sir," my father replies.

I note the honorific term use and struggle to keep myself from making a comment or rolling my eyes. At length, I look down at my book, still listening, but trying to make it seem like I'm not.

"I understand you are Blaine Christensen, no?" The nice-looking one says again.

My father nods. "Yep, that's me. What can I do for you?"

The mean-looking one narrows his eyes.

"We need to ask you questions about Stan Grilivan and Todd Larsson. You're their colleague in technical maintenance, right?"

I flinch at his tone. He sounds angry, and somewhat rude. I don't get the feeling that the combination is good.

"I'm more than happy to answer questions, sure. Yes, I do —" my father pauses, eyebrows furrowed, "—did work with Todd. Assuming Stan can still work, I do work with him."

The shorter and kinder looking Peaceholder smiles and puts up a hand.

"Please exit your domicile, if you don't mind. We want to question you in private."

My body explodes in fear, and I can't help but stand.

"Wait! What is going on?! Father, don't go with them," I say, louder than I mean to.

He puts up a hand and smiles disarmingly at me. "Korinne, it's no problem. I'm sure their questions are important. I'll be back soon enough, right guys?" my father asks the Peace-holders.

The shorter Peaceholder laughs at the use of the term 'guy' and the other scowls. My fear deepens at the reaction. I can't understand why my dad would rebel in such a way right now. I know he's in trouble; it's not a coincidence that two of his colleagues were punished or killed, and now they are here for him.

"I'll be back, no worries, okay?" he says, though I can see unease behind his eyes.

He exits our home, and the door shuts with a loud hiss. I can't help but think it's the last time I'll see my father. Despite my efforts not to, I cry.

8

MY FATHER NEVER RETURNS TO OUR HOME UNIT, AND I'M convinced he's gone forever. This day has been so terrible that I am afraid to stay awake any longer for fear that it will all just get worse. Despite my mother's insistence to spend time together, I retire to my room and go to bed early.

As my door hisses closed, I replay the image of my father going out our front door, his head turning around so he can look at me and give a slight smile. I can't imagine how he could even smile at a time like that. I know Peaceholders, and even though one was being nice, it's not comforting to me. I'm still crying as my mother tries to come into my room a few times, but I've engaged the lock.

When I started crying, my mother didn't understand why. She came to console me, sure, but she didn't think there was anything to cry over. She's deluded. How she hasn't considered the connection between the families being killed or punished and dad being taken is beyond me. Unless she's just pretending to not know for my brother's sake.

When I think about that, I decide not to judge her too harshly. Sean is only nine. As much as this is scary and disturbing to me, he's younger and innocent. I soon drift to sleep and am surprised to hear the speaker in the morning.

"Citizens of Safety, the time has come to get up. Clothe yourselves and prepare for the day. If you have not yet risen from your bed, motivation can be provided to assist you in doing so."

I roll over and, and for the second day in a row, glare at the space where a clock used to be. I slept through the first announcement. I'm lucky I didn't sleep through this one, because then I'd be getting a good shock awake. No one wants to wake up that way. Well, maybe Charlie. I shake my head at the thought of my friend and his odd decision to let the electric shock get him out of bed most mornings.

A pang of sadness rips through my chest as I recall the events of the night before. Tears threaten to come, but I push them away, focusing on my newfound hatred of the Creators and of this dumb compound. I don't know why they took my father away. I should be scared that they'll take me or punish my entire family like they did the Grilivans, but I'm still numb from seeing my father walk out.

When I dress and get out to the kitchen, I freeze, hardly able to believe my eyes. My dad sits at the table, sipping a cup of coffee. Without even trying to stop myself, I run to my dad and throw my arms around his neck.

"You aren't gone! They didn't hurt you!" I say, squeezing hard.

He grunts at my forceful hug. "Well, good morning to you too, Kor. Is there a reason for this treatment? Normally I just get to hear your complaints."

I punch his arm in jest. "Hilarious, dad. I'm just glad you made it back."

He looks curiously at me. "Now, why would I not come back? I have such great coffee to look forward to."

The comment is snarky and sarcastic, which is even more encouraging than anything. It's like the nervousness he had from the night before is gone. Part of me wonders why he's changed, but most of me doesn't care. Even though it was a short time when he wasn't acting normal, I still missed his true self.

"Oh, Korinne, leave your father to his coffee before you make him spill it over his work clothes," my mother spouts, moving from the kitchen to shoo me away, "I still don't understand the drama from last night about your father leaving. I told you everything would be fine, and see how I was right?"

My father raises an eyebrow. "Yes, I heard about your emotional response. I suppose it's good news that you love me enough to worry when I go out the door. I do wonder, shouldn't a fifteen-year-old be over her separation anxiety by now?" he smirks.

Naturally, I stick my tongue out at him.

"Oh, Korinne, would you stop that? You're fifteen, for Safety's sake, use words or something. Tongues are best kept in mouths," my mother fusses at me.

Sean rolls out of his room and brightens when he sees our dad.

"You're back! Why did they take you? Where did they take you? Are you in trouble? What's going on?"

My brother fires the questions out so quickly that I wonder if he's even taking a breath. No one scolds him though, because I suspect my mother and I both want to know the answers. I will ride along happily with my brother's barrage of questions.

"Well, I see we are quite curious about what that was last night," he says, inspecting us. "I don't know what you're expecting to hear. They had questions about Stan. I answered them, and we moved on. Wasn't that big of a deal. I do work closely with him, so it's unsurprising that they'd ask me questions." He says nothing else.

Wait, that's it? That's all he's going to tell us? I think.

I'm disappointed, but I shouldn't be surprised. Sean isn't having it.

"That's it? I was hoping to hear something more epic, like they have chosen you to be a part of an experimental study for super powers or something," Sean blurts, waving his hand in the air to show someone flying through the air.

His use of the words 'experimental study' irk me, and I resist the urge to say something. My father chuckles and my mother shakes her head.

"So—" I cut in, "—that's it? You aren't in trouble or anything?"

He shakes his head. "Now, where would you get an idea like that? I'm fine, no trouble at all."

I stare at him in disbelief. "Really? The fact that the Creators punished Stan Grilivan for something during his work —the same work that you've been doing—doesn't give you any pause?" I say skeptically.

He sighs. "Yes, Korinne, I am aware of the implications, but I am innocent. I wasn't involved with the Stan stuff. In fact, I had little to say to help them."

A chime dings above our heads and I know it's time to head to breakfast in the mess hall.

"Oh, of course. I just poured my tea and it's time to go. I guess that's what I get for staying up waiting for you, Blaine," my mother shrugs.

"Oh Elaine, you know you didn't have to stay up for me," my dad says, matching her tone.

"Citizens of Safety, breakfast will soon begin in the mess hall. Please proceed to dress yourself and make your way to the hall. Eating will begin promptly at 6:15 a.m."

My mother feigns annoyance, but my father stands up and moves to her. He hugs her tightly and they kiss. I wrinkle my nose at the sight and Sean groans, but I'm actually grateful to see that they get along. My father flinches as my mother puts her arms around his waist. I narrow my eyes, noticing the odd reaction. Fortunately, my mother notices too.

"Are you okay? Did I hurt you?" she asks, worried.

"No, no. Well—yes, but you didn't know, and it's fine. I had a bit of a fall down the stairs on the way home last night, and I've got a bruise on my side. Nothing to worry about."

"What? You never mentioned that to me when you got home."

"Dear, not now. I'm fine. Let's just get to breakfast before we are late."

My mother doesn't listen. She reaches over to his grey pullover shirt and pulls it up to see a purplish black bruise extending from his waistline to his armpit. My stomach lurches.

"Blaine! You ought to go to the medical ward and get this taken care of," she scolds him.

"Charred, that's a wicked bruise, dad. Too bad it doesn't have a cool story to go along with it," Sean says, admiring the wound.

My mind is spinning. I've never fallen down the stairs, but something doesn't seem right about the bruise. That it's so large gives me pause. I am trying to figure out what to say when another chime overhead reminds us we have five minutes to make our way to the mess hall.

"Later, dear. For now, let's just eat. I'm starving today."

He pulls his shirt down and a flash of silver catches my eye on his wrist.

"Okay, fine, let's just go. I guess it's going to be another morning without time to finish my tea." She grumpily pours her freshly made tea down the sink.

"You good, Kor? You look like you're still half asleep."

I realize I've been just staring at my dad the whole time, not saying anything. I probably even have a dumb look on my face.

"Hmm? Oh—sure, let's go," I say.

My mother leaves our apartment first, followed by Sean,

who is excited about the biscuits and gravy for breakfast today. I wait a moment to let them get ahead. My father notices this and raises an eyebrow at me. I know he likes to go out last in the group, so he can tell that I've lingered for a reason.

"What really happened, dad?"

His face softens at my comment.

"Kor, I fell down the stairs. Seriously. I'm getting older and I damage more easily. There isn't anything more to it than that."

Even though I can tell he's keeping something hidden, I shrug it off.

"Okay, if you don't want to tell me, then fine."

I'm not really angry, just concerned for him. I feel like if he doesn't tell me what really happened, then I can't help him. I laugh internally at the idea.

What could I possibly do to help him? I'm only fifteen, I think.

My father reaches up to his face and runs his fingers through his hair. It's getting long, and I am surprised that they haven't made him go to the barber. There aren't strict rules for how you have to style your hair, but you aren't allowed to grow out a beard or let your hair get too long. As he moves his hand, I see he's wearing his advanced access bracelet. His job requires more access since he maintains the systems and computers, but there is a small silver charm there that I've never seen before. I squint to inspect it. From what I can see, it looks like a set of rings set into each other, with a star overlaid through them.

"What is that?" I say, pointing to his bracelet.

He looks where I'm pointing and a look of surprise flashes on his face.

"Oh, this? It's just a new access fob that they've given to me and my colleagues—" he pauses for a moment and looks sheepish, "—my old colleagues. Anyway, it's nothing you need to worry about. As with the bruise, just forget it. It's going to come into question later at my tests, I'm sure, and my examiner is going to have a field day. But it'll work out."

I furrow my brow at the reference to his examination. He gave me a pointed look as he made the comment, as if he was trying to hint something, but I heard nothing. I wonder why he could say it without his brain getting attacked, but then again, he said nothing about what they actually do, which is maybe why he didn't get pain from the microbots. Still, it feels out of place.

Not sure how to respond to his words, I just shrug again and turn to walk out the door. I'm moving quickly to catch up with my brother and mother when I feel a firm hand on my shoulder. My father slows me and then whispers.

"I know it's weird and scary to have the tests administered now, but know that you'll be alright. If your examiner is anything like mine, you're in excellent hands."

Once again, the oddity of his comment is not lost on me. Sure, it's somewhat comforting to hear the words, but why bring it up at a time like this? I don't even have more tests for a couple more days. I've spent the better part of the evening and morning distracting myself from them so I don't have to be stressed.

"Um, okay. Thanks," is all that I can say to him.

He smiles and we hurry to catch up to the rest of our family.

When we get to the mess hall, I can't help but feel that there will be another terrible announcement saying another family is going to be punished or taken from Safety. Nothing comes.

"You seem on edge, Korinne, are you alright?" my mother asks as she finishes her most recent bite.

"Hm? Oh yeah, I'm just thinking about yesterday. I can't help but wonder what is going on with the Grilivans," I say, poking at my food with a fork.

My mother looks both troubled and annoyed. "I understand it's upsetting that one of the Larsson kids was in your class, but it won't do you any good to worry too much. You weren't close, were you?" she asks.

I shake my head. "Really, it's the Grilivan family that I'm more interested in."

I look up from my plate to see my father's reaction. It apparently struck a nerve, for I see his jaw harden and he fakes a big smile.

"Kor, I've already told you this. Stan worked with me, but I wasn't anywhere near him when he was accessing forbidden stuff. Our family is going to be okay," he says to me.

I'm not convinced by his words.

"I think the best thing we can do is live life normally, as best as we can. What happened yesterday was distracting, but life will go on, you'll see."

There is something else going on, but I can't say that because I know it'll make my parents annoyed.

"Okay, fine," I reply.

As if to emphasize his point, the speakers overhead crackle and the announcement tells us it's time to wrap up breakfast and move to our jobs. My only solace in knowing that breakfast is almost over is that my job today is food cleanup, which I don't mind. I stand up, my plate still full. My father eyes me, looking worried, but I take my tray to the ramp and drop it there. The contents clatter loudly.

They prefer us to get to the dish room early anyway, I think, moving to the kitchen door.

I'm stopped by a Peaceholder there and they scan my print to make sure I'm one of the kids meant for kitchen duty today. The man mutters something like 'approved' and steps aside. When I try to move past him, the door to the kitchen shuts just before me and I walk right into the cold metal. I grunt from the pain and turn sharply toward the Peaceholder who checked my identity.

I see the amused face of the Peaceholder and anger boils in my chest. He let the door go on purpose so I'd walk into it. It's the same Peaceholder whose boot I tripped on during breakfast yesterday. I want to scream and shout at him, but I know that'll get me into more trouble. Instead, I suppress the feeling and move into the dish room.

I won't assume anything is a coincidence. *Not anymore*, I think resolutely.

9

I hurry to a closet and pick up a plastic apron. Putting it over my head, I look at the wall to see the whiteboard with the jobs. No one has picked any jobs yet, so I write my name and Charlie's next to 'dish line'.

I rarely get here before everyone else, so I end up doing something terrible, like sorting through the gross food bits that come through on the plates. It's a messy job. But today I'm first, so I choose to handle the clean dishes as they come out at the end.

A couple girls from our group come in. When they see me, they scowl. It's Susan, my tormentor.

"Why are you here so early? Shouldn't you be out there complaining to your family about everything like you usually do?" Susan says to me.

"I thought it might be nice to beat you to the good jobs. Of course, I only did it to bother you. I can find happiness in this place sometimes, you know."

She scowls at me and turns to her companion, a chubby girl about my height named Lauren. Lauren's hair is brown and long, past her shoulders. Her skin bunches around her eyeballs from the extra weight there. Then Susan pointedly looks at the board.

"You aren't allowed to sign anyone up for jobs if they aren't here, that's against the rules," she says proudly.

I smirk at her. "Fine, be my guest." I move to the board again and wipe out Charlie's name. "Would you or your massive friend rather take care of the clean dishes with me? I think it'll be just *so* fun to work with either of you."

Susan's face turned red at the comment, realizing that she'd just backed herself into a corner. Charlie's name might not be allowed, but mine was legitimate.

"I think Lauren has a different idea of how things are going to go. You want a black eye? Or to lose a tooth?" Susan says, taking a step forward. Lauren, the large girl with her, glares at me.

Fear blossoms in my chest, but I make a show of not being scared, even though it's a lie. I crouch somewhat, hoping that I don't have to dodge anything but still trying to be ready for it. Lauren smiles at me, her pudgy face appearing more evil because of how covered her eyes become when she smiles.

One Peaceholder walks into the dish room and I breathe out in relief. Lauren will not attack me with a Peaceholder there. Sure, if she'd smacked me good while they weren't here to see, she would just get a slap on the wrist, but if a Peaceholder sees fighting, well, that's a different story.

Susan continues to scowl, but she and Lauren sign up to sort clean silverware when it makes it out of the dishwasher. It isn't the worst job, but it's not as easy as the one I signed myself and Charlie up to do.

As they walk away, Susan flips her perfectly styled brunette hair. She's a little shorter than me, but she packs a punch. Ever since we started schooling, she's terrorized my life. If it isn't making fun of my stringy hair, it's tripping me, or ridiculing me in any other way. What I don't understand is how Charlie can still be nice to her when he sees how she and her oaf friend treat me. But then again, Charlie's nice to everyone.

Soon Charlie walks in, and my heart thumps at seeing him. He's actually done his hair well today and his grey shirt is tight against his chest. He's grown recently and I know they just need to up the size of his assigned wardrobe, but it must not have happened yet.

"Oh, hey there, Kor, what are you doing here so early?" he says to me, looking confused.

"I just felt like leaving my table. I wasn't having a good time with the conversation."

He raises his eyebrow at me before turning to the whiteboard. "Nice! You snagged the first spot on the clean dishes. I'm guessing you wouldn't mind if I signed up to work with you?"

He says it as a joke, and the way he smiles at me makes me want to fall over, but I steel myself and join in on the banter. "I mean, I hoped that pudding-face over there would, but I guess she'd rather spend time with prissy pants."

I say it loud enough that they can hear me, and I see Susan stiffen at the words. Lauren must not be paying attention though, because she doesn't turn to scowl at me until after Susan gives her a meaningful whisper. I'm not breaking any rules, but the Peaceholder standing in the room doesn't look pleased with my comment. I smile at him and wave, trying to be annoying.

Should I provoke Lauren and Susan? Probably not. It will likely come back to bite me later, but I don't care right now. I'm still annoyed that my father is trying to downplay everything that's happened in the past couple days, even expecting me to forget about it.

"Don't listen to her, Susan, she's just having a rough day," Charlie says to her.

Susan turns and bats her eyes at him. I know she has a

crush on him. Okay, most of the girls in our class have a crush on him, but Susan is actually pretty. The rest of us, not so much.

I'm suddenly very conscious of my thin strawberry hair. Charlie must think Susan is prettier than me, and the idea is painful, but I push it away. I focus the energy into a comment.

"I guess it would be okay if you worked with me. You aren't too stinky today."

He grins at me, then writes his name next to mine.

Soon the other kids funnel in and the jobs are quickly taken. We don't start right away because one of the hired workers, someone from the outside and not a Citizen of Safety, has to go over the safety measures and whatnot. I think it's silly they have to go through the rules every time. We've only done dish duty a million times. It's not like we get new kids either; it's the same group every week. All the citizens are put here at birth, so this man repeating the instructions feels like a waste of time—we obviously already know the drill.

Still, the person tells us how to be careful with the hot dishes, butter knives and whatnot, to make sure we don't hurt ourselves.

Finally, when the man is finished telling us the same old information, Charlie and I move to the conveyor belt that comes out of the dishwasher. We aren't allowed to turn the equipment off and on—that's what the adult hired from outside Safety is for. He starts the belt and trays come through the narrow window from the mess hall on the other side. There are a bunch already stacked up from people who finished their meals early. Of course some of them are ours, since we had to come into the room to prepare for dish duty.

"So, what did you have to get away from at your table? I thought you and your family got along well," Charlie asks next to me.

As there are no clean dishes yet since the sorters have just started pulling out the silverware and garbage from the trays, we have time to talk.

I eye the Peaceholder standing to our left. They probably can't hear us, but I'm still suspicious they might.

"My parents and I just don't agree on how we should handle what happened yesterday," I reply.

Charlie raises an eyebrow at me. "You mean the Larssons? Yeah that's wild—rotten luck for them to get sick."

I stare at him. "And the Grilivans, you know, their family punishment. Did you see them today in the mess hall? I know I sure didn't," I say with contempt.

"Whoa, okay I see that it's a tough subject for you," Charlie says, putting his hands up in the air. "Families get punished. Sure, it happens sometimes. I mean, don't you get punished?"

I answer with a scowl. "That's not relevant. Sure, I've racked up a demerit or two, and so has my father, but what the Grilivans did must have been really, really bad. Why else would they be taken away and hidden?"

Charlie shrugs again. "I don't see why this bothers you so much. I can keep living my life and not worry about them. I mean, Therese was really nice, but they said the family was taken care of painlessly. And it sounds like the Grilivans deserved what they got."

I gape at him. "How can you say something like that? Are you okay with the Creators just killing people because they think it's the best course of action?!"

I get a little too animated with that question and the Peaceholder notices. He turns to me and glares, not hearing my exact words, but seeing that I'm upset about something.

I relax my face and turn back to the belt. By now the dishes are starting to come through, and we need to carefully pick them up to sort them into carts. They are hot so we have to be careful as we do it.

"I see what you mean, okay? But that's just how things work

around here, right? The creators make the rules—we'd be dead meat if we lived outside of here. If the sun hits us, we're fried. Or did you forget the picture we looked at yesterday?" he reminds me.

The image of the man bursting into flames flashes in my mind. Nausea creeps up at the thought.

"Yeah, I hear you, but couldn't they just have let them get better? Why kill them like that?" I ask incredulously.

"Sure, I hear you, but you didn't even know them that well, so why are you taking it so personally?" Charlie asks, hissing through his teeth as a hot plate burns his hand.

I pause, feeling like I'm being watched. I'm probably not, but what I'm about to say makes me feel like my family might be vulnerable as a result.

"Charlie, don't you realize? Those men were the only ones who worked with my father in technical maintenance."

Charlie's expression changes, a dark shadow passing there.

"Oh, charred," he says. He remains in a stupefied silence.

"That's all you can say?" I exclaim, exasperated. My tone and volume alerts the Peaceholder who starts walking toward us.

"Shoot, now I have to deal with him," I spit out.

"Is there a problem here? Why are you yelling at your groupmate?"

His voice is very low, and I wasn't expecting it. An internal struggle begins, part of me wanting to lash out at the man for interrupting our private conversation, the other wanting to lay it on thick to make him go away. The latter wins.

"Dear me, I'm so sorry. I wasn't angry, just nervous for my friend. He almost hurt himself on a burning plate and I was just trying to warn him."

Charlie raises an eyebrow at me, skeptical that my antics will save us.

"Ah, well perhaps you should look less angry when you warn him," the Peaceholder suggests. He pauses for a moment before turning and walking back to his station on the wall.

"I don't think he bought the act," Charlie whispers.

I turn my face away from the Peaceholder and scowl at Charlie.

"Hey, he went away, didn't he?" I say.

Charlie shakes his head and keeps pulling dishes off the conveyor belt, wincing a couple times as he picks up scalding ones.

"Charlie, I just have this feeling that my father—and my family, by association—are in trouble. I feel like we're being watched because of something those men did wrong. I think they suspect my father of something too."

My best friend eyes me with a sideways look. His green eyes are gorgeous. Part of me melts away at his look, but I steel myself and raise both eyebrows, trying to get him to say something.

"I don't know, Kor, it sounds like a stretch to me. Do you think your dad did anything wrong?" he asks.

I stare back. "I know my father, and if he did, he had a good reason for it."

Even as I say the words, I realize how off it sounds. Especially to someone watching from the outside. I decide to try another tactic.

"Do you think it's only coincidental that two of the families whose fathers worked with my dad got punished or killed?"

Charlie pauses for just a moment before continuing, pulling off large plates and cups from the belt.

"Kor, I think you're overreacting. They said the Larssons got sick, so they probably did. Why would the Creators lie to us like that? I don't know what the Grilivan dad did, but he probably deserved it. Trust your dad, if he says he wasn't involved, he probably wasn't." He sees the look on my face and can tell that I'm feeling invalidated and frustrated at his response. His expression softens, and he reaches out to take my hand, grabbing it firmly. I want to pull it away, but my head is screaming to leave it be. I feel warmth in my chest from the touch of his firm hand.

"I realize this is upsetting, but I don't know that you have to worry about it. They'd have come after your father if he truly got into something he shouldn't have. There are cameras everywhere, so they'd have evidence."

I pull my hand away and mourn the loss of his hand in mine. Turning to the belt, I grit my teeth and work hurriedly, focusing on the motions. Pausing, I consider my next words, eyeing the people around us. The hissing from the dishwasher steam echoes loudly in the room, so I hope no one will be able to hear as I speak through my teeth.

"They came for my dad last night."

Charlie now pauses next to me as I keep working. "What?!" he asks.

I nod. "Peaceholders came and took my dad away last night. I don't know where they took him or why, but I thought I wouldn't see him again." Tears well in my eyes and I force them back by sheer will power.

"He came back though, but he has a massive bruise on his chest and stomach, like he'd been beaten. He insisted he fell down the stairs, but I can't see how that could have happened from falling."

Charlie still stares at me and only continues working when he sees the Peaceholder is watching us again.

"Okay, I get it now. You could have started with that before I tried to convince you of something else. I'm sorry, Kor."

After picking up a few more dishes, we see that the clean plate cart is full and Charlie pushes it to the side while I rush to get an empty one.

When we're back at the belt, he continues. "I imagine the experiments aren't helping with your stress," he says.

I look at him sideways. That he brought those up seems ill-placed. Sure, they freaked me out, but they weren't that awful.

"They scared me a little, but it wasn't too bad when I was in there," I say.

"For reals? That's not how my experience was." Suddenly, he cries out and holds the back of his head. "Freaking stupid robots in my brain!" Charlie shouts.

The Peaceholder looks over at us again, face hardened. He sees Charlie holding the back of his head and nods in understanding. It's a well known rule that you aren't supposed to talk about the experiments, so he must have just figured.

"You can't tell me what happened, remember?" I say, nudging Charlie.

"Yeah, yeah, I didn't forget the rule, I just didn't think my brain would explode if I kept it vague."

He grabs my shoulder and looks me in the eye. "I don't know if you are just lucky with your scientist or what, but I've never been in so much pain in my life." He winces again as the microbots shock his brain. "Though these bots do hurt like being charred," he complains.

My mind thinks back to the scientist who worked on me in the exam room. She was pretty nice, and nothing she did to me was that painful. Did she do it wrong? Did Charlie have a meaner scientist working on him?

I want to ask a thousand questions, but I fear for Charlie. I also don't know if asking specific questions counts as discussing the details of the experiments, so I refrain for fear of getting hurt by the microbots.

"I'm sorry. I didn't know it was that rough for you."

Charlie shakes his head, wanting to say more, but knowing that he can't.

The shift moves quickly, and all I can do is hope that the rest of the day is normal with lunch, school, and dinner again.

I'm not sure that I can handle another crazy announcement from the Creators.

10

FORTUNATELY, MY WISH COMES TRUE AS THE DAY CONTINUES without incident. My parents aren't all that chatty for the rest of the meals, so we just eat in silence. Family time doesn't happen either, which is unusual for us, but I don't complain. I guess it's because my mother and dad are still upset with the things I said at lunch. I will not take them back. I really do think something is going on, but I try to forget about it.

The next day is normal as well, with no new announcements and no additional punishments. Charred, even the Peaceholders ignore me as if they don't want to get into a scuffle with me.

My parents act normal again today as well, which is both relieving and annoying. I don't know how my mother can get over the fact that my dad has a giant bruise and that his coworkers are gone, but my mind is on something else: I have to go to the 'tests' again today.

I'm dreading it the moment I wake up. I remember Charlie said a couple days ago that his were painful. Mine weren't, but that doesn't mean they won't be this time. I have a feeling they just got to the more intense stuff earlier with him because he's a guy. Maybe they'll get that way with the girls today.

This idea makes me even more terrified. In fact, I almost don't want to get out of bed this morning, opting to get the shock and a demerit because of it. At the last second, though, I jump out of bed and throw my grey clothes on. Staying in bed means I miss my opportunity for a hot shower, but it's worth it. Procrastinating getting up makes me feel just a little better, though not much.

When I exit my room into our family's main living space, my mother raises an eyebrow. She sees that my hair is ratty, and that I didn't bother taking a shower. She knows how much I love the showers, so she probably suspects that something is wrong.

"Have a rough night last night? You are typically up before now and ready to go," she asks me.

I shrug. "I'm just extra tired today, I guess."

My father, Blaine, comes out of his room and walks up to me.

"So it's that day again, huh? You ready for your experiments?" he asks me.

My mother looks at me with worry. "Is that why you slept in today? I'm sorry, I didn't think of that," she says, and she does sound sorry.

It's not that I think my mother doesn't love me or anything. She does, but she is a lot less observant of me, or perhaps just less in sync with how I'm feeling. Not to mention that she isn't at all okay with pushing back against the Creators and how they run things around here. I'm positive I'm just a thorn in her side.

"I'll be okay, just trying to come to terms with everything," I say, but my voice cracks as my fear leaks out in my tone.

My father puts a firm hand on my shoulder and I want to

cry, but I don't let myself. He squeezes softly and I look up at him.

"I wouldn't worry. I think your examiner is doubtless as good as mine is. She's the smartest and kindest one I could ever ask for."

He winks at me, and I scowl.

"How could you even know that? She's going to poke and prod me until I bleed to death," I complain.

Right as I say it, a sharp pain rockets through the back of my head and I bend over, gasping while I reach up for my head.

"Charred," I say.

My father grimaces. "Yeah, you shouldn't try to talk about it anymore, I don't think your brain will handle the bot attacks. I want you to grow up with some brain capacity, though it's clear the Creators don't care that much about our mental abilities. They would be fine with brainless grunts to package food for the rest of their lives."

Despite the intense pain I just went through, I chuckle at my dad's gibe.

"Blaine, you need to stop encouraging her. She's going to get us in more trouble," my mother scolds.

Just then, a hissing announces every bedroom door opening by the timed mandate. My brother groans.

"Hey! I wasn't ready yet!"

We look to see him wearing just his underwear, grey and unassuming. He tips over as he tries to get his foot into his pant leg and we just laugh.

"Sean, put your clothes on, it's time to go," my mother says, covering her own smile. Her teeth are stark against her dark skin.

He's still trying to get up as he puts his pants on and I roll my eyes, turning around. My mother does the same, though she's still chuckling.

"There, now you can get dressed faster. I'm starving, so could you please hurry?" I say.

Fortunately, this helps him get ready faster and we are soon on our way to the mess hall. It's waffles and bacon today, which is the best thing to have happened to me in a long time. I eat way more than I should, but I don't mind how sick I am after. It's definitely worth it to me.

At the end of the meal, I see a glint on my father's wrist again and I try to get a good look at the little silver charm that is there on his access bracelet. He told me it gives him more access to the compound, but I'm curious to know what access. I want to know why he has it now when he definitely did *not* have it before.

"When did you get that silver key thing, dad?" I blurt out.

My father has just taken a big bite of waffle and he stares at me while he chews. I see him thinking about a response as he chews, then he swallows and gives a fake smile.

"Why are you so concerned about it?" he says, holding up his bracelet. "It's not that exciting."

I shrug, but then tell him. "I just don't remember you having it a few weeks ago. Is it something new? Did they reward you for something?"

He chuckles at this. "I wouldn't say a key with more access is much of a reward, it means more work for me and my colleagues." He pauses then, brows furrowed. "Or at least whoever my new colleagues will be."

I freeze. "Wait, Todd Grilivan isn't working with you anymore?" I exclaim.

Even my mother stops eating and stares at my dad when he says this.

"You didn't mention that to me, dear—when did he get moved out of your workforce?" she asks warily.

My dad smiles, and he looks at us one by one. "You are all

still so worried about this whole Stan thing. Yes, he got in trouble. I'm not in trouble. I am continuing to do my work and minding my business. I'm lucky that I have a brain for technology, that's all. I don't know what Stan got into, but it doesn't concern me, or our family."

I hear his words, but still I'm gaping at him. The only person who doesn't appear to care is Sean, who is stuffing his face with third helpings of food. I want to smack him for how he is ignoring these developments, but I resist the urge. He's just a kid, anyway.

My mother's expression softens, and she resumes eating.

"I trust you, dear. If you say it's nothing to worry about, then I'll believe you."

I don't feel the same way. My eyes flick to the small silver charm on his bracelet, the set of rings with the star set in the middle, and I can't help but get uneasy. I want to ask a thousand more questions, but decide I shouldn't. It's because I don't think that my dad would like me to after the assurances he tried to give us, but also because breakfast will be over soon and it'll be time for our jobs. It's canning facility day, so my group will help to can something in our cannery. This is one job that rotates more regularly in the cycle because of how large the cannery is, and how much food needs to get processed. We won't be the only group there, probably one of five or six. I've never counted the number of groups that go each time, but it seems like a lot.

"I've got to get ready for my assignment," I say, eyeing the silver charm another time.

My dad sees my gaze and pulls his sleeve up over the bracelet.

"If this access key is going to be distracting for you, then I will just have to keep it out of your sight," he says playfully. He waits for me to say something back.

"Yeah, hiding it is going to help me forget about it," I say sarcastically.

He laughs and nudges me as I stand up. It's not a powerful push, and I know it's playful, but it still makes me lose my balance as I'm standing and I almost drop my plate. I glare at him, but only in jest. He bursts out laughing. We draw the attention of a few other citizens at tables around us and my mother gives me a sharp look.

I don't mind making her mad. My relationship with my father is too important for me to care much about pleasing her or the Creators.

Just before I walk away, my father calls my name.

"Hey Kor, just remember to be nice to your examiner, okay? She's just doing her job."

I furrow my brows at him and cock my head. I open my mouth to say something, but decide not to. I really am eager to get to work so I can take my mind off of the experiments.

How did he know my scientist is a woman? I wonder. Maybe all the girls get women scientists.

It's the type of thing I would like to ask my groupmates, but I know I can't.

I meet Charlie at the cannery, and we get a decent job of wiping off the jars after the processing seals them. The strawberry jam is in this part of the cannery, the sweet fruit making my mouth water even though I just finished eating breakfast not too long ago.

The work day is relatively normal, considering what I know is going to come later in the experiments. While I'm nervous, I'm still surprised at how life has returned to normal the past couple of days. The number of incidents and announcements that came at the beginning of the week made me feel like it would continue—that life would be very different.

At length, lunch passes and school comes. Today, it's math. I think it's a cruel punishment that they lined math up with the days we have the experiments, and part of me thinks the Creators are trying to spite me. But I know we're just a bunch of pawns to them—an obligation they doubtless just want to get rid of, but can't because they haven't found a cure yet.

I wonder how much money it takes to run this place, but then again I have no perception of money at all. We've learned about the United States history and the monetary system, but we have yet to see it in action. I have never seen a real dollar, or coins. Ironically, that was the only bit of math that fascinated me: the money unit.

I grit my teeth as our teacher goes on and on about how important pre-calculus is while I try not to feel rebellious. As much as I want to snap at her, I don't want to get demerits before I head into the torture chamber.

I watch the clock, my stomach clenching as I see that class is about to end early.

A small ding rings in my ear bud and overhead in our classroom.

"Group 55A, class is now over. Please proceed to the hallways where your examination rooms are."

A groan erupts in everyone around me, making me jump. I blush deeply at my overreaction and look around. No one seems to have noticed. In fact, everyone looks as nervous as I feel. Grace, the small blonde in the corner, looks green. James looks like he'll throw up, and even Charlie, the most positive kid in class, looks terrified.

"I'm not sure I'm ready for it again today," he whispers to me, looking down at his desktop.

"Oh, that's just too bad. Class is already over! I know you were enjoying derivatives as much as I was today," the teacher says with far too much enthusiasm.

I know you wouldn't expect me to clock you one for being so chipper, I think darkly.

I won't do it, of course, but I can't get in trouble for just thinking about it.

"Please take your holopads with you and complete the rest of the in-class assignment by tomorrow. It shouldn't be too difficult. Remember that you can access the answers, but only after you take at least one try. Don't forget, I have access to your data holopad history and can see if you peek at the answers before trying to solve it yourself." She smiles at us and sits.

Even with how much I hate math, I would actually rather sit down and work through the assignment than go to the experiments.

I can feel myself getting sick with the nerves. There isn't much talking at all as we gather our stuff and get ready to go. At the end of class there are usually happy and excited conversations going on, knowing that class is finished. I gather it's not just me who isn't thrilled that class ended early today.

Suddenly, an annoying voice speaks. "I am excited for the experiments. You are just a bunch of babies," Susan says, flipping her perfect brunette hair over her shoulders and forcing her oaf friend Lauren to push through us. Lauren looks even more grumpy today.

I turn to Charlie and give him a sad look.

"It's not like we're going to die," he says, trying to be funny. His eyes still convey his anxiety.

"Right, yeah, we'll be fine," I say, trying to be chill, but sounding like an idiot.

We part ways and I walk with the other girls in silence to the hallway where the trapdoor is. There are a couple of female Peaceholders there waiting for us. They activate the wall switch and the hall closes off before the door opens in the floor. We stay silent.

One by one, the girls in my group file down the steep stairs. I'm near the end again as we enter the locker room. It looks as clean and new as ever. An image of my face hovers over the locker assigned to me and I go to unlock it.

I undress as slowly as I possibly can, hoping I can reduce the amount of time I'll be in the room with the weird helmeted scientist. A buzzing in my locker door gets my attention and a robotic voice tells me to put in the ear buds again. I roll my eyes and do as it says.

"State your name, Citizen."

"Korinne." I pause then.

"Your full name, Citizen."

I grin, pleased at my stalling tactics. "Korinne Christensen."

"Voice match confirmed, please go to examination room 12."

It's the same as before, though I don't know why I wondered if it might be different. My nerves are spiked as much as they were last time, even though I've done all this before.

I am by far the last one out of the locker room this time, the other girls entering their exam rooms before me. Grace is shaking like a leaf when her door opens and she enters.

Soon, I'm at my examination room. The door opens for me and I see the same lab-coated woman sitting next to the exam chair. She is tampering with the computer and her huge helmet has its visor up. I almost glimpse her face before the visor hisses closed.

"Hello there, Korinne. I am glad to see you again."

Her voice is definitely feminine, but it's robotic from the enhancements of the helmet.

"Have a seat, just like last time."

I say nothing, but just walk to the chair and sit down gingerly.

"Your father said you were nervous for another round of tests. I assured him I'd take care of you, just like I take care of him."

I start, the earbud in my right ear coming loose and clattering to the floor.

"Sorry," I mumble, but I'm still distracted by what she said. "You know my father? Do you know my mother too?" I ask.

She pauses, appearing to hesitate. My head snaps up to her visor when she doesn't answer immediately, but the big helmeted head sways side to side in a head shake.

"No," the robotic voice says, "I just get to examine your father on his test days. Sorry to say, there isn't one examiner per citizen, you have to share."

She's teasing, I know, but I don't find it funny.

"Oh, I thought you only worked with girls." It's all I can think to say.

A light chuckle comes through my earbuds as it distorts her laugh.

"No, they just do that for younger kids. The Creators believe it will make it a better transition for you."

I nod, feeling my stomach get sick at the idea of a male examiner in here with me and this awkward blue robe.

She sighs and gestures to her helmet. "Yeah, I have always hated this thing. Mind if I take it off?" she asks.

I didn't expect her to ask me anything, so I just stare at her.

"I'll take that as a yes," she says as she pulls her hand up to her helmet and lifts it.

It hisses as the mechanism securing it to her head is released. Thick, rich brown auburn hair cascades out of it. Her face reveals almond eyes, a sleek, pointed nose, and vibrant green eyes.

Oh, she's gorgeous. Of course she is, I think to myself.

"The first day was a bit odd, so let's start again. I'm Lucia. I'll be your examiner most likely for the rest of your life. Or as long as you live here in Safety, at least. With any luck, we'll cure your sun allergy and get you out of here."

I hear her, but I am too distracted by seeing her face. That, and the fact that she just alluded to people not living in Safety for the rest of their lives. It freaks me out more than it should.

"Mmmk," I mumble.

She smiles. "How about you sit back so we can get started? I want to try different things today that we didn't get to last time."

Her chipper attitude only makes me more nervous.

<h1 style="text-align:center">11</h1>

THE ROOM FEELS COLD TO ME TODAY, BUT I THINK IT'S JUST because of how nervous I am. Now that I know she's going to try new things on me, I can't even rely on my one experience here. I don't feel like a human in this moment, more like a lab rat.

"I turned the air down, I hope you don't mind. There is a slight possibility that your body will overheat as we work through these experiments and I don't want you to get uncomfortable."

I chuckle, causing her to raise an eyebrow. Then my face turns bright red. At this point I'm incredulous about every claim of wanting to help. It's like the words that come out of her mouth just keep getting worse and worse, yet she sounds more positive than ever. The laugh that escaped my mouth was very unintentional, but my emotions have been building and building since I've been in here.

"Is something funny?" she asks me. I can't tell if she's annoyed or angry, but I just shake my head, my blush deepening.

"I'm not going to hurt you, Korinne, you have nothing to worry about," she says.

At this point the tears are welling in my eyes as I recall what Charlie said about his tests. What had he said? They were always painful? Even my dad hinted that when he and I first discussed the tests.

"That's not what my best friend tells me. He said it hurts like charred." I'm crying now, and maybe I should be embarrassed, but I'm not.

Lucia eyes me with a look of pity, then looks up at the camera.

"Your friend shouldn't be talking about the tests. The microbots in his brain should have prevented him from giving any details," she's explaining now.

I nod then say, "Yeah, they attacked his brain—don't worry, they did the job."

I don't know why I can't control myself. I'm mortified by this whole thing and especially my reaction, but Lucia doesn't appear angry.

"Well then, I'm glad to hear that."

I can tell my tears are making her uncomfortable, but she reaches over and pulls out a syringe, another large one connected to an empty vial.

"We'll get blood from you, as usual. We burn through what we draw very quickly, so we'll get a new sample each time."

I sniffle and nod, not sure if I can say much else.

The poke in my arm isn't as bad as it was last time. I think it's because I'm still trying to control my crying, to no avail.

Once she's done taking my blood, I am recovering. I have a slight headache now from the tears, and my pride is shot, but I wipe my face and look at her, waiting for the next action.

She pulls out another needle and sticks it in my arm, connecting a small tube to the end. The length of the tube is strung over a metal stand with nothing at the top.

"This is just an IV for precaution. I'll be doing different things with you today and it's never a bad idea to have support like this in case you present with unexpected symptoms."

Oh, so it won't hurt, huh? You're sure inspiring confidence, I think to myself.

When I don't say anything, she continues. I see her reach to the side of the computer stand and pull out several small wires with a circle sticker on the end of each one.

"These are electrodes. I'm going to put a couple on your head and chest. Can you please open your robe up just a bit?"

I stare at her, my fear growing inside. I had forgotten I was naked underneath this weird shiny blue robe, but now that she asks me to pull it open, I blush. Sure, she's a woman, but the circumstances of the tests make everything feel weird to me.

"You can keep the bottom closed, I just need to reach your upper chest."

I hesitate, and she smiles. "If you don't want to open it, that's fine, I'll just stick my hand in like this."

She reaches over and slides her hand into my robe, sticking one sticker and wire to my upper chest. Then she sticks one more on the other side.

"That should work just fine. See? I can see your heartbeat now."

I look at the computer and hear a rhythmic beeping that must be my heart rate. A line is squiggling with each of the beeps. There are a bunch of numbers and colors flashing on the screen too, but they mean nothing to me.

"Now your head," she says, putting a sticker on each of my temples.

"I'll be able to track your brain activity and response as we go through the simulation. How does that sound?"

I think that she's asking me to make me feel better, but I don't react. I'm not sure what to think about this whole process, and I'm just trying to make it out alive.

She pulls a pair of white goggles with large wires out of the back. The thick cords connect to the back of the computer.

"Alright. If you lean back and try to relax . . . ."

Sitting back slowly, I try not to panic. I feel like a creature of some sort with tendrils growing out of me. I've read descriptions of such things in the books that we have access to in the libraries. I can't remember what they're called at the moment.

"Your body knows it's allergic to the sun, so your brain should act accordingly when put through a limited simulation," she says, eyes watching me, "I assure you that you will be safe, but it will seem very real and even a bit distressing. Do you understand?"

I stare at her, not even close to understanding what she is saying. She nods and puts the goggles over my eyes. They cover about half my face, and there is even a part that covers my nose. I open my mouth and start breathing there.

"You can breathe normally through your nose, don't worry. It won't suffocate you."

The goggles are clear, so I can still see the fluorescent lighting on the ceiling above me. The whiteness of the light hurts my eyes.

"The simulation will start in three seconds."

I count down in my head, not because she asked me to, but because I need something to distract me. I don't really know what to expect, so when the room goes dark all of a sudden, I gasp.

"Just relax, it's going to be alright," she tells me.

I hear the beeping on the computer speeding up quickly and realize it's my heart thumping so fast, I wonder if I might pass out. I don't know why I'm so nervous, nothing hurts, and I'm technically comfortable, but this is so freaky.

"Alright, here we go."

The room changes and I see that I'm sitting outside. At least, what I think outside looks like. The sky is dark above, and

I see lights everywhere in the sky. I realize I can't feel the chair underneath me anymore, but instead, soft ground. I look down to see that I'm sitting in the middle of a field, grass growing up around me. Of course, I've never seen this before in my life. I only know it's grass because of the pictures I see and the things we learn in school. Looking up, I smile at the beauty of the sky. Stars are, once again, only things we hear about. The Creators could probably let us out at night, but they are too afraid that we'll get stuck out when the sun comes up and we'll die, so they don't even bother letting us out.

"This is weird," I say out loud. My voice is distant, and it echoes.

"Just enjoy what you see, alright?" I hear Lucia's voice say somewhere in my ears.

If I focus just right, I can sense the earbuds in my ears and feel a slight tickling in my temples where the stickers are. But when I look around this place; it's easy to lose track of the sensations. I breathe deeply and almost forget how afraid I feel. Instead, my brain revels in the beauty around me. The air is so cool and it smells incredible.

Is this what plants smell like? I think, closing my eyes. A breeze blows through my hair and I breathe through my nose again, reveling in the smell. I want so badly to fill my lungs with it that I open my mouth and suck in a breath. Unfortunately, that just brings me back to the examination room, as I remember that the strange goggles only cover my nose.

I close my mouth and keep breathing through my nose until I'm lost in the simulation again.

The grass sways around me and I realize I can see it more and more by the minute. Curious, I glance up to the sky and see that it's getting lighter. It's changing from a dark blue-black color into a lighter blue. I furrow my brows, curious to know what is changing. It gets lighter and lighter, and I turn to see that mountains, tall and angular, spread across the area far away. Colors explode in the sky and I notice they are changing. Then I see the edge of the sun.

My face falls, and I panic. Fear grips my stomach, and I gasp again. I jump up from my sitting position and frantically look around me for a place to hide—a place to get away from the sun. But there is nothing. I'm just in a massive field of grass, no trees or anything to be seen. I collapse and try to bury myself in the dirt, pulling the grass over my body to get away. Then the rays of the sun burst over the mountain and I squint as the sun hits my face.

My body explodes in heat. I scream at the intensity and I know that any moment I'll be in flames, burning to death as my body reacts to the allergy that keeps me in Safety. I try to cry, but I can't because of the heat that is coursing through my veins.

Then everything goes dark, and the room is back in my vision. I'm crying again and shaking as a firm hand presses against my shoulder.

"Korinne! Calm down, it's not real!"

I hear the words and remember where I was before I was being burned by the sun, but I can't shake the sensation of the heat radiating from inside my whole body. Tears are streaming from my eyes, dripping down my cheeks. I turn to see Lucia with a worried look on her face.

"Despite your reaction to the serum in our last session, I didn't expect it would be this intense for you. Based on how your mind reacted to the simulation, I can only guess that your body is extremely allergic to the sunlight."

I nod, but only because I have no words.

She bites her lip and I can tell that she does feel bad for what happened.

"I've only been a scientist for about ten years, coming in here and working on the Citizens, but never have I seen someone react that much to the simulation. It is a really good thing you were brought here before the sun could touch you. It would be the most excruciating way for you to die." She looks conflicted at this last statement, but the expression soon passes. Now she stares at me kindly, her hand still lingering on my shoulder. I squirm under her hand, uncomfortable with her oddly caring touch.

"Water," I say through dry lips.

She nods and reaches over to where a water dispenser sits. Before long, she hands me a paper cup full of the cold liquid. It feels like ice as it goes through my throat, almost burning with the coldness, but I welcome it. At least it's better than the hot intensity in my veins.

"Please don't say I ever have to do that again."

Lucia presses her lips together in a thin line.

"Not today, at least," she says.

My stomach drops. I want to scream, but I can't give her the satisfaction. I can't give the Creators the satisfaction of knowing that they are upsetting me.

"Fine. But why? You *know* what would happen if I went into the sun," I say grumpily.

"We're going to be administering a series of serums over time as well as other antidotes. Then we'll try the simulation again to see if the reaction slows down. Eventually, we are hoping to end your body's sensitivity to the sun, and the only way we will know is if we keep trying the simulation after the medicines. Trust me, it will get better. This is the only time we need to get the control data."

I raise an eyebrow, questioning.

"Control data—it's the information we get from a Citizen without any medication at all. The simulation provided—it's the worst-case scenario, so to speak."

Rage builds in me at this explanation, but I grit my teeth and nod again.

So they are *treating us like test animals*, I think.

"Under normal circumstances, I would give you our latest serum to see if it would help you even a little, but I promised to not bother you again today, so I won't."

Instead, she pulls out another large syringe and I see the contents are the same yellowish substance that she put into me last time. Panic rises in me again, knowing what it's going to do to me. I imagine the heat rising inside my body again and begin to hyperventilate.

"Are you alright?" Lucia asks, noticing my reaction.

I shake my head. "Please don't make me burn. I don't want to feel that again."

Her eyes soften, but she shakes her head. "I'm sorry, I know this is difficult for you, but this is why we are here. We can't find a cure for you if we don't continue with the experiments. This is a much smaller dose than last time, I promise. You will hardly feel any discomfort with this much of the serum. I can see your body reacts violently with exposure to the sun, so I don't need to confirm it again."

I lean my head back and just shake my head. "Fine," I say through gritted teeth.

She sighs at my reaction and then leans in over the tube in my arm. Before she injected the stuff into my muscle, but now she inserts the needle directly into my bloodstream through the attached tube. At least I don't have to deal with getting jabbed again right now, I think, grateful for the tube.

As with the last time, a warmth enters my arm and spreads throughout my body. It rushes up my arm and into my neck, while a line of it shoots into my chest. The heat floods my brain and my chest at the same time. She's right, though, this time it isn't terribly uncomfortable, it just feels like a pleasant heat. I sigh in relief and close my eyes. For a moment, I wish I had activated the music so I can relax during this, but then I hear Lucia gasp. The computer beeps rapidly.

My eyes shoot open as my heart speeds up, fear filling me.

All this does is cause the heat to spread even faster throughout my body. It covers every inch of me and then intensifies. It isn't uncomfortable yet, but feeling it getting hotter makes me panic a little. I think it might just get worse and worse until I end up dying—if not from pain, definitely from fear.

The computer beeps like crazy, and I can see it flashing in my peripheral vision. All of a sudden, there is a loud pop, and the screen explodes outward, the glass shattering.

Lucia yelps and I see glass slice across her face in a few places. She's quick enough to cover her face with her hands, but she gets cuts there too.

The heat still fills every part of me, but I'm kind of liking it today. Once I realize it's not killing me but that it's just warming me up, I revel in the feeling.

Lucia jumps from her seat and rushes to a set of drawers that, admittedly, I hadn't realized were there. She pulls out a syringe with blue stuff in it and rushes back to me. She inserts it into my tube and the coolness spreads throughout my veins. I sigh as it releases the heat.

"That was incredible," Lucia whispers.

I hear her say the words, but I don't know what to say. So I just ask.

"What is? What happened?"

She's staring at the computer, which is buzzing and sparking.

"Did I do something wrong?" I ask, nervous that I'm going to get a demerit for breaking her computer.

"What? No!" she says, "You did nothing wrong, Korinne. I've just never seen that strong of reaction before."

I furrow my brows at her. None of this makes sense.

"I thought you said the dose was lower than when I was last here?"

"It was, that's the strange thing. It's as if your body was primed by the simulation to react *more* with the sun serum. The energy of the reaction was so far off the charts that the computer couldn't handle it."

I level a flat stare at her, unintentionally showing her that I don't understand.

Lucia sighs, then speaks while she fusses with her injuries. "Your body hasn't had any exposure to the sun, or anything like the sun, until now. When I put you in the simulation and gave you the serum before, the cells in your blood essentially *learned* how to react to it. "

Once again, I just stare. I'm not sure if she's thought about how I wasn't aware my cells learned things, but scientist-speak is always a little above my head.

"You know what? Don't worry about it. Just know it's incredible that it happened," she explains.

I take a moment to inspect her injuries. She's still bleeding on her face, as well as a few places on her arms and hands.

"I'm sorry you're hurt."

She shakes her head and puts her other hand over the cuts on her arm.

"Don't worry about it, it's no problem."

I blush, knowing it's my fault that she's hurt. Then I notice a glint of something on the wrist of her hand. A silver charm on her bracelet is reflecting the light from the fluorescent bulbs above us. The symbol is a set of rings with a star at the center. It's the same charm that I recall seeing on my dad's bracelet earlier today.

"What's—?" I start to say before I stop.

Lucia looks over at me, her green eyes curious. "Yes?"

I can tell she's still marveling about what just happened with the computer, so I take advantage of her being distracted and shake my head. I know I shouldn't ask about the bracelet charm because it's none of my business. I still think I'm in trouble for breaking the computer, so I don't want to push my luck.

"If it's nothing, then you can go. I hoped to do a lot more with you, but without a computer, I can't do much else. It seems you get more free time today than either of us expected."

She looks at me and smiles, but there is something else in her eyes. It looks almost like she's afraid.

12

I RUSH TO THE LOCKER ROOM AND PUT MY CLOTHES ON AS QUICKLY as I can. It's strange being the only one in there, but I'm grateful. I don't like it when the other girls are here while I'm undressing. I pull the odd blue robe off and hang it in the locker. Right as I do, I notice the blue material on the outside of the left arm is blackened. Looking closer, I see there is a hole burned all the way through it.

My stomach turns at the sight and I close my locker quickly, not wanting to know how that could have happened. I check my arms to make sure I'm not hurt anywhere and sigh when I see nothing.

I hold my holopad tightly and move out the door and up the spiral stairs. When I get to the top, the Peaceholder raises an eyebrow at me. I open my mouth to say something, but then think better of it, still fearing I'm in trouble. Instead, I look down at the ground and move through the hall away from the trapdoor.

I'm not sure why the Peaceholder doesn't stop me. I'm not supposed to be done with the tests for another thirty minutes. I just offer a silent prayer to some god somewhere. I wonder if

I'm being watched even more now as I hurry through each hall-way. Lucia's reaction is playing through my mind over and over. I hear the glass of the computer break again and see the shards of the screen flying into her face and arms.

I'm blushing now as I keep my holopad pulled into my chest. I don't know where to go, so I head back to my home unit.

When I get there I rush in, hoping no Peaceholders see me. There are rules about being in your home unit without permission, but I'm not sure if this counts, since I was let out early from my tests.

The tests.

Every time the words come into my mind, I am irked. I hug my arms around my chest and just crouch with the metal door of our home unit behind me. Then I see movement in our kitchen and my chest constricts. I feel air wanting to escape my mouth in a scream, but I can't get it out. I relax when I see my father's face there.

"Kor? What are you doing here so early?" he asks.

The tension leaves my body, and I almost cry from relief. He sees I have crouched by the door and moves over to me, coming to my level.

"I—got done early with the tests. Lucia—"

I stop when I say her name, mostly because I know that I'm not supposed to talk about what happens in the test room, but also because I'm not sure she's told him she is the scientist for both of us. No pain twinges in my brain, so I guess I didn't break any rules.

"Lucia? As in, the scientist from the experimental room Lucia? How do you know her?" he asks me. Something in the way he looks at me seems like he already knew this.

"She's my examiner too. She told me she's also yours," I say.

I see an image of my father wearing the same ridiculous blue and shiny robe and I blush, knowing that he would be naked underneath that for the experiments. The thought is absolutely mortifying.

"That's great! She's been an amazing examiner for me," he says.

I peer up at his face, seeing that he looks happy. I note that he doesn't have any headaches so what he said must not be off limits. Still, something doesn't feel right; it seems like it should have done something to me. I've felt the pain a couple times even from just mentioning such few things about my experiments. Part of me wants to test it further to see what I can get away with, but then a thought comes to me.

"Wait, what are you doing back in our home unit? I thought it was against the rules to be here?" I ask. My eyes wander to the camera above our kitchen cabinets. It doesn't seem to be moving. I wonder if there is actually someone watching.

I shake my head at the thought. It moves all the time, so the fact that it's not probably means nothing.

My father sees me do this and his eyes remain on me, noting the action.

"I got off work early today. They had to refresh the systems of the office I was working on and they asked me to leave while they did it," he says.

A reasonable response. I've not learned everything that my father does, so I can't say if he's being truthful or not.

"Lucia is nice," I say randomly. I don't know why the words come out, but I just had to say them, partially to see if I get the pain in my head, partially to see how my father reacts.

He smiles at me.

"Yes, she's a brilliant examiner. I've had a few of them over the years, but she's by far the best I've had."

"Wait," I say, "you've had different scientists since you were eighteen? How many have you had? How often do they switch?"

I feel panicked inside, though I don't know why. Perhaps

it's because I know Charlie was terrified of what his scientist did to him. I don't want to cross paths with whoever does his tests.

"Oh, I don't remember. I've been doing the experiments for so long I kind of forget them. Maybe six, or seven. I can't be sure, they blend together," he replies.

Then he looks at me and chuckles.

"How about we move to a different place to talk? I don't think sitting by the door of our home is the most comfortable or the safest place to sit. I can see your mother rushing in here before dinner and tripping over us."

I cover my mouth and laugh at the idea.

"Okay, you're right," I say, standing. My head feels dizzy and I wonder what Lucia did to me. I don't remember feeling this way when I was coming back to our home unit, but now that I don't have the adrenaline from the fear, I wonder if it's been there all along.

"Listen, I'll make tea and we can talk more about the experiments," he says.

I stop and he notices me do this.

"In not so much detail, of course. I don't want you getting attacked by the microbots as much as I don't want to be attacked by them. You're obviously high-strung from something though, so it won't hurt to talk."

He moves to the kitchen and pulls out a mug for me, along with his own favorite coffee mug. I know my mother wouldn't be thrilled to hear about me drinking coffee, but my father will take the brunt of that fight if she ever finds out.

"And don't you worry about your mother," he remarks, noticing my hesitance, "you can have some of the herbal teas we've got lying around. Your mother doesn't like them; she thinks they're gross. I think she just doesn't want to have to drink anything without the caffeine in it," my father says before laughing.

I can't help but laugh, too. They both like their caffeine, just in different forms.

Before long, he's sitting next to me on our grey sofa and putting his feet up on the coffee table. I eye his grey slippered feet.

"Oh, your mother won't know about me putting my feet up, either. But if it's going to make you uncomfortable," he moves his feet off the table before continuing, "I can just put them down."

He looks at me meaningfully, waiting for me to say something, but I don't know what to say. We sit there in silence for a moment before he speaks.

"So what has you shaken up? Were the experiments that bad?" he finally asks.

Once again, I don't know what I can say, so I just shrug.

"It—didn't go very well, let's just say that," I say, taking a sip of my tea and wincing at the heat. My father has a tendency to overheat his beverages.

"What? You don't prefer it scalding? You are too soft like your mother," he teases me.

I make a face at him and blow on my drink.

He grins at my reaction and makes a show of gulping his coffee. When he does, though, he burns himself and sucks in air.

"Okay, okay, that's pretty charred hot," he sputters.

We both start laughing then. The tension leaves me almost instantly. It takes a few moments for us to stop because we keep fueling each other's laughter. When we can compose ourselves, I look at him, trying to choose my words.

He speaks before me, though.

"I know it is odd, the things they do to you in there, but they are harmless. I don't think that Lucia is trying to hurt us or treat us unfairly. She's a good person," he says, staring off at the wall.

I furrow my brows at the comment. I don't think the same

thing about the scientists. Anyone who gets paid to poke and prod a bunch of kids doesn't sound like a good person to me.

"Your definition of a good person is definitely a lot different than mine. Maybe I should go around stabbing you with knives and sucking your blood out," I say, more darkly than I expected.

He tilts his head and his eyes fill with something. Is that a pity look?

"That's not what I mean, and you know that," my father says, taking another sip of his coffee, "I mean, of the examiners that I've had, Lucia is definitely the most caring and gentle. I think having her rotated in a few years ago was a blessing in disguise. Perhaps God is watching over us."

I hear and understand his words, but they hit me like a powerful force. If he thinks Lucia is a more gentle scientist, what was he experiencing before?

My imagination gets the best of me and I worry about my classmates with their scientists.

I see my father staring off at the wall and know something is going on in his head that he's not telling me. I open my mouth to say something when a crackling sound comes on the speakers overhead and we both look up. I eye the clock and see that it's still an hour too early for the dinner announcement.

"Blaine Christensen, please report to sector 42A for a debriefing of your work for the day. You have ten minutes to comply before Peace-holders locate and subdue you for questioning. Please make sure that Korinne stays within your home unit until dinner is ready in the mess hall."

My skin crawls at the robotic voice and what it says. I've never been able to tell if it's a recording of the Creator's voice, or if she always speaks with a monotonous tone like that. It doesn't matter, for the words they speak weigh heavy in my chest.

I think my dad is in trouble.

He looks upward, his dark brown hair well kept and

smoothed back across his head. His blue eyes narrow at the ceiling. If there is any doubt that they have been watching us, it is completely gone now. They knew I was here and they want me to stay. The idea of being alone in our home unit freaks me out.

"But dad—," I say before he puts up a hand.

"Hold whatever you were going to say for when I get back, it's nothing to worry about," he assures me.

I can see he's got stubble from the day, his dark brown beard coming in after his shave this morning. I look nothing like him, of course, since he isn't biological family. It's an odd reminder, considering that he's my father, but then again, it's not like he adopted me. We were just assigned to be here together.

"Fine, but I think you are lying to me," I say, folding my arms.

He laughs at this. "You are a feisty one, that's for sure. Look, Kor, I promise this is just standard operation. They are watching me and my colleagues on camera all the time, but we are still working in systems and computers with highly sensitive data. They need to know what we've seen and where we've been working, just to make sure. There is nothing wrong, I promise."

His words are so full of surety that I just have to believe him. I don't think my father is a liar. I've never thought so. I nod and gesture to the door.

"Then I guess your interviewer is ready," I say sarcastically.

Fortunately, he picks up on this and fakes throwing his head back with a belly laugh.

"I'll tell them nothing of use," he jokes, winking at me.

There is still something that feels off, but I don't know why. The words he says and the way he says them are so reassuring. I shake the feeling away and think about how this weird break will be over soon and I can go to dinner as usual.

"See you at dinner, Kor," he says before walking through the door.

It hisses as it closes behind him. I recall him leaving with Peaceholders a couple days ago and how nervous I was for him then. In the scheme of things, the voice over the speaker sounded less angry than the Peaceholders who came to get him from our home unit. I relax a little, knowing that what my father said must be true. Leaning back, I try to not worry about the fact that I'm here alone. I know I'm safe, or at least that's what the Creators tell us, but I still feel weird being here alone. I sit up and look at the door.

I wonder how much trouble I'd get in if I left, as I don't want to sit here in the creepy quiet. I stand and move to the door. When I get there, however, it doesn't open. My skin chills, and I try to open it again. My ID bracelet is beeping and I see that a red light is flashing.

I guess I'm not going anywhere.

I move back to the couch and slump down on it. My tea is resting on the coffee table, and I slouch before grabbing it and taking another sip. It has cooled, and I sigh in relief. I lean my head back for a moment and think about what my father said about Lucia. He's got to know a bunch more about the experiments than I do, and I trust him.

I turn to look at where he sat and I startle at a glint of light that I see on the grey couch cushion beside me. Upon closer inspection, I see it's the same little silver charm that I saw on his ID bracelet earlier, the one he said gives him access to certain mainframes of the Safety computer systems. I eye the camera, not sure if the Creators would be mad if I try to bring it back to him.

I reach out discreetly and grab the small charm in my hand, slipping it in the pocket of my grey pants. I stand and move to the kitchen where I set both of our mugs. I turn to leave them there and sigh. My mother would know for sure I was here with someone having tea with them. Moving to the sink, I wash the mugs and place them on the drying towel. Sure, she'll see the mugs, but maybe she won't care as much about how they got there if they are washed. I step up to the door and hope it will open, but it still doesn't.

I place my hand on the door, waiting for the screen on the wall to flash, my bracelet telling the door it's me. Nothing happens.

I press my lips together firmly, my third failed attempt making me quiver. I reach over and try the manual latch to see if I can pull it open, but that doesn't work either.

I want to scream, both because I'm terrified of being locked in here and also because I'm angry. Apparently they didn't think I'd stay here when I was told to. I shake my head and sit back on the couch.

They must know me better than I thought.

I position myself so that my back is turned to the camera and hold my hands below the back of the couch to hide them from any other cameras that might be there.

I inspect the silver charm and consider what it means. That same symbolic charm was attached to Lucia's bracelet and I wonder why my father has the same access to rooms as Lucia does.

Deciding I should make sure to not lose it, I put the charm on my own ID bracelet and lean back on the couch. It seems like forever before my mother gets home. She looks exhausted and weary. It must have been a rough day in the canning facilities. All that hard work just to send the food away to who-knows-where. Sure, we eat some of it too, but without the plant in Safety, we are told the city outside of this horrible compound wouldn't have enough food.

My mother gapes at me, "What are you doing here, Korinne? You know it's against the rules for anyone to be in their home unit alone. Especially right now. It could be dangerous."

For some reason, when she says it, the thought sounds ridiculous even though I just had the same thought myself. I know inside I'm not unsafe here, but being alone in a place just does that to you, I think.

"Relax, Mother, I just finished my experiments earlier than —," I almost say her name, but realize my mother doesn't know who she is nor does she care, "—my scientist expected. I was sent to find something to do."

She narrows her eyes at me, not sure if I'm being honest. Still, she moves to the kitchen and goes to heat the water before realizing there is already warm water in the kettle.

"Did you have some of my tea? What kind did you use? I don't get these very often and have to ration them."

"No, Mother, we had dad's tea. The stuff you don't like."

She relaxes at that. "Well, that's good, then. At least there is still water in here. It means I can likely get a full cup in before the dinner announcement."

She warms up the water and is drinking a cup of her own tea when my brother huffs in.

"Ugh, I hate history," he complains, plopping down on the couch. He drops his holopad there, and it slaps against mine. I curse and run over to pick mine up to make sure it isn't broken. When I look there, I see he has twelve assignments for the day.

"Whoa, that's brutal. Twelve assignments for history? No wonder you aren't happy," I tease.

He glares at me, his blond hair coming over his forehead to just over his eyes. He's going to need to get a cut soon, otherwise he'll get in trouble. For a moment I marvel at the oddity of our family. I know nothing of genetics, but with my mom's dark brown skin and black hair, the paleness of the rest of our family unit's skin is stark. My own hair is strawberry, while my fathers is dark brown like my mother's.

Sean opens his mouth to speak when the speaker buzzes and the voice tells us it's time for dinner in the mess hall.

My mother purses her lips in the kitchen and eyes her mug. There is no way she finished it.

She says what we've all been thinking. "Huh, that's early for dinner. I wasn't expecting the announcement to come for another ten minutes."

I'm nervous now, though I can't describe why. My brother groans that he didn't get to wallow in his sorrow for long before dinner was ready. I punch him, and he winces, holding his arm.

"Stop, you two, let's get going. I'm starving today. I had a busy day at work," she sighs, moving to the doorway.

The three of us exit our home unit and I turn to watch the door hiss closed.

All I can think about is how strange it is that my father was called from our home unit. Well, that and my mind also dwells on the fact that it's pork and bean soup for dinner.

13

When we get to the mess hall, we stand in our usual spot, waiting for my father. As the time passes and we don't see him, I start to get nervous. He said everything was normal, that it would be fine, but he is usually here by now.

I stare at my mother, the fear obvious in my eyes. She looks at me and then scans the mess hall.

"I'm sure he's caught up with something at work. When did he leave the unit? Was it just before I got there?" she asks.

"I don't know. I was distracted, so I wasn't watching the time," I say, still scanning the room for signs of him.

"You need to be better at watching the time, dear. You are going to get yourself and our family into trouble again if you aren't better about keeping time."

I know she's lecturing me, and normally I'd have something sarcastic and snotty to say to her, but I am still too distracted that I don't see my father anywhere. At length, the line for the food gets shorter and we decide we should eat before we run out of time. I don't like the decision, of course, but I don't know how much longer I can listen to Sean complain about how hungry he is.

I'm so preoccupied with my father's lateness that I just end up getting the gross soup and bread. We lingered too long and now we get the stuff that was at the bottom of the serving dishes. The roll I have is soggy from all the steam of the hot rolls above it.

"So how was your day of tests, dear? Was it as horrible as you thought it would be?" my mother asks.

I start to speak but she interrupts me— "Without too much detail, of course."

I didn't need the clarification, but mothers will be mothers.

"It was fine, not what I expected, but oh well," I say.

I think my mother doesn't appreciate that answer, but she changes the conversation to talk about Sean's schooling. I'm not listening anymore, though, as my eyes wander to the small charm that is attached to my ID bracelet now. The set of rings is beautiful in a way, and the star is set so perfectly within them both. How such detail could be created into the size of my pinky nail, I can't be sure.

It's not like my father to leave something like this behind, and part of me wonders if he did it on purpose. My stomach tightens at the thought, and I put my hand down below the table, hoping no one noticed. I don't think it's wrong that my father had this, but I realize now it's likely not a good thing that I'm the one with it now. I'm just a kid. The Creators wouldn't relish the idea of me having access to other places here that I shouldn't.

My thoughts are interrupted with another complaint from Sean. I'm annoyed to discover he's *still* complaining about his History lessons.

"I don't know why I have to care about a bunch of random old dead guys from a country I haven't even seen. Shouldn't we learn just about the history of Safety?" Sean says, folding his arms. It's obvious he is still bothered by his large workload for the day.

I think he's kidding, but I understand his point about the uselessness of learning U.S. History. Why learn about a country that we have no connection with, other than technically living in it? We don't ever get to leave Safety, and I'm not optimistic that anyone will find a cure for our disease, but it's a nice thought he had—learning Safety's history.

My mind wanders back to Lucia and how I saw the same charm on her ID bracelet. Then I'm remembering the experiments again and seeing the sun rise above the mountainous horizon before I panic, knowing I will burst into flames. The memory of the intense heat exploding in my limbs rushes through me, startling me.

I drop my fork and it clinks loudly on the plate, making my mother and brother look at me.

"You okay over there? Are you trying to break your plate?" my brother asks.

I've turned the heads of a few families around us and I blush.

I open my mouth to answer when the speakers above us crackle for an announcement. I eye the clock again, knowing I don't need to see the time to know it's not a normal time for them to be coming on the speaker.

"Citizens of Safety, we are excited to say that we have some new arrivals in our compound. We have found and rescued others afflicted by the same illness. They've been in hiding for many years now. We are grateful that they survived and that we could rescue them."

My mind is reeling now. *What do they mean they found more?* We are brought here at birth, period. Are they saying that they brought new babies to us? They don't normally announce that.

We turn toward the main doors to the compound and see a young girl and boy walk through the doors. My eyes widen when I see how old they are. The girl looks my age, her hair cropped around her ears in a pixie cut, the boy a bit shorter. He looks to be a few years younger than Sean. They each have black hair. Her eyes are almond shaped and his are round and wide. They both look terrified to be here.

"Well, that's odd, isn't it," my mother says, her eyes moving to look at me, "how did the poor dears last so long out in the world without getting killed by the sun?"

I can't say I wasn't thinking the same thing, but that's not what I'm focused on. I know I wouldn't have seen the boy and girl before, but they somehow look familiar. It's an odd feeling when you are sure you don't know someone, but you also know there is something you recognize about them.

I turn to look back at my mother. "Where are their parents? How did they end up getting found?" I voice some of the questions that flow in my mind.

My mother shakes her head and keeps eating. Between mouthfuls, she answers pensively. "I'm not sure, but I'm glad they made it here alive. What a wonderful blessing."

Hearing my mother say that makes me remember the fact that my father isn't sitting with us at the table. I look at his empty place at our family's table and feel even more nervous now. The assurances he gave me last night flip through my mind. I know he's an optimist, but things have been strange around here in Safety for too long. For sixteen years, or as much of that I can remember, things have run smoothly. Not once has anything happened, other than old people dying, of course. Yet in the past few days, one family was killed to protect us from some random sickness and they punished another so terribly that no one sees them anymore. My father's been beaten, or so I believe. I've started these horribly terrifying experiments. And now my father isn't here when he should be.

My stomach is roiling so much that I put my spoon down on the table. I can't focus on eating anymore; I'm too distracted by the thoughts going through my head. This gets my mom's attention, and she looks at me, her face scrunched in worry.

"Korinne, are you okay? You've hardly eaten anything," she says.

Suddenly, I'm angry. It boils up inside of me.

"How can you even ask that?" I say, louder than I mean to. A few people around us turn their heads at my tone. "Dad's gone! Men that he's worked with are dead or in trouble. The past week has been so strange, and you sit there as if there isn't anything wrong!"

She's blushing now and looking down at her food. She knows what I'm saying is true, but she won't admit it.

I look around to see that more heads have turned toward our table, and a couple Peaceholders are making their way over to me. The blood drains from my face when I see this, and I sit quickly, shoving a spoonful of the cold soup in my mouth. The Peaceholders still come over and stand behind me.

"Is there a problem, young lady?" I hear a female voice speak behind me.

I'm terrified inside, knowing that demerits for my family will get us punished. We're already so low on the scale that too many more will make it so we have to leave the mess hall like that other family.

"I'm sorry," I mumble through my big bite.

"Excuse me? I couldn't hear you through your food," a male voice says over my other shoulder.

I gulp down the bite and repeat my apology.

"That's better. Remember your place, citizen. We can't have disarray in this place. It's for your safety, after all," the female Peaceholder says.

I still haven't turned around to look at them, because I don't trust myself to not do something stupid. I just nod profusely so they can see it from behind.

A body presses itself up against my back and I know it's the male Peaceholder from the pair, the one who threatened me before.

He whispers in my ear. "Good girl . . . keep that temper in check, or else you'll regret crossing me again," he hisses.

Chills run up my spine and I know with surety that it's him, the same man I tripped on last week. He is out to get me.

The rebellious part of me wants to pick up my soup bowl and toss it in his face. In fact, I imagine doing this and getting the satisfaction of seeing it smash all over his uniform. I don't do it though. I just lock my jaw and force another nod.

Soon they are gone from our table and my mother is inspecting me.

"Korinne, you must keep yourself together. Your father is going to be fine. There is nothing for you to be stressed about. He's just busy with work, that's it. Now, can you please eat your food?"

I don't respond. Instead, I just poke at my food while staring over at the orphan table. I see Charlie there with a bunch of other kids, eating their food. He sees my gaze and smiles, waving at me. Then he looks over at the new kids and points to them, his eyebrows raised.

I can read the message in his eyes. He thinks it's weird and impossible that these two kids have survived that long out in the sun. There is something else going on here, but I don't know exactly what it is.

Sean complains about something again and when I tune in to hear his words, I realize that he's talking about me.

"—going to get us in trouble because she's a baby," is all I catch of his words.

I squeeze my fist around my spoon and glare at him. "You aren't worried then?" I ask. The anger hasn't left my voice, but the loudness has.

He looks at me, then shrugs. "I don't know, he's had to work late before. It's not *that* weird."

What my brother says is true. There have been a few times my father has had to work late. But this feels different.

"He was off early, though. Why would he be off of work early, then have to go back to work late? I don't see how that could be normal."

Sean just shakes his head and eats more soup. My mother opens her mouth to speak.

"Korinne—"

My mother's words are cut off as the speakers crackle overhead. The announcement says that dinner is almost over and that we should go ahead to our family time. I grumble, knowing I'm going to have to worry about my father and pretend like I want to spend time with my mother and Sean. I stand up forcefully and turn from the table.

"I'll just meet you at the home unit, alright? I don't want to talk anymore."

I make a beeline for the food tray conveyor belt and drop mine there. The dishes clatter and a few heads turn my way. I hear someone mutter something about a temper and my face flushes yet again. Why I get so embarrassed, I'm not sure. I'm clearly drawing too much attention to myself by the way I'm acting, but I just can't help it.

Suddenly, there are two bodies behind me. I stiffen and turn to see the tan camouflage clothes and armor of the Peaceholders. Fear grips me, and I know they are going to take me. When they don't grab me, I almost dart around them and run. Something stops me, though.

"Korinne Christensen?" one asks.

I nod, unsure of what else to say. I can't get my voice to work.

"Please come with us," the same one says.

I want to ask why, but I still can't speak. Instead, I walk forward toward them. They each grab one of my arms and lead me toward the main door to the mess hall. My eyes dart over to my mother and I can see she's pale. Whether it's worry for my safety or worry that I'll get the family in trouble, I'm not sure.

I look over at the orphan table and see that Charlie's spoon has frozen halfway to his mouth. He looks nervous. I can feel tears welling in my eyes. Part of me knows I am in trouble, while the other part screams that I did nothing wrong.

My mind is flashing back to all the things that have happened in the past few days and I stop on the broken computer, the strange explosion of the equipment in my test room. Could Lucia have been lying when she said I wouldn't get in trouble? Why would she do that?

I turn to look up at one of the Peaceholders and he looks sideways at me.

"Please don't give us any trouble. We don't want to make a scene," he says to me.

I can't help but laugh out loud. It isn't a jovial laugh, just an incredulous one. How can he say that to me when they've already made a scene?

Heads follow us from the metal tables where people have pretty much already stopped eating, either because dinner is almost over, or because they are too busy watching me.

We get to the door. Then I cry.

14

They yank me through the hall now, not because I'm resisting them, but because I'm bawling and my legs aren't functioning properly. I feel the hot tears running over my cheeks and I'm even more embarrassed now. The only solace I have is knowing that everyone in Safety, save for a couple other Peaceholders, is in the mess hall right now eating.

They lead me through the metal halls silently. I can hear my own sobs echoing off the walls. Our feet clatter on the metal grate below, the fluorescent lighting shining up through the gaps at the edges of the floors along the length of the hallway.

It takes me a moment to realize they are leading me toward the same hallway that takes me to the experiment rooms. The fear deepens in my chest now as I see that's exactly where we're heading. We stop just short of the intersection to the next hall and the male Peaceholder to my right punches a code into the wall there. Hissing announces doors extending inward from either wall in the hallway. They close off the exit with a final thunk that echoes behind us on the metal.

The other Peaceholder reaches down and opens the door in the floor.

"Citizen, please go directly to your test room. Your examiner is waiting for you there. She'll provide an explanation once you arrive."

I stare at the steep stairwell and don't move right away. This awards me with a nudge from the Peaceholder on my left. It's not an angry shove, just an impatient one.

I'm numb.

What do they want from me? Why is this happening? I think, panicked.

Stepping carefully so that I don't fall down the steep stairs, I shakily make my way down until I'm at the metal hallway with doors lining each side all the way along its length. I can't remember the room number I was in earlier because of how panicked I am right now, so I just start walking, hoping I'll remember before I get to the door. I see a number over each of the doors and I'm trying to recall which one feels familiar.

"Korinne, in here," a woman's voice says to my left.

I jump at the words and turn to see a white-lab-coated person is sitting next to an examination chair. Her bulbous helmet is on her head again, making her appear like a creature instead of a person. The black plastic in front of her eyes is tinted so darkly that I can't see through it to her face. It's only her voice that gives her away as Lucia. At least it sounds like her to me.

"Umm, okay," I say, turning toward the open door and making my way to the lab chair. I feel overdressed right now, knowing that I am usually here wearing the horrible shiny blue robe.

"I'm very sorry for the trouble, but seeing as your last two sessions were cut short, I'd like to perform a couple tests today to get you caught up," she says with her robotic voice.

I hear her words and understand them, but for some reason I'm not processing them.

"Um, what?" I ask, staring at the place where I think her

face probably is behind the large helmet. My eyes are still blurry from the tears and I reach up to wipe them away.

"Yes," Lucia's robot voice says, "I haven't been able to gather enough data from you to keep up with your classmates in our study for a cure. Let's see what we can get done today."

The words don't come out fast, but I'm still having a hard time processing them. My brain is spinning.

"But—I thought I was in trouble for the computer, I don't —" I sputter, not sure what else to say.

Lucia sighs. "Yes, that is what's tricky about data. You need all the parts to create an accurate study. We still aren't sure how to deal with the intense response you have to the reagents." She sounds sad in a way.

"If you don't mind, please sit back and relax," Lucia suggests. Her voice does sound strange and robotic, but it's somehow soothing.

Still feeling uncomfortable, but not knowing what else to do, I sit back in the chair, the leather of it sticking to my sweaty arms. In normal conditions, the fact I'm so sweaty would embarrass me, but this time I can't think of anything else but how my father is missing and I might never see him again.

"I'm going to take blood samples from you again. Nothing unusual on that front, but I'll be performing live tests on the blood here. We need instant results if we are going to include your data for the past week."

I nod, still feeling like I'm out of my body, fear and worry ruling me.

I open my mouth to see if Lucia knows where my father is, but even if she did know, I don't think she'd be able to tell me. It's likely a security risk for me to know. I pause my thoughts when the needle enters my arm. I wince at the pinch, knowing it really doesn't hurt that much, but getting blood taken is so new that it still freaks me out.

Lucia extracts a few vials of blood before banding my arm.

"Okay, while I do these tests I'm going to run you through some of the same mental tests I did before. You'll be going to sleep this time and you'll experience a similar simulation to last time, though I won't pull you out as quickly. We need to understand how your brain will react to the sunlight."

I say nothing, knowing it won't matter that I don't want to do the tests again anyway.

"Good," Lucia says. I think she's smiling, which ought to make me feel more at ease, but it doesn't. She quickly attaches the same probes to me that she had before, though she has a little more trouble having to work around my clothes.

"I need you to drink this—"

"What? Why? What is it for?" I ask, my voice quivering.

Her eyes flash with irritation for a moment. "I need to fully understand your reaction in the simulation. I don't have time to explain, just drink it."

She hands me a small glass of liquid that looks like water. I don't like the idea of drinking it, but I don't have much of a choice. I drink the liquid, realizing it's not water by the bitter and lingering taste, but that's soon lost on me as my mind fogs quickly. I feel the urge to close my eyes. Rather than try to fight, I just do it.

My mind blanks out and I'm in the field of grass. It looks just like it did last time. A slight breeze blows through my hair and I can't help but smile and suck in the fresh air. I've been in Safety my whole life, so the idea of fresh air is ludicrous. I look to my left and note there are a bunch of dark outlines in the night: trees. There's a forest of some sort over there. Looking to my right, I see lights shining through the darkness of the night.

I think that, for a moment, I might move toward the town to see what it is. Then I remember that the sun is supposed to rise soon.

I panic.

The sky is already lightening and my eyes widen in shock. I

knew this would happen, because I've been here before, but I'm frustrated that I can't get away fast enough. I feel as if I'm being dragged backward and I turn to see Peaceholders grabbing my arms, keeping me in my place.

I shout back at them, but they don't listen.

The sky is getting lighter swiftly now. I turn to look at the spot where the sun rose last time and see that the sky is blue there. I scream and pull hard on the Peaceholders. Suddenly, they are gone, and I lurch forward. Turning, I run as fast as I can to the town in the distance. It's too late though. The sun peeks over the line of the landscape and I scream. Tears fill my eyes, and I know it's coming.

A beam of sunlight hits me and my blood burns. I'm heating up from the inside, like I might explode in flames like the man in the picture they pushed on us so many times.

I cry harder and fall to my knees, the intensity of the burning overcoming me. Then I pause.

I'm still crying, but I realize that the burning doesn't *hurt*. It just feels . . . intense.

Curious, I inspect my hands and see that I'm not on fire. In fact, nothing has changed. I suddenly feel a draw to go *toward* the sun, as if my brain wants to soak it in more. I'm so confused, the tingling of the burning filling every part of my being. A sound behind me makes me turn to see the scowling Peaceholders there. One of them is the same one who has been tormenting me in the mess hall. I glare at him, wanting to hurt him. Then Lucia's voice echoes in my mind.

That will be enough, she says.

I know she's going to pull me out, but I don't want her to anymore. I want to hurt that Peaceholder so badly. I reach out and scream, before a flash blinds me. I hear the Peaceholder shout in pain, but then I'm back in the chair of the exam room, gasping.

"—the char just happened to me?" I say, unabashed.

"Hurry, we don't have time," Lucia hisses.

I hear an urgency in her voice that wasn't there before. Her helmet is off and she's still as beautiful as she was the last time I saw her.

"What—?" I say before she shushes me harshly.

"Don't speak, do nothing other than what I instruct you to do. Understand?"

I nod, but the fear is back. Whatever lingering satisfaction I got from the strange simulation is gone as Lucia stares at me fiercely. She grabs my hand and a twinge of fear washes over me. She doesn't hurt me though; instead, she grabs my wrist and points at my bracelet with her free hand.

"Use this charm—here," Lucia says. She's pointing to the charm my father left behind.

My blood runs cold.

"Walk to the mess hall, but turn left down the first hallway, 34D. Use it on the door to the left. Wait for me there."

I'm so confused by what she says that I try to ask again. "What—?"

"No talking, just moving, *now*," she urges.

I glance around the room and see glass everywhere. There are spatters of red on the desk and floor. I realize only briefly that it's my blood before she pushes me off the chair.

Did the vials of my blood break? I wonder.

"34D, wait for me there. *Do not talk to anyone else*," she says.

Her words feel like a threat to me. I promptly turn to the doorway and move through it, my body feeling even more clammy than before.

Oh gosh, I'm sweating so bad, I think.

For a moment I make a beeline for the locker room, but then I remember I'm not wearing the weird robe today. There is a female Peaceholder standing outside the doorway and she stares at me. I blush and look at the floor.

"Well, are you cleared to return?" she asks me.

I'm frozen, and I remember Lucia's instructions. My hand casually moves to my bracelet and I cover it with my hand.

Oh no, oh no, oh no. It's been less than ten seconds and I'm already ruining Lucia's plan. I open my mouth to say something, but I'm sputtering. I can't form the words.

"Yes, we've got the data we need for today." I hear Lucia behind me and relief bursts through me.

The Peaceholder looks behind me, then back at me warily. "Fine, return to your quarters immediately. It's almost curfew," the Peaceholder says.

I startle at the revelation, feeling like I've only been here for a matter of ten minutes. The dream must have lasted far longer than I thought.

A hand rests on my shoulder and I tense.

"And don't forget what I told you, Korinne. I need you to rest up and be ready for our next exam," Lucia says. As she does, I feel her lightly tap my arm, the one with my access bracelet. She moves in front of me and addresses the Peaceholder, blocking my view of her. I shove my hand with the access bracelet into my pocket and move past them.

I stop listening to what they are saying, focused only on getting to hallway 34D. I know this one. Fortunately, it's not too far from here.

Walking briskly, I ascend the spiral stairs and reach the hallway. The two Peaceholders there, these are men, watch me with serious looks on their faces. I just bow my head and keep walking.

I can make it, it's not too far, I encourage myself.

It isn't far, but it feels forever away. Soon I'm rounding the corner of the mess hall and I see the glowing 34D sign over the intersection to the hallway. Another set of Peaceholders stands outside the mess hall door to my right and I look away sharply. The hallways are empty, save for a few members of Safety who are hurrying along. A clock on the wall shows it is only thirty minutes until we are to be in our quarters.

I move to the hallway and turn down it. It's empty, and I know I should hurry before a Peaceholder comes around to see me. I spot the metal door that reads *Personnel Only* on the left. They've embedded a key card reader in the wall just next to the door. Just before I get there, I hear shuffling behind me.

"Kor?"

I freeze, knowing the voice.

"Charlie!" I hiss, turning to him. "What are you doing here?"

"I was just talking to—" he stops and blushes. I realize he's not alone. Susan, the one and only bane of my existence, is smirking behind him.

"He was talking to *me*, in case you are wondering."

Charlie shakes his head and glances at Susan. "Actually, I was just trying to enjoy a few more minutes of quiet before I'm forced into the room with the other family-less kids. Susan chased after me without me asking."

My mouth drops open, and I pause. I'm angry, frustrated by what I see, but I know I don't have time to discuss the issue. Charlie does seem annoyed, which is odd for him. I force my mind back to the task at hand—I need to hurry. Lucia said I had to go right away. I glance at the door and then back at Charlie.

"Um, Kor, are you okay? What did they do to you? You look nervous," Charlie says, concern on his beautiful face. I feel the butterflies swarm in my stomach at the sight.

"Come here," I hiss.

I know this isn't what Lucia told me to do, but I have decided.

Charlie stares at me, confused, but he comes. Unfortunately, despite hating me, Susan follows him. The moment they are close, I whip my braceleted hand out of my pocket and wave it on the scanner. Sure enough, the silver charm my father left behind works. The light turns green, and it beeps loudly. I wince at the sound. The door clicks, and I push it open hurriedly.

"Kor, what the—"

Charlie doesn't get to finish as I shove him and Susan hard through the doorway. It's tricky because he's much bigger than me, but I get them in. Just as I'm turning to close the door behind us, I see the boot of a Peaceholder enter the opening of the hallway.

I pull the door closed behind us.

15

I'm gasping. It's partially from the effort I had to use to get Charlie and Susan through the door, but also because I'm gripped with fear. I know we went through a door we are definitely not supposed to be using. A Peaceholder, maybe more, is likely coming toward this door at this moment. *And* I just used an access fob that didn't belong to me to get into a restricted area.

Panicked, I look around the room to find a place to hide. I'm disappointed to find we aren't in another room, but in a hallway. It's long and narrow, made of the same metal on both sides, and it has the same grate below with the lights shining through. The only difference is that it's more narrow than the public hallways.

"Kor—what the heck are we doing? We are going to get in so much trouble," Charlie's saying. I turn to see that he's pale, contrasting with his dark hair. His gorgeous green eyes are wide with fear.

A hand grabs my arm and turns me sharply. I'm surprised by the strength.

"What the *char* are you doing dragging me into this? If you think you're going to get away with ruining my demerit-free standing here—"

I jump toward Susan and firmly place my hand over her mouth. She squeals underneath my palm and I press harder.

"I don't want you here, but I didn't have a choice. Besides, it's too late now. If any Peaceholder knows you even came in here with me, you are charred. So be quiet," I say forcefully.

Susan's eyes widen as she realizes what I'm saying is true. She can't go back without getting in trouble, whatever story she has to tell.

At this point she's stopped squealing, so I cautiously pull my hand off of her mouth. Her eyes are wide, the stark blue irises reflecting the overhead lights.

"What have you done?" Susan whispers, tears forming in her eyes.

I actually feel kind of bad, despite the things she's put me through.

"We just have to wait. Someone is supposed to come get me," I say, though just now realizing how stupid this sounds. Charlie and Susan must think I've lost my mind.

Looking not far down the hallway, I see there is a four-way intersection. Straight down the hallway, the way curves left and I can't see further than a few hundred feet.

"Kor, what is happening? How did you get the door to open? What are we doing here?" Charlie asks. When I look at him, he looks angry. I'm feeling even more guilty now for bringing him into this. Then again, part of me is relieved that I don't have to be here alone.

"In my test, my examiner, Lucia, she—well—I was told—"

I'm sputtering. I can't put words together and it's frustrating, but I'm so flustered I don't know what to say.

"Kor, I don't understand. What are you saying?" he presses, still confused.

Just then, a beeping sound behind us makes us turn

sharply. Susan squeals and Charlie gasps, backing toward the wall.

I freeze, my heart stopping with fear.

Oh shoot, oh shoot, my family is going to be banished for this, I think.

As the door opens, I position myself in front of Susan and Charlie. I don't know why; it's not like I would or even could defend them against someone like a Peaceholder. Maybe I feel like I need to make up for pulling them into this.

"—all doing fine. I'm just glad we could complete a test!"

The woman's voice is familiar, and I soon realize why. Lucia walks through the door with her head turned backward, speaking to someone on the other side of the door.

"Looks like business as usual in Safety and—"

She grunts as she walks right into me. I tumble backward, knocking Charlie and Susan down as well. I land hard on my backside, the grate cutting into me.

Lucia curses and slams the door hard behind her.

"Why are you standing in front of the door like that? You could—" she notices Susan and Charlie and her eyes widen in shock. "Who are they? *Why* did you bring them?"

Lucia looks angry, and the pit grows in my stomach. I didn't think about what her reaction would be to seeing two random kids in here with me. I obviously wasn't thinking when I pulled them along. But leaving them behind might have meant they'd get in trouble for doing nothing but being in the wrong place at the wrong time. What choice did I have?

She shakes her head and turns her back to the door, putting her finger to her lips and making eye contact with each of us before turning around to face the door. Lucia casually opens the door only slightly and apologizes to whoever she was talking to before.

"I just tripped on my own feet," she says, laughing forcefully, "Ah well, have a good one, Earl!"

I hear a man give best wishes before the door closes with a hiss.

"We can't stay here, follow me," Lucia whispers, a hardness still in her eyes. She looks at Susan and Charlie before saying, "All of you."

My face is burning, and I know I'm blushing. Lucia clearly wanted only me to use the access charm to get in here, and she's angry that Charlie and Susan are here.

"Do you still have the access charm?" She's watching me now, her hand outstretched.

I nod and hand over my whole bracelet.

"You two—I don't know who you are, but I need your bracelets too. Now," Lucia says. She sounds intense.

Charlie and Susan shakily pull off their bracelets and hand them to Lucia. Without hesitation, she tosses them down through the floor grate, the metal clanking loudly.

She says nothing else, but instead turns and rushes through the hallway, stopping just short of the intersection.

"We have little time—this way."

My mind is numb, but I follow with Charlie and Susan just behind me.

Lucia leads us to the left down a hallway, which looks largely the same as the others. Her auburn hair is curled today, and it falls over her back, stopping halfway. My mind is wandering now, trying to cope with the stress I'm under. I can't help but remember how familiar Lucia looks to me.

The woman stops so suddenly that I almost bump into her. I stop just short of her back, Charlie and Susan still behind me. She waves her own bracelet over the scanner next to a door to our left, and it hisses open. She peers in, then looks back at us.

"All of you—in here."

At first none of us move, but then Lucia waves her hand gesturing us into the door, a stern look on her face. Charlie jumps to it first and enters the room, with Susan close behind.

Still apprehensive, I follow. After we are through, Lucia comes in and closes the door behind us, the hiss feeling more final this time.

Lights automatically come on in the back half of the room. I gather that the other lights came on when Lucia first poked her head in. It's a locker room, with benches in the center and lockers lining all of the walls. An opening in the wall shows a bathroom connected to this room.

"Korinne, you've made this more complicated than it needs to be," Lucia says, looking at me harshly again, "I asked you to come immediately—not to pick up friends on the way."

I'm hurt by her words, but I don't know why. She isn't my friend. Still, the way she tried to keep me at ease during the experiments bonded me to her somehow.

"It was an accident, I just ran into them—" I try to say before Lucia puts her hand up.

"It's too late now, we'll have to make it work."

Lucia walks briskly around the benches to the opposite wall.

"Lock the door, now!"

I hear her voice echo in the tiled room, even though she doesn't turn. Charlie is the first to respond as he turns to the door and stares for a moment. He's scanning the door, trying to figure out how to lock it. He eyes me and I just shrug. The doors here look different from the ones in our housing units.

I jump when Lucia sighs and brushes past me, moving to the door and pulling a latch near the opening. We hear muffled hissing and metal sliding into place somewhere inside.

"Sorry, I forgot you aren't familiar with this part of the compound," she almost sounds like she means it. Almost.

She crosses back to the lockers and puts her hand to the wall of one. It scans her hand. I hear a robotic voice say *"Confirmed: Lucia Stromberg, Examiner, Safety level B"* before the locker hisses open.

Level B? I think.

We've not been told anything about other levels of Safety. Then again, only recently did I realize that there were even stairs down into the testing rooms.

Lucia pulls out a white lab coat and gestures me over.

"Well, get over here, we need to cover up your clothes."

I look down at my grey attire. I've chosen sweat pants and a simple short-sleeved shirt. Charlie is wearing the same, coincidentally, but Susan is wearing the dress version. Made from the same cloth, it hardly looks good on any of us.

Still hesitant, I walk across the room and take the coat from her with two fingers. It's the kind of coat she and the other scientists wear when they come to do our tests. Feeling strange still, I put my arms through the coat and am surprised to see it fits me perfectly.

"I only had one made to your size, Korinne. We're going to have to improvise with you two," Lucia grumbles, looking at the others. Once again, she reaches into the locker and pulls out a lab coat, this one bigger.

"I have an extra lab coat . . . and you—" she points to Charlie, "—will just have to wear this one. Don't put the coats on yet, there's something we need to take care of first."

She shoves the coat into Charlie's hands and pulls the one off of her body. Just before she hands it to Susan, she pulls her ID badge from the little pocket near the lapel. Underneath her coat, Lucia wears a smart, knee-length red dress. I'm struck by her beauty. The color of the dress makes the red in her hair pop.

"It's going to be strange going out without a coat, but I'll make do."

She reaches into her locker again and pulls out two clipboards with packets of paper on them. She hands one to me and the other to Charlie.

"You're medical students from St. Anstine's University. You

came here to see my work and learn more about the affliction of the people at Safety. Those—" Lucia points at the clipboard in my hands, "—are your notes. You will not answer questions and you will not speak. Let me speak for you. Understood?"

I'm nodding, but only because I have no idea what to do.

"Um, but who are you? Why are we here—?" Charlie begins to ask.

Lucia holds up her hand. "No time for questions. Once we're out of Safety, we can talk more. For now, we move."

"What?!" Susan squeaks. "You aren't taking me out of here! You can't make me!"

Susan's eyes are welling up and she's shaking. Charlie is grimacing, his own face betraying his fear.

Somehow, I feel more excitement than any other emotion at the idea.

"But—the sun—you know we can't go out in it," I say, trying not to think of the implications.

Lucia rolls her eyes. "It's night—didn't they teach you that the sun goes down at night? Besides, girl—" Lucia realizes she doesn't know their names, "—I can't leave you now. They probably already know you are here with me."

She slams the locker shut and I wince at the sound, glancing back to the door. It's not like she's been quiet since we first came in here, but I'm still worried by the noise.

"I'm sorry about this, but I'll need to cut you before we go further." Lucia grimaces as she says it.

I knit my brows at her words. Sure enough, she pulls a small device out of her pocket. It's small and silver, and looks to be made of some type of metal. Pushing a button, I see it flip open to reveal a blade.

My stomach turns. *Oh gosh, she's going to kill us*, I think, panicked.

I'm backing away now and she looks at me, her face softening.

"I know this is all going so fast, but *please*, trust me. I will not hurt you—too badly. I need you."

Lucia's eyes are pleading now and I see that she's pained by this need to hurt us. I break a little on the inside, seeing her reaction.

"I need to get you out of Safety, and we don't have time for more explanation," Lucia pleads.

Charlie and Susan have backed away too. I'm shocked that Susan is now being quiet, it's so unlike her.

"What do you need that for, then?" I say, pointing at the knife. My words come out much more angry than I expected, and I shrink back internally, thinking I've made her mad.

Lucia's face is still soft, and she folds the knife away, putting it in her pocket.

"There, it's gone for just a minute. If I'm going to get you out of here, I need to remove the tracking devices in your arms."

I start at the words.

This time Susan speaks. "Get the what? What do you mean? Why are we leaving Safety? We'll *die* in the sun! Maybe not tonight, but in the morning! I can't go out there!" Susan is yelling. She's also turning green, clearly beside herself at the idea of leaving.

Lucia sighs and gives me a pointed look as if to say *why did you bring her here?*

"Once again, no time. If you want to be punished beyond comprehension, and if you want me to get killed, then don't listen to me. If you want us all to live through this, then stop wasting time."

That shuts Susan up. She's hyperventilating though, but at least it's quieter than her yelling.

I stand up straight and though I'm still terrified, I nod to Lucia. I'm trying to be brave, though I'm not sure it's coming off well.

"To the bathroom, over there."

Lucia strides over to the next room and I see white-tiled floors that match the locker room. Only sinks and stalls fill the room. Charlie blushes when he realizes it's a woman's restroom. A slight smile breaks on my face at his adorable reaction.

My scientist stops by the sink and pulls out the knife again, watching my reaction. At the same time, she retrieves a small box made of metal. It is square and rough-looking, but it looks heavy. My thought is validated as she drops it on the sink edge, a clinking sound proving the material's weight.

"This was already going to be challenging with just one sensor, but our odds of success are greatly decreased with the three of you. Once I get them out, the sensors will send a distress signal to the Creators of Safety, and all Peaceholders will be notified of the sensors' location. This box can hide the signal for a few minutes, but not much longer. It will eventually go into overdrive and push out stronger waves."

I'm stuck on every word she says, but not caring what they mean. All I know is that she said she's getting us out of Safety. The idea terrifies me, but at the same time it's like a dream come true: something I've always wanted, but knew could never happen.

But it's happening now.

I step forward and submit my arm to Lucia's knife. She pauses.

"Actually, I'll do you first. Uh, what's your name?" Lucia asks, looking at Susan.

"Susan," she squeaks, her voice cracking.

"I get the feeling you will make a lot of noise and it will draw too much attention with two other trackers sending out signals."

Susan pales, but moves in front of me.

"Hold out your right arm, and—"

Lucia reaches into her pocket and pulls out a foam roll that looks like a red hot dog.

"—bite on this."

Susan takes the foam and puts it in her mouth. Lucia raises Susan's arm upward to poke her upper arm. She then puts a small device that she got from seemingly nowhere and holds it there. A beeping sound is slow at first, but then increases in speed as it reaches the middle of Susan's upper arm.

"Once this is done, I need you—boy, to take her place, then you, Korinne. We only have a few moments to do this before the sensors give us away. Once you are bandaged, put your coat on quickly."

Lucia marks with her pen on Susan's arm, then does the same to Charlie. After that, she comes to me and helps me lift my sleeve. The beeping device speeds up at a certain spot on my arm, and Lucia draws an 'x' there.

"Get ready," she warns.

We all nod, my own mind numb from fear.

"Three—two—one," Lucia counts, before diving the knife into Susan's arm. My enemy's eyes scrunch up in pain, and she screams through the piece of foam she's biting on. My stomach turns as blood runs down her arm and drips to the floor. I feel light-headed and have to look away.

I hear the squeals and then shuffling before turning to see that Lucia has bandaged Susan's arm and has moved on to Charlie. His eyes are wide and he's pale now, too. I look away before the jab comes to him.

Suddenly she's next to me, eyes wild, yet concentrated. She says nothing before she digs the knife into my skin. The pain lances up my arm and I grit my teeth. Susan is crying, Charlie is gasping, and I just feel pain. The warmth of my blood runs over my arm and I think I might pass out. Lucia straps a thick bandage over my arm tightly and turns, rushing to the box. She flips open the lid and tosses something in there with a clink. I'm guessing it's the sensors.

Lucia rushes to the sinks in the bathroom and begins scrubbing her hands. My vision is blurring and my head is foggy. I've never seen this much blood before. The scientist finishes washing her hands and dries them hastily.

Lucia glances behind and shouts to us. "Put the coats on now! Close them over your clothes."

I'm breathing heavily from the pain, but I do as I'm told. I am barely aware that Susan and Charlie are putting their coats on as well.

Lucia then turns to us. "Now, we run."

16

Lucia grabs my arm and drags me to the door to the hallway. I didn't realize it before now, but my face is wet from tears. Charlie's jaw is set and I know he's trying to hold his emotions back, though his eyes are watering. Lucia takes notice, pausing before the doorway.

"This is going to sound rude, but I can't have you crying. Medical students crying isn't uncommon, but in a setting like this, it will look bad," Lucia says. There is sorrow in her face, and I know she's not enjoying our pain and fear.

I take in a deep breath and wipe my face.

"The sensors haven't made it through the box yet," she states as she pulls out a holopad of sorts from a pocket hidden in her dress.

Charlie is breathing hard, but he's becoming more calm. I'm feeling like I can hide the pain, but Susan is still beside herself. Her blue eyes are red rimmed.

"Honey, if you can't get it under control, we're going to get caught," Lucia begs.

My mind flashes back to my dad, and I imagine him in trouble. I don't know what happened to him, but I don't want that to happen to us.

"Pretend she's sick. She couldn't handle something we saw. You are taking us somewhere so she can compose herself," I suggest.

Lucia looks at me curiously, then her eyebrows raise slightly.

"That's not a terrible idea. It'll have to work."

She sounds skeptical, but Susan is not going to calm down.

"We only have a few minutes, so we move—now."

The words feel final, as if this will be the last thing I'll hear before I die. I get the feeling that Lucia thinks if they catch us, that's what will happen.

But that's not what scares me the most. Sure, it doesn't make me comfortable, but I'm suddenly stressed about what we'll see if we make it outside. Lucia said the sun wasn't up, but what if she's wrong? We're taught that night is when the moon comes up, but we've never seen it. We're only working with what the teachers told us. Suddenly, my lack of trust in Safety isn't giving me any confidence to push back.

Lucia opens the door and stands up straight, striding out confidently.

"Now that you've seen the locker room, I think that concludes your tour of Safety. How was that for a first day?" Lucia states.

I'm impressed with her acting, though it makes me think I stick out even more because *I* have no idea how to act. Not knowing what to do, I just smile and nod, watching her. Once we are out of the room, we turn left. Lucia looks around, notices that we are alone in the hallway, and relaxes.

"Do you remember the way out from here?" she asks.

I'm staring at her again, forcing a smile.

Why is she still acting? There is no one around, I think.

Then I remember. Gazing up, I see the cameras along the ceiling. A pang of fright shoots through me at the thought that they might have seen me go through the door in the first place, but then I pause. If they had seen me, then they would be here to get us already. I wonder if Lucia tampered with the cameras in that first hallway before we went to the locker room.

I don't have time to think about it as Lucia walks briskly down the hallway. I'm not the only one struggling to keep up; Susan hobbles next to me, her face still pained. Charlie doesn't appear troubled by keeping up, but then again, his legs are longer. He's all leg and no body, as I like to tease him. *Still as cute as ever*, I think, looking over at him.

We're still moving fast and we come to another door. Just before Lucia grabs the handle, a red light flashes above our heads and a loud alarm goes off. My heart jumps into my throat and I almost pee from the shock. We hear a loud click as the door locks shut. Still, my scientist tries to pull it open to no avail.

Lucia curses. "Well, that didn't buy us as much time as I hoped," she says grimly.

For a moment, we stand there with the alarm blaring. A few Peaceholders run past us at the intersection behind. One of them breaks off and walks toward us.

I'm panicking, but I'm putting everything I can into a smile. It's got to look so fake. In fact, the Peaceholder—this one male, looks at me as if he's wondering why I'm false smiling.

"Hey, what's going on?" Lucia asks coolly.

"We've had citizens disappear. Their trackers were found in a locker room cut out of their arms. Have you seen anything off? Anyone alone?" he asks, looking at me again.

"Hm, no, not really. I was just taking these students out. We just finished their rounds in the compound and it's past hours for them."

Lucia honestly sounds convincing as she says this, but the Peaceholder is still watching me.

"They'll have to stay. It's lockdown until we find the missing citizens—" he pauses, then narrows his eyes at me. "—hey, aren't you that bratty girl from the cafeteria?" he asks, moving toward me. He looks angry now.

I'm suddenly kicking myself for putting up so many scenes. *Of course he recognizes me!*

Before anyone can react, Lucia is right in front of him, shoving her hand into his nose. I hear a crack and he screams in pain. She spins smoothly and lands a kick in his side. He collapses just after she chops him in the neck, making him go unconscious.

I'm beyond shocked at the sight.

"How did you—" Charlie asks before Lucia grabs my hand and yanks it forward.

"We don't have time. There is only one other way out left and I didn't want to have to take it, but we don't have a choice anymore."

There is something in her voice that sounds far more ominous than I want to admit.

I'm winded as she drags us at a break-neck pace through the halls. We run past a few guards, but they don't pay us much attention because they are focused on something ahead of them. Lucia stops so fast that I run into her.

"Hey! Dr. Stromberg? What are you doing out right now? Shouldn't you be home?"

The woman's voice sounds pleasant, and I soon realize it's the same voice that we hear over the speakers when the Creators put announcements on the overheads.

Lucia speaks through her own quick breaths, "Yes, I'm just trying to get these medical students home. They've had far too much excitement for their first bit of rounds," Lucia tells her.

I peer around to see an older woman, hair dark with patches of grey and pulled up in a bun. She looks attractive for someone so old. Her olive skin has wrinkles spread on her forehead as well as on the sides of her eyes, which are brown.

"Well, I'm afraid they can't go out—you can go to the lounge in the meantime," the woman says casually. She notices Susan is crying, and raises an eyebrow.

Lucia steps up behind Susan. "She's overwhelmed by the lockdown. I'm not sure she's cut out to be a medical student."

The woman furrows her brows now. "They do look quite young to be students—"

I think she's onto us when Lucia speaks up again.

"They are high school-aged, but they were home schooled. Part of the same cohort."

The older woman nods, still watching Susan.

"Well, get them to the lounge," she replies. Then, looking at Susan, "Don't worry dear, we have these people under control. This place is more secure than a prison. No need to fear them escaping."

I pause when I hear the words. *Why would they fear us leaving?* I wonder.

Lucia doesn't begin moving. Instead, she just presses her lips together. Her eyes flick to a door behind the woman and then back to her.

"Um, yes—well, we need to stop by to speak to John for a minute. I wanted to introduce them to him," Lucia says.

The woman folds her arms with authority.

"Dr. Stromberg, this student is clearly in distress. You must take them to the lounge at once. Let them rest, then you can introduce them tomorrow," she replies.

"I'm sorry for this," Lucia states hesitantly.

The woman looks confused. Then Lucia slams her fist into her face, knocking her to the ground.

"Run!" Lucia shouts.

She bolts to the door, and I stand in shock. Charlie and Susan somehow snap out of their confusion faster than I do and run after her. I see the woman, nose now bleeding, laying on the ground and almost don't move until I see her shake her head. She glares at me. There is something evil there. I'm gone then.

My heart is racing so fast, I expect it might stop from the pace. By the time I'm to the door, Charlie and Susan are through. Once I bolt through it, Lucia slams it shut and flips a deadbolt. I'm panting, and so are the others.

The door handle jiggles and we hear a beep on the other side. Just then, the deadbolt flips from the locking mechanism. Lucia flips it back to locked and the door is jostled once more. After a couple more times of this, it stops. Silence.

"We don't have time to rest, we—"

The speakers above us in the hallways crackle, and we hear a voice that sounds exactly like the woman we just left on the ground.

"All personnel in Safety, please be aware that Dr. Lucia Stromberg has the three fugitive citizens in her possession. She is aiding their escape. They were last seen escaping through wing 12R."

Lucia curses again and bolts to the left. The lights around us flash red. I can only assume the same thing is happening throughout Safety.

What will my mother think? My brother? I wonder.

I'm worried about them. The realization hits me that they might be punished for my disappearance. The guilt sets into my chest and I gasp from the onslaught.

"Here!" Lucia bursts through another door and pauses. Charlie runs right into her, and Susan and I barely stop before doing the same. My scientist stumbles from the collision with

Charlie, but they don't fall. Right before us are four Peace-holders holding black metal rods.

"Dr. Stromberg, you're to be brought before the Creators. Release the citizens for their punishment at once."

Lucia scowls at them, then puts her hands out defensively. "I'm afraid that's not happening," she says.

Terror catches me even more, I know we are stuck—there is no way out. The door behind us slams shut and we hear a lock engage.

Lucia puts her access bracelet behind her to unlock the door and it flashes red.

"Your access has been revoked from every doorway within Safety. You can't go anywhere, Doctor. Please, don't do anything you'll regret," a Peaceholder says. It sounds like a man, but I can't be sure because they all have their tinted helmet visors down.

I wonder why they're hanging back so far, as if Lucia might hurt them, but I don't know how she could. She doesn't have any weapons that I can see, just the bag she grabbed with the clipboards and pens.

The four Peaceholders are advancing slowly now. They are only ten feet away when Lucia slips her hand into the bag and pulls out a ballpoint pen. In a flash, the woman runs forward to them. I'm shocked by her speed. Her curly auburn hair is whipping through the air as she does. One of the Peaceholders swings their black rod and I hear the crackling of electricity.

They're electric? I realize at hearing the sound. I'm worried about Lucia, but it's unfounded.

Lucia dodges the one and slams the point of the pen into their neck. We hear a sound like compressed air releasing and the guard falls to the ground. Two others swing their rods at her, but she ducks to the ground and their rods hit each other. A loud crack sounds and they are thrown back into the walls, bodies shaking from the electric current. The final Peaceholder gasps and swings, hitting Lucia in the arm. Her body convulses and I see her drop.

No, no, no, I'm thinking as we see her fall, shivering.

The Peaceholder shakes their head, then turns to us. "Citizens, come now, or be subject to immediate death."

Charlie moves in front of me and Susan. He's standing up straight as if he'll protect us, but I know he doesn't have a chance against this man. The crackling of the electricity sounds louder now as the Peaceholder moves toward us. Just then, Lucia reaches out and grabs his leg. He curses, looking down at her. She's still not fully functional, but she yanks backward, making him trip to the ground.

Susan shrieks as he falls on his chest, the black bar inches from us on the ground. The two Peaceholders that were shocked are getting up now and I know we're goners. I'm not thinking, I just move. I jump upward and land a foot right on the wrist of the Peaceholder. He roars and lets go of the black rod. I grab the rod and hold it over my head. With all my might, I swing it and smack him on the back.

Electricity arcs from the metal into his body and he screams, convulsing.

I feel sick, but adrenaline is running through me. I'm running solely off of that. I swing again and he gets shocked once more, this time only gurgling. The other two Peaceholders are on their feet now. Flipping the bar left, I hit one of them in the arm and they collapse again, shaking. I try to swing to the right but I miss this one, instead hitting the metal wall where electricity rockets up and down.

I drop the bar, the force of it hitting the wall causing it to be pulled from my grasp.

The Peaceholder growls and raises their bar to hit me when they shake and fall to the ground. I'm so scared that I am quivering, and I realize that I've peed a bit from the stress.

Looking down, I see that Lucia has the other Peaceholder's bar and has touched it to this one's leg, shocking him or her.

She gets up unsteadily and shakes her head. "We need to move," she says again.

She's still not recovered, but she makes her way through the hallway past the unconscious Peaceholders. It's easier to keep up with her now that she can't move as quickly, but I'm not sure that's a good thing.

We reach a three-way intersection with a door right in front of us. I think she'll turn down a different hallway, but she goes to the door. No sooner do we arrive than we hear shouting from both halls on either side. I gasp and turn to see Peaceholders everywhere.

"We're trapped!" Susan squeals.

Lucia nods and pushes the door open.

"Hey! Stop right there!" A Peaceholder to our right is yelling at us and calling out orders. Once we are through, Lucia slams it shut.

"Fred! Need a little help here!" Lucia shouts.

A short man pokes his head out from a machine of some sort. I notice it's extremely warm in here, making me more sweaty than I already am—which is saying something. The man is small. He has a black mustache framing his mouth, and has brown skin. He nods to Lucia and runs to the door. The small man yanks planks of wood out from behind a set of shelves there and fixes them over the door, fitting into brackets to either side. Once a few are in place, he turns to us.

"I can't believe you made it. I thought you'd get nicked for sure," Fred says. He has a slight accent of some sort, but of course I can't identify its origin.

"Well, we can celebrate it later. We need to go. Is everything ready?" Lucia asks.

Fred nods. "'cept I haven't had time to turn off the incinerator, could be bad for us if I don't—"

"No time," Lucia interrupts, "the redirect will have to do."

"But—," he starts to reply. A banging on the door stops him. He curses and runs to a trapdoor on the back wall of the small room labeled 'garbage' and yanks it open.

I gulp. *They can't be serious*, I think.

"Alright, everyone in. I'll go first. Fred, you bring up the rear. Oh, please say you have my gun," Lucia says.

"But Luce. With the fire goin', we could get burned bad. I need to disengage it," Fred tries to reason. He hands her a weapon as he speaks. I realize it's a firearm and my eyes widen in fear.

Lucia takes the gun, smiling fondly at it. I wonder why she didn't have it all this time, but before I can wonder longer, she shakes her head at Fred and runs to the garbage chute, jumping in feet first.

Fred shouts, then curses again.

The banging on the door intensifies behind us and I know Lucia is right to not wait.

"She's right. We have to go. You—"

Fred points to me and I freeze, not wanting to go into the black hole. Another bang on the door changes my mind, though, and I rocket toward the space in the wall. I grab the wall on either side of the hole and lift myself in. My legs hit a metal slope, then soft hands push me from behind, forcing me to let go.

My stomach lurches as I slide down a steep slope of metal, a scream getting caught in my throat from the sudden change in my momentum and direction. I lean back instinctually and put my arms up over my head. It's pitch black now, which makes it so much worse. I'm still terrified and screaming, when suddenly the metal beneath me and around me heats up. It gets so hot so fast that I don't have time to react. My bare arms are slipping on the metal of the slide above my head and I gasp as the hair on my arms is singed by the heat. Suddenly, there is searing pain on the back of my forearms, so I lift them. I feel the heat under my grey sweats and lab coat as I slide down the chute, but it's not as painful because of how thick my sweats are.

The tunnel suddenly ends. Once again, a scream gets lodged in my throat as I tumble into nothingness.

17

As I fall, I realize two things. First, the air has gotten much cooler, and second, I can see again. Lights have appeared above me, small and not very bright, but enough to see how fast I'm falling downward. I see a black surface rising to me, when suddenly I smack into it and am enveloped by water.

The shock of falling into water unexpectedly combined with being out of breath from the sudden fall make it impossible to react, let alone breathe. I try to suck in a breath and the panic rises in me as water starts to enter my lungs. I flail, even more terrified now, when strong hands grab my arms and pull me upward.

My face breaks the surface and I heave the water out of my lungs, coughing and sputtering.

"Shoot! I forgot you don't know how to swim!" Lucia cries over my noise.

I hear another scream and a splash near me, followed by two more. There is so much splashing and gasping that I don't know who is near and who landed farther away. Finally, I feel Lucia drag me to the edge of the water and lift me onto the hard ground before she turns and jumps back into the water.

I'm staring up at a blackness covered in speckled lights. A banana-shaped light is there, casting a bright glow on the landscape. By the time I realize it's the moon we've learned about in school, I hear the splashing of the others near me.

"Well shoot, boy, who taught you how to stay afloat?" Fred asks.

I hear Charlie mutter something before he collapses on the ground by me. Relief floods me as I realize he's okay. I am still staring at the sky, wonder filling me. I've never seen something so amazing. The air is crisp and cool, and I suck in a breath, partially because I still feel starved for air, but also because it smells—well, it smells.

Though I can't place what it is, I know it's different from the air inside Safety. The dream Lucia put me into—the one of being outside Safety floods back to me.

This isn't a dream, though, I think in disbelief.

Naturally, I then imagine the sun coming up and fear grabs me again.

"We're outside—I can't—we can't, the sun!" It's all I can sputter out before Lucia stops me.

"It's night. There won't be sun for a long time. But we need to keep moving. Sorry to cut your sky watching short," Lucia says, regret in her tone.

Her hand grasps my arm and yanks me upward. I'm still coughing slightly from the water in my lungs, but the adrenaline is coursing inside me.

"The car is over here. Should be gassed up and ready," Fred tells us before moving that direction.

"Come on, we aren't safe yet," Lucia explains.

Just then, red lights and alarms start from the building high on the hill above us. I look up, seeing the tall stone building on top of a hill. I'm shocked at the size of it. Even looking left and right, I can't see where it ends.

I'm pulled into a forest of trees, and the smell of them is

overwhelming. I love it, but part of me still can't enjoy it still because of the mania from running.

The light is dimmer in here and I stumble on something, not sure what it is.

A bright flash of light blinds me suddenly, and I know I'm not the only one who shrieks this time.

"Sorry!" Fred says from behind the light, "Forgot the head-lights were so bright!"

I don't know what he's saying, but I just follow the form of Lucia in front of me. Once we move to the side of the bright beams, I see there is a vehicle of some sort, Fred in the driver seat. Of course we learned about motor vehicles in Safety, but I've never thought I'd see one. Only those who work in the shipping parts of Safety that packages the goods we work with and puts them on the trucks get to see vehicles.

This one is metal, as they all were in the pictures, but it's boxy. It looks like a brown-painted box on wheels. Lucia ushers me into the car and I land on hard seats.

"Where are we going?" Charlie asks.

Hearing his voice fills me with warmth. We've all been moving so hard and fast that I forgot that he and Susan might be as terrified and confused as me.

"In short, to a base of ours. It's not far from here but it will take several hours to get there. We need to make it far enough away that our car can blend into the regular traffic around us. With us leaving, the Creators will soon know about the chute redirect from the incinerator," Lucia states.

At the last part, she turns to Fred in the driver's seat and eyes him pointedly.

"Okay, okay, I get the message," Fred responds, putting his hands on the wheel.

The car roars to life and we speed through the trees.

I'm holding onto a handle in the car door next to me, panicked as Fred drives through the trees. At one point, I have to close my eyes because I am feeling sick from the motion and the sight of the trees flying past us.

"It's a wonder they haven't sent anyone to follow us," Lucia says.

I open my eyes to see she's turned around facing into the back seat where I am plastered against Susan. Charlie was last when getting into the car, Susan between us. I look over to see she has her eyes closed as well, and looks green.

Lucia taps me on the shoulder and I jump. She stares at me with worry in her eyes.

"Let's take a look at those cuts now. I want to make sure we don't have too much bleeding from any of you."

I nod and pull off the sleeve of the coat and my shirt. Once I see the cut, my stomach turns. It must be deeper than I thought, because blood is staining the bandage in most places.

"I'm going to take off the bandage now—"

Right as Lucia says this, Fred swerves around a tree. My head knocks into the window to my left, and I wince in pain. Lucia curses and scolds Fred.

"Hey, chica, maybe you should wait until the paved road to fix their wounds, no?" Fred replies.

Lucia rolls her eyes and pulls back my bandage. I have to look away for fear of vomiting.

"It actually looks pretty good, you're clotting up well, Korinne," she tells me.

I hear a ripping sound and peek again to see that Lucia has ripped apart another long stretch of bandage she's taken out of a kit in a compartment of the vehicle. She fastens it to my arm quickly as Fred continues to swerve around trees. The car rattles and bumps from our drive on the uneven forest ground.

Suddenly Fred says something I can't understand. I realize it's another language after a moment.

"They're behind us, look!" he exclaims.

Lucia was working on fixing Susan's bandage when he said it.

"How close are we to the main road?" Lucia asks.

"Close, just need to push harder," he says.

The car speeds up and I close my eyes again. The bumping of the wheels over the rough ground is even more intense now. It feels like my brain is going to rattle out of my head.

"Oh no, they're ahead of us too," Fred says.

Lucia has moved on to Charlie's cut now. She was whispering for a moment, but now she turns to look angrily at the driver.

"Get us out of here, Fred! I brought you here because you told me you could get us out of anything!" Lucia is yelling now, obviously upset by our predicament.

Opening my eyes, I see flashes of lights ahead of us through the trees. I'm guessing there are more behind us because the surrounding trees are lighting up as if there are cars bouncing around while following us.

"Hold on!" Fred yells.

Lucia barely has time to snag a handle above Charlie's door when Fred swerves to the right, causing my head to knock into the window again. I gasp and hold the sore spot. Then my stomach drops. I hear Susan scream out and I hold my breath as the feeling of falling overwhelms me. I'm hovering out of my seat for seemingly forever when I land hard back in my seat, a jolt running up my spine.

I hear coughing and look over to see that Charlie has thrown up between his legs. Susan looks to have passed out. I understand their reactions completely.

"Whoa! That actually worked!" Fred exclaims, apparently happy with himself, "Here's another road now."

The car bumps one last time before it's smooth. Fred presses the gas and we speed up again. Looking backward, I see a drop of at least ten feet behind us.

Did he drive us off that cliff? I think.

"Excellent work, Fred. Now get us somewhere safe so we can stop and clean up this mess," Lucia says, gesturing to the floor between Charlie's legs.

Charlie apologizes for the vomit, but Lucia shrugs.

"Honestly, I'm impressed with how you three have done so far," she replies before eyeing Susan. "Well, as long as that one isn't dead."

She says it so nonchalantly that it makes me uncomfortable, but I look over to see Susan still out cold. I can see her chest is still rising and falling.

"She's still alive," I say, "I can see her breathing."

Lucia nods. "Well good. I'd say that went well then, considering I was only prepared to smuggle one of you out of there. I had to improvise with the coats."

I can't tell if Lucia is mad or not that I dragged Susan and Charlie into this. Regardless, I'm kind of relieved that I did. Sure, Susan and I aren't on great terms, but it's relieving to know I don't have to do this alone.

Looking over at Charlie, it's easy to tell he is still sick. I reach over Susan's unconscious form and squeeze his shoulder. The look he gives me breaks my heart. He's terrified, but he's trying to hide it.

And this is all my fault. He could have stayed. *He could have been going to sleep by now,* I think.

I don't believe he's mad, but he seems to be having as rough a time as I am. Susan probably is too.

"Okay, looks like your cuts are healing. We'll be driving for a few hours now, so if you want to get some sleep, now would be the time," Lucia tells Charlie and me.

I nod and look through the window. I see trees flying past us so fast that I can hardly make any of the details out. Charlie sighs and leans his head back against the seat. Before I can do that, I have to ask something. There are dozens of questions I want to ask, but I don't know how to ask them all.

"Who are you really? Why did you come get us—me?" I correct myself as I say it.

Lucia has turned around and is facing forward, but she glances back at me again when I say this.

"All in good time, dear. You're safe now, that's all that matters. We are allies, and we want to free you from Safety."

The answer is simple, and it seems obvious, but it doesn't satisfy me. I open my mouth to ask again, or maybe rephrase it, but Lucia shakes her head and puts her finger to her lips.

"Not now. Get some rest. We can explain when we get to our base."

I look into her eyes and see something there. She's looking at me like my father does sometimes. There is a loving look there, something deep and unrelenting. It makes me uncomfortable to look into her eyes like that. I want to argue, but my body tells me not to.

Instead, I nod and put my head down on the cool glass of the window. It's not super comfortable, but I'm so tired that I close my eyes and immediately drop off to sleep.

18

When I wake up, it's only for a moment. The car has stopped at a well-lit building. Lucia calls it a gas-station, and I assume we're here to get fuel. There are a few other cars, and Lucia says it's not uncommon for people to be out this late. I immediately think about how they must not have curfews outside of Safety. Lucia and Fred clean out most of the vomit from underneath Charlie and then we are moving again.

As we pull away from the gas station, I look up into the sky to see the stars and moon are still shining. I've not seen something this beautiful in my whole life. Turning to look at Charlie, I see he's asleep again. Susan is still in the same position she was when she passed out however long ago.

I see the sky is lighter outside Charlie's window and I get nervous again.

"Um—" I say, "how much longer until we are there?"

The worry must be obvious in my tone, because Lucia stretches her hand over the front seats to put it on my knee.

"We will be inside long before the sun comes up, Korinne, don't worry," she tells me.

I think for a moment how odd it is that I'm letting some

unknown woman touch me, but then I realize I have little choice. I figure if she wanted to hurt us, she'd have done so already.

I laugh internally at this because she literally cut our arms open on purpose. Still, I'm not scared of her. Since I met her in Safety, there's something about her that puts me at ease. That, plus the fact she is also my father's scientist, and he said to trust her. That's enough for me.

Thoughts of my father come flooding in and I sit upright.

"My dad! Where is my dad?" I exclaim.

Lucia bites her lip. "I'm sorry, Korinne, we didn't have time to get him out too," she says.

Fred whispers something I can't hear from the driver's seat, and Lucia nods in acknowledgement.

"We'll get him back, don't worry, someday we'll get him," Lucia says.

I'm not comforted by her words. Tears are welling in my eyes at the thought of my father dead.

"But he's going to die, isn't he?!" I realize I'm almost yelling this as tears stream down my face.

Lucia's eyebrows shoot up and she shakes her head. Her hand squeezes on my knee, and then she's speaking.

"He's not going to die, the Creators have him secured for the time being," Lucia pauses and rubs her eyebrows with her free hand. "Now is not the time to talk about this, you need rest. Just know he is going to be okay, he's just in the hands of the Creators."

Once again, her words aren't overly comforting, except for the fact that she said he won't die. What it means for him to be in the hands of the Creators I don't know, but I try to relax, knowing he won't die soon.

"Sleep," Lucia commands me.

This time, now that the adrenaline and the idea of my father dying is past, my body responds to the idea of sleep.

Leaning to the side, I close my eyes again and drift into a heavy sleep.

I jolt awake and I'm thrashing around, panicked. I was dreaming about my father being pulled away from me, his hands outstretched and shouting my name. No matter how hard or fast I ran, I couldn't reach him. Somehow, in my dream, I knew he'd be lost if I didn't get to him. I never did.

Trying to shake off the feeling, I look out the window to see we are in a large, open room. There are other cars around us that look just like this one.

"Well, we made it," Fred says from the seat in front of me.

"Thanks to your effective driving. Remind me to convince the boss-man to give you a raise," Lucia tells him.

I look over to see Susan and Charlie have also woken up and are trying to understand where we are. Charlie is the only one brave enough to ask.

"So—where are we, exactly?" he asks.

Lucia turns and grins at us.

"Away from Safety and the Peaceholders, so that's good," she says.

We just stare at her.

"Wow, okay, apparently not what you wanted," Lucia replies after we don't react, "This is Nugennexx Industries, a place where you can be free."

I hear her words, but somehow they aren't reassuring. Charlie and Susan must feel the same, their facial expressions betraying their emotions.

Lucia sighs then. "Look, I promise you're safe. Let's get out of the car and get your arms fixed up. I did an okay good job of bandaging your cuts, but I bet we have something that can make you more comfortable."

I'm relieved to hear this. My arm is still throbbing from the gash she put there. I can't tell if it's still bleeding or not, but I can see the blood has soaked through the white lab coat I wear.

Lucia opens the door and steps out, greeting a few others who are mulling around in the huge room. I am hesitant to move. Charlie fiddles with the door for a moment, trying to figure out how to get it open, when Fred speaks.

"You pull the handle, see it there? Kind of grey?"

Charlie glances down and finally sees the handle.

"Sorry, I've never been in one of these before," Charlie says, blushing.

He looks cute when he's embarrassed, I think.

I'm glad he asked, because I would have doubtless run into the same problem. I push open the door closest to me and look back to see Susan staring forward.

"Come on, let's go out together," I reach my hand out to her.

She shakes her head at me.

I grit my teeth and grab her arm, tugging lightly.

She eventually gives in and we both step out of the car. When we get out, I notice just how many vehicles sit around me. Big bulky ones that look like the tanks from our history classes, smaller motorcycles, normal cars of many colors are all arranged randomly. There aren't many people here, but more than I'd expect this late.

I realize I don't know what time it is right now. When we left, it was the beginning of the night. Lucia said we'd make it here before the sun came up, but I don't know how long we were in the car. The fact that I didn't burst into flames suggests we got into this building before the sun rose.

I shudder at the thought of us sleeping in the car when the sun hit us and bursting into flames.

"Come on, kiddos," Lucia says to my right.

The few people who are here stare at us, some wide-eyed, some with thoughtful looks.

"Wow you went through the ringer, didn't you?" a woman with short-cut blonde hair says, eyeing Lucia and Fred. I didn't notice at first, but their clothes are dirty and torn in a few places. I inspect myself to see that the lab coat I wear is smudged with brown and yellow all over.

"So these are the rescues?" another woman asks.

"It was only supposed to be the strawberry-headed one, but we picked up some stragglers," Lucia tells the woman before looking at me. "She's a rebel like her mother."

Lucia's eyes twinkle, but my head buzzes in confusion.

"You... know my mom? How do you know her?" I ask, confused.

Lucia shakes her head, "We'll get to that later, let's get you all fixed up, okay?"

Her comment about my mother being a rebel confuses me. My mother is definitely nothing like that.

"I don't think Tom will be thrilled you extracted three. That wasn't the plan," a gruff man with black hair and a square nose asks.

"Chill out, Brennan, we didn't get captured, that's what matters," Lucia says, glaring at him.

I turn to the man who spoke and jump when I realize he's glaring at me.

"I bet you set off all sorts of alarms now. And did you get out undetected? Can you return to your post as an examiner?" the man says.

Lucia grimaces at that. "Alright, so we didn't get out without a hitch, but we can work with that later. We have these three. This could be an advantage," she answers him.

Brennan scoffs and turns away.

Fred speaks up then, "Oh don't mind him, he's just excited to see you."

I'm not convinced.

Lucia bids farewell to the others in the large room and leads us through a set of white double doors. The hallway we enter is so different from what I'm used to. The floor is smooth and grey, polished so it reflects the overhead fluorescent lights back up at us. The walls are painted a light blue, and there are railings along the side. My feet sound so different, flapping against the stone rather than metal grate.

"We'll stop at the medical ward, get you pain meds and maybe stitches, then we'll visit our leader, Tom," Lucia says without turning back to us.

I nod, not caring that Lucia can't see me and my apparent fascination with this place.

"When do we get to go back?" Susan asks with a shaky voice.

Lucia stops abruptly then and turns. She appears both sad and angry, though I'm not sure how that is possible.

"What did you say your name was again?" Lucia asks.

Susan doesn't respond but looks at the floor.

"Susan," I say for her.

"Ah, Susan. I am sorry for disrupting your normal schedule," Lucia tells her, "but there's no chance you can go back. There is zero tolerance for escapees from Safety, and there will be no leniency for you, even though you are so young."

Susan stares at her for a moment before putting her hands over her face and shaking her head. Her long brown hair is a mess from the night before.

I don't know why, but I put my hand on her back to comfort her.

"So people have escaped before?" I ask, curious.

Lucia presses her lips together, then shakes her head. "Not from Safety, but they drill the consequences of citizens escaping when we start work there," Lucia replies

She still looks sad, but Lucia turns and walks up to another white door with a small window at the top. A sign above the door says *Medical room*. A pit forms in my stomach when I realize it reminds me of the experiment rooms that they took us to back in Safety.

But this is a safe place, Lucia said it is, I remind myself.

She pushes the door open and we enter a medium sized room with medical beds separated by curtains. The room is empty, save for a bald man with dark skin. He wears a white lab coat like ours, but he has a badge that says *Dr. Johnson* on it.

"Hey Doc, you good to help patch up the rescues?" Lucia asks.

When he turns to look at us, a smile breaks out on his face.

"So you got her, then? That's great!" His face falls when he sees the other two, "And these others are—"

"An accident, but we'll talk about it later. Can you help fix up their arms? I had to dig into them deep to get out the trackers."

Dr. Johnson furrows his brows and stands. "How bad is it?" He moves over to me and lifts the white lab coat to see the bandage.

He leads me gently to one of the white paper-covered beds and helps me up. Before I can protest, he takes off the white coat and slowly unravels the bandage.

He tsks the moment he sees it. "Blast it, Lucia, I wish you'd have listened to my instructions on cutting these out. This is a mess," he scolds.

She shrugs. "We were in a hurry. I did the best I could. Couldn't risk getting caught. You know what they did to the last ones who tried to get out," Lucia responds.

The hair on my neck stands. "Wh—what? I thought you said no one has ever gotten out?" I say, shocked.

Lucia grimaces. "I did, and it's true. That doesn't mean people haven't tried," Lucia replies, biting her lip, "I believe you knew them as the Larsson family?"

My whole body goes cold.

"But—they got sick, that's why you were testing me and— my father . . . " I can't get any more words out.

She shakes her head. "They never got sick. It was a lie— among others told you by the Creators—to keep you in the dark. Mr. Larsson found information he shouldn't have. When he saw it, he tried to escape Safety with his family. They killed him and his wife, but I heard they wiped the memory of the two kids and gave them new identities."

My mind flashes back to the mess hall and the two new kids they found.

It was Therese, that's why she looked so familiar, I think. The revelation doesn't make me feel better.

"Lucia, I wish you'd have waited to tell her this, she's sweating something awful now from the stress," the doctor scolds her.

"She needed to know," Lucia tells him, before pressing her lips together once more.

"Alright, a small pinch," the doctor says before sticking a needle in my arm. My stomach turns at the sight, but a coolness enters there and spreads through my arm. The pain goes away instantly. I can't help but sigh out loud.

Doctor Johnson smiles at me. "Yes, I thought you'd appreciate that. Now let me get this stitched up," he says. I don't know what he means, but now that the pain is gone, I can't help but just let him do what he wants.

My mind is reeling. I'm grateful that I can think of anything at all. The pain from my arm is gone and I didn't realize how much it made me lose my ability to think. I recall my tests and how scared they made me. Inside I scoff, realizing how mild those were compared to now. Questions are coming to me, but one stands out.

"What about the microbots? Can we get these out?"

I feel uncomfortable knowing these things can still cause me pain.

Lucia presses her lips together. "Um, well I don't think we need to worry about that. During your second test, your reaction to the experiment fried the microbots. They're in there, but they are fried to bits is my guess. They didn't give any frequencies off after that," Lucia responds.

Stress releases in my chest. Still, something bothers me about it all.

"Why did they make us have the bots anyway? Why didn't they want us to talk about it?" I ask.

Lucia suddenly looks annoyed.

"Equal treatment, that's why," she replies. I think she might stop talking and leave it at that, but before I can urge her on, she continues. "Some of the other examiners were more–brutal with their tests."

Charlie shuffles next to me and I turn to see that his face has turned white. He looks like he'll be sick.

Lucia notices this too, a regretful look on her face. "They were afraid that if any of you found out that your examiners varied in their methods, there would be confusion, uproars and more. Anyway, we'll have to figure out how to deal with those microbots in your heads. If we can force a similar reaction in you two, the same thing should happen," Lucia suggests.

"Let's focus on one thing at a time. The microbots can wait," Doctor Johnson remarks as he continues working.

I think back to when my father and I had the conversation about my experiments in our home unit. It suddenly made sense why I didn't get attacked by them while we talked.

Then the thought of my father returns to me.

"Wait, but what about dad? Where is he?" I don't know why, but I'm panicked again.

Lucia stares at me, looking worried. "We—have reason to believe he found the same information Mr. Larsson did, and the Creators found out."

The world goes blurry.

"Wait, is he dead too?" Susan pipes up.

Lucia glares at her. "I don't think so. We think he's just being held by the Creators," Lucia says.

"Why didn't you take him instead? Why us?" Charlie adds out of nowhere.

Lucia glares past him. "Actually, he was our original target for escape. Unfortunately, they got to him before we could. Because of that, we wanted to get Korinne. That was part of the reason I had another lab coat, the larger one," Lucia pauses for a moment before saying, "I wanted to get you, Korinne. And *you* both weren't supposed to be there." She jerks her head toward Charlie and Susan at this comment.

"Yeah, you've said that, but why?" Charlie emphasizes. He looks upset.

Lucia sighs and puts her hands to her forehead. Doctor Johnson eyes her and shakes his head slightly.

"We'd best wait for them to see Tom—"

"Why? They'll find out eventually," Lucia interrupts him.

The doctor shakes his head again before speaking to me, "Alright young lady, you're done."

I look at my arm and see he's freshened the bandage, the cloth pure white. I still can't feel pain and I am relieved. He moves over to Susan and begins working on her arm.

Lucia looks me in the eye, then says something that makes the world spin.

"Korinne—they lied to you and your friends. Safety isn't a haven, it's a prison for people like you."

19

I hear the words, but I don't process them immediately. My theories are now proven right, and I should be happy, but for some reason I can't be. My head was already foggy enough before she told us. Now I'm not sure I can accept it.

"What—?" Susan says, her lower lip quivering, "That can't be. That's our home!"

She sounds defensive. I can understand why she's reacting this way; Safety treated her and her family far nicer than Charlie and myself.

Lucia grimaces at Susan's words before responding. "Only because it's all you know. There is more going on at Safety than even we can understand," Lucia says.

Dr. Johnson is shaking his head now. "Lucia, you can't leave well enough alone, can you?" he remarks.

"Hey, they asked. I answer. That is how I do things here," she responds before turning to me. She looks like she wants to say more, but holds back. I see the same longing in her eyes, though this time she's tearing up. I know she's keeping something else vital from me, but she won't say it.

"Well, we're done here. Are you ready to go see Tom?" Dr. Johnson asks us.

I shrug, but only because I'm still at a loss for words. The other two glance at each other.

Lucia is still staring at me, but she nods, then agrees, "Let's get going. There's a lot that we still need to tell you," Lucia says. She gives one lingering smile to me before gesturing that we should follow.

I take the lead, despite feeling totally disoriented at Lucia's latest revelation to us. Truly, though, I'm barely hanging on. To keep myself together, I continue to inspect the surrounding hallway. Although the floor is polished stone, and the walls are concrete, it somehow feels more comfortable here. I see the hallway is more lit up ahead. I freeze.

That doesn't look like fluorescent light, I think.

Charlie and Susan must think the same thing, because they pause as well.

Lucia notices us hesitating and turns, her eyebrow raised. "Is everything alright?" she asks.

I don't know how to respond, other than pointing to what I realize is a window with bright light pouring in. I've not seen it in real life, but my instincts are telling me to hold back. It's sunlight.

I've started sweating, and I back away from the bright square of sunlight that is shining on the floor and wall. Lucia's face softens, and she pulls something from her side. It's some type of squarish electric device.

"Can we close the shades in sector H for the next little bit, please?" she says into the device.

There is a crackling sound and a man's voice responds. "Roger, you got the kid with you, is that it?" the voice asks.

"Yep, they may not be allergic—" Lucia responds, eyeing me warily, "—but we aren't ready to find out what happens when they touch it."

A loud whirring sound fills the hallway, and I notice that the sunlit square reflecting on the wall and floor shrinks. The sound is coming from further up as well, and I notice there are another three or four windows up ahead that were letting in the sun. After a moment, the whirring stops with a few loud clangs.

"There, that should do it," Lucia says, satisfied.

I'm hesitant, but we follow her up to where the sun was coming in the window. When we get there, I see that a solid piece of metal has closed over the opening. I shiver, knowing that just on the other side of that metal is the thing I've been told would kill the three of us instantly. Lucia thinks there's more to the story, but the death by fire idea is still very real in my head.

I glance over to Charlie and see the same worried look on his face. He skirts around the closed-off window, Susan close on his heels. The moment he notices me, he winks, trying as usual to make light of the situation. I know he's scared too, but his glance makes me feel better. Susan glares at me, as if to perpetuate her thoughts about being dragged into this.

Trying to distract myself from the fire in her eyes, I ask the first thing that comes to mind.

"Is this place full of windows like this?" I ask suddenly. For some reason, I feel like it's a dumb question, but I came from a place without any windows.

Lucia chuckles. "Yes, some hallways have more than others. This is the hallway to Tom's office and he doesn't like the gloom, so we've got a lot of windows in here."

She leads us past a few more now-closed windows and then left through a double door. I jump the moment we do, because the floor gets squishy. I look down to see a really long and thick carpet, brown with black and white specks in it. Carpet is a rarity in Safety, and even when you see it, it's very short and rug-like. I've not seen carpet like this before.

I look around to see a single desk with a small bookshelf behind it. A woman sits there, reading papers on her desk.

"Hey Lorraine, I've got the package," Lucia says as she approaches the desk.

The woman looks up and stares at me before her face brightens. Her eyes are very blue and her brown hair is curled in huge ringlets. Her eyelids are purple and her lips are so red they look fake. I've seen makeup before, only in the videos of the Creators and on some employees at Safety, but this woman looks as if she painted her entire face with a whole bottle of the stuff, or whatever they hold makeup in.

"You look like you've been through battle. What happened to you?" the woman asks, not noticing us.

Lucia grimaces, eyeing her ripped and dirtied red dress.

"The trip didn't go as smoothly as I hoped. Let's leave it at that," Lucia responds.

The woman's curls bounce as she shakes her head. After a moment, her eyes wander in our direction and widen when they land on us.

"My goodness! They are darling! I am so glad that they made it out. And so glad you did too," she says.

For a moment, I can't understand what she says because she has a very thick accent, something I've not heard before. It reminds me of the cowboy videos we watched in our history classes sometimes. The vowels in her words are long and drawn out.

"Meh, it was all in a day's work," Lucia leans back and folds her arms, "Anyway, is Tom in? He said to bring Korinne when I could."

The woman nods.

"Head on in, he shouldn't be on a call or anything," the assistant says.

Lucia gestures for us to follow, and I once again take the lead, though Charlie doesn't appear as bothered by the place now. Susan of course still trails behind. She's folded her arms, but at least she doesn't look like she's falling apart anymore.

I follow Lucia through the double wooden doors and into a medium-sized room. It's full of bookshelves and has a fireplace set into the wall on the right. A man sits behind the desk, hair blond and wavy, coming just to the tops of his ears. He has a blond mustache that curls up around his nose. He's hefty as well; I can see fat folds under his chin and his round body betrays his volume.

"Well, I'll be. You actually did it," he says.

Lucia scoffs. "Why did you think I couldn't? I had to get her, I had to meet her—" she turns to look at me and I see the adoration in her face again.

I'm even more uncomfortable now.

"I'm eating my words, then. Now I don't regret letting you give it a go." The burly man stands from his chair and walks toward us.

I freeze, my body locking in place from fear.

"Sorry for my rudeness, I'm Tom. I'm in charge of Nugen-nexx Industries," his eyes look above my head and I see him nod at Charlie and Susan.

"And who might these two be, then?" he asks.

Lucia grimaces. "An accident, but we can't complain. More for us to work with," Lucia says.

What is that supposed to mean? I think, *She's talking as if we are some type of experimental material.*

"I guess you could look at it that way." Tom gestures to a few soft chairs in front of his desk, "Have a seat, you all look exhausted."

Hearing his words, I almost don't want to sit, but my exhausted body moves of its own volition. I'm sitting in one of the high-backed chairs facing his desk before I know it. Susan and Charlie follow suit. As I sit, I notice a symbol hanging on the wall in a nice-looking frame. I start when I realize it's the same symbol on the charm my dad left on the sofa. I check quickly to ensure I'm not imagining things.

Is this where my father got his charm? I wonder. Before I can get the courage to ask, Tom starts talking.

"Good. Now that we are all here, I think there are some things you should know," Tom turns so his back is to us. He's facing a beautiful painting of a landscape somewhere, the sun shining over a sea, the waves beating along the shore. It is breathtaking. I start to get lost in the colors.

Tom doesn't speak at once, and I wonder if he's trying to figure out what to say to us. During the silence, I turn to look back at Lucia, who is leaning against a bookshelf with her arms folded. She's staring at me again, and I squirm in the chair. Turning to the side, I see that Susan is spaced out, staring at the picture as well. I can't tell if she is still fuming from what's happening, but she isn't crying anymore. Charlie and I lock eyes for a moment and something passes between us.

What is going on? his eyes ask.

I shrug, understanding what he's thinking.

Finally, the tall and burly man speaks. "Safety is not what you think," the man says suddenly.

My stomach clenches at the words, but this time it's less of a shock. Lucia said more or less the same thing not too long before. Though I don't understand fully, there isn't as much of a force to the revelation as before. The room goes silent again, and I shift in my seat.

I am wildly uncomfortable with the whole thing, but my curiosity gets the better of me.

"What does that mean? Lucia told us that before, but I don't understand," I plead.

Tom turns and narrows his eyes at Lucia. She casually shrugs. Just like with Charlie and me, something passes between the two, though I can't be sure what it is exactly.

"How much has she told you, then?" Tom asks me.

I shift in my chair, remembering her words, but not wanting to accept them.

"She said Safety is a prison," I respond.

Tom nods thoughtfully, then moves to his chair.

"Yes, it appears that way, but we don't know everything about it. Your father—" he pauses, glancing back at Lucia for a moment before continuing, "—your father stumbled on information within the systems, a message from the government to the Creators of Safety. It's the same communique we've intercepted since we've been studying you."

My mind is spinning, and I'm completely lost. His words make some sense, but there is so much information missing that I can't grasp it.

I open my mouth to ask more questions, but Charlie pipes up this time.

"What does that mean? Who are you people? Why did you just take us from the only place where we are safe from the sun?" Charlie asks.

The bit about the sun irks me more, knowing that we aren't in a dedicated facility designed to protect us from the rays. My eyes shift to the door where I know the windows are. At any moment I feel like the door will burst open and we'll explode to death in flames, just like the picture of the man.

Tom shakes his head. "I'm sorry, I know this is probably overwhelming. Let's start from the beginning. We are Nugennexx Industries, a subsidiary of a much larger organization, Triloton Incorporated. We were the most recently contracted company hired by the U.S. government and the Creators to work on a cure for your disease. For the past five years, we've been tasked to study you to learn about your ailment. Our goal has always been to learn about your disease to create a cure or a way to allow you back into society. Lucia here—is one of our top scientists."

Lucia looks up from where she was staring at the floor and

nods. This surprises me; I've forgotten that she's a scientist at all, seeing how she maneuvered us out of Safety. I'd have thought she was a Peaceholder for the outside world, or whatever they call them.

"We've been sending in scientists since then, trying to learn from your sickness. That is, until five months ago," Tom says.

He shifts on his feet and eventually turns to go sit behind his massive redwood desk.

"Lucia, being the rebel she is, went against Safety's protocol and snuck some blood out of the compound. Safety has been adamant for years that every sample must remain to be tested within their internal labs. We have access to the data, and we can create our own simulated tests outside of the compound, but we could never bring out real samples," he shifts in his seat and looks me in the eyes.

He's lost me again, and I glance over to see that Susan and Charlie appear equally confused.

"Let me see—sorry this is so new to you. We've been testing your body tissues and minds to understand their reactions to sunlight. We've done this through simulated sunlight all this time, but Lucia here took a vial of your father's blood directly into the sun, and the reaction was something we did not expect."

I shiver at the thought of my body coming into contact with the sun.

"What happened?" Charlie is on the edge of his seat.

"The reaction was violent," Tom continues before looking back at Lucia, "and it almost hurt her, but the odd thing is that it did not harm the blood cells themselves."

I'm trying to follow, but they're losing me again. Tom must see my confusion, because he gestures for Lucia to water the explanation down.

"Honey, it means the blood cells didn't die or get harmed by the sun. The antibodies didn't attack the sun rays like a normal allergy would. It means we don't believe you are allergic to the sun," she says.

Those words hit home.

Susan speaks up this time, though hesitantly. "Wh—what? What are you saying? We'll die in the sun!" Susan's now shouting at Tom.

He shakes his head, a look of pity on his face. "It's a lie," Tom blurts before shifting his eyes to me. "Your father came across communications while working in the computer systems. It was a message from the U.S. government—our President and his cabinet."

By the way he says it, I know these are important people. I vaguely remember learning about the United States government, but I haven't cared that much. The only important people at Safety are the Creators. They are the government there.

"They asked," Tom continued, "if there has been success in learning how to remove your abilities, or how to remove the threat you are to the world."

Threat? I think, *how could anyone think I'm a threat?*

"When your father found veiled messages about the threat the citizens posed to the government, he hid it, very well. Lucia was placed as his examiner, for reasons we'll get to in a moment, but he eventually confided in her, sharing what he saw and heard. We've had our suspicions about what the sun *really* does to you all, but we haven't truly seen the effects until now."

Lucia jumps in now. "I had seen his blood's reaction to the direct sunlight, and I had to know what the truth was. When I heard what he'd read from the government, I knew something was off. I had only been placed with him to get closer to you, but this intercepted message made me more interested in what he found out."

I hear all of her words, but my thoughts linger on the part where she wanted to get closer to me. The way she's been staring at me has kind of been freaking me out, but I didn't want to say anything.

"Are you the ones who gave my dad this then?" I ask, holding up my access bracelet.

Lucia smiles, then nods.

"We managed to, after a lot of time, recreate the frequencies in the access pads. I'm the one who gave that to Blaine," Lucia confirms.

Tom grunts then. "Undoubtedly they've reworked their whole system so these access bracelets no longer work."

The plump man sounds annoyed. Lucia clears her throat at the comment, likely trying to move past Tom's disappointment about the fact.

"I'm still so confused, if Safety is a prison, why did you take us from it? Why are they telling us we are allergic to the sun and we'll die?" Charlie asks. I can tell he's getting frustrated with the whole thing. I am still stuck on Lucia wanting to get close to me.

Tom sighs, "Son, we don't know. But based on our tests, we don't think you are allergic to the sun. We think your bodies—your genetics, react differently to the sun, sure, but that it's not dangerous to you."

Charlie sits back and folds his arms. "So you're saying we have been stuck in a building for no reason?" he asks.

Tom shakes his head, "Not for *your* safety, at least."

This strikes me again. "For whose then? Why stick us there?" I am asking now.

"To protect the world," Tom says, "You aren't the only ones. Your compound is one of hundreds throughout the world."

My head spins.

"The genetic mutation from the sun's events affected the entire world, not just the United States. There are hundreds of compounds like Safety throughout the world. There are more than just the few thousand of you there."

I hold up my hand. The information, while helpful, sounds so far-fetched, so made up. I can feel anger rising in me.

"How are we supposed to believe any of this? We don't know you, we were just taken from the only home we know, and we're in a place we know nothing about. All I care about is why me—why did you have to come to get me from Safety, instead of my father, or someone else more helpful?"

Tears are welling in my eyes now. I miss him, I miss my mother and Sean, and I am somehow missing the familiar metal hallways of Safety.

The silence lasts only a few beats before Lucia speaks.

"Korinne," Lucia says from behind. I turn to look at her before she continues, "because I've been trying to find you for years. I—" she pauses, and I see tears are flooding into her eyes as well.

"I'm your mother."

20

MY mind reels at the words. Something stirs inside me at the same time, making the whole idea more confusing.

I stare up at the woman with brown and reddish hair. She is smiling back at me with that same endearing look I noticed a few times since we've been traveling with her. Part of me wants it to be true, while the other part of me is rejecting the information.

For years, I've wondered what happened to my actual parents outside of Safety. Here and now my supposed mother stands before me, and for some reason, I can't be happy. There are so many questions swimming in my mind, but only one pops out.

"Why—why didn't you tell me that from the very beginning?" I ask.

My voice comes out more harshly than I expected. I can see on Lucia's face that my tone stings her, but she holds her smile.

"Korinne, I couldn't very well have told you when we first met. Biological family members aren't allowed to visit or see any of their family once they get put in Safety. If the Creators found out I was your mother, they would have fired me. Char, maybe even killed me. Before I even applied to work there, I had to create a totally new identity, including changing my name. They couldn't know I had any relation to you."

Once again, her words make sense, but I'm still angry. I've met with her for tests a few times and not once did she let on that she was my mother. The heat in my chest builds and I want to scream, but I hold myself back, not wanting to embarrass myself. I can tell my face is red.

"Korinne, I am truly sorry. When I found where they'd taken you, I worked hard to get myself stationed here in your compound. I learned who your father was in Safety and became his examiner. I didn't expect to be assigned to you for another few years, but they lowered the examination age and I took advantage of it."

Tears start welling in my eyes. I can see Lucia cares—she is happy to see me, but I'm just angry. Not wanting to draw on the subject any longer, I change it.

"My father," I practically spit out, "where is he, will he be okay?"

Lucia's mouth hovers open, then she shuts it. When she doesn't speak, Tom responds.

"The information your father gained in Safety puts him in dire danger. He likely discovered they have lied to you, and the Creators aren't happy. We hoped to extract your father, but they got to him first."

Tom's voice wavers and I look at him. He clears his throat and shakes his head. I've heard this before, but I'm not satisfied. Just as I am about to ask for more details, Tom continues.

"Your father knew about us, that we weren't at the behest of the Creators. He knew we planned to get him out of there. If only we'd been there to get him earlier."

My mind flips back to when my father and I spoke in our assigned quarters. He did sound slightly off then. The way he reassured me about the tests and how I could trust my examiner. I can only assume what they are saying is true.

"Now what?" Charlie pipes in, "What's going to happen to Kor's dad? What's going to happen to us?"

Susan shakes her head and puts her face in her hands. I envy her. She feels like she can let the emotion free. I have tears welling in my eyes, but I won't let them fall. Not for these strangers, not even my biological mother.

"Well, we'll keep you safe. We want to continue trying to learn about your condition and how you react to the sun."

"So we'll just continue to be lab rats?" Charlie says, folding his arms. I can tell he's angry as well.

"Son, that's not—"

Charlie cuts Tom off sharply. "Not what? Not what you want to call us? That's what we'll be! You just want to test us and poke us like you did in Safety? Why not just leave us there and keep testing us? Why even bother taking us from what we know and putting us and Kor's dad in danger?"

They are excellent questions, and I've wondered a few of them myself. The fact that Charlie is asking them like this is encouraging, as it lets me know I'm not alone in my concerns.

Tom stands up swiftly from his chair and leans on the desk.

"Son! You've been in a prison. You may not have known it, but they held you captive. The government fears you and people like you. None of you deserved to be kept from the world, stripped of the freedoms you deserve. I understand you don't get any of this; it's all new to you, but you have to give us time."

Charlie speaks up then, "We didn't know we were captive. It wasn't great, but it wasn't horrible. For all we know, they are punishing our families because of us. If you cared, you should have just left us alone."

Tom takes a deep breath, then holds up a hand.

"They are monsters that take everything from the world.

They took my daughter from me because she was like you. For years I've tried to find her, but they placed her in a compound somewhere I haven't been able to find. I couldn't rescue her like we did you, because they know who I am and won't let me anywhere near her location. Still, they couldn't afford to not hire our parent company's teams of scientists, so I was assigned here, to Safety. Your families there in Safety aren't even your real ones. The world is a big place, full of freedoms."

Tom's tone is desperate, and his voice shakes at the mention of his daughter. Closing his eyes, he composes himself before continuing.

"If you want to help stop the government from taking more children from their families, then you will shut up and listen. You can't go back, just face it. Either help us or try to go back, but if you return, it'll be to your deaths."

Charlie is quiet after that. Susan has started to sob, likely at the thought of what the Peaceholders will do to our families. Tom's words just remind me of my father.

"What about my dad?" I press again.

Tom's face softens, and he looks at me before shaking his head.

"We don't know," he tells me, "The day before Lucia got you, we intercepted communications from Safety that they planned to take your father to extract what he knew before—"

My stomach drops when Tom doesn't continue.

"Before what—?" I ask, but I dread what I'll hear.

"Korinne, they are going to terminate your father in three days," Lucia says. I can tell she's upset by her tone.

Somehow my brain expected this to be what they'd say, but I can't accept it. I don't want to be here anymore. I want to go back, to be with my father, and to save him in any way that I can. My legs move before I realize it. I turn and run toward the wooden doors we came through and shove them. They swing wide and slam into the walls in the next room, making the woman sitting there yelp in fright. I hear Lucia call to me from behind, but I don't care, I just want to get away from this place; I want to hide somewhere and scream.

They are going to kill my dad, I think as tears start spilling out of my eyes.

I enter the hallway with the paintings and the now-closed metal shutters and turn left. It is opposite the way we came from. I'm not thinking about where I'm going, I just want to get away. The hallway turns right gradually ahead of me, and I follow it. I see doors to the right and to the left of me up ahead, and I pick one. Trying the left doorknob, I grumble when I find it locked. I quickly spin around and grab the handle of the right door. It spins easily and I rip it open, rushing out.

I'm blinded.

There is a light so bright, I feel the burning from its intensity. I gasp and cover my eyes. My arms heat up like fire. The heat spreads rapidly throughout my entire body and I scream in fear. Every inch of me is prickling with the heat.

I try to open my eyes but all I see is spots. I hear screaming around me. For a moment I expect it's my screaming, but when my eyes finally clear, I see there are people at tables pointing at me and running away. My brain is trying to comprehend everything that's happening, but it's having a hard time. My body still blazes with the intense heat, and I crumple to my knees.

It's then that I realize that the heat doesn't hurt. It's wild, and it's intense, but it almost feels—nice. Still crouched down, I hold my hand up to my face and see it's on fire. I squeal and shake my hand, trying to put it out, but it doesn't work.

I look down to see that my whole body blazes with the same fire. Flames lick every inch of my body, yet there's no pain. I stand up steadily and realize I'm filled with energy. I feel wide awake, alert, and oddly strong. It's as if I wasn't exhausted from the travel and lack of sleep just moments ago. I stare upward to see a massive blue canvas of nothing. A bright yellow orb hangs in the blank blue screen above.

Sunlight.

My brain is screaming at me to run, and I shake from fear, but the strength, the power, is intriguing me. I'm compelled to put my hand forward and open it. The moment I do, a ball of flame explodes from my palm and flies toward one table. It collides, and the table is engulfed in flames. In moments, it's gone, replaced by ashes and the smell of burning plastic.

I hear footsteps approaching from the hallway behind me.

"Korinne! You have to—what the—?!"

I turn to see Lucia covering her face with her arms. She backs away from the heat that must be emanating from me. I look down to see that the metal grate beneath me is red hot and spreading toward the doorway quickly.

Armored men and women appear from the doorway across the courtyard and raise their weapons to me.

"Korinne! Put it out! We aren't here to hurt you!" Lucia shouts through her arms.

I realize she's telling me to turn off the fire, but I don't know how. The power is surging through every inch of me, and part of me wants to keep throwing it out. I'm still terrified, but this feeling of power is giving me an odd and unfounded confidence.

"Korinne! You're going to hurt someone if you don't put it out!" she continues yelling at me.

I see Charlie run up behind her, his eyes growing wide. He looks at me, terrified.

Suddenly I feel guilty. My stomach flutters at the sight of him, as usual, but the way he looks makes me feel horrible. I'm scaring him.

The desire to turn it off flourishes in my mind, but I can't figure out how. It just keeps blazing. I take a step toward Lucia and she backs away.

"Hold your fire! She's not trying to hurt us!" Lucia yells behind me.

I realize then that the soldiers have weapons raised at me. The red-hot metal of the grate below me has reached the door and I see the wood of the frame catch fire. Lucia and Charlie back away down the hallway just as I step through the door into the hall.

The fire immediately snuffs out, and my eyes have a hard time adjusting to the dark of the hallway. Though the flames are gone from my skin, I still feel the heat and power within me. It's bursting and coursing through my veins. I'm still invigorated.

"Sheesh! I guess that answers the question of what happens when sunlight touches you," Lucia breathes out.

"What the—you were—fire," Charlie looks terrified as he backs away.

"Are you alright?" Lucia asks before looking me over, "I don't see any signs of burns or anything. Are you hurt anywhere?"

I'm shaking my head, but words can't seem to make it out of my mouth.

What is this feeling? *I feel like I could run for miles*, I think.

For some reason the pull to do so gets the better of me, and I start sprinting down the hallway.

"Korinne—wait!" I hear Lucia yell behind me.

I keep running. The wind of my run is whipping through my hair and beating in my ears. I haven't done much running in my life. We didn't have a dedicated space to do so in Safety, and running in the halls was prohibited by the Creators. The way the walls and doorways are passing me so fast, it makes me wonder if my speed is abnormal. I run past a few scientists in lab coats and they stare at me, perplexed. Right as I enter another doorway, I startle soldiers in camo uniforms. They shout at me but they are so quickly far behind me that they can't do anything about it.

Alarms start blaring around me, red flashing lights at the top of the hallway walls.

Shouldn't I be getting tired by now? I wonder.

I recall running with Lucia, Charlie, and the others when we escaped Safety and how quickly I got winded from the pace. I'm so full of energy now, I expect I could run forever. Soon enough, I run into a dead end and turn on my heels, bolting the other way. A few soldiers appear at the end of the hallway when I turn and I slide to a stop.

"Halt!" one of them shouts at me.

I stare wide-eyed at the guns that they hold up toward me. Unsure what to do, I back away slowly.

"S—sorry, I didn't mean to do anything wrong," I say, terrified now. The burning is still swirling and twisting inside and I want to keep running, to test my limits, but something tells me it wouldn't be wise for me to run past these two soldiers.

One soldier puts his hand to an earpiece and nods. "Tom has asked that we bring you to him. Please come quietly. We don't want to have to shoot," he says.

My skin chills at their words. Their formality and uniforms remind me all too much of the Peaceholders in Safety.

I finally nod, following one as he turns to walk. They lead me through a series of hallways, some of which I must have run through, but I don't recognize. Everything still looks the same.

I let my body follow the two soldiers, but allow my mind to focus on what happened.

After a few minutes, I feel the swirling heat inside me begin to subside. It's as if the battery of an electronic device is running out and needs a recharge. Before we make it back to Tom's office, it's nearly all gone. With the excess energy, apparently, went my normal energy.

I'm exhausted. My body aches everywhere and my head is

pounding. When the soldiers look at me, confused, I realize I'm gasping.

What the—? I'm out of breath, I think. And I am.

I'm heaving as the first soldier walks through the library before Tom's office. I've not felt this tired in a long time, perhaps never. I almost collapse before one soldier puts his hand on my arm.

"Are you alright, miss?" he asks me.

"I'm not sure," I respond.

I want to lie down and sleep. At the same time, I want to know where this power came from.

I want it back.

21

"Well, that was unexpected."

Tom sits at his desk while Susan, Charlie and I are in the chairs in front of it.

"Maybe we should watch it again," Lucia offers.

Tom nods, then turns to the flat television that is embedded in the wall behind his desk. He presses a button on a small remote in his hand, then the screen fuzzes, the figures moving backward.

Suddenly I'm there on the screen. They have cameras all over the place here in the base they didn't tell us about. I'm not surprised though, based on the other security we've seen around here. It makes me wonder what they're worried about.

The screen stops fuzzing and becomes clear. This camera shows a view from across the courtyard that I unwittingly stumbled into. We see the door fling open and a person comes running out onto the patio just in front of the stairs down to the tables. The moment the sun touches them, they burst into flames. The flames must be hot because you can see the air warping around the person as they flicker in the light breeze.

I didn't even notice the breeze.

The person is me. From so far away in the video, you can't see my face, either. But it's me. I know it, and they know it. I was on fire.

People at the tables below start screaming and jumping up from the tables. They scatter, some pin themselves up against the wall while some run below the camera through a door that is hidden from view. A few soldiers, relaxing during a break, hold their guns up to the flaming ball of a person.

My stomach turns at the view. I didn't realize how many of them had actually fired their weapons at me. I flinch at the sound of guns going off as a few volleys are fired at the flaming me. Flashes appear momentarily on the fire, showing where the bullets landed. I am unscathed, so the soldiers must have missed.

We watch as the metal below me heats, glowing red. The door slams open again and Lucia backs away, her hands covering her face.

Tom pauses it then. "How in heaven's name are you not hurt?" he asks, turning around and staring at me.

I look down at the floor, embarrassed. He has to realize I don't have an answer.

"You were on fire, Korinne, and you said you didn't feel any of it burning you?"

He asked me this already when we watched it the first time. I just shake my head. This, in and of itself, is challenging for me. The energy declined more rapidly once we entered Tom's office and now I am having a hard time staying awake. Whatever energy I got has also sucked my vitality out of me.

"Korinne, are you okay?" Lucia asks, noticing my drooping.

I shrug. "I'm exhausted, I don't know why," I say, still looking at the floor.

Tom grunts. "Honey, I'm shocked you aren't in worse condition. We didn't know, without physically testing, what sunlight would do to someone with your same gene mutations. While I don't love that this is how we found out, I'm glad we know—well, that you aren't truly allergic," he sits back in his chair as he says it.

Charlie perks up at the comment. "You mean you weren't actually sure that we aren't allergic to the sun? You were just guessing?!" He sounds mad.

Lucia shakes her head, a grim look on her face. "Hey, kid, we were sure, that's not the problem. We just didn't know what exactly *would* happen to you in the sun," Lucia folds her arms, then leans on the wall. "That would explain the violent reactions Blaine's blood goes through when exposed to the sun's rays. I mean, her blood exploded my workstation when I prodded it with the manufactured sunlight," Lucia puts her hand on her chin.

Charlie shifts his gaze to me, a mixture of worry and fright on his face.

"So, if I go into the sun—" Susan says suddenly, "that will happen to me too?"

She sounds terrified.

"I think we can only assume that's a yes, though we can't know until we try," Tom replies.

Despite her fear, there is a curiosity in her gaze that I can understand.

"But we won't do that if you don't want to," the leader shakes his head and gives Lucia a look that seems to ask if Susan is always so dramatic. Lucia shrugs.

I didn't realize Susan was such a softy until now. She always seemed so harsh and hardened when she was backed by her posse. Not now.

"And what is it you felt?" Tom changes the topic.

I'm still staring at the floor, forcing my eyes to stay open.

"I—I just felt hot, like I was burning on the inside," I start.

Then I pause, trying to remember. The recollection of the

feeling makes me long for it again. My mind locks on the sensation and I can't focus. It's like it has grasped me and won't let go.

"Korinne?" Lucia prods.

I shake my head and try to focus. "I felt strong, like I could go forever, like there was so much deeper energy that needed to get out of me," I reply, before something crosses my mind. I remember when Lucia injected me with the manufactured sunlight and the rash I developed. I turn to Lucia and just say the words, "Why did I get a rash from the tests in Safety, but not from the sun?"

Lucia's eyes widen slightly and I can tell she's considering the question. Finally, she replies, "My only guess is because the serum was made by us, it isn't truly sunlight. You may have been reacting to some other chemical or agent in the serum."

I nod absently as I'm distracted by the sensation I had while running.

Tom grunts, then waves a hand dismissively. "But I still want to know," he returns us to the prior subject, "why on earth did you run? Our guards almost shot you because of it. I can't imagine what made you barrel through the halls." He sounds both annoyed and impressed at the same time.

I'm embarrassed by his question, but it is valid. I don't know why I started running. I strain to remember what compelled me to sprint down the hall. Then I remember.

"I don't know exactly. I just felt a burning power inside of me that made me want to run and run. I've never felt anything like it before—"

I take a moment to get my bearings because I get dizzy from talking.

"Korinne, are you okay? You look like you are about to be sick all over the floor," Lucia pipes in.

I didn't realize that I felt nauseous until she said something. My face must betray how I feel.

"After the odd energy went away, I got exhausted," I respond.

"It must be a side effect of the sun's rays on your skin. What else did you feel?" Lucia asks, curious.

"Lucia," Tom says, "I know the scientist in you is intrigued by what happened, but we have to be cautious. We can learn about her abilities later. For now, we have to understand what she experienced so we can be prepared for the future. We can't have flaming kids running through our compound threatening the lives of those around them."

I blush at his comments. He makes it sound as if I purposefully put people in danger.

"Right," Lucia concedes, looking back at me.

"Well," Tom asks, "why didn't you stop?"

I shake my head to wake myself. "I felt unstoppable, like I had all the energy in the world. I don't know why, but I couldn't make myself stop."

I have to catch my breath again. A warm hand presses against my shoulder and I look to see a concerned Charlie sitting next to me.

"I didn't even get tired, I could just go on for a long time," I finish lamely.

Tom makes a concerned face, then nods. "I would like to learn more about this power you felt, but I can tell you don't have any more in you," Tom tells me.

He gestures to the side as a soldier moves from beside the bookshelf she'd been leaning against. I jump at the sight of her because I didn't even realize she was in here. She's of average height and has long, curly black hair. Her skin is tan, and her eyes vibrant green. She has earrings up the entire edge of her right ear.

"Shelly, can you please take Korinne and the others to their quarters? Make sure they're comfortable and can get some rest.

These poor kids have been up all night and doubtless could use solid sleep."

The soldier woman nods at him and walks toward me.

"Come with me," she says, her voice lilty and soft. I'm taken aback by the sound of it because I didn't expect that to come from a hardened looking soldier like her.

I stand shakily and almost collapse, my limbs tired and weak from who-knows-what. Shelly catches my arm and hefts me back up to my feet.

I mumble a thank you and blush at my blunder. She smiles and puts my arm around her waist, her own wrapping under my armpits. Together, we walk to the double doors at the back of Tom's office. Just before we leave, he speaks to us from his desk.

"Oh, and Shelly, please make sure they get an inside room. We don't want any unexpected combustions from the sunlight."

She nods at him and we walk out of the room. I had almost forgotten we had traveled most of the night. It seems like just a moment ago we were running through the metal hallways of Safety and sliding down a garbage chute. Now we're in an unfamiliar compound with apparently copious amounts of outside access. I had no idea the doors that I used earlier would lead outside, so I really didn't expect to run into the sun.

Footsteps shuffle behind me and I turn just enough to see that Charlie and Susan are following behind us. Charlie has his arms around Susan's shoulder as she continues to cry softly. He stares at me, a look of concern and fright on his face. His expression irks me more than I want to admit.

He fears me, or at least what happened to me, I worry.

"I must say that was quite the display you put on there," Shelly says next to me.

I turn to look up at her face and she's smiling.

"Never thought I'd get to see a human bonfire while I was on my lunch break," she chuckles.

I know she's trying to make me feel better, but it's not working. I have no idea what a bonfire is, but I guess it involves flames.

"Sorry to bother your lunch," is all that I can say.

She laughs again. "Girl, you didn't bother me at all," she replies. "Sure, I might have shot a couple slugs at you, but that didn't phase you." She sounds impressed and amused. That wasn't what I was getting from Tom and Lucia.

I just walk silently, relying on her strength even though I don't want to.

"It does make sense now why the government has you all shut up like that," she comments.

My mind flips back to Safety and all the other people who are allergic to the sun.

No, I think, *we aren't allergic. But the sun—* The moment I realize it, I gasp.

Shelly stops and kneels in front of me. "Are you okay? What happened?" she asks.

"Oh nothing, I just—I just realized that every person in Safety is like me, which means—"

I pause, not wanting to say the words *they'd all burst into flames in the sun like me.*

Shelly smiles. "Yes, if every person in there is like you, and I'm guessing you two as well," Shelly gestures behind me to Charlie and Susan, "I'd guess that the government doesn't want people with your power roaming the outside world."

That my father, my mother, even Sean would feel the same way I did outside in the sun gives me a thrill. I suddenly feel hope. All my life I assumed I couldn't ever live a normal life outside of Safety. I assumed they'd never find a cure for our allergy. But I don't even have an allergy. A little energy runs through me as I have the encouraging thought. It dissipates quickly though.

Shelly supports me again and we continue walking down

the hall. Soon we come to a set of double doors on our right, a sign above it that says *guest housing.*

She pushes the door open and leads us into a hallway with short carpet, red with swirling blue designs. A man sits behind a desk, clacking noisily on something with his fingers. I peer over the top of the high wall in front of his desk and see he's typing on a bulky computer. I don't have experience with the things because we only have holopads in Safety. My dad told me about them before.

"Can we get three keys for these kids? Something close together, so they can find each other easily," Shelly tells him.

He looks up from his desk. His black hair is swooped to the left of his head.

"Oh, sure thing. How long are they staying?" he asks her.

She shrugs. "Until we find more permanent quarters for them," she replies.

He furrows his brow and stares at her. "You're young for new scientist recruits," he says, "Then again, a love for science can't ever start too young."

"Nah, Scott, these are the rescues. The ones from Safety," Shelly tells him.

His eyes widen and his jaw drops. He scans over the three of us until his gaze locks on me.

"You're the girl—the one on fire," he says.

I blush, Shelly laughs.

"Yes, Scott, and if you aren't careful, she'll melt you to bits," Shelly jokes.

Scott rolls his eyes and reaches into a drawer below him.

"Hilarious," he replies, "now here are cards for rooms eight through ten." He hands them to Shelly, but she pauses.

"Aren't the odds the ones with actual windows?" Shelly asks.

Scott looks at her and nods. "Yes, what's wrong with—?" His eyebrows shoot up when he remembers seeing me on fire in the security footage. "Oh gosh, yeah—right, here's number twelve."

After they exchange cards, Shelly turns and leads us down the hallway. It isn't long before we get to the door labeled eight.

"Here is eight, ten is just up there, and twelve right around the corner to the left," Shelly says, handing me a card. "You'd better take eight, I'm not sure you can walk much further."

She hands the other two to Susan and Charlie, who watch her.

"Well, go on," she says. When none of us move, she laughs. "Right, you don't know how this works, let me show you."

She takes the card from me and turns to the door. "See the slot here?" She points to a slit opening in the door. "Just stick it in there."

We watch as she slides the short end of the card into the slot. There is a flashing light and the door swings open.

Inside, I see a room about the size of the gathering room in our assigned quarters at Safety. The floor is covered in soft, grey carpet. There is a doorway to another room just on the right, but I can't see where it leads. Straight ahead, I see the bottom of a bed, a large screen on a table, and a chair at a desk. My eyes shift up to a curtained window. I freeze.

The soldier notices my reaction and follows my gaze. After a moment, she chuckles. "Ah, yeah, that's just a fake window. There isn't any sun coming into the room, don't worry," she shifts on her feet as if waiting for something, "You can go in if you want. There isn't much to it, but then again, you probably had less in Safety."

I hear her, but I don't respond. I'm getting more and more exhausted as I stand here. I feel my legs go out from under me. The ground rushes to my face and then everything goes black.

22

I'M DREAMING. I KNOW I AM, BUT I CAN'T GET MYSELF TO WAKE up. I'm back in Safety again, but there are windows on every part of each wall. In fact, the left side of the hallway is completely glass. Sun is pouring into the room, touching my skin. My entire body is ablaze, a torrent of flames licking the floor and the wall to my right. Parts of the glass windows are melting from the intense heat of my skin.

I see people around me, dressed in their normal grey garb with little variety. They stare at me, terrified, as I walk toward them. I see people screaming and running in terror. My mother appears in the crowd, looking as terrified as everyone. I call out to her, but she just turns to run. I feel the power coursing through me just as before, so I break into a run. To my horror, my mother bursts into flames, screaming and collapsing.

I stare at her, shocked.

I just killed my mother, I think.

"Kor?"

I look up to see Charlie and Sean standing ten feet away. Sean looks scared but Charlie just seems curious.

"No! Stay away!" I yell at them.

Charlie ignores me and steps forward. Suddenly, he's on fire, screaming and collapsing to the ground.

I cry. I can feel the tears on my face for only a moment before the heat of the fire evaporates them. Covering my face, I fall to my knees. The screaming around me disappears and I look up to see I'm in an exam room, like the one Lucia tested me in back at Safety.

A man screams. He's in pain, I know it. I stand and breathe out relief when I see the fire is gone from my body. That relief soon disappears when I realize who's screaming in the patient's chair.

Dad, I think.

He screams out as one of four robed scientists jabs a sharp metal object into his ear. My stomach lurches when I see this and I shout.

The scientists can't hear me as they continue to poke and stab my screaming father.

"Korinne, help me!" he yells.

The scientists continue to ignore me as I shout for him, trying to get closer. I feel like I'm running through something thick. I can't move fast enough. I'm mortified by what I see. The tears are falling again now, and my emotions shift from sad to angry. As soon as the anger comes, the power bursts inside me. I don't know how, but I throw my hand out, the scientists being pushed through the air by an invisible force. They collide with the wall, collapsing without moving again.

I can move again, but when I get to the patient chair, my father closes his eyes.

I'm too late.

I gasp and sit up. I breathe heavily, trying to come back to reality. What I see when I wake up is an unfamiliar room. Somewhere I don't know. I'm in a bed with a heavy white blanket and thin white sheets. Right in front of me is a massive black screen. I look to my right and see a curtained window with dull light filtering through. I scream and throw my hands over my face. The moment I do, I gasp as pain shoots up my arm, the deep cut Lucia gave me still aching slightly from before.

When I don't burst into flames, I uncover my face, still breathing hard. I'm soaking wet. The sheets and blanket around me are wet too. The nightmare must have made me sweat enough to saturate everything.

My mind is working to understand my surroundings, but I can't seem to grasp anything. I look to my right and see a table there with a shining lamp. A note sits there with a white card that says *Room 8* on it. Finally, I remember what happened earlier. My mind calms down. I pick up the note and read it.

Sorry you didn't make it. I didn't change your clothes; I figured you wanted your privacy. I left your key here for you—don't leave your room without it. When you wake up, pick up the phone and dial 4862 to get something to eat - Shelly

An image forms in my brain of a powerful woman with long and curly black hair. Her many-times pierced ear draws my attention, but not for long. I'm soon remembering her incredibly green eyes.

This image in my mind comforts me, though I can't describe why. I don't know how Shelly, this random soldier-woman, gives me any reason to feel this way, but I trust her.

I look around again, trying to see what she means by "phone". I spot another piece of paper stuck to the lamp in the middle of the shaft. It has an arrow toward the wall and says *phone*.

I follow the arrow and notice a black box stuck there. It's the size of my shoe. Curious, I reach out and pull on a handle there. When a part of it pops out with a click, I yelp and catch it before it falls to the ground between the table and wall. A strange noise is coming from part of the device, and I put it to my ear. It dings before a robotic man's voice speaks back to me.

"Please select your department now. Press one for laundry, press two for receiving, press three for medical, press four for cafeteria."

The list goes on a bit more, but I stop listening. I stare at the note for a moment before pressing the number keys Shelly left in her note. I've not used a phone before, so I am concerned I did something wrong when it doesn't do anything. I'm about to put it back when someone speaks back to me.

"So you're awake then? How'd you sleep, Kor?" It's Shelly.

"Umm, hi—fine, I guess," I say, unsure how else to respond. I do feel a bit more rested, but the tiredness pulls at me still.

"Want something to eat? I can bring it up to you if you want," Shelly responds. "I said I could help you get something to eat."

I pause. "Sure, I am hungry," I say to her. As if on cue, my stomach growls. I blush, but I don't get the sense that Shelly could hear it.

"What strikes your fancy? Hamburger? Chicken? Salad?" Shelly begins saying. She lists off at least a dozen more things before she stops.

"Um—I don't know what I want. I'm just hungry," I reply.

I hear her chuckle on the other side before she responds.

"Fair enough, I can just bring you what sounds good to me. I promise it'll be delicious. Just keep resting and I'll be up in five minutes," Shelly says, then the phone goes silent.

I sit there for a moment, still taking in the room before I decide to get up. My bladder presses me to find a restroom. I realize then that it's been a very long time since I've been able to go. The room I'm in is so small that it can only fit a bed, desk and chair, as well as a TV. I remember abruptly the moment I first got to the room and saw a door to the right of the hallway. I gradually get out of the comfortable bed and step onto the soft carpet. Turning the corner, I see the door indeed leads to a tiny bathroom. I'm shocked at how much they could fit into the little place.

After relieving myself, I return to the bed and sit patiently.

I don't know if I lose myself in my thoughts or if five minutes just isn't that long of a time, but Shelly knocks on my door sooner than I expect. When I open the door, she's grinning at me. Her pitch black hair is tied back in a long ponytail today, rather than curled. The metal ring in her nose glints from the light in the hallway.

"I went with the burger, since it's pretty much lunch time. Did you realize you slept through breakfast? It's already afternoon—you slept nearly 24 hours." Shelly sounds incredulous.

She walks in casually and plops on my bed. She's still wearing her camouflage uniform, but she looks more relaxed than yesterday. Shelly nods and pats the bed next to her.

"Have a sit."

Smelling the food makes my stomach growl so hard that I almost feel nauseous. I sit next to her and grab a fry from the bag.

"Sorry the rooms aren't big enough for tables, we had to fit as many of them into a space as we could, so the designer went with a hotel-like room. Did you at least sleep well?"

I nod as I take a massive bite of hamburger. My eyes roll back in my head at the taste of the food. I'm not sure if she's expecting me to say anything else, but I can't with the food in my mouth anyway. Before I know it, I'm taking another bite without even swallowing the first one. My stomach is protesting from the speed of my eating, but my hunger makes me want to eat even faster.

"You know the food won't run away from you," Shelly chuckles.

I blush and put the burger on my lap for a moment. "Sorry —I didn't realize how hungry I was until now."

Shelly smiles. "You can eat fast, I just don't want you to

choke on your big bites," she laughs again. Her mirth is cut short, however, when the smile on her face fades and she looks at me seriously. "Are you ready for today?" She asks me.

I watch her, unsure of what she means.

"Tom and Lucia want to test your abilities," she says.

I stare at her, recalling that this was something Tom mentioned yesterday, but not understanding the implications.

She continues staring at me, a look of concern on her face.

"It means more fire, and not just for you, but for your friends as well. We plan to expose you to the sun again, though in a more—controlled environment."

My stomach twists at her words. From excitement? From fear? I can't tell. The look of worry on her face tells me she at least thinks I won't like this news.

It's then that I realize I'm thrilled.

As I remember the feeling of power and strength I got from being in the sun, my entire body aflame, excitement flows through every part of me. Sure, I got exhausted after the power, but the sensation before was incredible. It is something my body has been longing for ever since it happened.

I shrug and try to hide my enthusiasm. I'm embarrassed about how excited I am for it.

I get embarrassed a lot these days, I think.

Back in Safety I don't recall blushing so much, but things have been out of the norm recently. At the thought of Safety, I straighten up, remembering my family, specifically my dad.

"What's happening at Safety? Is my dad okay? My mother and my brother?" I'm speaking fast now, the thoughts flowing in my mind of what might have happened to them.

Shelly presses her lips together and shakes her head.

"We haven't heard anything yet from our men there. Safety has locked down all incoming and outgoing communications. They've shut the doors and aren't letting anyone in or out. We still have people there, but they can't tell us what they know, at least not for now," Shelly tells me.

My stomach twists at the thought of not knowing what's happening there. Images of my father being held prisoner flow through my mind. I think of my mother and Sean being put in the lowest levels possible, their lives ruined because of infinite demerits from me running away.

Suddenly, I want to cry. A tear wells up in my eyes and I look downward at my burger, forcing in another bite. Although I turned my face away from Shelly, she must have seen something, because she puts her hand on my shoulder.

"Kor, I'm sure they are alright. The Creators may hold people like you captive, but they aren't wild killers. Your family is probably okay."

I notice the pause in her words when she says 'your family' and my mind flips to how Lucia is my real biological mother. How long has Shelly known that Lucia is my mother?

Shelly checks her watch and huffs. "I hate to break this short, but we gotta get going. Lucia is ready to get started with the tests. We don't know what will happen with security at Safety once they find out how many of you have been taken. Lucia and Tom want to understand as much as possible about your condition so we can make plans of what to do about it," Shelly says.

I nod and finish the last couple of bites of my burger.

"Take a quick shower, get dressed, and then we'll head to the testing rooms," Shelly pauses before looking at me a bit sheepishly, "You—know how to use a shower, right?"

I can't help but laugh at her words. "Yes, we had showers in Safety," I laugh.

She nods curtly and walks to the door. The idea of a shower is incredible right now. I feel gross, a bit tired still, and ready for something relaxing. Even though this room is unfamiliar, it is small and safe.

"Enjoy the shower, but try not to take too long. It's time to set you ablaze."

I know she means this as a joke, but the words stir the excitement up again inside me.

A warm shower doesn't sound as exciting anymore.

23

THE SHOWER IS LARGER THAN THE ONE IN SAFETY, AND THE WALL has a bunch of buttons on it. When I press the button that says shampoo, images of feet appear on the floor below me and I'm instructed to stand on them. When I do, I feel cold, thick liquid drip from the ceiling onto my head.

Well, that's—convenient, I think as I try a dispenser that launches soap onto my chest from the wall in front of me.

The shower turns out to be a lot nicer than I expected, but I don't take too long. Sure, I get distracted by how the soap and shampoo are dispensed, but that doesn't take my mind off the idea that I get to experience the power inside once again.

When I exit the shower room, I realize I have nothing else to wear, other than the grey clothes I was wearing when I left Safety. I put them back on, feeling the grunginess from my sweating the day before and in the night. Normally I might feel weird putting on the same clothes from the day before, but I'm looking forward to the sensation I'll experience in the sun today too much to care.

I open the door to see Shelly staring at the screen of her

palm-sized device in her hand. Sounds play from it and she's smiling. When she sees me, she straightens up and nods.

"Ready?" she asks.

I nod. Her eyes look me up and down and she grimaces.

"Oh gosh, you need something else to wear, don't you? I didn't think about that. Did you want me to go find something now?"

I shake my head. "It's fine, they aren't that bad."

It's a lie—they're still damp from my nightmare, but I don't want to delay the tests. I'm eager to get going.

She shrugs and puts the device she was holding into her pocket. "If you say so . . . shall we?" She gestures to the left hallway before turning that way.

We pass the desk where we saw the man yesterday, but there isn't anyone there right now. As we exit the door, I'm shocked by the number of people who mull around. When I ran out into the sun yesterday and fled through the hallways, I didn't see a lot of people. Now soldiers, scientists in their lab coats, and others walk briskly around, some chatting, some inspecting papers or devices like the one I've seen Shelly use.

"It gets busy around here. You were lucky that your dash through the halls yesterday happened during a lunch break. The halls were empty then. There's even more bustle now that we have things to learn about you and your two friends," she tells me.

I feel overwhelmed by all the people that surround us and want to run back to my room. Shelly must pick up on this because she gently puts her hand on my shoulder and nudges me to the right.

"It's not too far from here," she assures me.

And she's telling the truth, because we only walk past two or three more doors before we stop at another set of double doors. She opens them and ushers me through. We enter another hallway, but this one feels much smaller because the ceiling is low. It only stands a couple inches above the doorway. I feel calmer now that we are in the small place. One, because there are no people, and two, because it's quiet and dimmer.

My comfort is soon gone as we follow the natural turn of the hallway and enter a massive room. I can't help but let my mouth drop open at the sight. The ceiling high above makes me gasp, but it's really the depth and breadth of the room that's shocking. I didn't see what this building looked like when we drove up in the car because I was sleeping, but based on the size of this room, it is much more spacious than I thought. The floor is shiny hardwood and has lines all over it. There is a square around the edge, and half circles on each end. I see a stand with nets on either side. Benches line the walls on all sides and they are tiered upward all the way to the top.

The worst part is that they are full of people. Okay, maybe not completely full, but there are tons of people. They go quiet when they see me walk in. I feel the blood run from my face and I get lightheaded.

"Well, I didn't realize you'd have such a great turn out. Apparently, lighting yourself on fire gets you popular around here," Shelly says next to me.

I know it's a joke, and honestly it's even funny, but I can't laugh, not with these people staring at me. My eyes drift downward to the wood floor and relief floods me. I see Charlie there, wearing his same grey clothes, and Susan as well. Seeing them makes me feel better. Charlie gives me his goofy smile then points at the people, shrugging as he does it. Susan looks at me and gives a half smile. It's good to see her not crying, to be honest.

Shelly and I walk across the massive floor to where they sit at a plastic table. Just before the table, there is a clear wall set up. When we get closer, I inspect the structure curiously. Lucia is at the table with her lab coat, along with Tom. There are several other scientists around, but I don't recognize any of them. Dr. Johnson sits off to the side with a bag of who-knows-what.

"Hey there, champ, you ready for today?" Lucia asks.

She notes my wary glancing toward the transparent wall and smiles wanly. "Just a precaution. We don't know the extent of your powers yet."

When I don't respond, she clears her throat and tries again. "Are you ready to give today a try?"

I look at her with a blank expression before mimicking Charlie's shrug. I don't know what else to say, so I glance around at the other scientists.

Lucia picks up on this action. "Ah, these are just other scientists who are invested in your—predicament. They have been going into Safety like me and testing the other people there. We wanted them down here with us to get a better view. Should we introduce them to you?" she asks.

I don't know why she bothered asking, because she does anyway. I half-listen to their names, realizing I likely won't remember any of them.

"They are as eager to see the sun's effects on you as I am. Some of our scientists got stuck in Safety after our escapade a few nights ago, but most are still out here," Lucia continues.

Tom clears his throat at the mention of the night we left Safety, and Lucia shifts on her feet.

"Anyway, we have exam rooms, but based on your reaction to the sun yesterday, they are way too small to use. So we improvised. This basketball court should be fine. We set up shields to protect onlookers from any potential singeing," Lucia explains.

"What do you need me to do then?" I ask.

"For now, just have a seat," Tom jumps in, "We need to figure out how we want to go about this."

Charlie folds his arms and looks around. "What exactly are

we going to be testing? I don't see any exam chairs or computers," he leans back in his chair.

Lucia grins. "I'm glad you asked. We have tested blood like yours and have also used mental tests, such as simulation dreams, but nothing has helped. We are going straight for the source." Lucia snaps her fingers as she does.

A loud grinding sound echoes in the vast room and I look up, jumping at the loudness. The ceiling far above us cracks in the middle and moves. Each half of the ceiling moves slowly outward. Once again, my mouth drops open. It's not just me that's shocked. I see the same reactions on Susan's and Charlie's faces. After only a moment, a bright light enters the room, a beam of sunlight shining directly on the floor all the way across the length of the room. Lucia raises her hand again, making the sound and the roof stop.

"We're going to give you a sunbath," she says.

My stomach writhes at the words, but I realize soon it's not from fear, but from excitement.

"You're kidding, right?" Susan jumps in. "You can't expect us to just go into the sun. Didn't you see what happened to Korinne yesterday! We could die!"

I can see Susan shaking from the news, and honestly, Charlie doesn't look too thrilled either. I move over to Charlie and put my hand on his arm. He jumps when I do because he wasn't looking at me when I came over. He was staring at the sunlight.

"It's okay, it really is. It doesn't hurt, it feels—," I pause, trying to find the words, "—incredible."

Charlie looks at me with concern, but then nods. He sighs and glances at the sunlight again. "I guess someone has to go first, right?" he says.

Lucia smiles and nods before waving her hand. The grinding sound starts again and the ceiling above closes. All eyes stare at Lucia, most questioning. A buzzing continues as all the people in the seats around us have their own conversations.

"Guys, I can't have you walking into the sun without you getting settled first. This floor is wood, you'd set it on fire instantly. You have to stand right there," Lucia points to a large piece of flat metal in the middle of the room. "We need you there before the flames happen, capeesh?"

Charlie and I continue to stare at her. I don't know what capeesh means, but I am too embarrassed to ask.

"Good call, Lucia, I hadn't thought of that," Tom agrees.

After a moment, all eyes look at Charlie. "Oh, I guess you want me to—okay, yeah," Charlie says.

He trudges to the metal sheet on the ground and pauses, looking hesitantly at it as if it's going to bite him. I can see he's shaking.

He's terrified, I think, *Charred, I'd be too, if I hadn't just run into the sun on accident.*

I move hurriedly to his side and put my hand on his. He jumps when I do, telling me just how on edge he is about the whole thing.

"Charlie, I know this is terrifying, but it's an amazing thing, trust me." I tug on his hand to make him turn around and look at me. "It doesn't hurt, I promise."

He nods at me and hardens his jaw. "Okay, I trust you," he tells me.

It isn't my first time hearing those words, but this time they send a shiver up my spine. It's doubtless because his fearful eyes stare fiercely into mine. I smile awkwardly and step back, tripping as my heel catches the ground, almost pulling me over.

His eyes twinkle at my clumsiness and I stick my tongue out at him.

"Alright, he's in position. Korinne, you probably don't want to be near him. We don't know if you'll get hurt by the reaction or not. Dr. Johnson, be on the ready. Just because Korinne didn't get hurt doesn't mean something won't happen to this young man," Lucia says.

The dark-skinned doctor nods at the words. I notice that his hand grips the handle of the bag next to him.

Lucia raises her hands again and we hear the grinding noise just as I make it back to the table at the edge of the seats. I see Charlie shaking again, though this time it's bad.

The sun peeks through the crack of the opening ceiling and spreads along the whole room again. This time, when it hits the metal platform, there is an alternative source of light.

Charlie is in flames.

These aren't the campfire flames that we've seen on the history channel videos we've watched at school. These are massive.

I wince as the heat laces on my face, thinking it'll burn me, but it somehow feels pleasant. I feel the energy coming off of Charlie's skin as he stands there. The fire is so high that it more than doubles his height above him.

I hear a noise from the flames. My skin crawls for a moment, but then I realize he's laughing. Charlie is laughing hysterically.

We watch as he holds open his hands and looks at them. It's hard to see through the blaze, but we can just see his outline. Suddenly, he turns and almost moves off the pad.

"Wait! Don't move!" Lucia shouts at him.

He hesitates and turns back to her. After a pause, he again begins to walk off the metal.

"Stop him!" Tom yells abruptly, "If he steps on the wood, he'll light the whole place on fire!"

No one can stop him, I think, fearful that he'll light the building on fire. *No one except . . .*

I'm moving before my brain catches up. My feet push me forward and I feel the heat intensifying on my face and skin. Once again, it doesn't hurt me, it just feels intense.

Before long, I'm right next to him. My body explodes with the same energy as the day before and I gasp at the sensation. A smile bursts on my face, but I shake my head and rush to Charlie. He's got one foot hovering over the wood floor as I throw my arms around him and pull him back.

Shocked, he stares at me wide-eyed. "Um, Kor, we're on fire," he says.

I laugh. He laughs with me.

We just stand there, bodies on fire, intense energy coursing through my body as the sun fuels me with something that I can't understand.

"Kor, I want to run, to just go. I could go forever." Charlie stares at his blazing hands.

"I know, but we can't. Look there," I point to the floor.

It's blackened, and the coating has melted away. The pull to run is tugging at me too, but I can resist it this time. Somehow, having done this before, I can fight the urge to test my energy.

"What does this mean?" Charlie asks.

I shake my head before saying, "I have no idea. But it's great, right?"

He grins at me.

Curious, I open my hand and look at the fire surrounding it and my arm. My eyes look to the side wall, a hundred feet away.

"Don't actually do it, but how fast do you think we could run to that wall? I think we can run faster now."

I point to the wall just then.

Right as I do, a ball of flames projects out of my hand and rockets toward the side of the room. The moment it collides with the wall, it explodes in a torrent of fire.

"Shut the roof!" I hear Lucia shout.

"Oh charred, oh charred, oh charred." I'm panicking as I see that I set the wall on fire. I have to resist the urge to run at it now. Men and women appear from the sides of the room and spray white foam-like stuff at it. The fire is gone in a flash.

The grinding of the roof starts again. Soon, the sun no longer touches our skin. The fire snuffs out around us, but the heat still lingers in every part of my body.

"Kor, I still feel it, it's all over me," Charlie tells me.

I nod and am about to say something when someone runs over to us.

"What were you thinking?! You just threw fire at the wall!"

It's a voice I don't recognize, and I soon find out it's one of the other scientists, a shorter woman, scolding me.

I open my mouth to say something, but when I pause for a moment, Lucia jumps in.

"That—was—incredible." Lucia comes in and hugs me.

This reaction causes the other scientist to scoff and hold up a finger.

"Oh, can it, Gillian, we knew this would be a dangerous test," Lucia cuts her off.

The woman huffs and hugs her clipboard to her chest.

"What do you feel? What's it like?" Lucia barrages us with questions.

So we answer them.

We find out that we were in the sun for five minutes altogether, but it felt like only a minute, like time had sped up. The two of us move to the table where they take our blood and begin tests. They've wheeled in equipment to test this and our other vitals. Every few seconds there is a gasp, or an 'ooh' or an 'ahh'.

I look over at Charlie, who has a smile pasted on his face. It's wistful and silly-looking, but it makes me want to hug him. Without thinking, I reach over and put my hand on his. He turns his hand and squeezes mine, our eyes locking.

"Kor, I feel incredible. The energy—it's going though, it's slipping away."

I remember how tired I got when it disappeared and bite my lip.

"I don't think it lasts forever. Once it's gone, you'll feel drained," I warn him.

After a few more minutes, that's just what happens. Charlie slumps in his chair and he goes pale.

"Oh gosh, I don't feel good," he comments.

Dr. Johnson moves hastily to him and takes his vitals again.

"Blood pressure is low, not dangerously, though. Pupil response is good. He is just showing signs of fatigue," the doctor replies.

Lucia looks at me.

"Are you tired too? This happened to you yesterday," she says.

I focus on my body and realize I'm not getting tired. The blazing fire persists in my veins.

"It's still there. I think that it's lasting longer than last time," I reply.

Lucia moves back to the science instruments and narrows her eyes.

"We see lingering effects on your blood; high nutrient content, as well as higher activity in all your cells. The effect has faded on Charlie's, but yours is still there. Somehow your bodies absorb the energy from the sunlight and use it for— well, whatever you just did over there." Lucia gestures to the wall that is scorched black in many places.

I blush at the sight.

"I wonder if the retention of energy is longer per exposure. You were exposed yesterday, Kor, so it must last longer this time," Lucia is concentrating on the readings of the instruments.

Hearing her call me Kor feels both wrong and somewhat comforting at the same time. I don't hate it, but I don't like it.

"How long will it last?" I ask, trying to force away the awkwardness of hearing her call me by my nickname.

"I can only guess. We'll have to monitor you to see how long the effect stays," Lucia moves over to Charlie and puts a hand on his shoulder before saying, "Good work out there."

She then turns to Susan, who promptly turns white.

"I—I don't know if I want to—" Susan stutters as she speaks.

Lucia sighs and looks back at me. Her eyes plead with me to convince Susan to do the experiment.

I shrug and move over to Susan. My muscles tighten harder than they normally would, and the same urge to run returns to me. My mind pushes the feeling away, but I still can move more quickly to her side, letting the energy push through me.

"Susan, it's not bad. It feels incredible, trust me," I tell her.

She watches me, fear in her eyes.

"I can come stand in there with you," I offer.

Lucia jumps in. "Ah, no, we need you to stay out. If we're going to understand the limitations, we have to know how long it takes for the effects to wear off," she moves to my side.

Susan looks at her, then at me again before nodding.

I'm instructed to go sit at the table, and I do. Dr. Johnson takes more blood samples as I watch Susan walk to the platform. She pauses, not wanting to enter the metal square on the floor. Pressing my lips together, I stand and move to her.

"Would you like me to stand right here?" I offer.

Susan turns and looks at me, hope now on her face.

"That—would be great," she replies.

I stare at her, the girl who ridiculed me, bullied me all my life, and I see how broken she is. A warmth fills me at how she feels, knowing that I'm here for her. It's as if all the bad things she's done to me don't matter anymore. There's something else unexplainable that bonds us now.

Despite Lucia's grumblings, they let me stay close. Susan steps to the middle of the plate and the ceiling opens. As expected, she bursts into flame once the sun hits her.

Susan's eyes widen as the heat flows off of her. I smile and step backward, moving back to the table once I see that she's comfortable now.

"Odd—her fire doesn't seem as strong as these two," one of the male scientists whispers behind me.

I inspect Susan's flame-engulfed form, but can't truly compare it to my own. I wasn't able to see what the fire looked like as it surrounded me, so I can't tell if what he says is true or not.

"I think you're right," Tom replies.

Lucia is nodding her head as well. After a few more minutes, she makes the hand motion for the ceiling to close above and it does almost instantly. I can see that Susan's eyes are still wide with wonder and she looks at her hands. I smile at seeing her feel anything other than sad. She's been depressed ever since we left Safety.

My mind drifts back to my family there. I imagine every person in Safety getting hit by the sunlight and bursting into flames. I think of Sean turning into a pillar of fire and thinking it's cool before blasting fire balls against the walls.

"Well, I guess it explains why the government covered this up," Lucia's words disrupt my thoughts. "How long have they been hiding this?"

Tom puts his hand to his stubbly chin and narrows his eyes.

"The more pertinent question is how did they expunge the information from all news sources? They had to have erased memories, even. The sun events only happened less than a hundred years ago." His eyes wander the ceiling.

"They kept one picture of it," I blurt.

I remember the picture of the man in the streets, flame surrounding his entire body. His eyes are wide in fear and people are shouting and screaming at him from the sides of the road.

"What?" Lucia asks.

"There was a picture in one of the hallways. They always

told us it was what would happen if we got exposed to the sun, that we'd burst into flames and die." I shift in my chair, remembering how scared I always was when I saw that picture.

"I mean, they weren't wrong," a voice says behind us.

I recognize the voice as Fred's, the driver from our escape yesterday, or two days ago, I guess, when you account for my day of sleep. In all the fuss with testing our powers, I hadn't noticed him coming into the room.

"Oh gosh, I don't feel good," Susan keels over and lands on her knees.

"Woah there, take it easy," the large doctor says as he lifts her by her arms. He gently puts her in a chair as her head bobs forward. She looks nauseated. Everyone's eyes shift to me to see what my reaction is going to be. I can tell the power inside of me is slowly disappearing, but I still feel energized and strong.

"Nope, I still got it," I reply, holding up my hand. The moment I do, it bursts into flames. One of the female scientists shrieks at the sight and almost falls over. I gasp and shake my hand until the fire goes away.

"Wait, can you do that again?" Lucia asks.

I shrug and open my hand, focusing the feeling of heat and power there. Right as I do, the fire springs up again.

"Huh, so you can bring the fire back, even after you leave the sun," Lucia writes on a notepad right after she says this.

"Holy char, her hand just lit on fire, and you're all okay with it?" Fred looks more than confused.

"It's a long story, Fred." Tom looks at Fred and raises his eyebrows. "The short version is that the government lied to these people and to us about the effects of the sun events all those years ago. Now, what is it you wanted? You came running in here like a madman."

Fred continues to stare at me, though he doesn't look scared, just curious.

"Huh, odd," he says, before turning to Tom, "They still

won't let our men and women out of Safety, and they won't let anyone in. But one of our scientists slipped an email out through their firewall. Our tech guys tried to reply, but the message failed."

Tom and Lucia perk up at the words.

"Well? What did it say?" Tom sounds impatient.

Fred looks warily at me, then gestures Lucia and Tom closer so that he can whisper.

He doesn't want us to hear, I think, feeling annoyed. I don't know why I'm annoyed. We are new here, and it's not like they should tell us everything.

I'm shrugging it off until I catch wind of them saying my father's name.

"What?" I say, more anger in my voice than I intended.

Lucia turns away from Fred and looks me in the eye. I know she wants to tell me something, but Tom puts his hand on her shoulder and shakes his head.

"What is it?" I put more feeling into my words, and this time intentionally.

"Kor," Lucia starts.

"I heard my dad's name. What happened? What's going on?" My imagination runs away with the thoughts of what could have happened to him.

My mind is suddenly catching every sound that I hear, the people in the bleachers are still chattering from the display of power. They echo all around, making it sound like even more people. I can hear myself breathing hard, and my heart pounds in my chest. Power gathers inside of me. It's as if the anger and fear are making it flare. My hands light on fire as I clench my fists. I grit my teeth, trying not to get more angry that they aren't telling us everything.

"Okay, okay, let's calm down now," one of the scientist men says, stepping backward with his hands facing toward me.

My eyes water, grief locking me in place. Somehow I know

my dad is dead, or dying, or something horrible like that. I just want them to tell me but no one seems to want to give me any information.

"Put the fire out, young woman. We can't have you hurting anyone," Tom says, looking stern.

I glare at him, and I have the urge to throw something at him.

Maybe they were right to lock us away, I think, feeling like I could attack any of them right now.

"Kor, your dad is not dead," Lucia says.

The words make my anger diffuse at once. My eyes widen and I open my hands, the fire snuffing out. The boiling anger and power inside of me subsides, and it's taking some of my energy with it, though some remains.

"He—he isn't?" I ask.

She nods, then glances at Fred and Tom. The blond leader shakes his head, but Lucia makes the same motion back.

"Korinne, they have him in lockdown still. The Creators believe he orchestrated the escape of you three from Safety. They have his execution scheduled for tomorrow afternoon."

Tom sighs and covers his face with one hand. Fred's eyes widen and he looks back and forth from Lucia to me.

"No—no, they can't," I am saying, but I feel lightheaded. The power inside of me is slipping away as if it's being sucked from me. I can't tell if it's because of the news or if it's just been too long since I was in the sun.

"She's losing it. How long has it been since she left the sunlight?" Lucia asks as she rushes to my side.

"Just over twenty-five minutes," one scientist offers.

The power leaving me feels terrible. I'm even more tired than the first time. I fall to the ground and am hardly aware of the people surrounding me. Then everything goes dark.

24

I wake up to the white ceiling of a small room. My brain tries to focus on what's happening, but it's foggy. I must not have dreamed at all because the last thing I remember was them telling me my dad was going to be killed.

The reminder makes me shoot up on the bed.

They're going to kill my dad, I panic.

Jumping out of the bed, I rush to the door. The moment I throw it open, a woman dressed in camo jumps up.

"Gosh, girl, what are you all bothered for?" she says.

I barely recognize it's Shelly, but I face her when I do, the blood rushing to my head from my quick burst from the bed.

"What time is it? When are they going to kill my dad? Is there a plan to save him?" I'm asking, practically shouting at her.

"Korinne, calm down," she says to me.

Tears are in my eyes now, and I throw my hands out to make her stop approaching me.

"I don't know what they are going to do. Lucia and the others are in Tom's office now discussing what to do. Girl, you were laid down in there, you ought to go back and rest before—"

She doesn't get to finish her sentence before I am running toward Tom's office. Or at least the direction I think his office is. I can't be sure until I see something familiar. I'm confident I at least turned in the right direction once I came out of my room. This is soon validated as I come upon the desk where the man gave us our room keys. He's sitting there today, and he jumps as I run to the door, throwing it open.

My heart races, and only now I realize that I'm very sweaty. It makes the air feel freezing as I run through the halls. I'm breathing hard as I bolt past a couple of men walking and chatting casually. They turn when I bump through them and keep running. I'm not tired, but I know I don't have that power that comes from the sun. However, I don't know what's pushing me forward. I just keep running.

Adrenaline, I remember from our science lessons in Safety. *Safety. My dad. My family.*

I'm cursing in my mind, but only because I don't think I could draw enough air to do it with my mouth. Soon I see the double doors that lead to Tom's office and I'm filled with intense relief. I know I'm safe in this place—at least I have been so far, but getting lost would have been both embarrassing and alarming.

I throw the doors open and step into the carpeted hallway. I notice there are no people here in the waiting area, and I wonder if Tom kicked them out or something. The last time we came, there was at least a secretary sitting at the desk outside his office. Now the room is empty.

Just before I wrench open the door to his office, I notice that the wooden door is ajar. That, and I hear my name.

"Korinne must be left alone. If she finds out any more, she might not handle it well," Tom says.

Find out what? I think, panic rising again in my tight chest.

I'm trying to hold in my breath so I don't gasp and give it away that I'm here.

"When do we leave?" another voice asks. I don't know this one.

"If we are going to gather the forces we need, it's going to take a few hours," this time it's Lucia.

"Leave before morning light, then," Tom says.

"How is this plan going to work? He's in a heavily guarded facility," another unfamiliar voice asks.

It's quiet for a moment, and I can only guess no one has a good answer.

"It has to work," Tom replies, "Blaine has the information and locations of all those affected like him. If our organization is going to liberate these people, we need the information."

"Sir, we could always bring the kids—," Lucia offers.

"No," Tom says, "They shouldn't even know about Blaine. Especially Korinne. She won't be able to function for the next twenty-four hours, I'm sure. And what if she uses her abilities out of anger? We have to learn how to harness them first."

"You think keeping this from her is going to help? She already knows, and she's going to ask—"

Tom's voice cuts over Lucia, speaking again. "Lucia, stop. This is much bigger than you and your daughter. I know you wanted to save her, but by grabbing Korinne and the other tag-alongs, you really messed this up. Blaine might have been able to talk his way out of this, but you took them. Now Safety is on high alert, and Blaine might die for it."

Silence again.

"Permission to stay with my daughter then," Lucia says suddenly.

"Denied," Tom's voice is flat, "you know Safety better than most, and you need to head part of the operation. We need to get through the gates, extract Blaine, and get out. Nothing else. Understood?"

I hear grumbling, but no one argues.

"Get some rest then, you leave at 0200 tomorrow morning." The words carry a finality to them.

Shuffling sounds come through the crack in the door and my heart stops when I realize it means they are headed this way. I panic and almost trip backwards, retreating to the hall. I know I don't have enough time to get out before they see me, so I open one of the double doors from the hallway and turn around, making it look like I just arrived.

I take a step forward right as I see the wood door swing inward.

The first man out is one I don't recognize. My heart beats even faster when I spot him, because he is massive. He has to be at least six and-a-half feet tall. He's bald and has a tattoo of a dragon from the top of his head running down the side of his face.

"Well, speak of the fiery devil, she's here," he says.

"What?" Lucia says, pushing her way past him. The moment she sees me, relief floods her face. "You're up already? Are you feeling okay? You were really out of it," Lucia rushes to my side and kneels.

I feel awkward that she's so close to me, especially after what I just heard in there. That she wasn't supposed to get me, but did of her own accord, makes me feel both good and strangely guilty. Part of it is that she could be the reason my dad is going to die. The anger inside threatens to make me lash out at her, but I push it back.

"Oh, I'm feeling okay. I just woke up and Shelly said you were here, so I figured I'd come see you." I stumble over my words, feeling ridiculous as I say them.

"Why? Is there something else going on?" she asks.

I pause, trying to filter out the things I just heard so I don't accidentally give away the fact I was listening.

"Umm," I say, "my dad—is he going to be okay? Are we going to get him?"

I didn't plan for the tears to come, and I'm embarrassed when they do, but at the same time, it's probably good because they add to the facade of what I'm saying.

Lucia's eyes change and I see something like pity in them.

"Your father will be fine, let's just leave it at that." Lucia squeezes my shoulder and stands.

"Sergeant, thank you for the meeting, let's discuss more later tonight—maybe in my office," Lucia tells the bald man.

He eyes me, then smiles. "Of course, I guess you'd like to spend time with your daughter now that she's awake." He nods and moves back through the other doorway into his office.

"Are you sure you are alright? You look sweaty and pale." Lucia is staring at me again.

"Yeah, yeah, I'm fine, just worried about my dad is all," I say.

The pity returns to Lucia's eyes and she nods in under-standing.

"I think he'll be okay; he's too good of a worker for the Creators to kill for no reason. He had nothing to do with you escaping, and when they find that out, they'll leave him alone," she says.

I'm staring at her face, trying to see any signs of lying, but she must be well practiced, because I can't see a thing. Once again, I'm at a loss for words. Instead, I focus on the plushness of the carpet beneath my feet. I forgot to put shoes on since I just jumped out of bed. The softness is even more exaggerated on my toes now.

"Did you want to get more rest? Or are you good for a little adventure?" Lucia asks me when I say nothing.

Adventure? What could she mean by that? I wonder. So I just shrug and continue inspecting the floor.

"Come on, let me take you somewhere I love to go."

Lucia grabs my hand and leads me out. Just before we do, Tom's voice comes from behind.

"Lucia, don't forget. We need you in the morning," he says.

She sighs, but turns to him and dips her head shortly. "I know, Tom, I'll be there—don't worry."

The blond leader eyes our holding hands, then looks at me and smiles, the worry on his face disappearing and being replaced by the mirth I'd seen before.

"And I'm glad you are doing better now, Korinne. I hope you are enjoying your room," he winks as he speaks.

"Yes, it's good. Thank you," I respond.

He waves goodbye and walks back into his office, the wood door closing with a soft click.

Once he's gone, Lucia eyes me up and down, a thoughtful look on her face.

"We should probably get you something else to wear. You can't be comfortable wearing the same thing you were when I got you from Safety," she says, "I'll have Shelly bring something to you later. I'd do it myself but I've got—things to prepare for. Come on, let's go to my favorite place on base really quick."

Lucia pulls my hand and we exit to the hallway. I try to remember each turn we take, just in case I feel the need to get away from the situation like I did earlier. After four or five turns, I lose track and give up. Every hallway is the same: cement walls and floor, the lights above us are fluorescent and bright like the ones in Safety. One of the more surprising things about being here is that our steps are so quiet. In Safety, you could hear footsteps easily on the grate. Here, there is only the slight echo of the sound on the cement. I almost feel the need to stomp to make things louder, if only just to feel like I'm not sneaking around. If any Peaceholders thought you were sneaking around, you'd get in major trouble, even if you weren't actually doing anything.

Lucia stops at an older-looking door, rust caking the hinges and the door handle. It looks like this might have been an original door that they built the rest of the newer place around. I've not seen anything like it before and I find it far more intriguing than I should. As I look closer at the substance, since I've never seen rust before, Lucia clears her throat.

"Um, it's just a door, Kor," she says.

I jump and turn to her. "Oh—yeah, yeah I know. I just have only heard of rust in school. I didn't expect it to look so—dirty, I guess." I put my hands behind my back and my face flushes.

She smiles and laughs at my reaction. "Come on, we're almost there, just a set of stairs," Lucia pulls the door open, the hinges making a terrible squeaking sound as she does.

I look around, half-expecting Peaceholders with their visors down to rush in and grab me before I enter. Of course that doesn't happen and Lucia gestures through the door.

"After you."

I shake my head. "No thanks, I'll follow you." I take a step backward to clarify that I'm not leading the way.

She furrows her brows, looking confused, then shrugs and walks through the door. Lucia reaches to the side and flips on a switch that illuminates a steep set of stairs with a yellow hue. I note that the lights above are not fluorescent, but are the yellow ones. Despite the light on the stairs, I don't feel comfortable going up them. Still, Lucia forges forward.

I tentatively step into the hallway, on edge that something or someone will pop out at me. When nothing does, I start up the stairs. By now, Lucia is already at the top, waiting at another door. I have no idea how large this compound is, and although I know I haven't been to every part, I sure have run through a fair bit of it. While I'm curious about the size, I've never thought much about it. We already climbed a few staircases to get to this point, so I can only guess how high we are up now. All of the windows are still closed, of course, so I can't see what things look like outside of the building.

"You aren't giving up on me, are you?" Lucia questions me.

I shake my head, but my lungs burn and I am panting. I'm not overweight due to the nutrition and weight management at Safety, but it's not like I'm the fittest athlete, either. I'm definitely not inspiring confidence by the way I'm moving.

"Umm, no I'm okay, just curious where you are taking me," I say.

The only thing on my mind now, save for where we are going, is that Lucia and some other people are going to get my father tomorrow. In my mind, I can only hope that they're successful, but based on the way they were talking in Tom's office, things seem impossible.

"Okay, ready?" Lucia asks.

I nod, though I'm not sure I'm ready.

She turns the knob on the door, this one also rusty and old, and pushes heavily on the door. When nothing happens, Lucia grunts.

"Oh, come on, they didn't seal this while I was away, did they? It's only been a few days since I was up here—"

Lucia continues to throw her shoulder into the door while she speaks and the door finally gives with a loud grinding sound.

"There we go, darn thing." She strides through the door.

Cool air rushes into my face and blows my long, scraggly hair over my shoulders. My stomach clenches when I realize she's taken me outside, and I throw my hands over my face, preparing for the fire to come.

When it doesn't, I peek open my eyes. I soon find out the reason I didn't explode in flames is because the sun is down. I see a dark sky and not much more.

Lucia laughs. "You thought it was day, didn't you? We ought to get you guys a watch or cellphone or something," she replies.

I know what these things are, but they were strictly prohibited for us in Safety. If they caught us using a Peaceholder's phone, or even trying to steal their watches? That was worth an insane amount of demerits. Big ones. The kind that ruin you and your family's lives forever.

"Sorry, I just never cared about when the sun was up until now," I reply, looking outward.

Lucia waves her hand and makes a dismissive sound. "Why are you sorry? It's fine, I get it," she then gestures to me, "come over here, take a look."

I hesitantly move out of the door and into the cool, fresh air. I can't help but close my eyes and suck in a deep breath. When I do, I want to cry. The air is so incredibly clean and soothing. The breeze runs past my face and makes my hair fly out behind me.

This is incredible. I can't believe I'm outside right now, I marvel.

"I can see you are enjoying this," Lucia is covering her mouth and stifling another laugh, "but you haven't even seen it yet."

Seeing where she's pointing, I move to a railing that stands at my waist. As I move to the wall, my eyes widen and I can't help but gasp.

I see bright lights flooding a field of green around us. When I make it to the railing, I stare in awe. Plants, tall and leafy, span into the distance in every direction. They're fields of crops, though I don't know what types they are. The stalks sway in the breeze and the sound they make is soothing. I want to close my eyes and bask in the sound, but I don't want Lucia to laugh at me again. Instead, I turn my gaze downward and almost stumble in fright.

Charred, we are up high, I think, grabbing onto the railing so hard my knuckles turn bright white.

"Woah, are you okay there? You look sick." Lucia puts her hand on my back, steadying me.

Once I stare at the ground far below us a while more, I look up again at the fields. Somehow I can see so much, even though it's dark outside, and I realize that there are lights placed throughout the plants, illuminating them. A road runs through the fields from the building into the distance, but I can't see where it goes. The lights end eventually.

"What do you think? It's so peaceful, right?" Lucia leans on the wall and stares into the distance. She closes her eyes and takes a deep breath, just like I did moments ago. "I come here when I need to think; to let off stress when I'm feeling wound tight."

I want to ask her why she might be stressed, but I expect I know the reason. She wants to stay with me, but they're making her get my father tomorrow.

My father.

I try to focus on the world around me to get my mind off of the conversation I overheard. It's proving more difficult than I thought. While I recede into my thoughts, Lucia does as well. We sit there in silence for some time. I don't know how long, but it feels like a very long time. The breeze flies past me and feels like it goes through me.

"I didn't want to give you up, you know," Lucia suddenly says.

My current thoughts are sucked away at her words.

"Wh—what?" I stumble.

"When you were born, I wanted to keep you with me."

The words smack me hard, as if I've just run into a solid wall. I open my mouth to respond, but have nothing to say. Or, at least, I don't know how to respond.

Lucia continues to stare out at the fields as if she's talking to them, not me. I look at her profile, her reddish-brown hair blowing around. She's wistful, I can tell.

"We never thought we'd have a strawberry blonde baby, but there you came. Your head lit up in the light," she folds her arms and chuckles, "How ironic, don't you think?"

She looks at me and abruptly she seems like a different

person. All I've seen was the hardened, tough-love kind of person since she led us out of Safety. As her eyes meet mine, I see that she's vulnerable. She has tears in her eyes, but they don't fall. For a moment, we just stare at each other, and I see the longing she must feel for a daughter she lost so long ago. Finally, she looks away from me.

"When they did the genetic test for the S12 chromosome and it came back positive, my heart just couldn't take it. I was in love with you the moment I laid eyes on you. Your father and I tried to convince the doctors we'd be careful, that we'd keep you out of the sun. They didn't let us. The government came in and whisked you away without even letting us have a say."

A hardness enters her voice then.

"The government that has lied to us for over a hundred years." Lucia turns to me, a fire in her eyes that wasn't before, as she continues, "And here you are—you've been touched by the sun, and you're thriving. Char, more than thriving."

Another chuckle escapes her lips, and she moves to me, putting her hands on my upper arms.

"Kor, I dedicated my life after that to finding a cure. Even though I had studied English in college for heaven's sake, I dove into science like you wouldn't believe after they took you from me. A decade later, turns out science is not too hard, and it's actually kind of interesting."

Lucia has a far-off look as her eyes connect with something in the distance.

I don't know why she wanted to share all these details with me, but I don't mind. Although, my mind is consumed by one thing.

"But we got you out of there, and I'm so happy to see you are okay." Lucia hugs me tightly, and I let her. It's awkward, but at the same time, the last couple days have been intense, and stressful. I wrap my arms around her and squeeze, reveling in the feeling.

When Lucia pulls back, I hope she'll continue talking about the past, but she doesn't.

"Well, I guess we better get back. I have an early morning," she says, "Tom wants me to meet with him early to discuss what our next steps are with you and your friends."

She is an incredible liar. I try not to dwell on it, because who knows what it could mean about all the other things she said. Still, there is only one question I need to know the answer to.

"What about my father—I mean, my biological one?" I ask, knowing Lucia didn't plan on telling me more. "I mean, don't I have siblings? When will he get here?"

Lucia's face falls, and she clasps her hands in front of her.

"Korinne, your dad—," she pauses when I wince, understanding I am thinking about my father still in Safety and in danger, "—your biological father. He died just two months after we lost you."

She looks at her feet, the grief clear in her face.

"I try not to think about that time. I was lost, confused, and angry. So many emotions threatened to rip me apart. His death only increased my want to get you back, to find a cure for your sickness. There were times men tried to date me, or tried to get me to settle down with them, but I didn't have time. The only thing I had time for was getting you back."

She looks up and smiles through the sadness. "And now I have you back."

I give a half-smile back, but it's hard to smile when I just heard that my real dad died and my other dad is about to get killed. The stress of the memory strikes me and I ball my fists, a mixture of anger and fear, knowing the Creators in Safety are going to kill my dad just because he came across information.

Lucia notices my reaction and moves over to me again.

"Hey, are you alright? You look like you might kill someone." She pushes the hair that hangs over my forehead behind my ear.

Oh char, she can't know that I know about their plan, I think. I don't know if she'd be mad that I heard their conversation, but I don't want to risk it.

"I'm fine, just tired, I guess," I reply, looking down.

She sighs, then nods sympathetically. "Yeah, it's past time for eating. Did you want to go to the mess hall to get some food? Or would you rather eat in your room?" she asks.

The thought of going into a room full of people I don't know to eat makes me want to hurl.

"My room, please," I say.

She cocks her head at my tone, but then shrugs. "Alright, let's get you back to your room, then. You can go to bed early if you want, that exercise earlier really seemed to take a lot out of you."

I think back to the gym earlier and how I felt during the sun exposure and even after. The memory of the power coursing through me is tempting, drawing me to it again. I shake my head and follow Lucia back to the old rusty door and back down the stairs. My thoughts drift to my father and his execution. Then my thoughts run through the hallways of Safety, to Sean and my mother. The thought of them makes my heart ache. Do they know the Creators are going to kill Dad?

How is it possible that I have two sets of parents, and after tomorrow, I still won't have any dads? I think. The anger is boiling inside me again. I don't understand how the Creators and/or the government could lie to us all these years, punish us, use us, and now ruin our families? *Do they really think we are that dangerous? A weapon?*

The last thought makes me freeze in my tracks. I don't realize I'm stopping until Lucia pauses and turns back.

"Uh, are you okay Kor? What's going on?"

I stopped because an idea hit me I didn't expect. A thrill

runs through me and I try to contain it, but I'm having a hard time. The feeling has spread to my face and I know it has, but I can't hide it.

"What's that look for? You look like you just figured out the world's most challenging puzzle," Lucia says, raising one eyebrow.

I just say the first excuse that comes to my head, "Being out here made me realize I'm not stuck inside forever anymore. I can go outside whenever I want."

Lucia grimaces. "Maybe not *whenever* you want. At least until we figure out more of what the sun does to you."

I chuckle, relieved that my distraction landed.

She smiles, then continues leading the way. I follow, but allow the tingly feeling to run through my arms and legs. I let the idea wash over me. The moment I heard they were going to get my dad, I wanted to ask if I could come. The reason I didn't was because I knew they'd say no. Tom already said to hide it from me.

But what if they don't know? I think, clenching my fists again at the thought.

There is no way I am going to live my life without any fathers. I'm going to smuggle myself into their group tomorrow. My thoughts return to the video we watched of me in the courtyard. I see a few guards fire their weapons at the flaming version of me. I'm not sure how I didn't get injured, but I didn't, and here I am. The memory of the sunlight pouring over me, filling me with immense energy, allowing me to go on forever, once again spurs that want inside.

It's not that I don't trust that they can get him before he dies tomorrow, but I have something that they don't. A word enters my brain, one that matches the feeling as well as the outside display of sheer power.

Sunfire.

25

ONCE WE GET BACK TO MY ROOM, I TELL LUCIA I'LL JUST GET MY own food by phone. To be honest, I'm not positive I know how to do it, but I figure I can do something like I did last time with calling Shelly. When I get to my room, I look for some type of instruction manual, but there's definitely nothing here. Right as I remember how the phone offered to connect me to the cafeteria last time, I hear a knock on my door.

I open it, surprised to see Shelly. She offers to run to get me food, and I let her. The moment she leaves, I peek out the door, looking to my left. Slipping out of the room, I walk two doors down, then rap on the door with my knuckles. I'm not sure why I feel the need to be quiet, but I just do.

After a few moments, the door opens and Susan stares back at me.

"Oh, it's you," she murmurs.

My eyes widen in shock. I assumed this was Charlie's room. I was wrong.

"Umm, sorry, I thought Charlie was staying here. I just wanted to see how he was doing," I say, "But you can keep resting."

I turn away, then realize that Susan was also drained yesterday morning after they exposed her to the sun too. I double back and smile at her.

"Are you okay? Were you as beat as I was after getting hit by sunlight?" I ask.

Susan eyes me, her face emotionless. "I'm fine, I slept most of the day."

She looks me up and down before continuing, "What were you going to talk to Charlie about?"

I harden my face, which isn't the right reaction, because she reads it at once. Susan narrows her eyes at me.

"What are you doing? You look like you're up to something," Susan says, folding her arms.

I shrug, trying not to let my face give me away more than it already has.

"I wanted to see how Charlie is doing, that's all. I feel like it's been forever since I've seen either of you and I wanted to make sure everyone's alright," I fold my arms and walk toward his room.

Susan narrows her eyes and follows me out of her room. While I'm turned away from her, I bite my lip. I'm panicked because I know she's going to hear what I want to ask Charlie. Knowing she's going to keep coming, I just move to door number twelve and knock on it. As with Susan's door, it takes a moment for anything to happen. Finally, a tired-looking Charlie opens the door.

"Oh, hey Kor, what's up?" He eyes Susan standing behind me and tilts his head, "And . . . Susan."

Still knowing Susan can't see my face, I widen my eyes and lightly shake my head to tell Charlie I don't want her here. Charlie and I have been friends for years, so he gets the message.

"How are you feeling, Susan? If you're like me, you're worn out and ready for more sleep," Charlie puts his hands in the pockets of his blue pants. I start when I realize he's not wearing the dull grey clothes that we wore in Safety.

How did he get new clothes but Susan and I haven't? I wonder.

I hear Susan make a sound behind me, a cross between a cough and a snort. It sounds painful.

"Yes, I'm tired, but I'm just happy I didn't burn to death," Susan says, sounding amused.

Charlie chuckles and I smile from her obvious joke. I eye Susan, noticing there is mirth in her gaze.

She's actually joking with us, I think, *maybe we can get along someday.*

"Though it did look like we roughed up their gym. So much for allergies," he says, grinning and staring absentmindedly off past us into the hallway.

His smile makes my stomach flutter, and for a moment, I feel lightheaded. My mind shifts to how cute he looks in the new clothes. I struggle to keep my face from showing my infatuation.

Finally able to get myself under control, I get hit with a thought I hadn't considered. This is the first time all three of us —char—the first time *anyone* from Safety has been able to discuss the fact that we were lied to. We can finally discuss the fact that the Creators of Safety convinced us we were in constant danger of dying to the sunlight. It's as if the three of us have something binding us together; a shared secret—not to mention the trauma of the past few days.

I suddenly feel guilty for trying to exclude Susan from the conversation I wanted to have with Charlie. Knowing Shelly will be back with food for me soon, I turn to look back at Susan and say, "I wanted to talk to you both about something."

It's not technically true, but I know they should both be aware of it. Especially if something awful happens.

Susan raises one eyebrow in curiosity and unfolds her arms. "Okay . . ." she says skeptically.

"Here, let's go in Charlie's room to talk more about it," I suggest.

Susan shrugs and walks past me into his room. Charlie raises his arm to let her in. Before I follow her, I glance down the hallway to make sure Shelly or anyone else isn't approaching. Once I'm through the door, I hear the soft click of the latch.

As I walk into his room, I note that it looks the same as mine. It's not that surprising, but it's somewhat disorienting considering there aren't any personal effects to differentiate the living space. I feel like I've just made it back to my room, although it does smell different.

My stomach flutters again at Charlie's smell, and I shake my head to get the thoughts away. When I turn around, I see both of my fellow Safety escapees watching me expectantly. Though it doesn't feel like I have been quiet for very long, their faces suggest otherwise.

I decide I should just get to the point, rather than wasting anymore time before Shelly returns. I speak the words that have been consuming my mind for the past few hours.

"I'm going back to Safety to get my dad." I look into Charlie's eyes when I speak. They widen and his mouth drops.

"Are you insane?!" Susan says, throwing her hands in the air. "Don't you remember what Lucia said about them punishing us?"

To be honest, I didn't expect this reaction from her. I still don't know what Charlie will do. His eyes narrow and he looks me up and down. It's obvious he doesn't approve, and he thinks it's a stupid idea, but he keeps his hands in his pockets while considering this. Meanwhile, Susan continues to sputter things about my being an idiot for breaking rules and leaving on a suicide mission.

I find it ironic that Susan has been so quiet—almost speechless since we left Safety, and now she's suddenly chatty and opinionated.

Charlie finally speaks. "Kor, I don't think that's a good idea. What happens if the Peaceholders—or the Creators for that matter—find out you are back and they try to hold you there?" he asks.

I hadn't really thought about that. Then again, when I decided to go with the group to get my father, I didn't care about anything but making sure he was safe. That hasn't changed.

"They won't get me. I'll hide and make sure they can't," I say matter-of-factly. Though my internal doubts are growing.

Charlie scoffs and shakes his head. "Kor, why would Lucia even consider letting you go back there to get your dad? I mean, you don't even know how to get back to Safety, so what are you going to do about that?"

His questions are very logical, though unfounded. It's then I realize they weren't there eavesdropping on the conversation earlier like I was. I press my lips together, considering what to tell them.

"I . . . overheard Lucia and Tom talking earlier today. They're going to send people to rescue my dad tomorrow morning. I'm going to go with them." As I say it, I realize how stupid it sounds. I'm a fifteen-year-old girl, planning to hide in the car with soldiers who intend to infiltrate a secure facility to get my father. Charlie and Susan must think so as well.

"That's ridiculous, you're going to get yourself caught, or—," Susan's eyes grow distant as she says the next words, "—or get killed."

The words still strike me. Fear blossoms in my chest, but I push it away. Getting my dad back is important, and I know I want to be there to help.

"Why did Lucia even say that you could come? That makes no sense, especially if she cared about you like she's supposed to as a mother," Charlie says, his face full of confusion.

I bite my lip and examine his room, choosing my next

words as best as I can. I notice his bed is messed up. It looks like when we knocked, he pulled the covers up and tried to make it look clean. The carpet beneath me suddenly feels squishy, the fibers going between my toes and up the sides of my feet.

"She didn't say I could come, I'm just going to hide in one of the cars," I reply. I'm suddenly realizing how crazy it sounds.

Charlie leans forward, a shocked look on his face. Susan gasps and I turn to see her put her hand on her mouth.

"Charred, Korinne, that's just dumb," Susan says, shaking her head, "You're going to get in so much trouble—"

I just hold up my hand, stopping her.

"So are you coming with me or not?" I ask Charlie before I eye Susan, posing the same question. He still appears shocked, and he shakes his head.

"Kor, I don't think I need to tell you how dumb that sounds. I mean, they had us in lockdown, and you heard how angry they are that we left. Lucia said they'd kill us if they got us back, and because of it, they are going to kill—"

He stops and looks away from me. I know he was going to say 'kill your father' but he goes quiet, knowing the words will hit hard to me. I finish his sentence for him.

"Kill my father," I say through a hardened jaw, tears brimming in my eyes. "That's the point. It's our fault—*my* fault—that my dad is going to get killed. Who knows who else is going to get killed for this because we left the place that kept us captive for all our lives? I don't care what happens, but I need to get my dad, and I know I can help. Charlie, you may not understand this, but my family is there. I'd do anything for them. I need them back."

I see Susan's jaw harden and she looks at her feet. Mentioning my family and how I'd do anything for them appears to have triggered something in her. She presses her lips and looks back at me. There is longing there now.

My mind shifts back to the blazing fire around me. I recall

the bullets being melted away when they were fired from the guards here at Nugennexx.

I'm struck by the thought of why there are so many guards here. *If this was supposed to be some scientific company to help find a cure for our ailment, then why is it so heavily guarded?* The question is fleeting though, as my mind returns to the task at hand.

"Kor, I'm not sure you should do this. I really think we should let them try to get to your father safely while we stay here."

Charlie's words sting. I can't be surprised; I pretty much dropped in on my best friend to tell him I was going to put myself in a dangerous situation the same day he found out he explodes into fire. Not to mention he's probably exhausted from the experience and still processing being held captive for his whole existence. Still, his words feel like a rejection.

I can't help but let the tears flow now.

"Fine, do what you want, but don't get in my way. If either of you say anything to Lucia or anyone else about this, I'm going to run away, even if it's during the daylight. I'll find my way back to Safety, whether I have your help or not."

"Kor, wait," Charlie reaches out to me, but I turn and glare at Susan.

She looks me directly in the eye. Her face is unreadable, but I wish I knew what she was thinking. As I turn to walk out, Charlie moves forward and snatches my arm.

"I can't let you leave, you have to stay here. I'm going to get Lucia, tell her what you're thinking—" Charlie threatens.

Anger flares up in me and I open my mouth to shout something at him, but Susan has already stepped forward and has her hand on Charlie's shoulder. She pulls heavily, removing Charlie's hand.

"No, let her go. She needs to do this. I—I wish I had the same courage she does, but I don't. Let her go," Susan repeats, more insistent this time.

I stare at her, shocked. Not once has Susan given me any sense of approval or friendship. While it's not direct help, she is showing more support than I could ever hope for.

Though I'm speechless, our eyes lock once more and she gives me a curt nod before pulling Charlie's hand away from me.

I immediately walk out of his room directly to my own. I scan the card I slipped in my pocket, the light turning green and the door clicking. I know Charlie is following me, but I hurry into my room and close the door, flipping the lock. Only moments after, I hear a knock on the door. Charlie says something, but I ignore him. He knocks once more, but doesn't stay much longer.

The tears continue pouring down my cheeks. I don't know why, but I feel betrayed by him. I thought Charlie would be more supportive. Isn't he as angry as I am that the Creators lied to us? That the government has kept us captive for all this time? That they kept us from our families? What if he or Susan say something and get me in trouble?

Somehow, I don't think they will. Not after seeing Susan's turnaround. While they believe my plan is stupid, I trust that they won't tell anyone to get me caught. Still, I wish at least one of them would have wanted to come with me.

Lucia comes into my mind, and I shake my head. I want to get to know her more, and I want to learn about my father and their relationship before and after I was taken. At the same time, I want to save my living father, and my mother and Sean, who are likely in far more danger.

26

The resolve I had earlier to go get my father returns and I stand up, clearing my throat. I move through my room and look around, deciding what to bring with me on the trip. My shoulders slouch when I realize I have nothing except for the clothes on my back. I sit heavily on the bed and listen to my stomach growl, the hunger still eating away at my insides.

After a moment, I hear a knock on my door. I ignore it until I hear the voice with the next knock.

"Korinne? You in there? I brought you food." It's Shelly this time.

My stomach growls at the mention of food and I rush there, practically ripping the door off its hinges.

The smell hits me before my eyes can catch up with the rest. Steam is flowing off of what looks like a pizza and French fries.

Shelly grimaces at the food. "Sorry, I know it's a weird combo, but they are some of my favorites, so I figured I'd just get them both."

Her black hair is still pulled back in a ponytail, her full face exposed.

"It's okay, I'm starving," I say, grabbing the food from her.

She laughs and asks if she can come in. I nod, and we move to the bed to sit.

I notice she has a bag that is full of something. Normally I'd ask what it is, but instead I take a huge bite of pizza, wincing at the heat. My eyes roll back in my head at the salty, savory taste of the cheese, sauce, and bread. Shelly looks amused as she watches me eat.

"Wow, maybe I should have gotten you more," she notes, seeing how quickly I am putting the food away. I blush, but keep eating.

"Oh, and I got you a few other things, some snacks to help tide you over if you get hungry later tonight. The mess hall closes after 8:00, so I grabbed more things for you to have in your room."

She pulls out bits of packaged food, things I don't recognize, and an apple. I take them gratefully and set them on the bed next to me.

"And I also got you clothes, so you can get out of those horrid grey ones." Shelly lifts the black bag I noticed at the door. "It's mostly shirts, jeans, and jackets. Though there are some sweatpants in here so you can be comfortable."

I nod, still eating my food with no thought for manners.

She laughs again and takes out her device, flipping through pages and reading things as she waits for me to eat. As I start to finish up the last few fries, I realize something that makes my stomach drop.

I don't know how to get to the room with the cars in it. When we got here the first night and they directed us to Tom's office, I wasn't paying attention. I know this place is huge, and I could be searching for the vehicle room forever. I feel hopeless my plan will work. Then I eye Shelly and an idea pops into my head.

Trying to not seem too eager, I take my time finishing the last bites of my food.

"Wow, thank you so much for that. I didn't realize how hungry I was until I smelled it." I lean back and sigh.

Shelly smiles and puts her small device away, glancing at me.

"Glad it hit the spot. So did you want to get more sleep? Watch TV or something? I can leave you alone now." Shelly stands up and moves to the door when I grab her wrist.

She pauses and turns to me, seeming thoughtful.

"Actually," I say, choosing my words wisely, "I was thinking it might be nice to get out of the room for a bit. I slept a lot today, so I feel pretty good."

"Okay, cool. We could walk the halls, or go outside for a while? Since it's night," she reminds me.

"Actually, Lucia and I went up on the roof earlier and that was great!" I feel awkward, as if I'm trying too hard, so I pull it back. "Umm, I was wondering if I could see the cars again. I've only even seen them in the videos at our school. They seem really interesting."

For a moment I think I've reached too far because Shelly raises an eyebrow at me. She looks confused by why I would care so much about them. Then her face relaxes and she nods.

"Alright. It's a strange request, but I don't see any harm. Let's do it," she says, standing up.

I once again exit my room and we take the normal path through the hallway. I make a point not to make eye contact with the man at the desk, as if he will be able to read my mind and know the real reason I'm asking Shelly to take me to the room with the cars.

"So—what makes you so interested in cars? You are technically old enough to drive them, you know." Shelly keeps walking down the hall without turning back as she talks. Her black hair is full and bounces with each of her steps. My own thin hair bounces too, but it doesn't look as luscious as hers, even when her is pulled back in a ponytail.

"I hadn't even thought about that. Kids can drive cars?" I ask, taken aback by the fact alone.

Shelly chuckles. "Yeah, with all the high-tech enhancements to cars, they lowered the age from sixteen to fourteen just twenty years ago. I think it's a dumb idea, but what do I know? You're around that age, right?"

I consider the idea of driving, but nod absently. "I'm fifteen, so yeah, I guess I can drive them," I reply.

"Well, there you go. You'd need to learn first before we'd let you behind the wheel." Shelly shrugs, then eyes me, "I guess there isn't harm in admiring the vehicles, if that's the type of thing you are interested in."

As we walk, I'm trying to make a mental note of every turn we make. If I'm going to make it to the room again, I need to remember. My eyes catch those of a soldier standing ready at a door. My breathing increases as my nerves shoot upward. I smile weakly and keep following Shelly.

Why are there so many doors guarded? I wonder, as flashes of Peaceholders in Safety whip through my brain.

I'm so fixated on this sudden thought that I'm surprised when Shelly stops. I don't run into her, but my vision becomes all camo as I come within inches of her back.

"Well, here they are . . . what do you think?"

Shelly is gesturing to an enormous wall, the top of which is completely windows. I walk up to the glass and peer through. Sure enough, I see the various sizes and colors of the vehicles. I admittedly don't know the names of any of them, or what they're used for, but there are about two dozen.

Then another thought hits me. *I don't know which ones they'll take tomorrow. How can I ask without being suspicious?* I wonder.

"Did you want to get closer?" Shelly asks me.

My eyes widen because I'm feeling sheepish about the fact I don't really care about the vehicles, but instead what they are going to be used for tomorrow morning.

"Oh, uh—yeah, sure," I say awkwardly.

Shelly opens the door to the room and waves her hand for me to go before her. As I walk, I tuck my hair behind my right ear. It's a nervous habit I've tried to manage, but haven't been able to get a handle on. Especially since I've left Safety.

"Seems like they're getting some of them ready to go," Shelly notes, pointing to our right.

Sure enough, there are men and women carrying various things and placing them into a few of the vehicles. These are the largest of them all. A few appear to be the size of a bus, the ones we'd seen on the videos about big city life, but they're all brown and musty.

"Hey, Carlos! What are you preparing for, a war?" Shelly asks, laughing out loud.

One man, also dressed in camo, looks up from a clipboard.

"I guess you haven't heard then, have you? Lucia is heading a charge to get one of the citizens. Seems he's in some nasty trouble back in Safety. We're going on a rescue trip."

My face pales at his words. *Oh no, oh* no, I think. My hands are instantly clammy and I don't know what to say. *Shelly is going to know I asked her to bring me here so that I could stow away. She's going to catch me and I'll lose my chance to hide in the trucks and—*

Shelly tenses and I see her look down at me from the corner of my eye.

"Oh, yeah, I heard he was in trouble. Good luck, then!" Shelly nods to them and I feel her hand on my back. She ushers me out of the room and back into the hallway. When we get out, she looks at me with pity.

"I'm sorry, I didn't realize your father was in that much danger. They've kept me out of the loop since they have tasked me with taking care of you and your friends. You doing okay?" She seems genuinely worried.

I open my mouth to speak, to say I'm sorry for planning to

stow away, but then I realize she's not asking me why I thought I'd go with them, she was just asking how I feel about it. Relief rushes through me and I try to recover from my panic just moments ago.

"Uh—I—," *the fact that I'm at a loss for words might be an advantage*, I realize now, "—yeah, I'm just worried about him. Is he really in that much trouble that they have to go get him?"

Shelly's mouth presses into a line and she nods. "I guess so, but I can't say I know much more. Look, you must be tired. Let's make sure you're all settled. You take a shower and I'll keep you company until you get to sleep, okay?"

I allow the fear of my father's death to bring water to my eyes. I close them to squeeze a tear out deliberately. It's not much, but it perhaps is enough for her to believe me.

"Okay, let's go," she urges, her hand nudging me forward.

Just before we go, I turn to see once more what the cars look like that they'll take.

Those will have to be where I hide, I think.

Before too long, we are back at my room and Shelly is sitting next to me on the bed.

"So, did you want me to get you more snacks? Would you want to watch TV?"

I shake my head, trying to think of a way to get her to leave.

"I think I just want to be alone, is that okay? Maybe I'll take a shower and just get some sleep," I say.

Shelly smiles and nods. "Okay, that sounds good, I'll just hang out outside your door, doing paperwork on my phone and whatnot."

I try not to panic again. If she's going to stand outside of my door, then I can't get out to hide in the cars.

"Um—no, it's okay. I bet you are super hungry. How about you just go eat and hang out with your friends?" I suggest.

I feel ridiculous telling a grown woman to hang out with

friends, especially since I don't even know if she has any. Still, it's the only thing I can think of.

She chuckles. "So you want to get rid of me, then?"

The fear once again strikes me and I bite my tongue, trying to keep myself from shaking or giving anything away.

"I get when a girl needs to grieve alone. I won't bother you. Hey, if you need anything—" she reaches into her pocket and pulls out a device, one like I've seen the others use, "—take this, at least." She hands me a flat and black rectangular box. I hold it in my hand and just stare at it. Shelly raises an eyebrow at my reaction.

"It's a phone, it's not that scary," she jokes.

I startle with realization. "Oh yeah, of course—yeah. We saw the Peaceholders with them every once in a while. I guess I just never thought about how they work," I admit.

Shelly reaches over and takes it from me before turning the bright screen toward me.

"See the numbers? Just hit 14435, then it will open."

I do as she says, my fingertips gingerly touching each number. When I'm done, the screen changes and I see a bunch of squares. There are pictures of people, and I can only guess that it's pictures of employees who work here.

"This is my old standard-issue device. I was supposed to turn it in last week, but I got a little busy. How about you hold onto it, just until tomorrow? If you need me, just hit that one right there," she points to a picture which is clearly her own.

"Okay, yeah—thanks," I say.

She smiles, then stands. "Well, I'll do what you say, I'll grab food and hang out with my friends," Shelly holds her two fingers on each hand in the air and bends them down in time with the last part of her sentence. With that, she turns and leaves the room.

I sigh with relief and move to the door. Peering through the hole there, I see she is still standing there. I hurry to the bathroom and flip on the shower, making a point to loudly close the curtain. After a few moments, I see her move away from the hole and hear her footsteps padding away.

I know I don't have a lot of time before someone else might come down the hallway toward my room, so I rush to the bed. I see the bag Shelly brought me with clothes and I rip it open. Ruffling through the cloth, I am overwhelmed by all the different colors and types of fabric. In Safety it was all the same, grey, yet soft. The idea of putting on something other than grey not only scares the char out of me, but makes me feel like I might stick out in the crowds.

Shaking my head, I try to remember I already do stick out in the hallways. Not only am I wearing the ghastly grey clothes from before, but I probably smell and I'm probably the youngest person here, except for Charlie and Susan.

I glance at the running shower and decide I can clean up quickly. After the warm shower, I move back to the clothes and dump them out on the bed. The nerves running through from earlier have made me tired. It's as if the cushion of the mattress is calling to me, making me want to lie down and get some sleep, but I shake it off, knowing I need to get out of the room and into a car.

I finally land on blue pants made of some stiff woven materials. They have the name Levi on them and I wonder if they took these clothes from some guy to give them to me. I blush at the idea of wearing boys' clothes. If they are for boys, they fit me well. There is also a black shirt that is thick and has some type of hat attached to it. It isn't until it's on me that I realize it's like a sweater.

I pull the pouch attached at the neck over my head and see how it comfortably covers my hair. Looking in the mirror, I am suddenly aware of how much I stand out with the shirt pouch covering my head and face. I pull it back and instead try to tame the wild strawberry blonde hair. I somehow get it into a ponytail and grab a cap with a logo on it. I don't know what NYU stands for, but I put the cap on anyway.

I leave the other clothes on the bed, grab the snacks Shelly brought, and pack the empty backpack. As I toss it on my shoulder, I spot the phone Shelly left with me. I almost leave it, worried that my lack of idea on how to use it might get me caught or in trouble, but I just snag it and put it in the pocket of my pants.

Before I can change my mind, I'm out the door in the hallway. Part of me wants to knock on Charlie or Susan's door to make sure they really don't want to come, but I just shake my head and walk down the hall. To my relief, the man isn't at the reception desk this time. Pulling open the door to the main hallway, I see there isn't anyone mulling about, and figure this is my chance.

I pause just outside the door to the guest rooms and close my eyes, mentally remembering the way to the car room. As soon as it enters my mind, I'm off. When I round the first corner, I jump when I realize the windows in the hall aren't covered anymore. My skin crawls at the thought of me sneaking around when I suddenly burst into flames, scorching the hallway or the surrounding people.

I slowly make my way through the hall, hugging the side opposite the window, when I breathe out a sigh of relief. There is only darkness beyond the glass. I have no idea how I managed to forget, again, that it's still dark outside. This day flew by far quicker than I could have expected.

Then I'm there. I see the wall made of half windows and peek around the corner to look inside. There doesn't appear to be anyone in there, but the lights are still on above. Just when I open the door to the room, I hear voices echoing in the halls behind me. Panicked, I throw myself through the door and dash to the side where the big transporters and the smaller vehicles sit. These aren't small, per se, but they can't fit forty people like the big ones. These look like a boxier version of the five-person car we used to get out of Safety.

Safety, I think, *I can't believe I'm trying to get back there.*

I rush to the closest car and look in the back window. There are supplies there covered in a blanket. I put my hand on the door and realize that I have no idea how to get it open, let alone unlocked.

I can't hear the voices anymore now that the door is closed, but I imagine they will come into view any moment and will see me trying to stow away in the car. My hands reach around the back of the car, shaking as I feel like I'm about to be caught. I suddenly see a black handle with a space below, about the size of a hand. Desperate, I reach under and pull the lever. The door pops upward with a thud and a wave of relief floods through me.

The back is filled with boxes covered with a blanket. I see there isn't much room, but I do find a seat-like spot on a few boxes where I can sit. Sliding in, my side gets jabbed on a hard and pointy object. Pain rushes up my side and I grit my teeth. I look down to see it's the butt of some type of gun. I stare at it, but pull my legs up into the small seat and yank the door down behind me. The spot isn't large, but I fit in just fine. Though the boxes cut into my back and butt, I can't complain because I made it into the car after all.

We will see how I feel in the morning, I think.

Sound gets muffled in here. I can't describe how I know, because there wasn't any sound outside of the car, but my ears feel like the pressure has changed in the air and I can't hear as well. I moved the blanket that was covering the things in the back of the car, so I pull the edge of it back toward me so it falls over my head.

I still can't believe I made it here without being stopped or seen, but it worked. I only hope the cameras that are likely hung up all over didn't make me appear too suspicious.

Now that I'm here, the tiredness rolls over me. I close my eyes and shift to get comfortable. Before I can let my mind drift, however, I remember the cell phone Shelly gave me. When I pull it out, I put in the number she told me to unlock the device. A few pictures of people come up, and I see the one of Shelly. For some reason, I feel like I betrayed her by not telling her my intentions, but it's too late now. I don't get the feeling Tom will be particularly happy with what I'm doing either.

At the bottom of the screen, I see a picture of something I don't recognize. It's a box with a circle in the center and a line coming out of the top corner. Part of me wants to push it, but another part stops because I don't want to do something that might make me get caught.

Putting my head back against the hard box behind me, I try to doze. Still, my curiosity gets the better of me. I lift my head up, open the phone, and tap the button at the bottom. Immediately, a sound erupts from a speaker somewhere on the device, and I jump, cursing as my side digs into the hard edge of the box next to me.

"—supplies packed, but I hope it's enough," a voice says.

I jump and drop the phone, but the sound doesn't stop there.

"And the extra weapons? We don't know what we'll need to get into that compound," someone responds.

My eyes widen when I recognize it's Lucia's voice coming out of it this time.

"Yes, ma'am, it's all there. Do you think we'll need it?" the former voice responds.

A pause.

"I hope not, but if the Creators don't let us in with our story, we'll have to force ourselves in. Blaine can't die, the information he holds is too valuable," Lucia says.

Her next words make me want to hide.

"If they don't let us in, we'll force our way in, and heaven help us if we have to do that."

I immediately push the side button like Shelly showed me and the sound goes off. I'm not sure how I tapped into a live conversation between them, but I regret it.

Is that why Lucia wanted to bring me and the others? To blast our way into Safety if they didn't let us in?

My insides buzz at the thought that I could make a difference, although I shudder at using my powers for destruction. *What if I hurt someone?* I think.

Even though I'm uncomfortable, I feel myself drifting off to sleep. Before I let it happen, I make sure the blanket is secured over me. I just pray that in the morning, there isn't anything else that needs to get packed in the back.

Finally, my eyes droop and sleep pulls me in.

27

A LOUD SOUND WHIPS ME FROM MY SLEEP, AND I GASP.

"What was that?" a strange voice sounds from somewhere to my side.

My mind is spinning for a moment as I try to understand where I am. It's dark around me and I'm hot and sweaty. Something sharp is pressing into my back and also on my right side.

"It sounded like—oh I don't know . . . maybe I should check the back?" an unfamiliar voice replies.

I hear one of the car doors open, but a woman's voice speaks. "Aw, don't worry about it, we're probably just hearing things."

"Fair enough, you're the boss-driver," the man replies before I hear the car door slam shut and his voice re-enters the vehicle. "What are we carrying back there, anyway?"

The car roars to life and begins moving. The sound of it running makes it hard for me to make out exactly what they're saying. Still, I focus my attention so I can hear them.

"—said it was extra weapons for—" we move over a bump and the boxes around me rub together, making me lose audio on them again. " . . . think we really need them? How much actual fighting—" the voice is interrupted by another bump.

"Look I don't know," the woman is speaking again, "but I guess it won't be bad to have them around."

I peek out of the blanket and look through the back window. The ceiling of the room with the cars is passing overhead, the bright lights flashing through the small gap I can see through. Suddenly, the lights are gone.

"Hey man, I appreciate you being the one to come with me, but I don't feel like talking. It's freaking early right now and I just want to be in bed. How about you get some shut-eye while you can? We are several hours away," the woman states.

"Fine, but if you fall asleep at the wheel and kill us, I'm going to be annoyed at you," the man teases. She snorts, but then there's silence.

I sit there, the thoughts of what I just did flying through me like electricity.

What am I doing? I worry. When I decided to come to help rescue my dad, I didn't realize that I would actually be able to. Sure, I did my best to not get caught, but I guess there was a part of me that thought they'd catch me and I wouldn't make it.

Now I'm in a random vehicle with people I don't know, heading back to the place that held me and my family captive for my entire life. *And* I'm sitting on a char-ton of weapons.

My eyes shift downward, and I shudder. I have no idea how they work, but the idea that I'm hiding on top of a bunch of things that can take someone's life freaks me out.

I suck in a deep breath and try to focus on being calm. I think about the conversation I had with Charlie the night before, when he told me he wouldn't come.

The anger and sadness that hits me makes me shy away from the memory. Instead, I think about my family. It feels like ages since I've seen my parents and Sean. I can't even remember how long it's been, because without my normal schedule and speakers to tell me where I need to be, I have a hard time keeping track.

I jump at the sound of the radio being turned on. My heart races for a moment before I calm it down.

I wonder what my family will think when they realize they've been held captive their entire lives—that they aren't allergic to the sun. *Instead, it powers them up like a light switch and—*

My eyes shoot open and I slap my hand over my mouth to keep from gasping again. I didn't realize I had closed my eyes at all, but I look upward out the back window above me. *If the sun pours through the window, I'll light on fire*, I think.

I remember Tom said they were leaving in the early morning, but I know nothing about the sun. What if the sun comes up while I'm back here and I get hit with the light? What happens when weapons get lit on fire?

My stomach twists, and I think I might vomit. I hold it in. As calmly as I'm able, I reach up to the blanket above me, pulling it down to cover as much of me as possible.

Before long, I'm letting my mind flip to things I remember from Safety, just to pass the time. I think about my mother and what would happen if she met Lucia. I think about my dad and whatever information Lucia and Tom say he has that they need. I think about my old room and the electric shock from the bed that gets us up in the morning. While I'm grateful to know what I know now, there is a longing for the familiar, for the things I know. Until now, I'd not known anything else.

I'm consumed by my thoughts, realizing I've not had any moments to just sit and think. I didn't realize I had so much to think about. Now, as I'm hiding in the back of a car, it all comes rushing out. My trip from Safety felt like a long time before, so I'm surprised when I hear the woman speak again.

"Hey, Reg, we're about twenty minutes out. You ready?" the woman asks.

I hear a grumble and some groaning from the man. "Ugh, why did you have to wake me up already?"

She laughs. "Well, be glad, because it gives you time to wipe up that drool and slap your cheeks." The man curses in response.

How did we get here so fast? The drive felt so long when we left, I think.

Then again, I fell asleep pretty quickly after we left the Nugennexx compound, so I don't know how long it was. My nerves flare up again. In my thinking, I'd calmed myself down by focusing on memories and thoughts of what happened over the past couple of days. Now that we're so close, I'm panicking again.

I realize I didn't come up with any plan in all my thinking. I grit my teeth and think about what happens when we get there. *I can't just jump out of here and run into Safety, can I? And what happens when the sun comes out?*

As if hearing my thoughts, the man speaks. "Oh good, the sun is rising, that'll help me wake up."

I peek out from the blanket and see the small bit of sky through the back window is lightening. I calm myself by breathing in and letting it out slowly. Pulling the cover over me more tightly, I duck my head and close my eyes. I have no idea if the sun coming up is enough to make me explode in flames, or if the sun has to hit me directly, but I still hide as much as I can under the blanket.

A little more time passes, then I feel the car rolling to a stop.

"And just like that, we're here," the woman says.

"Gretch, do you really think this is a good idea?" the man named Reg asks.

"Dude, we don't have a choice, we're here. Lucia's going out to talk to the border control."

Hearing the words makes me want to throw the covering off my body and look out the window, but I hold back. I imagine the sun pouring in through the window somewhere and me accidentally landing myself inside of it.

Silence again.

"Well it doesn't look like it worked," Gretch says, "Lucia is heading back to the cars."

I hear a crackling, then a voice comes from somewhere else. The voice is Lucia's.

"Yeah, they aren't going to let us near the front. Transports two and three head to the west entrance; try to be diplomatic and see if you can gain entrance there. If not, pull back and call me on the radio. Maybe the side entrance isn't as heavily guarded and we can get in with our ID badges."

The car turns off.

"So we're just gonna wait? That's boring," Reg complains.

"What, you want to just run up there, guns blazing? I don't think that would go over well," Gretch sighs. I hear a whirring sound before a rush of fresh air blows onto me under the blanket.

"Geez, it's a chilly morning, isn't it?"

The woman laughs. "It's honestly not, I think it feels amazing. You spend too much time inside, I guess." I hear her breathe in deeply.

Suddenly there's another sound, an echoing voice.

"There will be no experiments on the citizens until further notice. Maintain lockdown. Personnel may not enter Safety at this time."

My senses perk up at the sound. It's the same voice I've listened to all my life. There must be speakers on the outside of the building. Of course I've never thought about this, because I was always inside.

"Huh, surprise, surprise, they won't let us in. What was Lucia thinking bringing us here? When they saw all of us, they probably locked up even tighter," Reg scoffs.

I hear a thud and who I assume is Reg complaining. "What was that for—?"

Gretch cuts him off. "Do you even realize why we're here? The man we came to get holds information that can help us liberate every one of these people. They've been lied to and imprisoned their whole lives. Get over yourself and just shut up."

Before I can think much more about this, I hear the crackling sound again and a voice.

"*Lucia, do you copy?*" I hear more static and then, "*—really bad—saw you coming—faster now—*"

I hear Reg say something, but Gretch shushes him quickly. I can't be sure where this voice is coming from, but my eyes snap down to the old phone Shelly gave me and I am tempted to turn it on to see if that's what it is. I resist, knowing that if I'm wrong I could reveal myself.

"*This is Lucia. Do you copy, can you hear us? The connection is unstable, over.*"

When Lucia speaks, a warmth eases its way through my chest and limbs. I can't say I'm one hundred percent comfortable with her yet, but she's been the only constant since we left Safety.

"*Lucia—Blaine—execution—*"

Lucia's voice comes over again, but this time, she sounds frustrated.

"*Soldier, we can't hear your words. What is it? Is Blaine not here anymore?*"

Silence for a moment. Static starts again.

"*Blaine—execution moved up. Not this afternoon—ten minutes.*"

My whole body goes stiff. I know what I heard, but my brain is denying it. Lucia and Tom said his execution was scheduled for later this afternoon, but did that man just say he only had ten minutes? *Ten minutes.*

"Holy char, we need to get in there," Gretch says.

I hear a weapon load and the car doors open, but I'm hardly

listening. My dad's face swims into my mind's eye and I can't think of anything else but saving his life.

My body moves without me controlling it. I throw the blanket off myself and push on the door next to me. When nothing happens, I quietly growl in frustration, searching for a handle. I finally notice a black thing that looks similar to the ones we saw on the door of the car we took to the Nugennexx compound.

The moment I step out of the car, the sun hits my skin. Heat explodes up my arm, but this time I accept it and open my mind to it, letting it course through every inch of my body. My skin hasn't erupted in fire yet, but it burns intensely inside.

Then, I smile.

Hello there, friend, I think, greeting the encroaching power.

28

THE NEXT THING I HEAR IS CURSING TO MY RIGHT. MY HEAD SPINS in that direction, moving much more quickly than I expect it to. My reflexes are faster than usual, my brain processing things more rapidly.

A woman who can only be Gretch stares at me, eyes wide. "What on earth—how did you get here?" She raises her weapon and points it at me. "Honey, this ain't the place for you to be. You ought to—"

Crackling comes over Gretch's phone and I hear Lucia again. *Engage! Get in there NOW!* Lucia says over the system.

I look down at Gretch's belt where the phone sits, and she follows my gaze.

"Oh, no no, don't you even think—"

I release the fire within. The flames spread almost instantly over every inch of my body. Letting it go is both relieving and somewhat overwhelming.

Gretch says some choice words, then fumbles for her phone. "Lucia! Got a situation here at the west door, the girl snuck in and—"

I don't wait for the last words. Instead, I vault past her,

making the woman soldier yelp and dive to the other side of the car where Reg is standing with his weapon toward me as well.

I know she'll move, but at the same time, I didn't care if she did. My mind has locked onto getting my dad. I know I can't lose him. I shake my head, coming back to reality, trying to get ahold of the blazing power inside. Part of me fears it will make me ruthless, validated by the thought I just had about Gretch, but I force it down, focusing on the one thing I need to do.

Ahead of me, I see there is one of the large transports which likely holds a dozen or more men. I don't know if any of them will stand in my way, but I hope they don't. I look at the sun and smile, taking a deep breath before I focus forward.

Before me stands a tall fence with sharp metal jutting out at the top. Beyond that, a metal wall, and beyond that, who knows?

There are double doors going through each of the two barriers. I know I don't have too much time to calculate how to get through, so I just follow my instincts. Holding up my hand, I focus on the heat in my palm, hoping something actually happens. When a ball of fire appears, the thrill flares up in my chest.

At my will, a mass of flames about the size of my head springs out of my outstretched palms and slams into the entrance of the fence, the metal exploding into hundreds of pieces. I guess I wasn't expecting explosive fire, but I'm feeling pretty elevated; *I wonder if my mood affects the intensity of my fireballs*, I think.

That's when the alarms begin. Red lights flash around the building and roof, and men and women shout.

More cursing from behind, though this time it's Lucia's voice I hear over a radio. "*Stop her! Stop her now! They'll kill her!*" She sounds panicked.

Hearing the tone of her voice breaks me a little inside. I can tell she cares for me, though I don't understand why. She never really knew me. Tears well up in my eyes, knowing I am likely putting myself in immense danger.

But I can't let him die, I think.

I walk toward the fire which is now blazing on the ground around the broken door. The second door crumples as easily as the first. Before I walk through it, I look down the length of the metal wall on either side. There are guards running toward me, black visors down, the same brown uniform I have stared at my entire life. They raise their weapons toward me and I hear explosions, loud popping from the guns.

My stomach clenches at the sound, yet I feel—nothing.

Either their aim is terrible, or . . . I think.

Sure enough, I see a flash as something hits my blazing skin and disappears. Deciding I shouldn't wait, I hold out my hand and let more power flow outward. Men and women scream as intense heat flies at them. Then I jump through the now-broken gate in front of me.

I see the grey stone building a hundred paces away. There is a door there, and two guards are shouting something while holding up their weapons. I grit my teeth and fling more flames in their direction. They dive out of the path.

Gunshots ring in my ears, but this time it's from behind. I whip around to see Gretch and a dozen other soldiers behind her.

"If we can't stop you, we'll at least back you up," Gretch yells over the alarm. "Get us in there girl!"

A smile spreads on my face. I feel better knowing I have them behind me. When I reach the door, however, the fire dies out on my skin. I look up to see that the building is shading me from the sun. It's just like before. The sun stops touching me and the fire goes away.

A bit panicked, I search inward for the power. I sigh in relief when I find it still blazing away. Rather than blast this door in, I walk up to it calmly and put my hand on the handle. It melts instantly, the door scorching on the surrounding metal.

"When we get in, fan out, find Blaine and let's get him out of here," Gretch says. She points to people and begins grouping them.

I don't wait any longer before I push into the room. The second I step through the door, I hear guns firing down the hallway, followed by screams. I freeze as I remember that the fire no longer protects me. My head snaps to the right to see three Peaceholders leveling guns at me.

"Freeze, now! Or we'll drop you!"

The rage takes over again and I throw my hands out in their direction. A blast of energy warps the air between us and slams into them, throwing them backward. The woman's uniform on the left starts on fire and she yelps, rolling on the ground.

The Peaceholder in front curses and yells something into a black box. "Breach, west door, it's one of them! Repeat. It's one of the lemmings, need backup, NOW." Then he raises his gun and fires.

A searing pain erupts in my shoulder and I scream out, my brain trying to process what just happened. Putting a hand to my shoulder, warm liquid pours through my fingers. My stomach turns when I see blood.

The Peaceholder stands, smirking. "Well, well, you aren't invincible like we thought. Time for you to—"

Gunshots ring from behind, and I squeeze my eyes closed and turn away.

"Char it all, Lucia's going to kill me," Gretch says. I realize it was her that shot and not more Peaceholders.

The pain is blinding and I am crying, but the power is still blazing inside. Somehow I know I can use it. The unlimited energy is urging me to use it. I focus the heat on my shoulder and it collects there, burning with an intensity of its own.

Then the pain is gone. I move my hand to see the wound isn't there anymore.

"Okay, now that's just charred cool," Gretch replies.

"We gotta go now, they'll be swarming here soon," she says, nodding to me.

I nod back, then take a moment to inspect how I feel inside. The heat is still there, but it feels slightly depleted. I recall how it lasted such a short amount of time before, and suddenly I'm even more uneasy. Gretch is giving orders to the other soldiers, but I'm not listening.

It's going to end soon. *I have to find him*, I think.

"Lucia said he's being held in—sector 23B of the compound. Do you know where that is?"

I shake my head, despair creeping into my body.

A man next to her cocks his weapon before speaking. "Then I guess we'll just have to ask," I recognize the voice as Reg's.

My mind whirls, thinking about how big this place is. If we only have ten minutes, even less now, we can't just run around.

I think about the experiments and the rooms hidden below. It's kind of a long shot, but I don't know where else to look.

"We need to get to the mess hall, there are rooms hidden in the hallway floors, maybe that's the right place," I say.

"The experiment rooms?" Gretch asks, "Why would they hold him there?"

The tears well, but I hold them back. At this point, I can't help but shout.

"We don't have much time to wait, we have to find him," I say pleadingly.

I shake my head and wipe the tears away. Drawing on the heat inside, I let my body move, using the seemingly unlimited energy. The speed at which I vault forward even shocks me.

I'm not sure where to go, but I know we need to move. My eyes are flipping side to side, looking desperately for something that is familiar. I've lived here my entire life, so I know the places I've been to a lot, but this is unfamiliar.

A sign above points to the right and says 'Citizen Housing.'

I immediately turn, rushing down the hall. Just before the door at the end, I see a single armed Peaceholder. He shouts while I run at him, but I thrust my hands out, the same wave of heat energy as before knocking him backward into the door. He collapses.

Something inside of me twists at the sight of him falling like that. Part of me hopes I haven't killed him or the others, while another part screams in my head that they deserve it—for my dad, for my family, for the entire lie.

When I get to the door, it's locked. There isn't a handle on this one, and I take a minute to remember everything here is automatic and requires an access bracelet. Sure enough, there is a black pad to the right of the door waiting to scan one. Without hesitation, I put my hands out, willing the heat to build there. Before I can let it out, I feel a firm hand on my shoulder.

"Hey there, pyro, let's not blow everything up in here, okay?"

I turn to see that it's Reg with a big grin on his face. "While it's cool to see you go all fireball, let's try not to hurt any innocents if we can avoid it," he says.

He leans around me and scans an access bracelet he has clutched in his hand.

"I snagged one of the scientist's access chains you knocked out back there, so this hopefully will get us wherever we need to go," he slides past me as the door hisses open, peeking around the corner. He nods and waves his hands forward over his shoulder, beckoning us to follow.

The hallway we enter feels so familiar. Just twenty paces to my right is the doorway to my family's housing unit. I turn left to see the scratches in the metal wall a few paces away to make sure it's the place I think it is. When I see them, everything shifts into place. It's as if my life has been a giant unknown for the past few days. I have seen nothing or any place remotely familiar since we ran out of Safety those days ago. Now I know where I am. Now I know where to go.

An urge shoves its way into my mind to go check on my family—to go into the housing unit to see if they are there, but I shove it down. I'll get my dad first, then I'll see them.

"I guess we split up and try to find him," Reg says before I hold up my hand.

"No need, I know where to go," I respond, confidence flaring, "Just try to keep up."

Gretch and Reg share a look only moments before I barrel to the left down the metal hallway. The pounding of the grate beneath my feet is loud and familiar. The fluorescent lighting below and above it is somewhat soothing.

Suddenly, the speakers above crackle and the same voice speaks.

"Code black; intruders in the west wing, citizen housing floor one. Engage all hostiles, remove the threats immediately."

"Uhhh, please say that's someone else they are announcing and not us," Reg says.

I don't answer, because he knows what I'll say.

Grinding sounds echo through the metal hall. They sound familiar to the ones I heard back at the compound where Lucia took us. When I try to find the source, I see there are barriers coming down slowly from the ceiling on various parts of the hallway.

Oh no, no, no, I am thinking, panic rising in me.

"Faster!" I shout, pushing myself, feeling the energy inside surging through my arms and legs. I hear gunshots behind me and grunts as well. I easily make it through the closing barrier in the hallway, then turn to see Reg and Gretch trying to catch up. Reg ducks under it just in time, but Gretch has to fall down and slide under.

The wall closes with a thud.

I realize all the other men and women with us are now trapped in there with the Peaceholders.

It's my fault, I got them killed, I think, *but I have to get him.*

"Okay, note to self, don't slide on metal grating. That sucked," Gretch complains.

I whip around, checking to see the damage. Fortunately, the barriers only came down behind us, though I know it will be a short time before more start closing.

"Come on!" I say, turning to run again.

More cursing from my companions, but they keep pace.

I round the corner and almost barrel into a group of adults and teenagers in grey clothes. They gasp and back away toward the wall.

"Sorry!" I say, stopping abruptly.

They cower against the wall, some of them eyeing the guns in the hands of the two soldiers behind me.

Then I hear my name. "Kor? I'll be charred, it's you."

I know the voice, and a strange sensation fills me. Sean stares at me, standing next to my mother, who is crying and has her hand by her mouth.

"What—what did they do to you? What are you wearing?" my mother asks. Without being able to stop myself, I run into her arms and hug her.

She grunts in pain and tries to push away. "Ugh! Korinne! That hurts!"

I remember then that I'm filled with the power of the sunlight and back away.

"You probably bruised me," she complains, then her eyes dart behind me, "what's going on, why are we being told to secure ourselves in classrooms?"

I open my mouth to speak, but pause when I hear the

speakers in the mess hall to my right. I can barely make out the words, but they are instructing everyone there to evacuate the halls and head to secure classrooms.

I see a flood of grey-clothed people heading into hallways, their kids directing them to their classes.

I didn't know what time it was, but I realize it's breakfast time based on how many people are coming out.

"No time! Sean, go to your class, we'll get you later. I have to save dad!" I say, turning away.

My mother grabs my hand and flips me back toward her. "Where is Blaine? What's going on?! Is he okay?"

I see the same fear in her eyes that I probably had when I heard the Creators had him imprisoned.

"Not now—I will come get you later. Please, just get some-where safe," I say.

Just then, I hear Gretch's phone crackle and an unfamiliar voice comes on.

"Peaceholders exiting on the east doors, they are opening fire!"

Popping sounds come through before the speaker's connec-tion goes out.

Another voice comes on: *"South side as well—we are getting heavy fire here."*

Then Lucia comes on. *"Defend, but don't rush in! Keep as many as you can busy from the outside while we rush in the north entrance. We have a lot to get through, but we'll do it."*

I remember the voice on the speaker saying to engage the hostiles, but I didn't think about Lucia and her group.

"Numbers are heavy here. On second thought, we might not get in," Lucia says.

"We're locked out on the east as well, there is no getting in there, should we retreat?" The same unfamiliar voice says.

Gretch holds it to her mouth and speaks rapidly. "West side convoy is in Safety, we are being led by the fire girl, over."

A moment of silence before Lucia comes on. She sounds

angry. Around her voice is the popping of gunshots. "Did you just say 'fire girl?'" She curses. "Korinne is with you?!"

Gretch winces at Lucia's tone, but speaks into the phone. "Affirmative, she's leading the way," Gretch responds.

Lucia speaks some more choice words before addressing me. "Korinne, I'm going to kill you when we get out of this, how did you get here?—shoot!"

Lucia is gone for a moment and while she is, I see my mother looking between me and the two uniformed people behind me.

"What does 'fire girl' mean, who are these people? What's going on?"

Gretch's phone interrupts us with more sounds. "*You have to be kidding me*," Lucia says.

The sound stays on for a moment while we hear explosions and other sounds far bigger and louder than guns. I realize I not only heard them on the phone speaker, but also echoing quietly down one hallway.

Lucia comes on again, in a more frantic tone. "Korinne, you got your friends to follow us too?! Girl, you are in so much trouble." We hear more rocking explosions. "*And yet, I could kiss you. They're getting us in.*"

A warmth fills my chest at her words. It's not the same as the power that is flowing through me still, but one of love and friendship. She said 'my friends'.

Charlie, Susan—they came, I think.

And suddenly things feel more possible.

29

REALIZING CHARLIE AND SUSAN ACTUALLY SUPPORTED MY PLAN doesn't last long before the urgency returns. I know we must only have minutes before they kill my father. My mother and Sean try to stop me, but I turn to run past them. My father never told me where his exam rooms are, but I figure there can't be that many of them. Still, I'm feeling hopeless that we'll find him in time.

Gretch and Reg follow behind. I can't run as fast as I was before, because of the masses of people around us. We weave in and around them, the noise of the many feet pounding on the grate below.

Before long, we reach the hallway where my exam room is. All of the people are going the other way, so the hallway is mostly empty. I slide to a stop as two Peaceholders make eye contact with me. I grit my teeth and back up.

"Halt! Stop there, or we'll shoot!" one of them says, holding up his gun.

Screams echo behind me as the innocent citizens of Safety see the guns and hear the words. They are further down the hallway, but I'm positive that no one is prepared to hear the words 'shoot'.

Reg calls for me to duck and I do before shots ring out from their guns. I look up to see the Peaceholders on the ground, one of them completely still. The other is holding his leg and points his gun at me. Instinctually, I throw my hands out. The same ripple of power flows through the air and slams into him, pounding him into the wall behind him.

He lies still then.

"Come on!" I hear myself shout before I break into another run.

"Geez, how are we supposed to keep up with you?" Gretch yells behind me.

I think she must be referring to the fact that the sunlight strengthens me, making me faster. At this point, I can't tell since it feels so familiar to me. Searching internally, I realize the reservoir of powers isn't waning too quickly, but when it does, I may be out for days.

If I even survive it, I think.

I don't know what will happen to someone like me if they take in this much power, but I do know that I'll find out soon.

I slide around the corner and enter the hallway where the floor opens to my examination room. Looking to the wall, I frantically bang on it, hoping something will happen.

"Try the bracelet on this wall! Right here," I shout, pointing to the reader there.

Reg catches up and I have to repeat myself. His eyes focus on the wall there and he squints.

"Where? I don't see—"

Gretch, still heaving, snatches the bracelet from his hand and swipes it over the reader. The light above it flashes red and a robotic voice says, "*you are unauthorized to access this point.*"

I grow cold. "Try again," I say.

Gretch looks at me with pity but flashes the chain again. The response is the same.

"Hey! Stop right there!"

My head whips around to see four more Peaceholders holding their weapons aloft. Gretch and Reg fire quickly into them, dropping a couple, but the remaining two fire at us. Gretch gasps and collapses on the ground, holding her arm. I feel stinging on my shoulder and cheek from a couple of bullets that grazed my skin. I duck and push my hands out again, tossing the two Peaceholders to their backs. Reg rushes forward and slams them with a few shots. They don't rise.

"Fire girl, we can't wait here forever. We need to get somewhere and deal with Gretch's wounds," Reg says, moving to his companion.

I distinctly note he doesn't say we need to heal my own wounds, but then I realize I have the ability to heal them myself. Even as I move, I focus on the pain I felt moments before. Warmth gathers in the areas and the pain dissipates quickly. I can't help but sigh at the instant relief it gives me.

I don't want to admit it, but I know the Peaceholders could just keep coming and coming.

Reg and I help Gretch to her feet and we move in the opposite direction of the hallway we just came from and toward where the last Peaceholders followed us. I'm trying not to cry, feeling certain we won't find my dad in time now. The moment we turn the corner, we come face-to-face with more Peaceholders. I toss my free hand out, pushing some to the ground, but three still stand. Reg takes one out before the other two fire at us. We duck behind the corner again.

I'm shaking now. The adrenaline from before is wearing off. The power inside is waning slowly as well.

"Shoot, shoot, shoot," Reg is saying, "We're in trouble, hun."

Just as he says it, we see the flash of the Peaceholders' uniforms around the corner. I gasp and try to throw my hands out to push them, but we hear loud gunshots. I close my eyes, expecting the pain, but feel nothing. When I open them, we see the Peaceholders on the ground.

"What the—" I hear from beside me.

"Looks like you could use a hand," a familiar voice says.

My body floods with hope and I turn left to see a group of others standing at the end of the hall. Lucia, a few guards, and —*Charlie*, I think.

I let go of Gretch, making Reg grunt from the woman's full weight, then run as fast as I can into Charlie's arms. They wrap around me, so warm and safe.

I take a moment to realize his skin is unusually warm, hot even. The heat doesn't hurt me, but I assume it must be from the effects of sunfire.

"Young lady, you are in so much trouble, when we get out of this . . . ." Lucia says, looking at me sternly. Then she drops down and embraces me.

"And also, thank you," she says quickly. "Without your fire-power—no pun intended—we wouldn't have been able to get in."

Reg has made it to us by then. "A royal mess they've caused though," he replies, letting Gretch rest on the wall.

Lucia presses her lips together, thinking through our predicament.

I take a moment to turn and look at Susan. She smiles awkwardly and waves a hand.

"Hey," she says.

I can't help but laugh. "You came—you both came. Why?" I ask, euphoria still flowing inside.

Charlie shrugs. "You can thank her." He jerks his head toward Susan. "I was so worried about you, Kor. I wanted to come, but I doubted. Susan is surprisingly convincing, to say the least," he tells me.

I eye Susan and she blushes. "He may not have family in here, but I do. I understand, Korinne," Susan says.

Smiling widely, I throw my arms around her, sniffling from emotion. She gasps, but I feel her arms softly return the hug.

Gunshots and footsteps echo on the metal walls around us, men and women shouting, an explosion here and there. I pull away sharply, my mind locking onto our situation again.

"Blaine's being held in sector 23B. I never had access to that wing," Lucia speaks bluntly, then holds up an access bracelet, "but I believe this man does."

She presses her lips together in a determined way, then moves off down the hall.

"We'll get him," Charlie says, shaking my shoulders softly, "he's around here somewhere, I'm sure of it."

The encouraging words are pleasant, but I still feel dread. We walk a minute more, not sure exactly where to look.

"We need to get him, now," Lucia urges, "only a few more minutes before they'll kill him," the tone of her voice makes my skin crawl. We start moving again, quickly.

I didn't realize it, but at some point I reached out and started holding Charlie's hand. His fingers wrap through mine. I can feel the heat even more intensely between our clutched palms. Susan notices our touching as well and rolls her eyes. Even though she is annoyed, I wink at her.

We lapse into an intense silence while we follow behind Lucia. She leads us down the hallway away from where my exam room was. Our footsteps echo loudly with the size of our group, putting me even more on edge. Finally, unable to walk quietly any longer, I turn to Susan and smile again.

"Thank you for coming. I didn't think you approved of helping me."

Susan presses her lips together. "I'm scared as char, but I knew we couldn't leave you alone. This guy was all talk and no action,"

Susan points her thumb to the side at Charlie before continuing, "I only came because I didn't want to be left in that creepy place," she scowls, but there is a slight turn in her mouth. I chuckle, allowing the levity of her comment to ease my stress slightly.

Lucia shushes me, then we go silent. My eyes shift to Charlie and he's studying me, relief swimming there. He squeezes my hand. My breath catches in my chest and I shake a bit. I don't know how much more of this I can take before the power runs out and I collapse, either from fear, loss of power, or both.

Gunshots still echo from far away places in the network of hallways. I press my lips together, wondering how many of Lucia and Tom's men are getting killed just to get my father. I still feel guilty, though I know they were planning to come anyway. I wonder if it would have gone differently if I hadn't blasted my way in.

I open my palms and inspect them as we walk. Charlie notices me and raises an eyebrow, wondering what I'm thinking at the moment. The middle of my hands seems normal, considering I just launched volleys of who-knows-what from them.

"Here it is," Lucia says, interrupting my thoughts, "we have to be quiet as I unlock the way. If they hear us talking, they'll be on us in seconds."

Lucia eyes each of us and puts her fingers to her lips.

Satisfied, she pushes a loose hair over her right ear and turns to the wall. At first glance, nothing seems to be out of the ordinary. Then she holds the access bracelet to the wall. I suddenly realize there's a small square there and the design meshes into the rest of the silver metal. My guess is the others with me didn't notice it either, because I hear quiet whispers of surprise.

A small glimmer of light flows back and forth across the square, and we hear a beeping. A hissing sound announces the wall sliding inward just in front of where we stand. It isn't large, just the size of a normal door. We'll have to enter single file to fit through.

"*Class A clearance, access granted. Welcome back, Steven Alright.*"

Lucia bites her lip, then says awkwardly, "Thank you Steven, whoever you were."

The way she uses his name in the past tense makes my stomach turn.

Lucia gestures to us to follow her as she enters the space. As we move, lights flash on, one after the other, responding to our movement beneath them.

Lucia enters first, then a couple of soldiers. I didn't realize it, but Reg had been working on bandaging Gretch's wound. A thick white cloth now wraps around where the bullet hit her.

"You can't very well leave me, so let's get going," Gretch says as Reg eyes her on the ground.

"Kids first, we'll bring up the rear with this chum." Reg points up to the last soldier, who is at least twice his size. He keeps a flat expression and just stares at Reg.

"Wow, buzzkill, aren't you?" Reg replies when he sees the man's deadpan reaction.

I stifle a laugh, enjoying the small comic relief that Reg provides in this stressful moment. Seeing Susan and Charlie won't go first, I enter the doorway, the metal walls feeling tight now that we left the larger of the hallways. Susan follows, with Charlie after her. I smile, knowing he presumably wants to keep a watch on both of us.

He is protective, isn't he? I think.

It's something I don't dislike about him. Do I wish he came in right behind me? Sure, but I also love that he cares enough to hold back to watch out for Susan as well.

The hallway is dim with the single lights spaced out along the middle of the narrow passageway. Our footsteps echo even more here since the floor is no longer made of the same metal that the other parts of the building are. Instead, they are solid metal with textured studs, perhaps to prevent slipping from anyone traveling through them.

I hear quiet voices ahead of me and my body tenses. Part of me wishes it's just Lucia and the scientist, *Steven*, I remember his name now. One voice does sound familiar, but not Lucia familiar.

It sounds just like the voice on the speakers.

My skin crawls as I realize what I'm hearing is not a voice over technology, but the real, echoing voice of the woman I've heard my whole life, in person.

Natalie Yurislav. The moment she caught us before we escaped Safety last time flashes in my mind and I shudder.

We catch up to the soldier as the voice gets louder. I realize we must be nearly in the next room away from the place she is speaking. There are two other voices, another man and woman, but these I don't recognize.

Lucia slides behind the soldiers and looks at me. She gets down near my face and whispers as quietly as I think a whisper can be. Her reddish-brown hair reflects the light from above, and I take a moment to wonder how she gets it so shiny.

"I know you miss your father, but you have to take it slow. Don't do anything when you see him, stay back, and let us handle it." Lucia grabs my left arm and squeezes it. It's not a hard squeeze, but it's firm enough for me to know she means business.

The soldiers in front of us move forward. My mind forces back the panic, combined with hope that I'll have my father back with me soon. Lucia stands up and follows behind. In moments, we enter a room with computers and tables all over the place. We're moving quietly, and the voices echo louder now. I realize the tables and computers are arranged in a circular pattern around the center of the room, which holds a single examination table. It is surrounded by a large bubble of clear material. There, on the table within the bubble-like shield, is a man wearing only blue pants.

Dad? I think, and my body tries to move on its own.

Lucia must have been expecting this, because I feel her grab my arm and hold me back. My lungs gasp for air as I try to take in what's happening. My father is lying on the white-paper-covered examination bed, but he's not moving. Wires connect to his limbs, head and chest. I see a needle in his arm, connected to a clear tube with liquid in it.

For a moment, I forget about the voices we heard talking, but it all comes back to me instantly when they go quiet.

"Ahh, and here they are," the familiar woman's voice says, "take them out, please."

Gunshots ring in my ears and I scream, throwing my hands over them and ducking down. Bodies fall around me and I sob, not wanting to see who they are. I just see camo uniforms, but I refuse to look further.

"Grab them, fast!" One of the unfamiliar men's voices calls.

Powerful arms grasp me from behind and hold my hands there. My heart is pumping so fast, I worry I might have a heart attack. Lucia is cursing next to me, and while I'm terrified at being restrained, I am relieved that she wasn't one of the people killed.

A gun cocks and Lucia sucks in a breath.

"Actually, keep that one alive. She is one of the scientists who might be intrigued to hear what we have found," the speaker-woman says.

I shift enough to see Lucia. She's gritting her teeth and her eyes are full of anger.

"Natalie," she spits. "The maniac who runs this singe-hole. You knew we were coming."

We're dragged into the open, and I can now see the entire room around the computer screens. Standing to the side of my unconscious father are two women and a man in white lab coats. On the left chest pocket is a golden symbol of half-circle leaves wrapped around what looks like a diamond shape.

Behind them, at least two dozen guards. My heart sinks. We're outnumbered.

"Well, now that it's just the four of you alive, we can talk business, can't we?"

Natalie is the one speaking. She has olive skin and dark brown hair that greys in a lot of places. Her face is covered with thick makeup, lines running from her eyes outward. My guess is that she tries to hide her age, which is evident from her wrinkles. Next to her, the other woman has dark brown skin and pitch black hair. The other man is blond and sports bright blue eyes.

"What, no proper greetings for the Creators who brought this together? You should be thankful we've provided this center for you to live. You've been safe here, after all," Natalie says.

I'm at a loss for words. I'm trying to process everything, but my brain can't keep up. We're stuck, outnumbered, and restrained. The power is barely flowing in my veins and I almost push out with it, throwing the Peaceholders behind me back, but I know the dozens of Peaceholders across the room will shoot me in seconds. That's not what my brain is struggling with, though.

She said only four of us are alive. I look around and realize Reg and Gretch are gone. Anger wells up inside of me, and I'm yelling.

"You killed them! You are a monster! You took my father and—" I am forced to be quiet as a rough hand covers my mouth.

Natalie smiles. "Now, now, let's be quiet while I share with you what we learned from your father, hm?"

30

MY MOUTH HURTS AS THE ROUGH HAND OF THE PEACEHOLDER restraining me pushes inward. I try to bite the fingers, but they are pressing too hard on my mouth.

"What do you mean? What have you done to him?" Lucia demands next to me.

Natalie eyes my father lying on the examination bed, still unconscious. My gaze follows hers and my eyes widen when I inspect him. His hair is more grey than normal, and I could be wrong, but he has more wrinkles, as if he's aged. I try to look over at Lucia but the hand pressed on my face prevents me from turning my head. Lucia's voice is almost as desperate as I feel right now.

"Well, we lucked out with this one. His dabbling into our computers gave us the okay from the higher-ups we needed to run more—volatile tests," Natalie raises a hand to her mouth and squints her eyes as if she's trying to think of something.

The other scientists around her shift on their feet, appearing uncomfortable with what she says.

"I became a Creator here to make improvements, to change things that would not only allow us to make life and energy more efficient for those living in Safety, but also for the government. We can run this place almost for free with the changes I've made around here," her face tightens, hostility entering her eyes, "But still they denied me my permits to run more extreme tests on live citizens."

Her voice gives me the chills, my body shaking from nervousness.

"Then your father and his colleague happened upon information that gave me the excuse to do what I want. Their deaths would be excusable, should the government find out what happened to them."

My mind is whirling, trying to understand what she means by my father's colleague. I'm feeling lightheaded with the hand over my mouth, and I soon realize I was trying to breathe through it rather than just using my nose, which is mercifully uncovered.

Oh, she means the Larssons! What did she do to them? I think.

Then it makes sense. Lucia told me the Creators killed the Larssons, but the idea that they would put Therese's parents through something like this horrifies me, even though I don't know exactly what it is.

It's as if Lucia reads my mind. "What did you do to him and his wife? Why send the children back but not their parents?" Lucia asks through almost gritted teeth.

The woman waves her hand nonchalantly and glances at my father again.

"Oh, the children. While I wanted to experiment on the kids, some of my colleagues—didn't approve. A simple memory wipe and appearance change, and they went right back into the system. "

I remember the new kids who appeared out of nowhere. I didn't know it at the time, but Lucia told me later it was Therese and her brother. I knew even before she told me that something was familiar about them. Hearing from Natalie that she experimented on their parents and only narrowly avoided doing the same on the children makes me sick.

"What about his wife? Where did she end up?" Lucia asks again.

I think I know the answer.

Natalie's mouth turns up in a semi-smile.

"They're ashes, I'm afraid. They couldn't withstand the experiments before Blaine recalibrated our formulas. Though, it would have been nice had we not failed with the experiments on them," the woman slowly walks down the few stairs to my father's form on the bed. She gently lays a hand on the shield-bubble surrounding him and caresses it fondly.

I'm sick from watching. I can hear the screams in my head, and feel them trying to break free from the hand covering my mouth, but they aren't escaping.

"Fortunately, Blaine helped us solve what we were missing. No one asked him to, but his natural problem-solving and mathematical inclinations helped us find the solution we needed. Who knew a sheltered man like him could solve problems we've been trying to crack for ages."

I hear Lucia struggling to get out of the grip holding her. There is a thump and a grunt before she is in my view. She vaults toward the woman speaking, but a gunshot sounds and then Lucia collapses.

I scream, seeing her fall.

She isn't dead, and I know that because she pushes herself up, her hand pressing against her upper arm.

"Come any closer, and I'll make sure my soldiers hit you somewhere more critical," Natalie threatens, looking bored. "I only kept you alive for a little longer so you can understand the revelation which will change the world; the one that will turn the plague of these—*abominations* and their power from the sunlight."

I start when she says this. For some reason, I hadn't thought about the fact that they would know the extent of our abilities. The way she looks at me now, and at Charlie and Susan, tells me they know more than we thought.

"Oh yes, people like you have been imprisoned for years and years, but not because we fear your death. No, we fear the death of others, the potential fall of society. People like you," she points at me, spit flying out of her mouth with her next words, "are a threat to the world. We had to lock you up. Sure, at first there was time dedicated to fixing you, giving you a chance to return to society. I've known from the moment I learned of people like you that it was a waste of time. I wanted to use you for something else."

Lucia gasps on the ground. Air hisses between her teeth, as I know she's trying to deal with the pain of the gunshot. She glares at the older woman, and I know that if there weren't at least forty guns pointed at Lucia, she probably would take Natalie out.

"If I'd known we'd be talked to death, I might have brought my ear plugs," I retort, some odd bravado surging through me. The moment I say it, I wonder if I'll regret it.

This makes Natalie laugh. "Oh yes, you are a feisty one, aren't you, dear? I can't wait to extract *your* energy once we're done with your father," Natalie replies.

"Anyway, I had to work my way up within Safety to become a Creator. After I made improvements to our system, we increased the experiments. We tested applying sunlight in small doses to the citizens here. By extracting their energy, we could use it for ourselves. We're talking almost immeasurable energy from the sunlight. Something more powerful than solar panels by at least a thousand percent. We were never able to get enough, though. Not without more invasive procedures."

Natalie walks slowly around my father's transparent prison.

"Then, the perfect opportunity arose. I was finally able to

test my science to its full extent. Unfortunately, the early attempts of extraction resulted in, well, death."

She says the words so matter-of-factly that it sounds even more disturbing.

There is movement from behind the white-lab-coated woman, and I see the other three scientists—or Creators, I assume—are shifting uneasily on their feet. I don't get the sense they are as excited about this as Natalie. I focus on my father's body, trying to make sure he is alive. I'm guessing the beeping of the machines connected to him means he is, but I'm relieved when I can see the subtle raising and lowering of his chest.

The computers surrounding him are flashing different numbers and graphs. There are colors and other pictures moving around, things that I can't understand.

"Your father is truly an extraordinary man," her eyes are now on me and the fear flashes inside my stomach like a massive wave.

She's watching him again. After a moment, she moves near his head and pats the barrier around him once more. Nausea waves over me again at the sight of the endearing look on her face.

"I don't know how he knew—how he could figure out something so complex, but he did. How he managed to tamper with our machines is beyond me. Still, his skill with computers allowed him to adjust the calibration just so. Not only did he protect his own skin by making it possible to extract energy without stopping his life force, but he created the improvements Safety needed for better sustainability, and a better life for humankind. With his adjustments, we could finally extract the power from him successfully. Of course, he didn't know exactly what he was working on. To him, it was like a hobby puzzle to solve. But we've stored up thousands and thousands of units. All from a few hours of exposure to the sun. Though, it does seem to take its toll on him."

The wrinkles on his face make more sense now, as well as his grey hair.

Lucia growls, then speaks. "You're sucking the life out of him. How can you do that?" Lucia glares at her, then shifts her eyes to the others, "How can you let her do this? This is more inhumane than keeping these people locked up!"

The other Creators shift in their spots again, but the blond man finally looks up.

"Sacrifices must be made to further our sustainability, it's not unusual," he says, a slight accent in his voice.

Natalie scoffs, "And we can eliminate threats as well. I've already sent the plans to the government and all the other facilities around the globe like this one. Before long, we'll be harvesting this power and building a better future. While subduing the horrid plague these people are."

"You are hideous monsters! I won't let you do it!" Lucia tries to stand, but a Peaceholder materializes behind her and yanks her back. She lands hard and gasps from the pain of landing on some stairs nearby.

"You may be angry now, but you'll thank me someday," Natalie says. She peers down at Lucia before she turns to my father once more.

"How about we show you what we mean? Lorie, please turn it on."

The other scientist woman moves to one computer behind my father. She types something quickly on the screen. Then we hear a loud grinding sound from above. I strain my eyes upward to see what's happening. Just like back in the arena at the Nugennexx compound, the ceiling moves. After only a moment, a sliver of sunlight seeps through the opening crack and lands on my father. His breath sucks inward and his chest puffs out. I can almost feel the reaction his body is having from the sunlight, because I remember it. My body is trying desperately to pull me toward the sunlight. I once again remember I can easily pull away from the soldier holding me from behind, but I know I'll get shot quicker than I can move. That, and the power inside me is waning even more.

There has to be something we can do, I think, more angry now at seeing what's happening.

My father growls, the sounds muffled by the material surrounding him. He throws his hands upward toward the glass and we see a ripple of energy fly outward. Unfortunately, it hits the clear shield, awarding him no success. He reaches down and tears out the heat-resistant tubes and sensors attached to him. Monitors and machines beep loudly when he does. He balls up a fist and slams it into the material. The sound echoes loudly through the room, and I notice many of the Peaceholders across the room tense up at his reaction.

"The sun makes him strong," Natalie says. Then she looks at me directly. "It makes all of you strong, but we melded this composite from the strongest materials. Even he can't break out of it."

Natalie looks at Lorie, who is still standing uncomfortably behind the computer. "Drain him." Her voice is flat and emotionless.

Lorie types something on the computer, then we see the bottom of the bubble, the part that connects with the floor, pulse with light. Suddenly, my dad starts shaking. I breathe quickly, the panic rising again. My dad struggles to sit up. He holds a hand up to his chest and sways more. For a moment he tries to get up again, then our gaze connects through the glass-like material. His eyebrows shoot up in surprise, but then his eyes roll back and he tumbles to the ground.

I look at Natalie. I can't help it anymore. I let the power inside fuel me, the burst of energy making me brave, if only for a moment. I bite down on the gloved hand covering my mouth and feel my teeth break through what's hiding underneath it. The leather glove of his uniform holds, but the man wails in pain and his grip loosens.

"Turn it off! Turn it off now!" I shout. I feel the draw to pull away from the man, but I still am afraid of the guns pointing at me.

Natalie turns to glare at me.

"Ah, yes, the infamous daughter of the man who changed everything," her face contorts into an ugly look that makes me want to run, "I knew you were trouble from the beginning. Whether it was your dad who taught you to be this way or not, it doesn't matter. When we are finished with him here, you'll be next. We haven't been able to test if different ages produce different energy levels."

She smiles evilly at me. "I can't wait to find out." She claps her hands together in front of her.

The lights pulse and my father is still shaking on the ground. Tears are flooding over my vision, and something just snaps inside me. I don't care that I could get shot, I don't care that this could be the end of me, I just act.

Drawing from the power inside, which I know is only minutes away from being exhausted, I push heavily backwards on my arms. Even though the power has been waning, it's still enough to push the two Peaceholders into the wall. They shout in surprise as they thump into the metal and collapse on each other. I hear a few gunshots and feel them zip past me, but my body moves more quickly with the sunfire. It takes only a moment for my mind to catch up to the fact that my body is speeding through the room, but then I'm in the sunlight and my blood ignites on fire. The dwindling well of power explodes with intensity and I can't help but laugh out loud.

31

A yelp from the side reminds me that Lucia is on the ground with a gunshot wound. I glance over to see her shuffling away from my blazing body.

"Shut the roof!" Natalie shrieks, "Lorie—shut it now!"

Gunshots ring out and I know that some of them must have hit me because the fire flowing around me sparks as the bullets collide, but I don't feel them.

Lorie types frantically on the computer while the other scientists scream and hide behind the computers ringing the center. I hear the roof begin to close and look up, realizing my time is short. The wedge of sunlight wanes swiftly as the doors above move. I look at the Peaceholders with their guns raised. I could kill them. I know I can, but I won't do it. I'm not a murderer. Instead, I focus on the feeling I had earlier when I pushed out waves of power. With a silent prayer to something or someone out there, I push my hands outward, hoping it's not fire that comes out. Luckily, it's not.

A blast of heavy energy ripples almost imperceptibly through the air and knocks the Peaceholders in every direction.

A flash in my peripheral vision makes me turn that way,

and I see Susan has entered the light as well. Her face is determined as the fire surrounds her body. She blasts waves of energy from her hands toward the seating across from us. Peaceholders return volleys of gunshots.

Seeing the girl who acted frail and scared stand confidently in the sun is striking. The fact that she rushed forward to help me shocks me, but I'm relieved knowing she's here to help. While she focuses on them, I put my hands on the hard surface separating my father and me. Channeling the power from the sunlight above, I throw what I can into it. The lights pulse quicker when I do, and I feel power being drawn from me. My eyes snap open and I pull away, cursing.

"It drains me too!" I shout, looking at Lucia. The sunlight is a mere crack now, and I reach my hand to keep contact. I throw out energy, but it bounces off the spherical wall as if it carried no weight.

My heart sinks. The lights keep pulsing, taking the power from my struggling father. I see more of his hair turn grey and a few more wrinkles set in his skin.

"Turn it off! Do something!" I'm screaming, yelling to someone I don't know.

Lucia stumbles up and shuffles to the computer where Lorie worked. I'm not sure when she got it, but she has a knife in her hand. She holds it up to Lorie. Natalie's dark forehead has heavy beads of sweat threatening to drip down. She stares at me, panicked, and backs toward the overwhelmed Peaceholders.

"Get him out of there now, or I'll carve you to pieces," Lucia steps forward and looks so menacing with her bloody gunshot wound that I can understand when Lorie submits.

Loud beeps sound from the machine and the clear barrier hisses, separating in the middle and disappearing into the floor. The roof stops moving inward, a sliver of sun still flowing down the center of the room. The fire no longer engulfs me without the direct sunlight, and I make a point to stay out of the rays.

I rush to my father's side and duck down to his unconscious form. A few gunshots from above make me duck behind the table, but now Charlie has joined the throng. He and Susan hold one hand up into the sliver of sun, their bodies engulfed in wild flames. They throw more energy into the air and the bullets stop.

Lucia is by my side, reaching out to my father's body.

"Freaking scientists! They are a bunch of nutjobs!" she says as she runs her hand over his shoulder and neck, "He's still breathing, and there's a heartbeat, but that couldn't have been good for his system. Can you carry him?"

I realize she's asking me and I stare at her.

Under normal circumstances, no, I couldn't lift my father's limp body, but perhaps—trusting my recharged energy from the sun, I put my hands under his back and lift, clenching my core and back in anticipation of the weight, but I hardly feel it. His body feels as light as the pillows back at the compound. My eyes widen, but I nod at her.

"Good," she inspects the gunshot wound in her arm, "any chance you can cauterize this wound?"

I stare at her, not understanding. "I—I don't think so—"

She shrugs, "It was a long shot. I'll make do, but we need to get out of here before we're overrun. Our only hope is to go back the way we came."

"Come on!" I shout to my friends who are poised facing the opposite side of the room.

With a grim determination, they each blast one more bout of energy before turning and gesturing for me to go. I run up the stairs toward the opening in the wall where we came. I'm at the entrance in seconds, so I turn to see Lucia is still stumbling up.

"Oh gosh, I've lost blood," she says. I can see she's paling.

Suddenly, Charlie is there. His body is no longer covered in fire, but I know he must still feel the power inside. He scoops her up and holds her comfortably.

"Sorry it took so long to get them off of me," Charlie apologizes.

I wave his comment away, indicating it's alright.

"Let's go," he says.

My heart flutters at seeing him hold Lucia with ease. I kind of wish it was me in his arms.

Shaking my head, I turn and lead the way into the dark hallway. The way back feels shorter this time, even though I'm not overly sure how long the tunnel is.

When we get to the end, I pause and hold up an arm. Peeking through the small crack of the slightly ajar door, I see two Peaceholders standing outside with guns pointing at the opening.

I steel myself for what I have to do, then focus on the flowing heat inside and try to forget about the lethal weapons they hold. With an exhale, I push outward, the door ripping from its hinges and smacking into them with a metal clang. They are instantly unconscious.

"Dang girl, you got some power, don't you?" Lucia whistles behind me.

I roll my eyes, then enter the hallway.

My mind spins, trying to get our bearings within Safety. Finally, I realize where to go.

I turn right and start sprinting down the hall back the way we came. The echoing of feet behind me assures me that Susan and Charlie follow. Just as we are about to bound past the mess hall, I remember I told my mother and Sean that I'd take them with me.

"We have to make a stop!" I say.

I slow my pace and then dig my feet into the metal grate. The standard issue grey flats I have on grind into the metal and

I almost topple over as the top half of me, weighed by my unconscious father, pitches forward. The sounds of shuffling and grunting behind tell me Charlie and Susan had similar problems slowing down from our rapid pace.

"What? You have to be crazy, Kor. We need to get out of here," Charlie says, exasperated.

As if to prove his point, there's more shouting and gunshots echoing through the hallway.

I know he deserves an answer, but I also know that we don't have time. Instead of explaining, I bolt down the right hallway to the classroom areas. Fortunately, there were enough times I went to pick Sean up from his homeroom class when he was smaller. We stay in our same classrooms during our childhood until we turn eighteen and the Creators assign us a job.

Well that's how it used to be, I think, not sure if I'm sad about not knowing what my future holds anymore.

The lights above and below us flicker as we hear more gunshots. It's only a minute or two before we slide to a stop in front of Sean's classroom door. I'm breathing hard, but I don't feel tired. The well of power throbs inside me, pushing me to run harder, to blow something up. Shaking my head, I try the door. When I push the button, the door hisses and slides open.

A few people shriek.

"It's okay! It's just me—Korinne," I say, putting up my free hand.

"Oh, Korinne, you are alright?" I hear my mom's voice say. She stands up from behind a turned over desk then gasps, her hand flying to her mouth. I can see she's mouthing my dad's name, but no sound comes out. Her eyes pass from my face to his body, confusion evident there.

I hear Susan sigh behind me before she rushes past me into the room. A woman stands there, sobbing loudly as she throws her arms out. Susan rushes forward and hugs her. It takes me a moment to realize it's her mother. A man stands next to her, his eyes brimming with tears. The way Susan switches to hugging him makes me think it's her father.

I can't believe our luck to find her family in the same room as mine, but I send a thanks upward to—well, any god who is listening.

"We have to leave!" I say, searching frantically for Sean, "Where is—"

My eyes lock on my smirking brother and I deflate, relieved.

"You weren't worried about me, were you? I'm the resourceful one in this family." Sean folds his arms.

I roll my eyes, then duck instinctually as echoed screams and gunshots sound behind me. They are too far away to hit me, so I shake it off.

"We need to get out of here, now," I say to Susan and Charlie. I lace my voice with a dose of anger to prove my seriousness.

They nod and inspect the other few people hiding in the room. I didn't notice them at first because they are crouching low behind desks. There is another woman with two smaller children and another few teenagers huddling near the back, a couple of them crying. They stand shakily. One says something, but I shake my head.

"No time to talk, let's go before we are surrounded," I say.

"How can we trust you? Why would we follow you?" a woman asks, her voice hard.

I clench my teeth, then turn to her.

When did I get so forward? I think, feeling the confidence burst inside me.

"You have no choice, unless you want to stay and incur the wrath of the Creators and Peaceholders. Who knows what they might do to everyone here when we leave," I make eye contact to convey the danger.

Even as I say the words, the dread fills me. My mind flies through the possibilities of everyone being killed for my actions. I don't know what that horrid woman is capable of.

Part of me is glad we didn't kill her or the other three Creators, but another part regrets it.

"What?! No, no, no—" Susan cries.

My head snaps toward her, hairs raising on my body. I don't know why she is making that noise, but I soon see that there isn't any trouble. I walk quickly to her, my heart breaking at the sight of her crying. I've seen her cry a lot during the past week, but this feels different.

"What happened?" I ask, awkwardly placing my hand on her back. I've not touched her in this way, so it feels unnatural, but something about how she pushed Charlie to come here with us and how she saved me makes me feel like I owe her.

Susan continues crying, and I notice that her parents look grave.

"My—older sister—she got killed in one of the gunfights," Susan manages to get out through her sobs.

My skin chills. Most families have two kids, and there isn't anyone else with Susan's parents. I open my mouth to console her, to say I'm sorry about her sister being gone, but I'm interrupted. The speaker above crackles and it's as if the olive-skinned devil herself heard my thoughts.

"*Attention, Peaceholders, the main perpetrators, the ones to blame for the breach, are in classroom 85 in hallway 25R. Please block their way on every front.*"

I curse.

"If it isn't our favorite old croon," Lucia mutters behind me.

My eyes flick to the top of the hallways where the cameras stare back at us. I lift up my hand and send a wave of energy at one pointing at me. The camera explodes with the impact.

"Charlie, hit the cameras," I say.

He nods and begins blasting the cameras he can see along the ceiling down the hallways. The citizens gasp and cower at the sight of Charlie's actions. A couple of them jump back behind desks to hide. I set my jaw, knowing how scary this must be but also aware of how little time we have.

I gently lay my father on the ground. My mother runs to his side and starts fussing over him.

"Mom, we don't have time for that. He just needs sun, then he'll be fine," I reply.

Her reaction is something between horror, shock, and anger.

"Korinne, why would you—why would you do that?!" she says frantically before putting her hand out to stop me.

That's when I remember they don't know that he and everyone else here isn't allergic to the sun. I squeeze my eyes in frustration, then think of the fastest way to explain it all.

"Mom, we aren't allergic to the sun. It heals us. The Creators lied to us. Now we need to move," I say, leaping to her and nudging her away. Her body flings further than I expected with my powered strength.

"Ow, Kor, no," she's saying.

I pause and put my hands on her shoulders.

"Mom, trust me, just come with us. You'll be safe," I say.

Our eyes lock for a beat and I see the fear in them, the fear ruling her. Finally, she nods and her demeanor changes to determined.

"Lead the way, then," she says.

I hoist my father back onto my shoulders, making a few of the people around us gasp and whisper. Until now, I hadn't thought about what it looked like to have a teenage girl carrying a bulky grown-man with ease.

I chuckle, awarding myself with odd looks. I turn to Lucia and see she's looking back and forth between me and my mother, her mouth a thin line.

She's never met my mother, I think. *Oh, my family is so much more complicated now.* "Let's go," I say, then I turn and run down the hall. I don't move as fast as I know I can, because I know the other citizens aren't used to running like this.

The gunshots are drowned out by the sheer noise of the group running behind me. I curse when I forget I was supposed to be taking out the cameras. Spotting two, I fling my hand out and knock them down easily.

It wasn't fast enough. The speakers crackle again, Natalie coming on.

"Peaceholders, they are proceeding through hallway 25S toward the bend."

I'm trying to navigate back the way we came, hoping there aren't a ton of Peaceholders blocking the way out. Unfortunately, that isn't the case. I have to stop unexpectedly when we reach the bend and face at least a dozen Peaceholders. All at once, the hallway that crosses behind us floods with more. We're surrounded.

Oh no, I think, *we're all going to die and it's my fault.*

Their guns raise and cock.

"Please put down the fugitive and surrender, you have nowhere to go," a woman in the front says.

"Like char, blast them, Kor," Lucia says smugly behind me from Charlie's arms.

My stomach clenches. The Peaceholders tense and raise their weapons more.

I put up my hand in panic. "No, no I won't. Please just let us out! Let's just talk about this!" I don't know why I try to talk to them. They won't see reason.

The speaker crackles and I hear Natlie again, her voice sending chills down my spine. *"There's no need to keep the girl and her friends alive, we just need the man. Eliminate her as soon as possible."*

My blood runs cold. I see a sly smile from one of the Peaceholders and I focus on him. I recognize him immediately. It's the same one who gave me trouble for the past few weeks. The dread of being surrounded and outnumbered settles in as he speaks out.

"I'll take care of this snotty girl, she's been a pain in the rear to me," he says.

He moves in front of the group, then aims at my chest. As much as I want to fight back, there are too many people around who might get hurt if I use my powers. "Say goodbye, sweetie," he chuckles.

I hear the gunshot just after I squeeze my eyes shut.
Nothing.

I open them to see my mother standing between me and him. My heart stops.

"NO!" I scream, catching her as she falls to the ground in her blood. I grunt from the effort with my father balanced on my shoulder. Somehow, I managed to hold him still.

Susan steps up next to me, Charlie following suit. They position themselves in front of me and throw their hands outward. Gunshots sound around me again, along with shouts from the other Safety citizens with us.

My eyes focus on my mother, lying on the ground beneath me. The sounds of gunshots and explosions drown out as tears fill my eyes. I slip my hand under my mom's head as her eyes flutter. For a moment I think she's already gone, but then her half-closed eyes wander to my face. When she sees me, she smiles. Her hand moves slowly to my cheek and caresses it.

"I'm so proud—of you," she says, her voice weak. I might not have heard if not for my enhanced senses. She coughs, then locks eyes with me again.

"Don't—change—" her eyes unfocus and she leans back against the floor.

"No! No—mom, don't go!" I'm shouting.

I can't tell if she hears me, because she keeps smiling. Then her hand falls to the ground, and she goes still.

For the third time today, something snaps inside me. I don't think—I stand sharply and push outward with my hand, a massive wave of energy flying past Charlie and Susan and into the group of Peaceholders. A couple of gunshots ring out and I hear sounds of surprise behind me. Every Peaceholder in front of me flies backward, most screaming. My friends spin back and stare at me in awe.

My mind is moving so fast and I try to catch up. I realize we are so close to the doors, to the place where we can escape this horrid place, but the Peaceholders are in the way.

I look up at the top of the hallway, knowing it's a long shot. I can't take it anymore though, as I try not to stare at my mother's body lying beneath me. Then I draw on the power within, I grab everything I can. The pulsing speeds up, and I feel like I'll burst. I scream, then push my hand outward at the upper corner.

What flies out is nothing like I've ever seen. It is a combination of flames and the same rippling energy from before. It slams into the top corner and tears a giant hole in the metal. Just as I'd hoped, the sunlight comes pouring in, hitting me like a massive wave. Just then, I hear gunshots and feel a couple of them enter my stomach and chest.

But the sun's there.

I soak it up like a sponge. The wounds heal rapidly, the bullets falling to the ground where the tissue heals. My father gasps and stirs on my shoulders. Susan and Charlie stand up straight to my side, each a blazing wonder. We lock eyes and they nod to me, turning back to our assailants with determination. Screams sound from the Peaceholders and those behind me. When I turn, I see them.

The citizens who are with me, the ones still alive, are surrounded by the flames. Eyes wide, they stare at me in confusion.

Then I smile. It isn't a cheerful smile. No, there's no joy as I remember the death of my friends, of my mother. It's a vengeful one.

"What—what's happening?" my father says from my shoulder.

I put him down and stare into his eyes.

"I'm getting you out of here," I say, then turn to the side and throw the biggest wave of energy I can at the Peaceholders.

32

I STAND ON THE ROOF, STARING AT THE MOUNTAINS THAT RISE UP in the distance. Desert grass flows as far as the eye can see, both north and south of the building. The wind blows through my hair, which is still wet from my shower earlier. The sun has fully set, but the faint afterglow remains to let me gaze out away from where I stand. As I look outwards, it baffles me that there can be something so large cutting off the view of the sky.

I laugh internally. *As if I have any sense of how the outside world should work*, I think, amused.

It's only been two weeks since I escaped Safety with Susan and Charlie, and it has been even less time for my father and Sean. Just after I broke a hole in the wall of Safety, igniting the other citizens around me, everything happened so fast. Lucia called backup before they met with us, so they flooded the compound with soldiers Tom had been requisitioning for months in various places surrounding Safety in other parts of Kansas. We got many of the captive citizens out of Safety, but there were many we couldn't. When government troops showed up an hour later, they had to evacuate. My mind is reeling thinking about what could be happening to those left behind. I hope with everything I can that they aren't going to be used in the way my father was. The hope isn't strong. Natalie didn't sound like she planned to back down, and she survived at our hands.

I try not to think about the citizens left as a loss, because there were so many others lost in that moment.

Gretch, Reg—my mother, I remember.

A pang of intense sadness rocks me inside when I think about my mother. She was so close to getting out, to really understanding what life could be. That opportunity was stolen from her, all because she loved me.

A few tears fall from my eyes, the wind making my face cooler where they trail. My entire life, I never felt like I had a connection with her. I recall the times she scolded me for getting us in trouble, or for being impolite. It wasn't that I never felt loved by her, I'm sure she did love me, but it was just —different.

I feel so much regret knowing I'll never get the chance to fix things, to apologize for all the things I put her and my family through. In the end, she proved her love by saving my life.

Footsteps sound behind me, though I can only barely hear them through the wind whistling in my ears.

"This place is cool, huh?" I hear my father say.

I sniffle, wiping the tears from my eyes, and nod heavily so he can see it from behind. I don't want him to see me crying. It seems there has been too much of that recently.

His firm hand grasps my right shoulder.

"I never thought we'd really make it out of there, let alone end up in some place I've never even heard of," he says, coming to the side of me to lean on the railing.

I shrug. "We haven't heard of most places," I say sarcastically, "they didn't emphasize geography in our classes in Safety."

And they didn't. When I'd heard from Lucia that Safety was

in the middle of rural Kansas, near a place called Wichita, I stared at her like a little kid trying to learn to read for the first time.

My dad chuckles. "Glad to know that even though you are still grieving, you haven't lost your sass," my father looks at me fondly when I turn to him.

I sigh, but let a smile spread across my face, despite my emotions.

"It won't do me any good out here, there is so much to learn, I don't know if we'll ever be able to blend in with the other normal people," I say, shrugging.

He furrows his brow at me. "Kor, we are normal people, don't you forget that. We just get a little hot-headed," he grins stupidly at me while I groan.

"Ugh, can you hold off on the horrible jokes? I may finally feel somewhat happy, but not enough to handle those." I shove him for emphasis.

"Couldn't help it," he says, holding his grin. "Besides, if anyone is ready to blend into the real world, you are. You've been able to stand being in the sun without bursting into flames, no one else has done that." He punches me lightly on the shoulder.

"Yeah, yeah, how fancy is it that I can go into the sun and not explode in flames." Sarcasm laces my tone, but I know what he means.

Since leaving Safety with the other citizens, Tom ordered the evacuation to another of their secret facilities further west. This one is parked at the base of the Rocky Mountains in some desert place in Utah. As a whole, there isn't a lot to see except short shrubs and tall mountains covered with rocky cliffs and tall pine trees, but there's still a peace to it somehow. It appears that Natalie didn't report it when Charlie, Susan and I escaped, but she couldn't cover up what happened after we rescued my father. Now that the government knows of our escape, Tom and his organization have had to slip into hiding. If the government finds us, I doubt they'll be lenient.

I breathe in deeply, thinking of how much this facility feels like Safety. We're allowed to move around freely, and we aren't held to a strict schedule other than set mealtimes, but there are cameras everywhere. Soldiers patrol the halls and we are restricted to specific areas of the building. I shudder slightly, then force my mind back to the current conversation.

"How do you keep the fire in, by the way? Any tips to share?" he asks.

My eyes shift to the west where the fading light of the recent sunset is going, and fairly quickly at that.

"I don't know, Dad, it's just . . . I can just hold it back," I say.

Part of the reason I escaped to the roof today was because I know none of the other citizens of Safety can come out in the sun without bursting in flames. Despite everyone's training and all the experiments, I'm still the only one who can hold the fire at bay. Sure, when I come into the sun, I still feel the explosion of power, the heat swimming within me, but that's where it stays. If I will it to stay, at least.

He sighs and slumps. I know he's exaggerating, but I also know he wants to figure it out.

"In theory, you could go out there," he gestures out toward the desert grass of the valley to the north, "You could blend in and have a normal life."

My stomach clenches at the thought.

"None of it feels normal," I say, looking down, "Not without you, Sean, and—mom."

I struggle to get the words out, and the moment I say them, I regret it. The jovial smile melts from my father's face, and his mouth quivers.

"Kor—I can't talk about your mother right now. I miss her so much—"

He puts his face in his hands and sobs for a moment. I move

to his side and hug him around his stomach, squeezing tight. In reality, seeing him react this way makes me feel validated. He loved her more than I can even describe. Despite the arranged marriage and family combining, he loved her.

For a moment, we sit there, the wind whipping our clothes and hair around us. We stare at the eastern mountains as they fade further and further into the darkness. Then we hear a knocking behind us and someone clears their throat.

"Uh, is this a bad time?" I recognize the voice as Lucia's.

Turning around, I shake my head. "We are just—enjoying the air," I say.

Lucia's brown-red hair is curly as usual, but it's pulled up in a loose bun at the back of her skull. She's taken a moment to apply more makeup than she did when we first met her, and she's wearing a slim purple dress that hugs her shape, along with a matching blazer. Since leading the successful mission in Safety, she's been promoted to something-or-other. Anyway, she's dressed more fancy ever since.

She notices my father was crying and presses her lips together. "Are you alright, Blaine?" Lucia seems worried, her eyes inspecting him.

He nods, then reaches out and grabs her hand, squeezing. She puts her other hand over his and smiles.

"Is it her again? I'm so sorry for your loss—"

My father puts his other hand in the air, stopping her. "I want to remember her for the good things, the good times, but try to focus on the future. There are still people to love."

My father looks deeply into Lucia's eyes and I see her face flush.

It was clear from the beginning there was at least a friendly connection between the two. The way Lucia talked about my father before we went to get him, the way she reacted when she saw him on the table in the hidden experimentation room, it was apparent. I'm not eager to forget about my mother, but it seems that at this point, my father and Lucia could have some sort of relationship. I don't love the idea of it yet, but at the same time, it's wonderful to think my actual mother could be—will be a part of my life from now on.

"Yes, you know I am a perfectly lovable person," Lucia says, batting her eyelids for emphasis.

My father and I laugh at her reaction.

"Uh, mind if we join your party? I know it's only family so far, but I can make the case that we are part of it." Charlie's head pokes out of the trapdoor to the lower floors.

"Get out here. You know you are always welcome," I say, moving to wrap my arms around him. Susan follows closely behind, a smile on her face.

"Wow, it's only been, what, a few hours since you last saw me? What's this for?" he asks, putting his own arms around me.

The flurries of tingles are springing through my stomach and into my chest. I've always loved being with Charlie, even though I knew we wouldn't be allowed to be together. In Safety you couldn't ever choose your partner, or your family. The idea of children was out of the question. Now—it's possible.

"You are family to me," I say, peeking up at his green eyes and disheveled black hair.

He winces. "Ooh, I hope not too much like family," he says.

I lean back and punch him in the bicep. He feigns pain, then smiles at me.

"Not like a brother, no . . . more like a boyfriend," I say, though it makes me blush something awful.

That awards me a wide grin from him.

"Well then that's the type of family I can accept being." He holds out his arm for me to loop mine through, and I do, still giddy from thinking about a future with him.

Susan makes a face like she's going to throw up and I roll my eyes. She smiles at my reaction, then moves closer. I surprise her with a hug of her own.

I feel her arms tighten around me, the hug returned. In the past two weeks, Charlie, Susan, and I have been inseparable. Charlie has always been a best friend, but Susan has bonded with us from the craziness of the past weeks.

"I mean, you know you needed a sister. Who else can you complain to about your brother?" Susan asks, nudging my arm.

I chuckle.

"What a family we are," my dad says, "we can enjoy quiet while your brother isn't here." He gives me a wink.

Sean has taken to being out of Safety far better than I did. He acts as if he owns the place. The moment his body erupted in flames in Safety, his ego exploded to an incomprehensible size. I smirk at the thought.

And yet he can't even control the fire, I think.

"I can't believe this is happening. I always go to sleep at night hoping I won't wake up to find it was a dream," I say, the emotions swimming inside feeling overwhelming: sadness, fear of the unknown, pure joy, excitement, so much more.

"It's happening, Kor, and it's only going to get better," my dad says, moving closer to Lucia and putting his arm around her shoulders.

Charlie holds me closer and we stare out at the last bits of sunlight disappearing behind the mountain. I feel Susan lean closer on my other side. Our hands clasp at our sides. The three of us stand together, friends bonded forever.

Now that we have freed hundreds of others like us, I don't know what the world will be. As a group, we aren't likely to be welcomed by normal people for a long time. We look normal, act normal, but I know there is something that distinguishes us from the others. It's something we must learn how to control, to live with, so we can live among them without trouble.

Tom plans to begin sending out groups to the various locations where the other people like us are held. He hopes I can pave the way for our kind, to teach them how to control the fire within. We'll try the diplomatic approach at each holding facility, but worse case scenario, we're an arsenal all on our own.

I close my eyes and find it, the very thing that was the reason I and the others were held captive. It swells within me, wanting to explode outward. I feel the urge to light something on fire, but I gently persuade it away.

As the sunset completely disappears and we are dropped into the darkness of the desert, I can only wonder what the country—what the world will be like now that we have been freed. There are so many still in captivity, but Tom wants to work to liberate them all, and then who knows what will happen. We are different, after all. There is something within us that normal people will likely always fear. Maybe they are right to fear it in the wrong hands.

I take a deep breath and revel in the feeling once more.

Sunfire.

Loved it? Hated it? Please leave a review!

ABOUT THE AUTHOR

Dan lives in rural Idaho where he happily lives with his wife, six children and numerous goats, chickens and a cat named Wilma. Aside from writing, which he'd happily do full time, Dan spends most of his time outside in the homestead he built with his wife. When he's not writing, he spends his time with his nose in a fantasy or sci-fi book.

You can connect with me at https://www.dankenner.com

ALSO BY DAN KENNER

www.dankenner.com/books

<u>Epic Fantasy</u>

Shielded: A Prequel to The Lightbearer Chronicles - Get the Ebook
FREE at www.dankenner.com/free

Awakened: The Lightbearer Chronicles Book One

Transformed: The Lightbearer Chronicles Book Two

Ascended: The Lightbearer Chronicles Book Three

<u>Young Adult</u>

Sunfire

<u>Middle Grade</u>

The Search for Silence

A Voice in The Noise

The Thundering Echo